T0028925

GOLD IN PEACE, IRON IN WAR

ANTHONY FLACCO

SEVERN RIVER PUBLISHING

Severn River Publishing
www.SevernRiverBooks.com

ISBN: 978-1-64875-552-1 (Paperback)

ALSO BY ANTHONY FLACCO

The Nightingale Detective Series

The Last Nightingale

The Hidden Man

Vengeance For All Things

Gold in Peace, Iron in War

To find out more about Anthony Flacco and his books, visit

severnriverbooks.com/authors/anthony-flacco

Readers are advised to remember that the Devil is a liar.

— C.S. Lewis

Without me, you would die.

— The Devil

PART I

PROLOGUE

EARLY FOG HUNG THICK OVER San Francisco's waterfront. It was still dark out, and he should have been safe in his hidden sleeping spot, tucked up in the great beams beneath Pier 7.

But this time darkness and fog were not enough to conceal him. The deadly Old Ones somehow found him there beneath the wharf, and in a few frantic moments they were on him like buzzards. The surprise attack caught him off guard. He knew the strange ones came out in full force during the dark hours, but he could not understand how this batch of random Old Ones discovered his hiding place.

Concealment, after all, was one of his essential survival skills. How could they have located him so easily under the wharf? It felt as if they possessed some evil twist on a bloodhound's abilities. He managed to bolt before any of them drew close enough to touch him, then dashed away followed by raggedy skeletons who hurled drunken catcalls when they realized he was outrunning them. He was a natural sprinter, and it always felt good to unleash his legs and let his feet eat up the ground, kicking it behind him. The sound of wind rushing in his ears gave him a confident sense of control. He was generally safe if he had room to run, especially if he could work in a little head start.

For the sake of a quick exit, he left his knapsack behind. His day had begun like this several times since he fled New York for California, but he figured he could get away again this time if he really put his feet to it. So far, he had always been able to surprise the drunks with his speed.

1

CITY SQUIRE HOTEL – ELEVENTH FLOOR (PRIVATE)

LOWER MIDTOWN, MANHATTAN

February 15th, 1920
* 1:00 a.m., Eastern Time *

THESE WERE THE DAYS WHEN SHE survived by keeping her focus tight to the moment. Like all who live in chronic pain, she had learned to value the art of deep concentration. She felt only slight reactions to heat or cold. Her eyes and ears took in no more than was necessary to perform a given task. As for the sense of smell, in her occupation it was best unused.

One productive trick was to deliberately take pleasure in tiny details of the moment: the comforting feel on the soles of her feet of the luxuriant carpet on this private floor. Much more luxurious than that of the rest of the hotel. Since she was ordered to appear at the party wearing a fresh uniform, barefoot, and without underwear, the softness under her feet made for a good point of distraction.

The piano music was also something to focus on. A gifted player was out there at the end of the wide hallway, sending up lush romantic art songs. She had seen him adjusting his bench while she was on her way in and managed to avoid catching his eye before she ducked into the cloakroom. It was better not to know him at all, but that made no real difference. There would be a new piano player next time.

The familiar party noise outside her door floated over the music. Tittering female laughter rose and fell in waves, as if endlessly amusing observations were being exchanged. She had learned enough of their language to make out most of what she heard, but as human beings the women behind the voices remained opaque to her. They appeared to be the crème of society to anyone who did no more than look. Anyone who knew nothing about them. She found herself observing what might as well be another species while their escorts dropped off coats and wraps worth enough to buy her out of her contract.

Every minute or two, she heard the men out in the hallway burst into manly laughter over nasty words, but less so as the party continued and serious deeds were anticipated. Soon, the catch of the month would be filed in, cuffed and chained, paraded, then posed for choosing. White slaves straggling out of the Baltic regions, following the same Great War that had killed most of what was left of her spirit. She knew what these auction parties were because she had no choice but to know. All too well, as it happened. She had starred in her own, before the Devil put her where she landed. Now the parties that were not really parties at all played out before her—while what was left of her wandered in a stupor.

The unseen crowd began to grow very quiet, as if anticipating the arrival onstage of some great diva. It took no words for everyone there to notice that nobody had departed yet, thus signaling to one and all that everybody was on board with the occasion. Liquor flowed from the open bar next to the piano while everyone was served by indentured servants who would be replaced with the next boatload.

She could see enough of the hallway to follow all eight couples while they filed by, heading for the music area to watch the auction and then repair to the private rooms. Nobody made any announcement about it being time to begin; they all just formed up like migrating birds, still talking back and forth, but quietly now, almost whispering.

They were primed for the arrival of the reasons they were there, waiting with anticipation. Everyone faced down the long hallway to see the indentured ones brought in, but at first there was nothing to see except the single wide hallway and its doors leading to large rooms equipped with royally large beds—and nothing else. None of the rooms had so much as a spot to hang a hat or jacket.

The fine hallway carpet stopped outside the room doors. The floors inside were of hardwood, but they were easily cleaned. Fastidious visitors would appreciate that.

She gently pushed one of the wheeled coatracks close to the door and stood behind it like a rabbit watching a gathering of wolves. She knew those people were deadly, but they would fit right in with any major social event. Fashions of the day were still wrapped up in the late Edwardian Era with full sleeves, fitted waistlines, and dresses done in rich silk reaching ankle length. Long pearl necklaces and drop earrings were everywhere. Women's shoes were all alike: thin, form-fitting leather fastened with laces and running all the way up past the ankle. If their feet were the same size they could have swapped footwear and gone home without knowing it.

Sometimes party guests chose to wear masks, but tonight's group seemed to feel no need to hide. Hats were also off and heads were all bare, with the men's fedoras and newsboy caps hanging in her cloakroom next to the women's velvet helmets and silk turbans. This in itself was message enough of illicit things to come.

Thus the casual state of attire signaled the determination of eight obscenely wealthy couples to ignore social boundaries and numerous laws, partly for pleasure, partly for future profits, and mostly because of the joy in flaunting the ability to get away with it. Deep doses of exhilaration were to be found in daring the civilized world to come after them, knowing they would dodge prosecution even if they were caught.

Moments later she heard the rattling of chains, and an excited murmur went through the guests while eight individuals who had either been kidnapped from the Baltic region or deceived into coming on their own were led in by one of the revolving staff. She knew they were used in the running of the hotel but had no idea what ever happened to them after they disappeared.

The auction was over in minutes, with the bidding done as a silent dance of hand gestures. Tonight's group consisted of three women, three men, and two children, a boy and girl of perhaps eleven or twelve years.

The victims were lined up and scrutinized, selected by one couple or another, then separated from the others and moved into one of the private rooms containing nothing but large beds. The captive adults all went quietly, resigned. She knew they had all taken thorough beatings already, including the children, to ensure cooperation and silence.

The private eleventh floor of the City Squire Hotel fell silent after the piano player and the bartender disappeared. She walked out of the cloakroom and began cleaning up the bar area, hearing nothing more than occasional bursts of laughter or grunts of pain. This was a moment she could only endure by jamming her emotions so far down inside of herself she was nearly an empty vessel. She had just filled a bus tray full of glassware and empty bottles when a young girl's scream rang through the floor.

One of the room doors flew open and the girl came rushing out, half-dressed and carrying a bundle of clothing.

The bus tray full of glassware went crashing to the floor. All restraint shattered with it. To observe this helpless child desperate for escape flooded her with rage. Before she had time to think about it, she found herself yelling for the girl to follow her, then led her to the fire stairs. She pushed the girl through the door into the stairway, telling her, "Run to the street and head for the train station. You can blend in there."

The girl said nothing but spun on her heel and fled down the stairs.

Other room doors began to open while occupants shouted complaints about the noise. Mister Clayton and his wife, Allison, came out of one of the rooms followed by the governor's chief of staff and his wife, with a confused adult female looking on behind them.

"What the hell is going on? Where is that kid?" Mister Clayton hissed at her.

"The little girl went that way, but I did not see her," she told him. She pointed toward the end of the hall. "Maybe into one of the rooms?"

Mister Clayton and his wife wasted the next minute or two asking guests to step outside and confirm that nobody had entered their room. The girl was gone. Once all the rooms were searched, he came back and pulled her into the cloakroom, slammed the door, and twisted the lock.

He grasped her by the throat with both hands and squeezed until her breath locked up. She knew better than to fight; experience taught her fighting only made him more determined to inflict pain. Her hands instinctively grasped his wrists, but she did not try to pull them away.

"You helped her get out, didn't you? Why would she know how to find the steps so quickly, eh? You sent her down the stairs!" He released her throat long enough to allow her to take a few shuddering breaths, then grabbed her again and reapplied the pressure.

"Now I know it. You helped the boy run too, didn't you? Everything you told us about him supposedly disappearing was a lie, yes? We'll find that girl back down on the street, but I'm not letting you lie your way out of it anymore. You know where the boy is, don't you?"

He squeezed until her knees began to buckle, then released her again and allowed her to take a breath. She knew from experience he could strangle her into unconsciousness over and over again without actually killing her. He called it foreplay. "Tell me where—or this time I won't let go until your body goes cold."

She considered dying an attractive offer, but the instinct to get her airway free again was too powerful. The words seemed to come from her lips on their own. "San...San Francisco."

"San Francisco? All the way across the country? Are you trying to tell me he's been out there for the past six weeks? Hell, it's been nearly *seven* weeks now!"

She dared to sneer at him, but her voice came out hoarse and weak. "You can't have him."

He responded by tightening his grip again. The pressure he applied was so intense, pain exploded in her chest from heart and lungs desperate for air. She began to feel herself go light-headed.

In the past, he had always stopped just short of killing her, making an art of dangling her over the precipice of death. This time, while she felt her consciousness go dark, she could only hope he would bring her back from the dead as he had in the past. Not that she cared much for life anymore, but instinct commanded her to breathe.

2

LAZY ANA BONE'S PLACE
TENDERLOIN DISTRICT – SAN FRANCISCO

February 15th
* 6:00 a.m., Pacific Time *

ANARCHIST BOMB MAKER ANDREA SALSEDO had just concluded his scheduled long-distance telephone call to check in with Clayton Mannerly in New York, where it was nine in the morning, but it galled him to do it from a beggar's stance. He regretted being such a good soldier and now wished he had skipped the call and invented some excuse. Despite the welcome order to return to New York, he considered Clayton Mannerly a perfect example of what the worldwide anarchist movement was created to fight.

Instead he had paid a premium-rate bribe to use the house phone at Lazy Ana's place and made the call from the kitchen of the well-heeled whorehouse. Apparently there was a going demand in the prostitute community for someplace to have a private phone call.

Even at the age of thirty-eight, Salsedo's sense of himself was tender enough that he smarted over the new order to kill a child.

He glanced around to be certain nobody was watching him. A house of ill repute was the only place with a telephone available at that hour, but even such a place had its limits of tolerance when it came to the presence of men wanted for multiple murders.

He made his way to the back door and sat down out on the porch, glad to still be cloaked in darkness at that hour. Shame radiated from him. He was thankful to feel grounded by the combined stench of seashore, city, and whorehouse garbage. Despite his slovenly appearance since going on the run, it cheered him to smell better than his surroundings for a change.

At last he permitted himself a smug smile, because despite his denials to Mannerly, of course he already knew where to find the boy. He had seen him with his own eyes, down at the Embarcadero, where so many of the beggar kids liked to corral the travelers and press them for coins. It had only been Salsedo's second day in town when he spotted him down near the Clock Tower with a bunch of other raggedy kids.

He just figured the kid must have gone on the run from New York to escape being used as property. *Oh, look: the Rich Bastard's slave kid over there with the orphans. Must've run away.* It was nothing to him. As a wanted man on the run for his life, he barely noticed.

So was Mannerly lying? Did this odd kill order really come from Boss Mario Buda? Salsedo cared nothing for the Rich Bastard's opinion, but it hurt him to think Boss Buda viewed him as a mere hired murderer. What would Salsedo's wife and two small children say to such a thing while they waited in New York for his return?

Cursed with undue optimism, he decided if he ignored the kill order, then his required check-in call to Mannerly had actually brought him good news: Boss Buda wanted to see him back in New York. Surely, he thought, a summons like that meant Buda knew of Salsedo's special skills. To be directly acknowledged in that way was a badge of honor in itself, golden confirmation of the value of his skills. It would finally lift him far above Mannerly's mere chore-work.

He reminded himself he was a typesetter by trade and bomb maker by profession, but not a hunter of the very young. Never. An anarchist, not a madman. One simply did not point out a child to Andrea Salsedo and issue a kill order. To comply would make him the same monster in the closet every child grows up fearing. He remembered that monster himself.

He had retained his humanity and would never cease believing the deaths of children would never aid the anarchist cause *unless they died in droves.*

To create a large enough shock wave to rock all of society, spectacular suffering was required. Child deaths were only permitted as part of the larger toll of random victims. In that way, infanticide was blurred over and the public outrage dampened by the blood of older people who probably deserved it.

But now, today, this new order to commit directed personal murder was so abhorrent, it iced his spine. A flash of anxiety ran through his bones and seemed to shriek, *Do something!*

Yes, do something, but what? Nuanced reasoning was never his strongest power.

Do something! His stomach twisted with the hunger for revenge at this insult to his very humanity. He felt as if he could live without eating for a year if he could somehow create the opportunity to blow Clayton Mannerly, Rich Capitalist Bastard, to his final end.

While he made no claim to understand that thing called the human soul, whatever it might be, he experienced it as the presence of something within himself he valued, something he wanted with all his energy not to defile, whether he was imagining it or not.

He leaped to his feet, leaned forward with his hands on his knees, and vomited, which immediately cleared his mind. He stepped his way around to the front of the respectable whorehouse feeling determined not to sink any lower.

The sun peeked over a rare clear horizon. Down at the docks, strong pink light flashed over the form of a female motorcycle rider dressed in full leathers and piloting a large Harley-Davidson through morning air redolent of seashore, diesel, and horse. The big bike had an empty sidecar that looked like a tiny boat on wheels, and the driver wove the vehicle in and out of traffic with the smooth ease of a tailor threading a needle. Despite the extra girth of the sidecar and the early morning fog, she skillfully zigged and zagged around motor vehicles and wagons pulled by draft animals. Male drivers occasionally honked their horns or shook their fists and leveled brazen insults, whether outraged by her close maneuvers around their vehicles or offended by the sight of a female on a large motorbike and disgusted by her obvious joy in nonconformity.

She ignored them all, instead focusing on a group of street kids working the crowd around the Ferry Building. At the age of twenty-four, she was thankful her own life on the streets was in her distant past, but the long list of things she would never get out of her mind included the fear and insecurity of fleeing the orphanage for the streets, with no idea if she could manage to survive them.

She quickly pulled over near the kids, cutting off a taxi driver and ignoring him while he loudly wished her damnation for her crime. She killed her big engine and sat back to observe the street urchins while a smile spread across her face.

Salsedo walked along among the other laborers heading to their workplaces. He felt certain he could sense the quiet frustration radiating from every one of them, no matter what their station.

He figured about ninety nine out of a hundred would walk off their jobs if they only had a chance to hear Signore Galleani speak to them about the plight of the workers of the world. There was willing soil here, in these beleaguered laborers. That soil was ready to receive the proper seeds. That was the work. The good work. Not murder for hire.

He didn't know what would cause a boy so young to run off by himself and apparently ride the rails all the way across the country. What could make him so determined to get that far away?

In the end, it made no difference. Mario Buda was in charge, and according to Mannerly, he had issued a direct order to Salsedo. Buda was in charge because he spoke for the entire American Anarchist Movement since Luigi Galleani had been deported. But the kill order? Clayton Mannerly was a rich capitalist bastard whom he would not trust with a spare nickel.

He had to wonder, was the assignment even real?

He walked through air briny with the presence of the sea and swirling with fog. It reduced visibility to fifteen or twenty meters. Before long he found himself down by the wharfs, maybe fifty meters north of the trolly turnaround in front of the Ferry Building with its tall Clock Tower. Here the potpourri of scents carried on the breeze was joined by a top note of ozone from electrical bus lines.

Troops of kids were already running through the area, panhandling dockworkers and tourists alike. Pick-pocketing if an opportunity arose. Some moved like true street sharks, but most were merely desperate children unlikely to make it to adulthood. Salsedo never liked thinking about them.

He snapped to attention when half a dozen children came rushing out of a nearby bakery, fists and faces stuffed with snagged pastries. The outraged baker quick-waddled to the front door, waving a broom and shouting, "You thieves stay out of here!"

The kids' laughs of triumph were muffled by the pastry, and they passed by Salsedo without breaking stride, all of them with bulging cheeks. Then it happened.

Shit! The boy. Right there before him.

Was it a sign? In the first hour of the first day of his new orders, here was the kid. All Salsedo had to do was look in the same spot where he spotted him before. The kid's height made him stand out. At first most of the little beggars seemed younger, but after a second look, Salsedo realized they were more likely to be malnourished kids of about the same age. He wondered if they packed up like that for protection.

A bunch of them moved along the sidewalk together, as if to protect themselves from the world while they made their way. The kid moved with confidence. He called out to the younger ones with instructions they more or less obeyed. He displayed a natural bent for leadership that could be productive if he survived long enough to become a free adult.

The street kids worked the crowd with a loose plan. A couple of them distracted the marks by begging while others slipped up from behind and hit the pockets. It was a fascinating ritual of survival for small people with no other resources.

The public let it all go by without reaction. The sight of renegade children barely drew a glance from most people, taken in context following the bloodiest war in living history. Terrible problems of survival lay in every direction. The nation was just beginning to recover from waves of mass murder so barbaric and horrendous, it was dubbed "The War to End All Wars" by people unfamiliar with human nature.

Salsedo knew better than to keep himself exposed out there on the streets like that, with the ever-present possibility someone might have seen a wanted poster, or perhaps even recall his face from his former days on the streets as a Galleani enforcer. It pained him to admit that his biggest mistake, barely four years ago, took place in this very city when he allowed the Galleanists to persuade him to trade the exquisite and explosive language of his bombs for the cowardly act of ramming a garbage truck into a policeman on a motorbike. Nobody ever told him why. And for all he knew, the man he killed was also a believer in the cause, caught up in a job he hated. Perhaps a brother in spirit.

Salsedo got away clean but suffered for it every day since. The murder of a single man for someone else's personal reasons was not a revolutionary act against a corrupt society. He could not hide the term "a coward's act" from himself, regardless of approval from others in the movement. Whether they realized it or not, he had allowed them to stain his honor.

He was condemned to a lifetime of fear, now. With no statute of limitations on murder, the hazard of sudden arrest was now a permanent boarder with its own room in his skull, an undesirable guest who would never go home.

That unpleasant business haunted him while he searched for a safe spot to watch the urchins. Nothing to do until he left for New York, anyway. He sat and allowed the morning fog to cook off while he stayed far enough away from the Clock Tower to avoid being noticed. He made it a point to behave casually, showing no overt interest.

Nobody had reason to suspect a thing.

3

SAN FRANCISCO – THE FERRY BUILDING

UNDER THE CLOCK TOWER

February 15th
* Approximately 7:00 a.m. *

ELEVEN-YEAR-OLD DANTE WATCHED CLAYTON'S MAN loitering back there in the morning shadows cast by a few parked work trucks. The sun was barely at the horizon, but the sky was already light. The stranger's face caught Dante's attention as soon as the man approached, setting off a silent alarm: *Old Guy trouble*. Recognizing dangerous Old Guys was not a skill he assimilated by choice; his expertise came through experience.

He recalled this particular Old Guy as a visitor to Clayton's penthouse back in Manhattan. Dante had lived in the place for nearly a year, but that proved to be eleven and three-quarter months too long. He left the dubious creature comforts of his foster home by keeping his ticket money in his pocket and instead leaped onto an empty boxcar of a slow train.

Dante turned eleven on a flatcar train hauling scrap metal westbound out of Kansas City, not long after running away. He had been pleasantly surprised to find himself alive, traveling toward California and the great Pacific Ocean. Moving, perhaps, toward safety and freedom. He came across plenty of other kids his age on the rails and in the trainyards, but all they would talk about was food and destinations, never their personal experiences. It was as if they had all been created yesterday.

He understood the unspoken sentiment. To ask them about any of the terrible things done to them, things they only knew because they were forced to know them, was obscene in itself. Obscene to them. It seemed like more pain than anyone could carry.

For the same reasons that kept the others silent, he had climbed up to ride on top of the lumbering freight cars whenever they passed through open terrain, up there away from nosy citizens and police. He found the winter temperatures made it easier to avoid rape by wizened men who smelled like sour wine and piss.

He knew their game when they came skulking around. They tried to amuse themselves by shocking him with filthy talk, but he shocked them back bigger and then laughed at them. When they came after him, he danced away, climbing up, scrambling around, and leaping along the cars, avoiding one and all, until every single one of the pursuing crowd of ill-nourished alcoholics felt their strength failing them.

They always gave up, for the time being, but Dante was still a boy in a man's land. Potential attackers filled his days and nights, forcing him to keep his antenna honed. Strangers practically sniffed him like dogs.

He had no memory of Old Guy's name, which meant he had seen him but they never actually met. His memory for names and faces was nearly perfect, an ability he frequently risked his life to employ on the streets at games of chance.

Since he was already aware of his unusual memory powers, it was no surprise to pick out Old Guy's face in a crowd of other old people. Dante had that face trapped in his memory the same way he had the faces of everyone he had ever met or given so much as a good clear look.

No, this was one of Clayton's men. He watched Old Guy from the corner of his eye while he helped the kids swipe food from sidewalk venues. A moment later he began to perform childish noises with the other kids and hopped around making googly eyes and generally pretending to be a lame brain, which usually took adult suspicion right off of him.

He sat down on a cold bench and pretended to munch a small baguette while he continued pretending not to watch Old Guy, who was pretending not to watch him.

Dante would ordinarily feel no concern at seeing a familiar face, even here so far from New York City. Such a thing would be coincidence. He knew people needed to travel for all sorts of reasons.

Still. The man was clearly trying not to be noticed. Why would he need to be sneaky?

Dante's mouth went dry while he pretended to chew and swallow. A deep wave of dread ran through him and settled in his stomach. *That Old Guy is wrong out here. A wrong thing.*

He moved slowly to avoid any appearance of fear while he stood and began to meander toward a different vendor booth, farther along the Embarcadero. There he used excited childish noises and an exaggerated happy face to trick three of the kids into going with him in expectation of some new source of food, profit, or at least entertainment. They made a pleasant little gang of side-walk rascals while they giggled their way toward a nearby sausage vendor.

Dante's idea was if Old Guy had some innocent reason for being around, then this would bring it out. The man would break off and go on his way, no harm done, and Dante would be free to worry about a million other things besides getting spotted by one of Clayton's men.

He bent over as if to remove a stone from his sock and sneaked a look back, hoping his pursuer was gone.

No luck. Old Guy was bearing straight down on him, sending a flash of fear through him like an electrical shock. He had just proved this man was hunting him down; the reason didn't matter. Old Guy had to be there on Clayton's orders.

Dante had already taught the other kids to scatter on the cry of "Police!" They had used it to their advantage a couple of times already. Now he stood and shouted at the top of his lungs, "Police! Police! Police!"

It not only worked, the group with him was joined by the ones they left behind when they leaped to their feet and scattered in all directions. A few old people grabbed at the kids to restrain them for whatever reasons, unwittingly helping Dante by amplifying the chaos.

The trick usually allowed him to disappear in a cloud of confusion. Not today. He glanced back to see Clayton's man pushing other kids out of the way while he bore down on Dante. This was concerning, but Dante still had the relatively open spaces of the waterfront ahead of him. He could outrun most old people.

Clayton's man made a show of keeping his face calm while he accelerated toward Dante. If his pursuit was harmless, he would call out and say something, would he not? *Hey, Dante, what are you doing here?* Or maybe just, *Hey, kid, ain't you from New York?*

Nope. Clayton's man was keeping quiet to avoid alerting witnesses.

Dante abandoned all pretense of doing anything other than fleeing at top speed, leaving the others to go back to their panhandling once things quieted down. If he ditched Clayton's man, he could always circle back around and rejoin them.

But zigzagging through traffic slowed him. He stayed out front but was not leaving his pursuer behind. And still, Clayton's man never called out, never tried to get Dante to acknowledge him. Whatever his motives, he needed to keep them secret and avoid public notice. He knew there was nothing but bad news in that.

He had only survived so far by being unafraid to make risky moves. Without any sort of warning, he leaped over to an outdoor café table and flipped it on its side, scattering drinks in all directions and causing the four diners seated there to jump up and bellow in indignation and create another blur of commotion. He sprinted north along the Embarcadero toward Washington Street and took the corner on Washington at a dead run, now heading directly away from the ocean. He had the good fortune of slow speeds from the freight trucks trundling along the Embarcadero, allowing him to run between them at will.

One large town car nearly struck him, and the driver laid on his horn like he was trying to stop a freight train. The horn blasts caused drivers in the area to also begin honking, with some honking to tell the others to get moving, and others honking to make the honking stop.

Dante's foot hit a fresh pile of horse flop from one of the hansom cabs that cruised the wharfs for ship travelers. He went down hard, causing several motor sedans to jam their brakes and nearly collide. He leaped to his feet again amid shouts and more honking, but the instant he tried to put weight on his ankle, he realized it had twisted in the fall.

The ankle joint felt so stunned, he had no real idea how badly he might be injured. He was out of options for now. His legs felt heavy. He had to clamp his groin muscles to keep his pants dry.

In the background, Clayton's man continued to close the distance between them, and Dante rose to hobble away, but his movements were too slow to effect an escape. There was no need for a doctor to tell him he was done running for the day. When he tried to speed up, he put too much pressure on his damaged limb and fell again.

The second time he hit the ground, he nearly went under the wheels of a large motorcycle/sidecar combination. It skidded to a stop inches from his face and, luckily, close enough for the vehicle to block him from sight and prevent Clayton's man from spotting him.

Dante noticed the guy riding the big motorbike wore a full leather suit, topped by a leather helmet. He looked like an airplane pilot on a magazine cover. The pilot gestured to Dante and then surprised him by calling out in a female voice.

"Get in!" She pointed to the sidecar. "You've got maybe ten seconds."

Okay, so a lady pilot. Still an old person, though. Not to be trusted. Problem being, right now it was Old Pilot here or Old Guy himself, only a few yards away and closing in.

Dante dove into the sidecar and curled onto the floor. He felt the vehicle rocket away even before he had the chance to sit up in the seat, forcing him to hunker down with his arms protecting his head. They peeled away down the road, and his body slammed back and forth against the sidecar walls like the clapper of a bell, batted by every pothole and again with every sudden swerve.

The driver turned off of the Embarcadero and onto Broadway, accelerating with a roar that filled Dante's ears. The rain-gutted roads bounced the cab, slamming away at his body while the pilot drove in swoops and swerves around the motor traffic, the horse-drawn traffic, the trolley traffic, and the pedestrian traffic—ultimately carrying him away from the haunting face of Old Guy, the determined pursuer. He quickly lost his sense of direction while they moved through parts of the city he knew nothing about.

The pilot drove like she owned the whole place. Within a few more moments she lost Old Guy among the early morning street traffic and countless pedestrians.

At last, after enduring more of the sidecar beating than Dante would have thought he could stand, the pilot pulled her iron beast to the side of the road. She cut off the engine and then just sat without moving, taking in a few deep breaths.

With great and deliberate care, she unfastened the chin strap and slowly peeled the leather helmet off her head, as if it might stick to her hair. It did not.

When she turned around to look at him, he involuntarily threw up his forearms to protect his face. Whoever she was, she was one of the Old People, and they were never to be trusted, certainly not within arm's reach. Dante had saved himself on many occasions, avoiding a blow more times than he could count only because he maintained that small amount of distance.

His arms stayed up. Nothing happened. He and the pilot each stayed in place. Neither moved.

At last Dante felt foolish enough to force his arms slowly downward, first one, then the other. He kept his eyes on the cab floor, knowing a direct gaze toward one of the Old People could easily spark something bad, earn back punishment of some kind. They didn't go for that eye-contact stuff unless you were listening to them lecture you.

He awkwardly climbed to a seated position in the cab, all the while keeping his face averted. Then, with his best imitation of a grown-up, "to Hell with it" sigh, he raised his eyes to look the female pilot straight in the face.

4

SAN FRANCISCO – EMBARCADERO DISTRICT

February 15th
* Immediately Following *

"VIGNETTE. VIGNETTE NIGHTINGALE..." She pointed to herself. "Vignette. And you are? ...Uh, speak English? *Mi español no es muy bueno.*"

"Yeah-yeah! It's okay. Got it. Thank you. Thanks for helping me. But I...I don't have any money, so you might as well let me walk away now. We don't need any cops or anything, right?"

She snorted and repeated, "No money. Got it." She stuck out her hand. "Pleased to meet you. Like I said: Vignette Nightingale."

He looked at her outstretched hand as if it represented some sort of trick.

Vignette kept it there. "So, Nightingale, like the bird, and Vignette, which is what they call a little scene in a play: a vignette. See? Ta-dah!"

Dante continued to regard her with a strange look while he clasped her hand in his. His grip was gentle but firm.

"I'm Dante," he replied. "Just that. Anyway, why did you help me? I'm sure we never met. But I have to tell you," he abruptly barked out a laugh, "that was amazing! You just swooped in! He was gonna get me for sure. No doubt. And then, and then, and then there you were! How did you even know to do that? And where did you get this...machine? I never saw a woman ride one of these things. How could you possibly—"

"Slow down! It's okay to—"

He continued on momentum. "Where did you come from, anyway?"

She figured that last question could be a good place to start, so she smiled and shrugged. "A new client stood me up for a meeting, supposed to be at the Ferry Building Café at six thirty. It happens. I bill 'em for it anyway. So I was just about to head back into the home office when I saw you take off running. Brother, the way that man was going after you, I thought I'd better tag along and see what was going on."

She looked away from him before she finished, "I don't like it when a grown-up chases a kid with that kind of anger."

"Wait. You—you decided to jump in the way you did just because of seeing that old guy after me... Why would you do that?"

"All right. Want to know the truth? I know he was going to have his work cut out to capture you, even without my help. I just thought we should hop to it and get your inevitable escape out of the way."

"What's that mean?"

"I thought it'd be fun to mess up his plans and help you get out of there."

Dante laughed again. "It was fun enough for me, I'll tell you!"

"Fine, but do you know who that man was?" She dropped her voice to a melodramatic tone. "Are you a dastardly villain?"

"I'm no villain! That old guy is one of Clayton's men."

"All right, then. Who's Clayton?"

"Back in New York. He was supposed to be my..." He let out a sigh. "I don't know what he wants with me, but it's nothing wholesome."

He hopped out of the sidecar and stood massaging his sore ankle while he looked over the bike, the driver, and her outfit, then broke into a wide grin. "Never seen one like you, lady."

"Vignette."

"Vignette. I never seen one like you and never heard the name. Is it real?"

"Sure it is." She leaned close to give him a fake dramatic whisper. "I picked it out myself."

"Ha! You too? I picked mine last year! This man, Clayton, he and his wife supposedly adopted me back in New York City. They got me a new birth certificate and told me to change my name. Fine with me. I never liked the other ones."

Vignette looked closer at him. "New birth certificate?"

"Yep. They had different names for me. I didn't know my real one. I don't talk about any of that. So I picked out Dante myself." He beamed at her. "I haven't actually read *Dante's Inferno* yet, but I sure like the title. Anyway, they said, 'From now on, your birthday comes on the first day of the year.' Good enough. It's easy to remember. They put it in that fancy writing."

"Does the fancy writing give family names, from where you originated?"

"It did. I saw it plain enough. But I tell you, I got shed of all that."

"You did what?"

"I got shed of it! Got it behind me, like 'Get thee behind me!' I'm just Dante now."

"Son of a gun, kid, you ran away all the way here from New York? From this Clayton guy and his wife?"

His eyes narrowed, and a shadow crossed his expression. "You gonna rat me out?"

"Not a chance."

"Well, Miss Vignette, I'm not going to be talking about Clayton or his people."

"What's the problem?"

"The problem is that the things they do, you can't talk about."

"Everybody does things you can't talk about."

"Not like this. You can't get near them. Everything's dangerous around them. Clayton told me he has an invisible army. I think it could be true. And that Old Guy back there was one of them."

"What old guy? The man I saw was young enough."

"How could you tell from that distance? I mean, don't old people lose their eyesight?"

"Answer me carefully now, as if your life depended on it, which it may: Just what age do you believe a person has to be to qualify as old?"

"I don't know." He looked away from her. "How old are you?"

"Jeez! I turned twenty-four last month!"

"...Sorry."

After an extended pause, they locked eyes and immediately burst into laughter.

Vignette regarded him with a steady gaze and held it on him for a long spell before she came to a decision and spoke. "So. Would you like a lift someplace? You know, beats walking, and all that."

Dante looked from Vignette to the sidecar, then into the distance down the street. He took a careful step away. "Miss Vignette, I hope you don't mind me asking you who you are."

"Nope. Don't mind. And it's just Vignette, no 'Miss.' But let me give you one of these." She reached into her jacket and produced one of her business cards. "Ta-dah!" she sang for the second time. "That's a new design for this year, right there."

Dante took it in both hands and squinted at it for several seconds, then sounded out the words: "Vignette Nightingale, Private Investigations, the Blackburn and Nightingales Detective Agency."

"Hey, nice reading. Somebody taught you well."

"My auntie started me, then I mostly taught myself. Anyway, this detective work, has it got anything to do with running down escaped kids?"

"Oh, hell no! I run down husbands who won't keep their vows, sometimes a wife or two, the odd crook. Got a company embezzler one time. How'd you manage to teach yourself to read?"

"I have a dictionary."

"But how?"

"It's not that hard. When you try to read something, you start with the small words and then look up anything you don't understand. After a while, you don't need it so much."

"And she, your auntie...or somebody, told you to do that?"

"Nobody told me not to!"

Vignette snorted in surprise and then laughed, clapping her hands together in delight. She regarded him for another moment, then took a deep breath. "So. If you want to take a chance on me and climb back in, I'll bring you back to our place for a hot meal."

"Our place? You married?"

"No, I'm not going to be doing that. I live with the man who adopted me. Randall Blackburn. He's the other name on that card."

Dante warily regarded her. "Excuse me, I don't mean to be slow, here, but you're all grown up. And you're still with the man who adopted you?"

"Seems like the best place for me so far."

He shook his head, trying to swallow the idea. "You stay there on purpose?"

"I do. He actually took in my late brother first, then me too. It all worked out."

Dante's expression darkened. "Your *late* brother."

"Yes. His name was Shane." She reached under her shirt and pulled up a teardrop-shaped bit of chromed metal about an inch long, hanging from a thin chain around her neck like a pendant. "This was the magneto switch on his motorcycle. I took it from the wreckage. He was killed four years ago. Not by Randall, either. Supposedly an accident, but I didn't see it happen."

Dante nodded as if some suspicion had been confirmed. He vigorously rubbed his hands over his face, then said, "The Movers did that, didn't they? He got too close?"

"I don't know about any 'movers.'"

"Yeah." He took a loud breath. "Clayton calls 'em that. I don't know where he got it or what they call themselves. All they do is move people around. Plant kids where they want. Old Ones too. Make 'em do whatever they want. I bet they're the ones who put you in with this Randall."

"Dante! Listen to me. Nobody 'put' me here. I pushed with everything I had to go live with Randall and...and my brother. It was flat-out the best thing I ever did."

He struggled to digest that before he responded, "So, you're saying you can just *leave*, then? You aren't indentured."

"No, no, I am not 'indentured.' Nothing like that."

He paused again and held it for so long, Vignette decided the thing to do was wait and let it play out. She started counting the seconds in her mental clock and got as far as seven. He spoke up just before the count of eight.

"So this...Randall guy. He's all right with you?"

"Best man I ever knew." She jerked her thumb at the sidecar. "What do you say? Free lunch?"

Dante looked both ways up and down the street, shook his head in some sort of resignation, and let out a deep exhale while he climbed back into the open cab. "First off, I got a knapsack stashed down under Pier 7. Traveling light. You know."

She smiled. "Understood. We can fetch." She fired the engine and revved the accelerator a few times, sending up the roar of a mechanical lion. She let the idle fall back down before she spoke up. "So, is this knapsack where you keep your dictionary?"

"Yeah, it's little. Just a pocket version."

"Ha-ha!" Vignette hooted and revved the engine again. "Pocket version! He carries a dictionary, everybody, but it's only a pocket version! I get it. You're traveling light." She gave the throttle a double twist. Dante was savvy enough to hang on hard while she did a fast release with the clutch and held the fanning rear tire roughly to a straight line of motion. The big bike blasted away, and when the front wheel tried to rise and tilt the sidecar backward, she threw her body weight forward over the handlebars and powered the vehicle out of the air and back onto the street.

Vignette looked over at him and seemed to read his thoughts. She bellowed hard over the noise of the engine and rushing wind, "These tires hold the road like glue! Best there is. My brother taught me about them!"

At that moment, as if to prove her point, an automobile crossed their path and halted, leaving them aboard a three-wheeled missile bearing down on the stopped car. With no other recourse, Vignette threw the combo-bike into a high-speed skid, trailing the sidecar on the backside while they carved their way through a wide arc—which carried them around the obstacle.

She kept right on going after she pulled the bike back to forward motion, straightening the wheel and powering away on a narrow path between a dump truck and a lamppost. The big bike shot into clear road space, and she glanced down at the boy again to see if he was frozen with terror. Dante was clinging to the sidecar grips, but as soon as his eyes met hers, he threw both fists in the air and screamed with delight.

5

SAN FRANCISCO CITY HALL
OFFICE OF MAYOR JAMES "SUNNY JIM" ROLPH

February 15th
* 8:00 a.m., Pacific Time *

AT CITY HALL, RANDALL BLACKBURN, PI, stepped into the office of James "Sunny Jim" Rolph in response to a summons delivered by private messenger. The underling had offered no further details, leaving the big detective to arrive blind to the meeting's purpose. In the past, the few times he had heard from the mayor, serious trouble was afoot and an investigation required someone less "constrained" by legal procedure than the civic authorities. *All right, then, there's nothing else for it*, he thought. No matter the outcome, the day would prove to be novel.

At the sight of Blackburn, the portly fifty-year-old politician happily cried, "Aha!" and jumped from behind his massive desk. Blackburn braced for some of that old political sunshine while "Sunny Jim" circled around to grab him by the hand and slap him on the shoulder.

"Randall Blackburn! Just the man I need to see!" He leaned toward the door and shouted, "Virginia, hold all my calls. No visitors!" He glanced at Blackburn and winked. "Important stuff here today!" Then he closed the door, hurried over to put his arm around Blackburn's shoulder. He spoke in confidential tones—*just you and me, pal.*

"Good to see you, Detective. Good-good. I trust your family is well? The kids are fine?"

"My daughter is fine. My son is still dead."

"Great God, how crude of me! Forgive me, Detective! Of course I know all about that tragic accident. I shouldn't have allowed it to slip my mind."

"Been nearly four years, please don't give it another thought, Mr. Mayor. What can I do for you?"

Sunny Jim took Blackburn by the shoulders and guided him toward the sofa across from his desk, saying, "I fear I am about to tell you something only a few others can be permitted to know. Please sit down."

He gestured to the sofa and resumed his seat behind his desk. Blackburn repressed a sigh of resignation and sat where he was asked.

The mayor said nothing at first; tapping out a little rhythm on the desktop, he seemed to daydream for a moment. He snapped to and gave Blackburn the ol' Sunny Jim smile.

"So! The years pass, but you and I remain, eh, Detective?"

"Knock wood. For the time being, anyway, Mr. Mayor."

"Time being? I'm not running for governor. Why would you say that?"

"Say what, sir?"

"You heard a rumor? Someone looking to do an end-run?"

"No, I meant in the larger sense. Life. We all pass at some point."

"Ah! Yes...*yes*! Excellent. Perfect way to lead into the topic at hand."

"Mortality?"

"Well, no. More as to the level of misery that can be directed at a person while they are still on Earth. The mayor of New York has confirmed they are seeing the same things we are. I am talking about the buying and selling of children, Detective. Indenturing them for much of their lives, working them to death. Domestic work, farm work, factory work, sex... Women and men, too. Mostly young, some old. Old ones are cheap. Buying and selling people."

"Illegal, though, Mr. Mayor, yes? The Emancipation Proclamation was over half a century back, and the White Slave Act passed ten years ago."

"Mmm. Yes—yes and no—and no. Yes, slavery is largely illegal these days. Yes and no, it's not entirely illegal. And no, it's not gone."

"Give me a minute..."

"Never mind. We've all heard about the famous 'orphan trains' bringing kids who lost their families in the Great War out into the heartland for adoption, yes?"

"I've read about them. People trying to do right for strangers."

The mayor regarded him for a moment and nodded to himself. He took a deep breath. "I have learned to trust you, sir. In my line of work, trust is golden."

Blackburn decided to keep it simple. "Thank you."

"Here it is, then: the same anonymous forces that plagued our city before the Great War have returned. If they were ever truly gone. Two days ago, I sent three officers to intercept the train and detain all the children until we could find out who they really were. The train arrived, the kids got off and dispersed. My officers vanished. From the scene, from their homes, from town."

"I never heard anything about it."

"I saw to it that it was never reported."

"Ah."

"I was already on the phone with Mayor Hyland for a long time yesterday. This morning, too. He's having the same troubles with staff and officials not following orders. He called wanting to know if I had anyone I could trust to look into this. Hear that? He's the mayor of one of the most powerful cities in the world, and he wants to know if I have anyone I can trust."

Blackburn nodded. "Proving no amount of authority is worth a tinker's damn if the people tasked with carrying out your orders can simply ignore you. But sir, in this day and age, how could anyone, any group, set up something like that and get away with it?"

"Doesn't matter how. Evil is never short on innovation. And there's no way of knowing how long these people, whoever they are, have been dumping orphans in this city or across the country. With the war on, nobody was paying any attention, and since it ended, everybody's busy with reconstruction."

"How can you keep something like that quiet? You had three officers, I assume with families, just disappear."

"Yes, and all these corrupted individuals needed to do was recruit three men who felt no particular devotion to their families and could be tempted by a cushy payoff. We realize there are plenty such men, yes?"

"Judging by the number I've had to put in jail over the years..."

"Yes. So what you will eventually hear are rumors of an on-duty car crash, remains too damaged for an open casket, and the burial of three empty boxes. These men may be still alive, but I am declaring them dead."

"Very good, sir. To Hell with 'em."

"The fight's going to be trickier this time, Detective, I can tell you. The Great War we just slogged our way out of, it left us with more than a few real curses."

"You know, some people are calling it 'The War to End All Wars.'"

"You believe that? A war with the power to end all future wars?"

"Not for a moment, sir."

"Thank you. We toil in the field of human nature. And the variation on human nature we find ourselves up against today is dark. The opportunity to own and control another human being is the sort of thing that overrides well-meant kindness and generosity. It tempts people who have been decent all their lives to react like starving wolves."

"It overrides them using what?"

"Hellacious greed."

"Yes, but how, specifically?"

"Specifically, the entire orphan train enterprise was infiltrated by organized criminals at some point along the way."

"You would think children represent a financial loss. A bunch of hungry kids you have to feed every day."

"No-no! Think labor! Free labor for the life of the child, or at least until adulthood. And cash—you need cash? Why, you can always sell the kid to somebody who can afford the nominal upkeep of a barn animal, you know, just a bit better than you can. It's far better than selling drugs or alcohol or food, because the human animal is a product you can sell over and over again, pulling out value the whole time."

"God. Like work horses."

"Cheaper. They eat less. So these corrupted people pick up orphans in Ukraine or anywhere in Europe where people really took a pounding. They insert them into the American orphan train system for later sale. Bribe a few inspectors. No real strain."

"Who pays for all that transportation?"

"Private church sponsors buy their tickets. Do-gooders. We don't know if they realize it, and I hope they don't, and all of us here, we just hope…" He drifted off for a moment, then snapped back. "Anyway, we don't know who is doing the buying and selling, but it's obviously not restricted to the East Coast anymore. It's here, and it's been here since the war, when the first orphan was abandoned at the station."

Blackburn nodded, then let out a great exhale. He realized his misgivings were valid when he first walked in. They formed a warning to turn around and leave. He had ignored it, and now here were the consequences —another City Hall horror show. Time to pull the plug.

"Sir, I'm sure you have a reason for telling me all this."

"Oh yes. I need to use your good working relationship with a certain easy-society madam. She's been running a cathouse down in the Tenderloin district since before I took office. Now she's got herself a brand-new nightclub, with a respectable public image."

"Ah. That would be Louisiana's place."

"The same. I wonder, is she 'Lazy Ana Bone' at the cathouse and 'Louisiana Bone' at her nightclub?"

"Can't say. I haven't spoken to her since she opened the new place. Maybe I could get you a couple of tickets?"

"Too late. Prohibition's here."

"You're joking."

"Of course. I can go whenever I want. Perquisites of office. Now, my plant at the telephone company says there have been a number of calls back and forth to New York City from Bone's public phone over the last couple of weeks. Far more than usual. There could be other calls from other places, but that brings us back to not having reliable information. So go down there and get her to agree to cooperate and funnel any information that comes in to us. If she balks at the invitation, remind her about

Prohibition. Ask her what regular surprise inspections would do to her new business."

"I guess what you mean is, give her a good scare to get her to talk."

The mayor held up his hands in defense. "Your words, not mine. No, fact is, she can put ears to countless men in this city, and more than a few women as well, to hear her tell it. One of them knows something. Maybe a bunch of them do. Impress upon Miss Bone, if you are able, that her ticket out of trouble lies in the information. She can live safer if she or one of her employees finds out what we need to know, that's all."

"I'll try, but I don't know how much cachet my name has on the street anymore."

"Listen, I'm not looking to make her life hard. Hell, Blackburn, you can bet she already knows what I think of this 'Prohibition experiment.' Why would I support closing down otherwise law-abiding tax earners when I can just look the other way once in a while, you know? The whole damned city knows I sent a bottle of champagne to every member of our civic government on the day that horse-hockey amendment passed into law. Ha! Come and get me!"

The mayor leaned in over the desktop, dropped his voice to a determined tone while he stared into Blackburn's eyes. "Detective, I am betting my political future that somebody in the employ of Miss Louisiana Bone knows these people or knows about them. Maybe she knows, herself!"

"How do you see that, sir?"

"With our old parade bombing case, you're the one who taught me the telephone can be a powerful tool for law enforcement. You think I could forget? I've been tracking the cathouse phone calls because I'll wager every cutthroat in the city passes through one of her establishments. And so somebody out there, some group of somebodies out there, knows that what others are publicly calling an 'opportunity for orphan children' is nothing more than an underground railroad for child labor."

Blackburn held up his hands. "I understand why you associate me with this issue, because of Shane and Vignette, but I never had to go through the authorities when it came to taking them in. Times were different. This was right after the Great Earthquake. Their papers were destroyed in the office fire at their former orphanage. I only got official help with identification papers after they were already with me."

"Understood. Apples and oranges, night and day, not why I called you. Detective, you maintain a far better street network than I can. We have reports of children pulled off the streets of our city and sent away for sale. Those reports come from the rare children who escaped and lived to tell about it. They talk about being bought and sold over and over, used for common labor, even as small children. Used for carnal purposes, Detective. Sold for sex. We have stories of small children being passed around from one house to another. Once they're four or five, I guess it's pretty much open season on them. Before that, they're too much trouble."

"Why would anyone lust after someone so small?"

The mayor spoke in a faint voice while looking down at the floor. "Simple. They can't fight back."

"Son of a bitch!" Blackburn felt like he had taken a punch that rocked him back on his heels.

"Yes. And there's no truthful way to soften the news. It's true whether it offends us or not. So, if you can make yourself picture all that, then congratulations, you have just met the enemy. Otherwise, we wouldn't know a thing about this. Think about that! A nationwide organization, perhaps an international organization, dealing in human misery and servitude, all in secret, right under the noses of all of us, of society itself. It makes you want to shout it in the streets!"

"I don't doubt you would, if you could get society to believe you."

"You see the problem. I'll shout it, all right, but I have to offer something people will accept. Something to cause them to take action. Otherwise the truth is so dreadful people will mock it to death and dismiss it altogether, just so they can return to the comfort of their uninformed lives. The perpetrators can only do this because nobody's watching! But all of it has an origin somewhere. Use your contacts to find out who is in charge, and let me know. Where are they?"

"I'll go start with Louisiana Bone."

"Yes! And if your investigation takes you to Chicago, or New York—"

Blackburn stiffened. "Wait. Mr. Mayor, I can't leave town for any extended—"

"Bring your adopted daughter."

"Vignette Nightingale, sir."

"Good-good. Now let's be frank, as two gentlemen ought to be, and acknowledge that this plague is coming from somewhere east of here. I'll say it: I see you and Miss Nightingale on a train in the near future. Detective, I am not tasking you with fixing the problem. You just find out what in the hell is going on."

"Good for us, sir. If we can do it."

"It will be very good for you, if you can, Detective. Very good for me, too." He picked up a dark wooden box of fine Spanish Cedar graced with ivory carvings. The lid was hinged in gold. Sunny Jim opened the top as gently as if baby chicks huddled inside.

He smiled and looked up at Blackburn.

"Cigar?"

6

CITY SQUIRE HOTEL – TOP-FLOOR PENTHOUSE

LOWER MIDTOWN, MANHATTAN

February 15th

* Late Afternoon *

CLAYTON MANNERLY HELD THE CANDLESTICK phone as if he wanted to choke it to death while he growled into the speaker cone. "You don't mean that, Salsedo. What you are going to do is put that out of your mind. And don't ever say it, don't even think it again. You do that, and between you and me, it's no harm, no foul. We'll just let that one lie there and both walk away. It's simple for you, Signore Salsedo. Simple for me, too."

Salsedo's voice had that same tinny, long-distance sound as their last call early that morning. This time he was obviously phoning from somewhere on the waterfront; ship's bells rang out in the background. "No. I thought about it, Mr. Mannerly. And I won't do it."

"Wait! Wait before you make another sound, *Signore*, ask yourself—"

"Mr. Mannerly. Sir. I don't go after kids as targets. I am a political animal, not a mere criminal."

"Are you, now? Find religion, did you?"

"I don't need religion to tell me it's wrong to target a little boy. I will honor Mr. Buda's request to return to New York City, but from now on, I deal with him. I am a Galleanist, and so is he. You? I don't know what you are."

Clayton Mannerly had not risen to the intersection between the smuggling line from Europe and the financial lines to this country's elite without consistently honing his ability to think up a lie quick as a blink and deliver it like a priest. "So you're going to hang up before you hear about the surprise we have for you, then?"

"What's that?"

"I talked it over with Buda and convinced him we don't need to chance getting rid of the boy. Too much risk of attracting unwanted attention. What we want to do is see if he talks at all, which he may well not do. Then if he does, we simply discredit the hell out of him. He's a godforsaken runaway."

Mannerly was making it all up in free form, now. He skated on the surface of his own stream of bovine feces like Hans Brinker on his silver skates.

"We'll just say I gave him a chance and he threw it out like garbage. We can bury him under so many accusations he'll never dig himself out. Safer for us to do it that way."

"All right! There! Good! I agree with you all the way. I don't care about some kid's stinking reputation, as long as we leave him alone to live his life. We have more important fish to catch."

"For once we're in perfect agreement, *Signore*."

"Tell me, do you pronounce 'signore' that way when you address Signore Buda? Always with you there is the tone of a problem."

"My problem is that you called to refuse my order before you knew I changed my mind!"

"So what?"

"Oh, so what? So, the next time I see you, sir, I will be the one to ask you why it matters that you refused my order before you knew it was cancelled."

Mannerly toggled the telephone's fork-handled receiver with his fingers until he heard the line go dead, then replaced the black ebony earpiece on the polished metal receiver arm.

He muttered to himself, "By then, we'll both know the answer." And Salsedo's opinion would be irrelevant. Mannerly had other soldiers on the payroll. Nobody would ever question the simple disappearance of a runaway, and he had delivered Buda's message to come home as instructed.

And if the boy was found dead, who in this world had the time or inclination to investigate it? He would be another nobody, quickly forgotten.

Louisiana Bone hustled Randall Blackburn into a private parlor deep within her "original establishment," as she liked to call it. The parlor was an ideal, task-specific place to talk and perhaps share a glass of wine. The nearby bed was well made and tastefully appointed. She sat him down at a small table, closed the door behind them, pulled up a second chair, and plopped down on her ample rear with an audible thump.

"Damn it all, Detective, you can't be talking out in the open about things like that. These girls don't just have ears, you know. They have mouths! Big ones, some of 'em, and you can never tell which direction things will spread. There's no controlling it."

"I realize that. But you were trying to hustle me out the front door, and I was just hoping a little commotion would help put you in the mood to talk. Seemed to work."

"Hustle you out? That's your imagination working against you! I would never give you the bum's rush. We go back."

"Well, good. So give out."

She pointed at his crotch. "You just remember you're a private dick now. Not on the force, eh?"

"I never forget that. Not a chance."

"Good. And since you're all private now and don't have City Hall breathing down your neck all day—"

"Amen."

"—then I guess you know what I mean about 'certain things.' Certain things we got to play close to the vest."

"Don't we all. Now about the phone call..."

"To begin with, that phone is one of four others all on the same line in this house. People who want to borrow it never ask if the line is private, so I don't mention that I can listen in any time I want. It's my damn phone!"

"Maybe legal, maybe not. Depends on your attorney, most likely."

"You want to hear this?"

"You want liquor inspections?"

"What? You would never."

"The phone call. You already mentioned it downstairs. So give."

"Damn! We listen in to get information to help to...to *encourage* our wealthier clients to pay fair, ah, *remittances* to the girls. And the house."

"So blackmail, then."

"No need for rudeness. If they didn't say it, we couldn't use it."

"Which one of you caught this information?"

"One of my employees, Detective. That's all I have to say there."

"All right, so this long-distance phone call comes in, and you said downstairs that whoever answered the call hears him mention Mario Buda and somehow gets the reference?"

Louisiana Bone exhaled and dropped her gaze to the floor, shaking her head. She appeared deep in thought for a moment, *beat...beat...beat...*then straightened up. This time she nodded.

"Look. No, I didn't take the call, okay? But my girl who was on the phone repeated the name out loud. 'Buddha,' like she wanted to get it right. It was quiet enough in the house just then for me to overhear. Anyway, so I picked up the extension phone and gave a listen, and this man tells my employee he owns the City Squire Hotel. I know of that place. Fancy. I already told you I was coming to you with this."

"Except you didn't."

"Not *yet*. Anyway, he's calling for a guy who left him this number, name of Andrea Salsedo."

"Why call here?"

"Customers sometimes leave this number with people for remote calls. Maybe things they can't talk about in their lives. I charge 'em a fortune to use the phone and they keep on coming. Gambling, whores, and expensive phone calls, they can't figure out why they don't get ahead in life, eh?"

"The call."

"So who knows if he really owns the hotel, but he sounded like class.

Educated. Name of Mannerly. He was in a big hurry to have a conversation with a man I happen to know for a street thug. So I break into the call and tell him, 'Your party's not here now, but he drinks here on a regular basis and I expect him in later.' When he hears that, he says have Salsedo call him back immediately, that same day. Urgent! You know those guys, everything is urgent-shmurgent."

"Did he sound anxious? Panicky?"

"Nah, too cool for that. But does it not strike us both as odd that some bigwig calls across the entire country because he needs something important from some louse?"

"You already know this Salsedo guy?"

"Not personally, but I know he used to work for that Galleani character. That's enough."

"Miz Bone, I need to be certain here. By 'Galleani' you mean the anarchist who was in town when the parade got bombed?"

"Oh yeah. I heard him talk to a pretty big audience of working people, down by the docks before it all went nuts. Mostly men, for sure, but some women, too. Anyway, when this Salsedo character comes back in, I tell him about the message, and I mean he *jumps* for the phone. Then I go upstairs and pick up the extension. I was just in time to hear the caller tell Salsedo that 'Buddha' has ordered him to return to New York City for some kind of mission, but I missed the part where he said why."

"Buddha. A mission. Could he have meant Mario Buda?"

"No way to know. That's why I was gonna call you. But now that you say Mario Buda, I recall that name from the parade bombing, right?"

"Right, it's spelled B-U-D-A."

"Yeah, that's it! That bastard Buda! I tell you, I will never allow a single person to pass in front of me who's got any tie to that bombing. I will turn the bastard in, no matter who it is. Regular customer worth hundreds of dollars a year? Poof! Gone like that. Good riddance."

"Fine. So if I boil this thing down, what we have is: a guy named Salsedo and our old pal Mario Buda have some sort of 'mission' going that requires Salsedo to be in New York. Highly suspicious news, but not what I came here asking you about, is it?"

"Yeah, okay, like you asked me *in front of the other customers*, I never use any kidnapped girls here. Never would. Are you joking? Try to imagine all the extra management headaches of housing prisoners. Please. My girls love to work here. They're safe, and the money's good. Anyone who works for me can head for the door anytime they want. And as far as children go, you know there's never any kids around here, Detective. I tell you, hand on the Bible, best I do for a kid, when one comes to the door sniffin' around, I run 'em on an errand for a couple coins. They don't even come inside."

Blackburn nodded. "It's all right, I'm with you, here. Never saw you in the company of any children over the years."

"Mm-hm. Course, you came here knowin' that..."

"I came here hoping this thing doesn't even exist. I'm hoping no matter how rich someone is, they can't get away with running a smuggling ring selling men, women, and children all over the world with the help of powerful politicians, and do it in secret."

That one stopped her for a moment while she waited for a punchline that never arrived.

"Jesus. You got to be exaggerating that, right? To get my help or something, right?"

"That's the case as it was presented to me."

"Stop it. We done away with slavery in this country!"

"Well. We made it illegal."

"Damn straight, we did!"

"Mm, yes. Prostitution is illegal. Robbing banks is illegal. Mugging a street whore is illegal, stealing from the poor box at church is illegal."

"All right."

"And since January of last year, every drop of booze served here is illegal."

"Okaaaay. So?"

"So there's illegal for you."

Neither one spoke. Neither moved. Their facial expressions did not alter. It might have been a moment frozen in time but for the patient ticking of the grandfather clock in the next room.

The clock helpfully selected this moment to ring its half-hour chime, which served to break the freeze and cause Bone to take a huge breath. She jabbed her elbows onto the table and rested her face in her hands.

Blackburn's years of experience interviewing witnesses and perpetrators from every walk of life advised him to push her one step further. "If they're doing it, they get away with it for the same reason you get away with operating your business here. I'm sorry to say it, and I don't mean to insult you. We both know there are wide variations in the evils of this world. Some we can live with and control, some simply destroy us if we get too close. If adults choose to drink and have sex, that's one thing. When we kidnap victims and force our will on them, when we do it to children..."

Blackburn leaned close. "I'm hoping somebody up in the ranks is bucking for a promotion and merely dreamed up all this garbage for effect. But the cruel reality is, the hunt is on now. It stays on, whether either of us likes it or not. So please. They want to know everything there is to know about any sort of underground organization trading in people—especially kids—no matter what label it hides under. Anything you hear, anything you can find out."

"Well, hot stinking damn, for once I agree with you, Detective. Straight up and down."

Blackburn pulled a business card from his pocket and placed it on the table before her.

"Ask every one of your employees and promise them they will be rewarded: Are any of the ladies working here controlled by an outsider? If any female, of any age, tries to come to work for you, and you get the feeling they're controlled by somebody, you will call me, yes? Say yes."

"Wait, all you want is for me to single out women who don't appear to be here under their own power?"

"Any such woman, call me right away. Then I can interview her before she gets wind of me and disappears. We don't have any desire to interrupt your business. We just have to track this supply line all the way back to the source."

"We do? Which 'we' is that?" She stared at him for a beat. Blackburn wondered if she was waiting for him to laugh or at least crack a smile. Instead he leaned toward her and fixed her with a direct gaze while he kept his voice soft enough to protect against being overheard by the staff. "Louisiana Bone, if you don't find out what they want and they begin to think you're dragging your feet, they'll wonder if it's because I'm being soft on you. Understand? It won't matter what I tell them; they'll replace me with someone who will occupy your home and businesses with undercover agents. You and your girls, your women, will be used as bait against criminals. We can arrest or kill the targets, but we cannot guarantee the safety of your employees. Or their clients. Or even any random bystanders."

He sat back up to a full upright position, and his expression managed to convey a powerful desire that she not bring the authorities down upon herself.

Bone looked into Blackburn's eyes and appeared to see those of a friend. She broke a small smile and replied, "You're an honest man, Detective Blackburn."

A moment later, she turned the quality of her smile to one of sultry seduction while she held his gaze a bit too long for polite society. She only broke eye contact to look down at the calling card on the tabletop while she reached to pick it up. She held it between her fingers and placed her tongue just a touch out of her mouth while she slowly moistened her lips.

It took a moment, as if her lips were quite dry. Then Louisiana "Lazy Ana" Bone stuck his calling card between two things the public could no longer hire her to display. Old habits.

Blackburn smiled. "Miz Bone, I'm on the job."

She laughed at her own audacity. "Hoo-ey, I crack myself up. Anyway, don't you worry. I can put more ears out into the world than you can imagine. Not just here, either. Why, the things people will reveal at home in front of their domestic help, I tell you, it's appalling. Every servant in the city knows I pay for good information, Detective. Every single one of them."

"What about new employees coming in who don't know about you?"

"What's that thing they say money does?"

"...Ah."

"Believe it, they all find out soon enough. The grapevine knows we're reliable and pay good. Some of them household domestics might even want to come forward for free, once they realize somebody out here actually gives a damn what they know."

Blackburn nodded. "I hold out my expectation that you will rise to this for me, Miz Bone. One piece of good information. Get us started. "

They each stood, and she stepped to the door, opened it for him, and stood waiting. He straightened his jacket and stepped from behind the table. "All right, then," he said. "I'll make sure Mayor Rolph gets the message that we'll hear whatever you know, and we'll get it as soon as you know it. In return you can trust me to make him understand there's no reason to get harsh with you, a cooperative witness."

"Does he have to listen to your advice?"

"He does not."

"Well, he damn well better. The stuff I've got on half the people in his administration..." She gave him a leering smile. "Present company excluded."

He snickered and shook his head. "Just stay focused on getting the information. A result like that could keep the city off your back for years to come."

"Off my back for years to come? Ha! On a more humble level, do you think there's any chance at all the mayor at least knows how to protect me, if and when word gets out saying I passed on extremely delicate information?"

She dropped her voice to a whisper: "Not that I intend to be anybody's victim, any day of the week!" While she spoke, she slowly pulled the hem of her skirt until it rose high enough to reveal a small-handled eight-shot revolver, with the holster strapped to her naked thigh.

He smiled and pitched his voice to the same level of whisper. "You're a prudent woman, Miz Bone."

"Louisiana."

"Beats 'Lazy Ana,' I do admit. But private guards will serve you far better than the city, believe me on that. Plenty of large-sized, out-of-work dockworkers are milling around the Embarcadero. They'll fight like dogs for you in return for a decent wage. You might need them. Because the kind of thing we're talking about—the kind of people who are in it up to their necks, they're going to fight to the death. They pretty much have to."

"Son of a bitch, Detective, you trying to scare me? Good job. Maybe we both fight our share of real-life demons, but taking children who have already been orphaned by the war and then, why, if this organization even exists—it's run by monsters."

"Agreed. They're so cold-blooded, it makes you wonder if they look like reptiles or more like regular demons."

The elder madam shivered and wrapped her arms around herself. "I'll take the reptile demons any day."

"How's that?"

"Regular demons can look like anything they want."

Blackburn also felt the urge to shiver at that, but his sense of pride forced him to ignore it.

7

THE BLACKBURN-NIGHTINGALE RESIDENCE
GOLDEN GATE PARK, SAN FRANCISCO

February 15th
* That Evening *

BLACKBURN PARKED HIS WAVERLEY in his rented spot at the electric stable a couple of blocks from the house, silently pulled nose-in to the wall charger, and hooked it up. He made the quick walk home in three minutes. When he approached the house, he was glad to see Vignette's Harley-sidecar combination parked out front, but it was a surprise when he turned onto their walkway and saw Vignette skipping down the path to intercept him. Interceptions always preceded big explanations. He sensed one coming.

"Hi! Hello there! Welcome home!"

She was too cheerful. It was odd. "Howdy."

"Got a surprise inside..."

Blackburn smiled and shook his head. "Uh-oh."

"No, no, nothing bad. Just an eleven-year-old boy. Runaway."

"Another run—"

She held up the flat of her hand to stop him...waited...then pressed on.

"Living on the streets. Says his name is Dante. I picked him up this afternoon to help him escape from a shopkeeper after he and his cohorts stole some pastries."

"All right, and he's here because…"

"This is the part you need to hear me out on. I mean, I can see how a person could get the wrong idea on the surface of it."

"The wrong idea? Vignette, you keep finding strays and bringing them home for a meal, which is all well and good, but after you have to turn them loose on the street again, you feel lousy for days. That's the part I don't get."

"Okay, this one's not like that. Come on in the house! You have to meet him! He's in there right now preparing our dinner." She giggled at the thought.

"He's what? An eleven-year-old?"

"No ordinary eleven-year-old, let me tell you. And he was the chef's helper at the last home he was in."

"An eleven-year-old chef's helper. How come he's not back there now?"

"See, that's the intriguing part. He ran off, won't say why, exactly. Something made it worthwhile for him to jump a train and ride across the country all alone." She noticed his eyes widen, so she pressed on. "He doesn't want to give any details, but I want to find out why."

"An orphan riding the train from New York? There must be something in the wind. Let's go on in."

Vignette took him inside and walked him back to the kitchen, where she made the introductions between Blackburn and their new visitor.

Blackburn was surprised to meet Dante and discover him working their large gas stove like a professional. It appeared that Vignette had truly found an extraordinary kid this time. He was a bit tall for his age, with an open face and an easy smile.

"Dante!" Vignette said. "This is Randall Blackburn. Randall, this is Dante."

Dante put down a spatula and stuck out his hand. "Pleased to meet you,

Mister Blackburn. Vignette told me all about you and how you work together as detectives."

Blackburn shook his hand and regarded the boy with interest. "Hello, Dante. You cooked all this?"

"No, no, Vignette helped."

"Actually, I didn't do much except—"

"She organized the whole thing. I'm just taking care of the cooking. I sure hope you don't mind me working in here like this. I have experience."

"Well, no. No, that's fine, Dante. Appreciate your help."

Vignette pulled Randall close and whispered, "He had some cleaner clothing in his bag, so I let him use the bathroom to wash up and change. He's been using the public washroom at the docks. He wasn't that dirty, considering."

"That's all right. Rather have a clean guest who knows where the commode is."

"Yes. And I showed him the clean towels."

Blackburn could see this boy was unique among the other urchins Vignette brought home, something she began doing after she bought the new Harley with the sidecar after Shane was killed. While those other unfortunates tended to be dimmed by malnutrition and loneliness, this boy appeared bright and alert. Blackburn decided either Dante had been on the streets for only a short time, or he had natural survival skills few other orphans possessed.

Dante smiled at both of them and held out his arms. "I can finish up here. Why don't you both go on out and have a seat? Relax. I'll let you know when it's time."

Blackburn slid a surprised look at Vignette, who beamed in response. "We've been talking all afternoon, Randall. He's something, isn't he?"

"Yes, indeed," he agreed. "Good to meet you, Dante. Just, ah, give a shout when you're ready."

"Or if you need some help," Vignette added.

Blackburn found Dante's level of poise and self-awareness to be reassuring. He had already decided the boy could be trusted with their food. Vignette spoke of spending hours with him today and was clearly convinced about him.

He gave himself a silent order for the old beat cop inside him to relax for once and forget about all those gruesome homicide scenes he had encountered over the years. Instinct honed by experience told him although there was always a certain level of vulnerability in allowing a stranger into your home, there was no danger here.

~

Fifteen minutes later, Blackburn was seated at their dinner table while Dante and Vignette brought out steaming dishes from the kitchen. "Here we go!" she cheerfully called.

"Nothing fancy," Dante chimed in. "Pork chops, baked potatoes, green beans, corn on the cob. No time to bake anything."

"You can bake, too?" Blackburn gave a low whistle. "Dante, I'm very impressed a boy your age could produce a whole meal like this."

"I just had to learn it, back where I was, that's all. They said if a boy's old enough to operate a loom for a full shift, he can learn his way around a kitchen. Besides, their chef needed a helper."

"You were working a loom? Where, in a factory?"

"Just that one summer."

Randall rubbed the back of his hand over his eyes. "A lot of kids get put to work too early, if you ask me. My dad let me wait 'til I was fourteen before I joined him at the sawmill in the afternoons after school, but I still say that was on the young side for such dangerous work."

"Did you like it?"

"I broke out and headed for the city on the day I turned eighteen."

The three were quiet for a moment, then Blackburn drew a deep breath and said, "Well, then! Let's pass these dishes around, shall we?"

Vignette smiled. "We ate a couple hours ago, and I'm hungry again!"

Dante grinned. "For me to say I'm hungry just means I'm awake."

They began passing the dishes around, helping themselves to a plentiful dinner.

"Dante," Blackburn spoke up, "we have a tradition of saying a prayer before the meal. We take turns saying it, but guests get first choice." He glanced at Vignette and reached out to take her hand.

She took his hand and reached out her other arm, but hesitated, unsure whether to extend it toward Randall or Dante.

"Up to you, son."

With a shy smile, Dante reached out both hands and grasped each of theirs. He closed his eyes and spoke in a whisper.

"Lord, I know you've sure been good to me today, and I thank you from my heart. I can see you been good to Vignette and Mr. Blackburn here, too, by the life they have. So you got us all this far, and we're grateful for that. We hate to keep asking you to sort things out for us, so we'll keep doing the best we can right here. Amen."

Blackburn chuckled. "I'll 'Amen' to that."

"Me too." Vignette nodded. "Amen."

They released their hands, helping themselves to the meal, then set to their plates.

"Oh, this all smells so good," Vignette enthused. She picked up a glass water pitcher and filled their three glasses.

Dante said, "I hope you like chops cooked this way. I slow-cook it through to get it done right, then pull it out and fire up the pan until it's scorching hot, then lay 'em back in for about ten seconds on each side. That gives it the little char on the coating."

Randall spoke with his mouth full. "Best pork chop I ever had, right here. Tender inside, crispy on the outside, almost a burnt flavor, but not really burned, it's just a...a..."

"A char?" Dante smiled.

Blackburn raised his fork. "Here's to the char." They smiled and nodded in agreement but did not stop eating. He turned to the wine cabinet behind his place at the table, pulled out a bottle, and opened it with a corkscrew, saying, "Dante, I usually serve red wine with dinner, but I think it will have to be water for you."

"I've got the water right here, Mr. Blackburn. A lot of old drinkers end up in the same alleys we sleep in, so I get the picture."

Vignette sighed. "Yep, this Prohibition thing they started last year isn't doing anything but making it harder for people to keep on doing what they were already doing in the first place."

"I've heard about Prohibition. I mean, everybody has if they can read.

All the posters make it pretty hard not to know. I just figured it was something too complicated for me, or that I'm too young to understand how it can work."

"I'm forty-nine, and I'm too young to understand how it can work."

"Make a lot of smugglers rich, I suppose," Vignette said. "Hey, is that it, Dante? Were your foster parents smuggling liquor? That might explain—"

"No. No more talk about that." His tone made it clear the topic was off-limits.

"Fine, then, but I think Randall should hear what you told me today. At least a little of it, can't you? You're safe here with us." She sat back as if to say she was done talking until he gave the answer.

Randall was wise enough to stay out of it and let Dante work it out himself. The room took on a thick silence while the boy stared at his plate, idly pushing the food around with his fork. When he reached his decision, it showed on his face. He kept his gaze on the food but began to speak.

"There are parts... I'll only talk about the train trip. Things like that. Not..." His voice trailed off.

"Fine, Dante," Vignette encouraged him. "You decide how much to say."

He took a deep breath and began. "I came along first. Just me. There was only enough for one ticket to San Francisco from New York City."

"Why San Francisco?" Vignette prompted.

"I picked it. It's about as far from Clayton's house as you can get. I ran first because she was going to hang back for just a couple of days to push the idea that I must have been kidnapped. To keep reminding everybody I would never leave without her, which is the truth! We did it that way to throw them off track so we could both get out and then meet. Get far enough away that Clayton and his men can't find us. Only she keeps not showing up, and there's no way to find out why."

Blackburn was leaning forward now, wide awake. "Who is she? Your mother? Sister?"

He shook his head. "My auntie. Eliana. The only family I have. She should have been here days ago."

Vignette chimed in, "They were supposed to meet in front of the Clock Tower down at the Ferry Building. He's been waiting for over six weeks."

Dante nodded. "If she's alive, she's back there with Clayton."

Vignette quietly added, "His name is Clayton Mannerly. Big hotel owner. Eliana works as a domestic."

"So you see," Dante went on, "I have to go back now. I gave it one more day today, even though I already knew something was wrong. I have to find Eliana and make sure she's okay. I made a mistake to run from New York like that, but I've learned a lot out on the streets."

"How does anything you learned on the streets help you with this?" Blackburn asked.

"I learned how I should have done it. I was right not to spend money on the tickets, but I should have used it to hire a few giant guys instead. They can walk her out of there and dare anyone to stop us. Disappear before anyone can get the police to show up, whether they own a telephone or not."

Blackburn shook his head. "I spent twenty years putting the guys you're talking about in jail, Dante, and I know you can hire them for muscle, but they're unpredictable as hell, those men. That said, I respect your goal. If she wants to work somewhere else, or if you two want to live somewhere else, you shouldn't have to fight for it. She's an adult, she's your relative, and she's all you've got."

"Right, I guess."

"That settles it. Nobody can stop you both from doing that. Your real question is, where is she right now? If the police aren't holding her for something, she has to be allowed to travel wherever she wants."

"Randall," Vignette quietly said, "maybe we could check on this for him. You know, unofficially. Ask a few questions?"

He regarded her with a wan smile, realizing this was where they were headed all along. As usual, his adopted daughter had exercised that same unique form of instinct he had witnessed in her behavior over the years. It had somehow compelled her to find this boy, out of so many other rowdy street kids, and to recognize the rare spirit in him that brings a story like his to light.

He gave a sharp nod and rapped on the table. "All right! You have officially piqued my curiosity. I think we should be able to find out what is going on with your Aunt Eliana."

For a moment, Dante's face resembled that of a trusting four-year-old.

His voice came out in a whisper. "Could you do that? Vignette, Detective... Mister...Blackburn, I'd be so grateful. Hell, I am already!" He exhaled a long breath and slowly sagged in his chair. "Thank you both."

He gave another deep exhale while a weary expression crossed his face, as if he had just put down a heavy load after a long journey. In spite of his fatigue, he beamed a grateful smile at each of them. With that, Dante pushed his dinner dishes aside, folded his arms atop the table, and—still smiling—lay his head on his arms and went to sleep.

Randall and Vignette looked at each other in surprise but remained silent.

Dante's breathing quickly became deep. In a matter of seconds, he was nearly unconscious. The only sounds were the clip-clops of heavy hooves while a draft wagon rolled by out front.

Vignette kept her eyes on Dante and whispered, "Okay, I've never seen anybody do that before."

Blackburn quietly said, "Wonder how long it's been since he felt safe enough to sleep?"

"His bag was stashed under Pier 7. I can't imagine trying to sleep down there in the cold."

"With more than a few dangerous adults for company. You better get him a pillow and some linens. I'll carry him over to the sofa."

Blackburn had napped on that sofa often enough to know it made a good bed. "This way we can let him sleep in, send him on his way in the morning with a hot meal and a sack lunch."

Vignette knitted her brow. "What? That's it?"

"We're on a case. I'll tell you about it as soon as we're done here."

Vignette looked unconvinced, but she hurried off to get the pillow and linens anyway.

ST. ADRIAN'S SEMINARY

AT BROOKLYN STATE HOSPITAL FARM COLONY – QUEENS, NY
February 16th
* 8:50 a.m. *

CLAYTON MANNERLY STEPPED OFF THE EASTBOUND Long Island Railway car from Penn Station at the Queens Village stop promptly at 8:50 a.m., satisfied that at least the cumbersome journey took only half an hour, once the all-aboard was called. His private automobile and driver usually transported him, but today's task was bathed in secrecy. He could ill afford to leave any record of his travel with the help.

He knew truth often died boiled in a pot of gossip. Especially truths like these at hand this morning. They required a world of explanations and critical thinking, all of which were a waste of time to the popular culture, since so little would survive the streams of gossip, anyway.

Example: Today's little jaunt involved a journey to an ersatz seminary school run by a charlatan of a priest directly under the noses of the guards and inmates at one of the local state-run insane asylums, right over the East River in Queens.

Such things could play poorly for all the other hoteliers on Wall Street.

He had never made the trip by choice. But no matter how tenderly the invitation was delivered by Father Young, this morning Mannerly moved under strict orders.

Few people alive could summon him to their door, fewer still force him to make a morning train trip, despite his need to be at the desk tending to the plans and working the phones. His schedule allowed nothing at all for free time. He was riding herd on a massive strategy, an ingenious concept marred only by too many loose ends. Each and every one had to be anticipated and patched before Election Day in eight months, and prudence required as few people as possible to be in the know. Leaving much of that heavy load to Clayton Mannerly.

To his chagrin, he knew there was no substantial financial relief coming before the presidential election. The Movers were demanding nearly all the proceeds from the smuggling operation and parting with less and less of it as time went on. Nobody had the wherewithal to fight them over it. That left Mannerly vulnerable to the threat delivered with an arrogant telephone call to his office the prior evening, when the Reverend Canon Richard Young, head of St. Adrian's Seminary, gently informed Mannerly he would be attending a private meeting at Young's "humble seminary" at nine sharp the next morning. "But come round to the Housing Building, this time—not my office." The priest had hung up without waiting for any sort of response.

Mannerly still seethed. This marked the third such "summons" in the past few weeks, sapping energy he already struggled to maintain. He awoke that morning with pain in his jaw from grinding his teeth in his sleep. A toxic mixture of outrage and indignation was building to explosive levels. It was only the need to cure his anxieties that put him on the train.

He tightened his butt muscles and hiked, step by extra-long step, directly past the hapless souls laboring on the hospital work farm. One of them waved his shovel in some sort of mock greeting and giggled. Mannerly looked away and quickened his pace.

After another hundred yards he passed the front of the main building, which shared an entrance with the seminary. He continued around to the side of the main hall as he had been instructed in his summons, to the set of heavy buildings that once housed the armory and an indoor shooting range. The thick-walled structures were clearly designed to minimize any ammo explosions.

The gated sign at the front entrance boasted a whitewashed background bearing tall black letters in chipped paint: *Brooklyn State Hospital Farm Colony*.

He had once asked Father Young, "Why would the Catholic Church put a seminary in an insane asylum?"

The priest responded without missing a beat, "The Church, in its mercy, ministers to all the unfortunates of this world."

He felt no concern over whether the priest believed his drivel or not. It sounded great. It sounded real. It had all the public relations value he needed to connect the immigration line he used in his hotel employment practices with the supply of boys for the seminary, young girls for pleasure work, and older females for domestic labor.

The privileged few adults got hotel work, but only if they were very good, like Eliana. Quiet of comportment, willing to sometimes work long hours, fine to look at, broken in spirit, pliable in bed.

Asylum for the troublemakers. They just disappeared. If a few of them had others on the outside who demanded answers for their absence, a determined spewing of bureaucratic nonsense eventually caused the complainants to give up in frustration and go back to their mayfly lives. The Lunacy Commission of New York State needed justification for its existence as much as any bureaucracy, but the silent system supporting it required no public record.

This method of obtaining the enslaved services of people who were only allowed to exist to serve others, and do so under the noses of so-called polite society, was worth protecting for some of the most wealthy and powerful people in the nation. Perhaps the world, for all he knew.

New York City was that kind of town.

He reached the front of the Seminary Dorm Building to find his host already waiting. The Reverend Canon Richard Young stood attired in his formal priest regalia, framed by the open doorway and wearing the familiar smirk he used for a smile. He stood taller than Mannerly and was more robustly built. Thick swirls of silver-gray hair topped his head and gave him the general appearance of a saintly man. It accented his sparkly blue eyes and signaled a priest of compassion and good humor.

Patients had to be crazy to refuse to trust him.

Father Young raised his eyebrows half an inch by way of greeting before he turned to walk back inside, leaving his visitor to follow. Mannerly stifled an indignant remark at this rudeness and tromped along behind him.

Once inside, Mannerly blinked while his eyes adjusted to the low light. When he turned his focus upward, he realized the hallway ceilings were draped with a string of low-wattage bulbs. They barely illuminated Father Young's receding form.

The rooms he saw at first were empty, though all showed evidence of recent occupancy. Each had its own dim ceiling light, most of them dark, since the missing residents were apparently out and about with what the priest had called their "therapeutic outdoor work." One room offered up a major surprise, illuminated by an additional table lamp placed next to an inmate who lay silent on the bed while another slumped in a nearby chair.

A few moments later, they were looking in on yet another inmate-resident. So far, Father Young had made no attempt to engage with either Mannerly or the others. He simply stood back, allowing Mannerly to soak in the sights and come to terms with the sort of lives these most unfortunate people were condemned to lead if they could not or would not live as obedient servants.

The thought ran through him, *"Seminary," for God's sake!* He had to check his facial expression to avoid giving away the revulsion gripping him.

The damned priest appeared to consider his message an important part of their business together, and while the arrangement had served Mannerly and the new missus very well for over two years, there was a reality here completely new to him.

But as far as he was concerned, the impact of the message stalled inside the darkened building. The depressing sights only deepened his state of outrage over having been summarily summoned and then treated in this fashion. Yes, misery was rife, and here was the world's misery at rock bottom. Why tell him that? He understood. He got the point.

Mannerly's rage grew over the slow roll-out. He decided to try an attitude test on the priest. "Whatever your intention, Father, wouldn't we have had a better guarantee of anonymity at your place at the institution on Blackwell's Island instead of here in Queens? Perhaps we could postpone..." He trailed off.

There were no indications Father Young heard him at all. They had gone beyond mere awkwardness. Clayton Mannerly felt his pulse begin to hammer, as if his body knew of some threat his brain had not yet recognized.

At last, the priest stopped at the last room on that hallway, peered inside and gave a nod to himself, then turned and stood away from the doorframe. He gestured for Mannerly to have a look.

He did so without hesitation, anxious to get things moving, but as soon as he looked inside the room, his knees nearly gave out beneath him. The room was shadowy and dim, with no light overhead. The air hung thick with feces, urine, and vomit. One small lamp shone a watery yellow cone of light over a narrow canvas cot with a patient sitting upright. The man may have been in his fifties but looked much older, thin and decrepit. He sat with his back to the wall and knees tucked to his chest, with his arms wrapped tight around them. Trembling, he muttered under his breath while he stared around at the room with an expression of great anxiety.

His eyes tracked invisible things. He did not appear to be aware of Mannerly and Father Young at all.

Young spoke in his full, sonorous voice, so perfect for delivering homilies from a pulpit and capturing the ears of his flock. While he spoke, he indicated the patient with his gaze.

"This one completely rejects our work here."

"What's...what's his name?"

"Name? Oh, I don't know. He was with us a long time. Back in San Francisco, he was known as Friar John, more of a title than a name, really, and he was headmaster of our orphanage operation. After the earthquake fires destroyed everything, he took it as a sign of Divine punishment instead of seeing it as the natural catastrophe it was. Went through some kind of transformation. We put him in a silent meditation monastery, but after a while they could not shut him up anymore. Do you hear me? Could not. See, that's the important part of the story: the potential for the wrong words to get out."

"This is why you called me? To see this?"

"Even after a stern warning, he went out on the streets. Started to talk about things we cannot, simply *cannot* have floating around out there. Clayton, you know yourself there's already a lot of resentment against the clergy. Driven by the Devil. Anyway, soon as the cops pulled him in and called us, we were able to get him back here."

"God have mercy on him."

"Perhaps."

"How long has he been…"

"In treatment?"

"Treatment. Yes."

"Oh, he's in the early stages, I should imagine. Plenty of hours of therapeutic treatment left to go: hydrotherapy, temperature therapy, sleep-deprivation therapy. Sometimes the truly guilt-ridden respond well to humiliation therapy. Many of them feel they deserve it, that sort of thing."

"But he came here when?"

"It's been a few months, but as you can see, Friar John can hardly be said to be responding well, so far. We'll have to stiffen our efforts on his behalf. We go the extra mile for those who were once one of our flock."

Mannerly squinted in the dim light to take in more of the man's features. The news was all bad. This was a broken human being, gone in health and surely gone in mind. His yellow skin stretched over a cadaverous skull, and his teeth were all missing from his slack mouth. He showed no awareness or concern over the long string of drool hanging from his chin to his lap.

Mannerly gasped in shock when Friar John suddenly lifted his head and turned his eyes to meet his. In that moment, his clouded gaze cleared. The old friar tried to say something, but his throat seized under the effort and his breath came out in a soundless rasp.

He swallowed and tried again, and this time got out, "Cahhhhhh…"

Mannerly turned to Father Young, who simply raised his eyebrows once again and made it a point to turn back down the hall, as if studying shadows.

Friar John swallowed hard two more times, then made another try. "Can you…ask them…if I can die now?"

"Bwuhhh!" The shock exploded out of Mannerly. He would not have been more horrified if a ghost jumped out of the ground.

"They won't tell me!" Friar John tried to shout, his voice cracking. The words came out in a rasp.

Mannerly staggered backward until he ran into the doorpost. All he could think of was to give this creature whatever it wanted and then get the hell out of there.

"I'll find out for you! I'm sure you can—uh…"

He stumbled down the hall constantly checking over his shoulder. It took only seconds to catch up to Father Young but felt like half an hour.

Young made no reaction to Mannerly's anxious state when he arrived panting and fell in beside him. The priest also exhibited no curiosity about the shouting from the patient's room. He seemed to understand, and somehow, to approve.

But as far as standing up for Friar John, it struck Mannerly that Father Young surely knew everything he needed to know about this man already, this pitiful creature. The seminary had been housing him for months, and it was now the erstwhile Friar John's permanent home.

So it followed, there was really nothing for Mannerly to tell Father Young on the crazed friar's behalf about his desire to die. He asked himself, Was that not so? Priests tried to help people to live, and if it was time, a priest would help them die. But they did not facilitate suicide. Their answer to anyone's request to die had to be, *No, you can't commit suicide because your flesh pains you. No matter how great the pain. Instead, turn your eyes to the Cross and give your pain to your Savior.*

So it was simple. There was nothing to ask on Friar John's behalf. Clayton Mannerly and the Reverend Canon Richard Young had far more urgent concerns than the fate of an inmate already halfway into his grave. He did not ask himself why Father Young would adhere to this particular rule against assisting suicide when he disregarded so many others.

There. That was it, then. This conclusion released Mannerly from any obligation on Friar John's behalf. What the broken man asked was impossible. He could not be given assistance with suicide, not even in the form of benign neglect.

A flash of anger went through him. Why wouldn't Friar John realize that? Why would he ask the impossible of another human being? *What a selfish bastard.* The man had to be delirious.

Without looking over at Mannerly, Father Young muttered just loud enough to make himself heard, "Poor soul. He forgot, *silence* is the watchword." He took a deep breath and once again produced the smirk that passed for a smile and raised his finger to his lips. "Come along, I'll walk you to the door."

At the exit a moment later, Father Young paused just inside the building and stopped Mannerly by holding out his fingers so they barely touched Mannerly's chest. It was the slightest touch, just enough to command his attention. Father Young kept his fingers there while he stepped in close enough for his breath to convey the remnants of that morning's porridge. "So! Much for you to see here today. Yes, Clayton?"

"Well, yeah."

"This calling takes all my time, though. I can't be worrying about your organization."

"How is my end of it any of your concern?"

"Because I have to answer to the bishop. Don't think just because he introduced us, he will be unwavering in his support."

"Support? All we need from him is the supply. I don't see that man talking to any outsiders."

"Unless politics forces him to. You don't think we have politics in the church hierarchy? There is little else but politics in the ranks, and if he has to burnish his image by nailing us to crosses, he'll do it faster than you can think the thought."

Mannerly's contempt for Father Young nearly regurgitated into his throat. "I run a hotel, Reverend. I don't pose as anything holy."

"Irrelevant. You were to guide your foster boy, bring him along with us. But you've had escapes. Recently an important one."

"Dante?" Mannerly whispered. "That's what all this—"

"Ran away, did he?"

"I'm already dealing with him."

"Good, good. You see, I know this organization, Clayton. Because they checked up to see how his first training session went. Disaster, as we know. So you are here to be reminded—if that boy talks, why, it was *you* who talked." He made a show of turning and looking back toward the cell where the former Friar John sat holding his knees and begging to die.

He turned back to Mannerly and repeated, "That's what they want me to tell you. I am but a humble messenger in this world of pain. Today's message is as simple as anyone could ask."

The Reverend Canon Richard Young lowered his arm to let Mannerly pass and turned to walk back into the dormitory. He spoke over his shoulder without looking back.

"If he talks, it was you."

9

THE BLACKBURN-NIGHTINGALE RESIDENCE

SAN FRANCISCO

February 16th

* 9:00 a.m., Pacific Time *

THE TELEPHONE BOLTED TO THE kitchen wall rang at the same moment the wall clock chimed the hour of nine. Blackburn left Vignette and Dante at the breakfast table and stepped out to answer it, wondering how people were supposed to keep their sanity among all the ringing bells. He closed the kitchen door for privacy.

"This is Blackburn."

A woman's voice came over the line. The sound of it was thinned by the long-distance signal, but it remained strong in its tone. "Detective. This is Deputy Commissioner O'Grady, NYPD. I got your message to call but decided to speak to Mayor Rolph first. He just told me you're coming in on the investigation into the slave traffic infecting our orphan trains. Says you're coming to New York on his invitation and asked me to cooperate with you."

"Yes, ma'am, Mayor Rolph has reason to believe there is a slave line running from Europe throughout the United States, because some of the youngest ones have ended up in San Francisco. Story is, adults are being brought in on supposed employment contracts only to find out they are indentured slaves, but the children are just bought and sold like cordwood."

"And your investigation so far bears this out?"

He lowered his voice and replied, "We just began. But I happen to have an orphan boy visiting right now, at my house. He came out here on his own from New York City, but he talks about the so-called 'orphan trains' being used to ship children to fake foster homes, where they are put to work. He got this from kids who escaped and took to living on the streets. We already know they tend to gang up together for survival. He says there's a lot more to it all, but right now he won't say what. I tell you, this is one cocky kid, self-sufficient as any child I've ever seen, but even so, he's still afraid to talk about it."

"What can I do for you from New York, Detective?"

"Probably nothing until we get there, Commissioner. The mayor warned me I might have to make the journey when I signed on for this, and he was right."

He heard her chuckle in response. "Uh-oh. Fell for the old 'Sunny Jim soft sell,' did you?"

Blackburn laughed at that. "So you know about him, even all the way over on the other side of the country?"

"Blame the telephone, Detective. Gossip travels at the speed of light."

"He's colorful, but the man's got a backbone. I've known him for years— as much as you can know a politician—and I think he's on the square. I'm certain he's got no part in whatever's going on."

"I'll accept that. He's a lifer like me. Some of us want to keep a clean wake behind us."

"I believe it, Commissioner, but the parade bombing four years ago was part of a much larger plot, and it had plants all through the government."

"Your point being that a lot of us lifers had to go along with that level of corruption?"

"No offense, ma'am. I have to look at every angle."

He heard her sigh from thousands of miles away. "I understand. I wish I didn't, but I do."

Blackburn continued, "I'll be coming with my partner, Vignette Nightingale, who also happens to be my adopted daughter."

"A family business."

"Very much so."

"And this boy you mentioned?"

"His name is Dante, and he speaks fluent English but I believe he originally came from somewhere in Europe with the influx of war orphans. He's pretty desperate to get back to New York for his own reasons, so I'm thinking about offering to take him with us. He says he's got an aunt still there in the city, stuck working for the same man he ran away from."

"So she's there on an employment contract? Those are tough to crack. I have a senior detective who's tried a few times. I should introduce you to her."

"That sounds good, Commissioner. For now, the odd part is whatever the boy was running from and why his aunt can't join him. The family she works for are the people who own the City Squire Hotel."

"Who? You mean Clayton Mannerly? And his wife, ah, Allison, right? They make the society pages often enough. Mousy little flat dot. So they took in an orphan boy, but now he's run off—and that's who you have with you?"

"So he tells us."

"Hell's bells, that's just odd, isn't it? Why would he leave? Those people appear to be rich enough to leave him set for life."

"We can't get him to tell us that part yet, but I'll work on him during the train ride."

"Good enough, Detective. Your mayor tells me they dug up a budget to sponsor you for a first-class ride on this investigation, so I'll welcome your help."

"Yes, ma'am, and to be perfectly frank with you, when I got through to you I was deliberately making contact with a woman with decades on the force. You must have avoided useless conflicts with men who just want to fight you for the sake of it. You succeed by striking that balance. That means you know things I want my daughter to know."

"Ha! Not often I hear a father talking about how to get his daughter a career as an investigator, public or private! With my schedule, best I can do for her is to make a couple of calls. But you know what? I do have just the person for her to meet. Isabella Goodwin. She's been a first grade detective on the force for over seven years."

O'Grady let out a hearty laugh. "She's got a poor appreciation for authority too, but she made so many good arrests they could never fire her." O'Grady laughed again at the thought. "So we had to give her an all-female squad of her own. She's got six of 'em reporting to her."

"I'd love for Vignette to meet them. One other thing, ma'am. The boy, Dante."

"What about him?"

"He's convinced his foster family will try to force him to come back. Basically kidnap him, if you will."

"Do they have their foster papers?"

"Apparently they faked up a set of papers when they took him in about a year ago. Ma'am, I'm only bringing him back to try to reunite him with his aunt. I don't want to return him to a place he seems to hate and fear so badly."

"Tell you what, until we find out the status of his paperwork and get to the bottom of his complaint against the family, keep him in your custody. You can get here in a week. After you arrive, we'll see about the boy. We can underwrite you here, if need be. Can you take care of him in the meantime?"

"Gladly," Blackburn replied. "I doubt Vignette will give me any choice."

Moments later he returned to the kitchen table and took note of what a good job Vignette and Dante were doing of pretending they hadn't listened in on the call. "It looks like the taxpayers are sending us to New York City, first class. You too, Dante."

Dante's eyes grew wide. "They are? That's on the level?"

Blackburn laughed in response and turned to Vignette. "We'll take an express train on the Overland Route. Our first cross-country train trip!"

"Old hat," Dante said with a grin. "It'll be my second."

"Yeah," said Vignette, "but this time you'll have a ticket and they can't kick you off! We get to sleep in beds and eat in the dining car!"

Dante smiled at the thought and stared into space, as if visualizing the train car. But a moment later, his face darkened. "Even if I have a ticket, I could still ride up on the roof, though. I mean, if I want to. Couldn't I?"

Vignette looked meaningfully at Blackburn, who responded, "It's so dangerous. What makes it worth it to you to ride up there, when you don't need to do it?"

Dante dropped the question and sat quietly staring into space, like a cat watching shadows people can't see.

～

Later that morning, Blackburn placed his large house key on the mayor's desk.

"This one does the front and back doors, Mr. Mayor. I appreciate your help with this."

"Least I can do, Detective. I'll have my secretary put this in a file and hold it for your return. After you depart, I'll have my staff go over and double-check that nothing was overlooked in preparing the house, and then triple-check all the locks."

"Thank you, sir. I've got us on the Eastbound Express at nine a.m. on the twenty-fourth. Less than a week. There won't be much time to put the house in order for a long trip."

"Yes. I realize it's hard to plan for being gone when you don't know how long the trip will take. What about your automobile?"

"It'll just stay hooked up in the electric stable up the street and present no problem. Vignette's motorcycle will be all right in that same garage."

"Can you take time out for this case exclusively?"

"We can. There were some calls to make, but it wasn't that hard to clear our business calendar."

"Did it all by phone, didn't you? No need to send messengers or to go to see them in person, correct?"

Blackburn laughed and nodded in acknowledgment.

Mayor Rolph laughed along with him, saying, "Lazy bastard! Makes you wonder how we ever lived without these things, doesn't it?"

"Oh yeah. The phone makes my business much easier. And we're betting it'll get better as more people get one installed."

Sunny Jim dropped into his trusty conspiratorial whisper, the one that got bridges built. "Good point! Good point! And it brings this to mind: what do you say—once every household has a telephone installed—voting by phone! Eh?"

He brought his voice back up to a debate hall shout: "Voting by phone, my friend! Who cares if it's raining or snowing? Vote by phone! From the comfort of home!" He threw his arm around Blackburn's shoulder. "Take away all the excuses every lazy citizen ever had for failing to vote! Eh?"

Blackburn had long since accepted that some truths, expressed, caused nothing but trouble. This man was not really asking for his opinion.

"Vote by phone. Sounds inevitable."

"Yes! My sentiments exactly." Sunny Jim triumphantly shouted. "Huzzah! He understands!"

"I understand. It's coming."

"Vote by phone!"

"How can we not?"

"All right, then!" Sunny Jim grasped Blackburn's right hand and squeezed hard. "We'll look out for you on this end and wish you Godspeed, sir." He handed Blackburn a slip of paper. "This is my private line at home. Call me if you need anything off-hours. And Detective Blackburn," he dropped his voice to a whisper, "we have betrayers among us again, and until I root them out, please don't communicate with anyone here but me—directly—about your work."

"Gladly. I've never liked guessing games."

"Me either, but they have forced me into one, and believe you me, I am going to clean this house with an iron fist. If I don't, we are going down before them."

The mayor still had a grasp on Blackburn's hand. He squeezed it again and whispered, "Watch your back, my friend. Anyone there you don't personally know is a potential enemy. Hardly a pleasant thought, but one that could keep you alive."

Blackburn showed a rueful smile. "I can believe that. Wish I could take an extra set of eyeballs for all the watching."

"If I thought it would help, I might let you take mine."

Neither thought the line was especially funny. But they were each in the rare and perhaps final moment of being with someone they could actually trust, so they chuckled anyway.

That evening, on an express train traveling the Overland Route from San Francisco to New York City, Andrea Salsedo sat staring out the window and smoking one of his last buttery cigarillos, a gift from Cubano partisans who appreciated his work on some difficult explosive devices.

"Ticket, please, sir?"

He jumped in his seat at the sound of the authoritative male voice behind him. Old habits. A moment later, he steeled himself, straightened, and slowly turned. It was the conductor. Salsedo looked the man directly in the eyes and made himself calmly smile, as he had been trained to do. Keeping himself even and cool.

Three days had not yet passed since he had learned of the plan to bring him home, meaning no passwords were in operation for him. The machinery was not yet in place to pass him anonymously through the system.

Yet a newly resolved Andrea Salsedo considered all of that good news. Fine news. Because the rich hotelier bastard had done nothing to help him, meaning Andrea Salsedo owed him no gratitude at all.

He smiled—but not too much—then pulled his full-fare ticket from his vest pocket and handed it over like the winning card it was. His fellow anarchists in Lynn, Massachusetts, were also avid Galleanists. They joined with their brethren in Manhattan, who were surprisingly good to him and generously so, paying for his ticket to New York. No questions asked. They did not even require him to confirm his identity before setting him up with a ticket at the San Francisco station. Communication was practically instantaneous and felt like a miracle to him.

Why, they even got him back his old job at Canzani Print Shop, down in Brooklyn, to help him remain undercover while he performed his mission for Buda, whatever it was to be.

He wondered if they would use his old "Tony Tazio" alias there, but he didn't care much either way.

Most surprising, the New York-Massachusetts branch of Galleani's followers did it all with a level of speed and organized efficiency he had never seen his fellow anarchists display. This was all the more surprising for the points of authority required to ensure cooperation and complete such an undertaking. Organized authority was not part of any anarchist's best day.

The boy? Well, that part was obviously a bump in the road, nothing more. They had already figured out how to neutralize him, even if he yet lived. Even if the kid opened his mouth about how they got rid of the rejects, he would be thoroughly discredited as nothing more than some orphan with a grudge. So what?

Yes, it was a good plan. He wished he could have thought of it himself. But no matter, the plan was in place, and because of it, the boy was no longer a threat. Meaning Andrea Salsedo was back in good standing with the American Anarchist Fighters.

Or ought to be, as far as he saw it.

He trusted his reputation with his fellow anarchists to remain strong. There was no other choice for them, really. He assured himself of that. Why, based upon his valuable skills with explosives and his record of loyalty, he had more than enough status to cover himself despite his so-called insubordination.

But even as he sold himself on that idea, it struck him that logic meant nothing in this. For them, the thing was his refusal to follow a direct order.

He felt a stomach-flipping moment of clenched muscles and clamped teeth while the clarity of the revelation ran through him. He saw it now. He turned to the window and blew a thin stream of smoke at his own reflection.

The refusal was the problem. The rest was window dressing.

Yes, he saw his mistake now, but was it too late? He had missed the sea change in attitudes within the anarchist ranks during his brief months on the run. It happened fast, and the knowledge of that burned him. He had isolated himself for safety while the law searched for him, but that same isolation tripped him up. If only he had kept up with the news, he would have detected signs that the American Anarchist Movement itself was suddenly experiencing giant increases in thrust and power and becoming much more publicly visible as a result.

Salsedo was a loyal follower of the movement, but also a practical man, a typesetter who knew one error could ruin an entire message. He knew it was no joke to say "the Devil is in the details," because the damned Devil really *was* in the details, every single time. He also knew the hours spent carefully proofreading and re-proofing actually represented time saved from the consequences of misprints. Therefore the obsessive typesetter in Salsedo had to ask himself, on behalf of his more reticent side as an anarchist bomb maker, *Where the hell could all this new money be coming from?*

Magic money? The comrades he stayed with during his flight from the authorities all seemed to be flush with cash now. Capital was pouring in for the American Anarchist Movement. That alone should have set off bells and whistles to the loyal followers. What did it mean? Money to make bail, money to pay bribes, money to pay for printing and distribution costs, for weapons, for ammunition. Money to sway public political opinion in directions of the wealthy elite's choosing, punctuated with explosions and shrapnel.

The money seemed to be converting a lot of anarchists to support something closer to Communism. Here was the glory of money for nothing. Manna from Heaven.

All that sudden cash was more divisive to their movement than the efforts of a thousand spies. Because as always, the presence of the cash inevitably begged the questions: Who controls all these new things we can buy? Who holds onto the weapons? The ammunition? The money itself...

Salsedo regarded the quandary and wondered what to do. He was one of those anarchists-in-the-know who realized people would never voluntarily give up their precious systems, because they wanted all the stuff those systems delivered. But what if, as Salsedo's role models reasoned, people could still get the *same* bounty those old systems provided, but without the systems themselves?

The smarter anarchists knew that would inevitably lead to failure. Human nature would guarantee it. Problem being, the failure might take many years to manifest in collapse of the government. Far too long. Bombs were the answer. Bombs were the stimulant toward a new age.

He saw it; didn't everybody see it? What the American Anarchist Movement actually needed were bombs, and the only thing it needed cash for was to build more of them. If a new system rose from the ashes and failed at fairness, bombs again. Bombs large for cars and trucks, bombs small for suitcases and postal packages. Bombs sized for a person to carry strapped into a shoulder harness to be worn by an idiot—almost always a young man or boy who failed to ask himself why the bomb maker did not wear his own device.

He briefly wondered why more women didn't strap on a bomb and blow themselves up. He was aware some few did, but they usually needed to be broken-hearted first. The question made him tired, and he dropped it.

The anarchist movement needed men like Andrea Salsedo, who knew how to design and purpose-build the necessary explosive devices. Because Americans were fat fools who believed the aftermath of "The War to End All Wars" was going to be an ever-rising stock market for an ever-rising economy in an ever-rising American nation.

Sadly for Salsedo, there was a fly in the soup; making a bomb required knowledge and skill, but was not as difficult as learning to play a musical instrument, design a huge building, or pilot a tall ship, and yet there were plenty of people who did all those things every day.

Therefore, Salsedo realized with cold certainty, even if he could make bombs the way Mozart played piano—not really a stretch, in his view—he could nevertheless be replaced with little difficulty because *they didn't need Mozart*. They only needed people as good at bomb making as the grade-school piano teacher was at *playing Mozart*.

The level of brilliance his creations displayed was superfluous to the worldwide anarchist movement. As long as you could do it and not blow yourself up, that was as good as you needed to be. The incompetent were self-eliminating.

The ignorant rich could always find bomb makers of middling ability, along with bomb-making teachers whose humble skills could be just enough to create more bomb makers of middling ability. Ending with bomb makers with mere "functional" bomb-making quality, which was all the ignorant rich needed. He knew it. The thought put a stitch in his side.

They honestly believed themselves to have vanquished the iron of war for the gold to be had in peace. But in all of history's long list of failed civilizations, human beings had created systems of authority. Then whoever held the controls bathed in that deeply pleasureful experience of indulging any appetite, any taste, any little hobby one chooses. The pull emanated from the fine ability to take far more for yourself than those around you, plus the privilege to take anything else you wanted, on any pretext. History showed it to be irresistible.

In this way, the limited humans who wore the masks of overlords had revealed themselves. The American Anarchist Movement saw such overlords when they looked at American governance.

That could no longer be permitted. It only stood to reason.

Signore Galleani hit the nail on the head the first time he said it: *America had to fall.*

10

CITY SQUIRE HOTEL – TOP-FLOOR PENTHOUSE
LOWER MIDTOWN, MANHATTAN

February 23rd – One Week Later
* 11:00 p.m., Eastern Time *

"IF MY MOTHER WAS STILL ALIVE, she'd be rolling in her grave." Allison Mannerly arched her back to press her breasts into her thin silk nightgown. She continued tweezing her eyebrows in the vanity mirror while she quietly put all her attributes to work on getting things softened up at home.

Because it sounded to her as if Daddy had more or less just told her she had to go to work. Which amounted to the exact opposite of the reason she was with him in the first place.

His message seemed simple enough, on the face of it: They weren't going to be doing the parties for fun anymore. Things had changed, and they were under terrible pressure from ruthless people. Opposing them was to guarantee a bad death. Choice had been removed. Now they would hold the sales parties because they had to, whether or not they needed indentured help for the hotel or commission on the sales.

She had to do it. Whether they felt like it or not, whether she felt like it or not.

And with that single twist, her plan for the evening collapsed. The opportunity disappeared for her to sit down with her husband and calmly explain, *Dear, while I accept your sexual proclivities, as you know, I can't keep up. I can no longer even attempt to keep up. You are free to do as you will, if you are discreet.*

Her plan was to invite him to tell people she was feeling ill for this party, to hint at something serious enough to make them want to leave the topic alone. And then he could just *attend the parties as a stag from then on.* Why not? He was a stag anyway.

There it was: a free ticket for him with passable social appearances. In her plan, it was supposed to be the bait. Certainly more than enough to motivate a man like him.

Instead, it all went out the window. Clayton's little proclamation of the terrible danger they were in had her trapped. Because of him. Because of the very thing she was planning to get away from, in trying to leave him.

She knew all about the Movers. All about Clayton's dealings with them. All three "party" sites: their hotel, Father Young's little seminary in Queens, and the big party site out there on Blackwell's Island, useful for running dozens of guests and indentured servants through at a time.

The reality was Allison could do massive damage to people all through the fields of banking and show business, as well as politicians, from local aldermen to the state and national congresses, plus various levels of the Catholic Church. There were even Texas oil barons along with all the other customers willing to pay, pay, pay for their very own slaves, each one thoroughly beaten into submission and terrified into compliance.

A round of hydrotherapy generally ensured a rate of cooperation at nearly one hundred percent. The few failures were so rare, so separated in time and location, nobody ever put them together. Society in general had little time for such issues. There was a post-war world to rebuild, and nobody liked to think of such things. Neither did Allison.

～

Clayton watched his beautiful wife like an appreciative backstage Johnny, staring at the stage door for a glimpse of his diva. In the eighteen months since their marriage—had it really been so long?—he was still not tired of the sexual energy she radiated. Her sustained naïveté in worldly things cost her absolutely nothing in the mating department. It made her fun to play with, but at times like this, her crude intellectual powers were painfully obvious. She thought herself to be manipulating him, setting him up to be asked for something, some special thing she wanted at the moment. The pattern was beyond familiar now; it had simply become routine.

Nonetheless, Allison was still a living gift of mercy whose presence in his life was not to be taken lightly. He knew how to appreciate a woman, but he knew how to control one, too.

"I mean it, Clayton. Are you listening to me?"

"Of course, dear," he said, easy as an exhale.

However—and this was all the *however* he needed—Allison's failure to warm to the proper bedroom discipline was far exceeded by her successful assistance in procuring other eligible game. At twenty-three, she was fifteen years his junior. Sure, he had married a dummy, but she was hardly stupid. She had a gift for buddying up to younger women and girls, making them want to follow her just long enough to take them somewhere they would not be able to leave, once the fear set in.

He had made it clear to Allison that if she kept the honey pot open for him, she could float through life on a full pass. It was all she had to do.

But she had to do it. Anything less was unacceptable.

Just like he had to make the hotel function while he secretly ran the supply lines. The struggling post-war economy was taking its time to get things right, and by the time it did, he knew he could easily be on the street watching the authorities load his household onto trucks, hauling everything away after padlocking the hotel doors. The City Squire would hardly be the first New York City hotel to fall victim to financial chaos. The secret human supply line was actually his lifeline. It was a relief that the Movers wanted him to know nothing more about them than his job required.

Mannerly's clients were painfully aware that if they suffered exposure and lost their position of privilege in that elite world, there was no other world open to them. They were universally despised by everybody except the other elites, and perhaps those who thought if they were given a bit more time, they could join the group, too.

Otherwise, nobody in the working world had any welcome in their heart for the elites. It was one of the reasons those of lesser means got treated with casual disrespect or even bald-faced contempt; the elites knew those same people would never tolerate such treatment if they were on equal footing. They would fight back.

Fear was the thing, and it ran in both directions. No other lash would control the grand elites except the fear of seeing their true selves exposed. Clayton Mannerly controlled them in that regard, but they also controlled him with their expectations. Their demands.

"Those women do nothing but glare at me all evening long," Allison complained. "Jealous old biddies. And I believe we've already spent time with everyone you would be inviting. Personal time, Clayton. I thought you didn't like going back for seconds."

"No need to belabor the point. Two of them are repeat clients. That's actually good. When we undress, so will the others, and put pressure on everyone else to join in."

"What if they don't want to?"

"Who cares what they want? We know they want to take their new slaves home, so the rest doesn't matter. They need product, and I've got it."

"Do you have to say 'product'?"

"It's what they are. Best product in the world."

"It's harsh talk. Pointless talk."

His face darkened. He responded softly in his best negotiator's voice, "Maybe your talk is pointless, Allison. Careless, even."

"What's that mean?"

"You demonstrate carelessness by taking your new life for granted and failing to live up to your end of the bargain."

"What the hell? Bargain?"

"There's no other honest term for it. It's so obvious. And it's fine. Really. You live the life of a princess on my money, and in return you keep things lively in the bedroom and recruit new dummies for me. Some we pay off and let go, some we turn into product. Through you, I can reach into the world and pluck those girls right out of mama's house."

His reply left Allison looking like a deflated balloon. She was at her least attractive in that condition, so he tried to think of something to cheer her up. "I'm giving you more responsibilities to show how you have earned my trust. This new batch is coming in from eastern and southern Europe. Blondes, brunettes, all sizes and shapes. They unload tomorrow sometime after sunrise. So all you have to do is have a driver take you down to the Ellis Island Receiving Center and watch them offload. There are supposed to be a few dozen of them. Ignore the weaklings and the mutts, but make a note of every desirable. Any good females belong to us. Make a list."

"But you're always the one to do that."

"Yes, and it seems to have been a mistake. You need a better appreciation of how delicate our positions are. So. As soon as they offload, present your list to the dockmaster. What we need is a little different this time. No kids, no old domestics. All transportation costs have been paid, so don't let anyone tell you different. But on top of that, what you do is offer him sixty dollars a head, paid cash on the nail, for each one he delivers up to the Blackwell's Island facility for tomorrow night's party. I will be there to make payment. Demand a minimum of twelve this time. Otherwise, he's got no deal at all. Hit that part hard. Let him know I am developing a secondary supply line in case his dries up."

"Are you?"

"At some point. Now, this guy won't need persuasion. He knows he will make, in one day, more than a year's salary for an officer in the NYPD. You'll be surprised at his cooperative attitude."

"What about the others?"

"What others? The mutts?"

"I mean the ones you don't want."

"Allison, when you harvest wheat, you have to throw away a lot of chaff, do you hear me? You grind it up with the grain and then you toss it up in the air, over and over, and you let the breeze carry away the dust and the fine-ground chaff, and that allows the good wheat to fall to the ground."

"The mutts are chaff?"

"The mutts are chaff. They blow away and are your concern no more."

"What will they do after that, just wander around?"

"The truth of them is, they won a game they didn't even know they were playing. We buy 'em by the batch and take what we get. Handling the mutts is lost time for us. Cost of doing business. For them, they've been rejected from lives of servitude. They're so glad to be on their own in America, they're not about to complain to anybody.

"Now the stupid ones, they'll die right out. You watch. Find 'em passed out in alleys, getting arrested for petty crimes. The ones with some spark, some determination—why, they'll see this as their big break and head for the hills. Travel on foot, sleep rough, live off the land until they can snag some job, maybe do something nobody else wants to do. And begin to put together a life. Lucky bastards."

Allison felt a headache coming on. "The authorities—"

"Are busy trying to rebuild a post-war society after the worst conflict in history. They won't even look, unless someone complains. Even then, it has to be a very credible complaint. These people have no standing."

"And if one of those very credible complaints actually comes in?"

"Then we pay a fortune to make it go away. Like last time."

Clayton waited for her to reply, ready to rebuff whatever response she made. He felt loose in the limbs and intellectually invincible.

Allison fell back on old tricks. She sighed a pretty sigh, the sight and sound of which had earned her bits of jewelry on more than one occasion. She tilted her head so that he would see her mouth reflected in the mirror while she painted her lips. If she could get him aroused enough, he would be malleable. It usually worked in her favor, even if he was slow on the grasp this evening. She hoped it would take effect before he wondered why she was painting her lips before retiring. If she had to explain, she could make it about wanting sex. Men always believed that.

She spoke up, "Once they're delivered and you pay the man, can we just go home then, instead of joining in?" She ran the tip of her tongue across her upper lip as if it had something to do with getting the makeup right.

She yelped like a puppy when he flew across the room, grabbed her under the arm, and lifted her out of her chair. In that instant he became a different man.

"You will *not* do that tonight! None of that shit works to change anything! We have to get this done, and you have to help me. Listen: one of our clients in NYPD administration says the department is in touch with some big-deal private investigator from San Francisco. Randall Blackburn. There's a name you're going to hear more of. Now, you like the life we have here? You want to keep it? Here's news I bet you never considered: the post-war economy might lift us all up, but it hasn't done it yet. The traveling public still isn't traveling enough to support us. By the time they do, *if* they do, we could've already lost the hotel!

"Allison. We have to deliver for our clients at Blackwell's Island tomorrow night, not just to make the sales and take their fees but to demonstrate to the Movers that we have everything under control. We have to do it. You have to do it." He dropped her into her chair, turned his back, and walked away, staring toward an outside wall as if he could see through it and discern something on the other side.

"You never told me this hotel is supported by the work you do for all those people."

"I don't understand your hesitation. One way or the other, you were going to attend most of these parties. Now you just do all of them on a regular basis while you also help run clients. They only come here because they need a place to purchase these people in secret. This hotel is our power base."

There was a long pause. Neither looked at the other. He walked up behind her and gently bit her neck while he massaged her breasts. She stiffened—from pleasure, he assumed.

"Once you pay the dockmaster, the products belong to you. They'll respond to any show of authority, so make it seem like it's an official matter and assure them when they go with you it'll just take a few minutes."

"How do I do that?"

"Some of them might not know any English. So make this gesture, see? Thumb and fingertip half an inch apart. Keep saying, 'A few minutes, a few minutes.' Get them to go with you without having them dragged off. They will have arrived still believing they're getting regular jobs. You can't just handle these people like dogs. You'll start a panic."

"Damn, Clayton. I understand, all right?"

"No, it's not all right unless we do this perfectly. Some of our clients will travel for days to get here, just to get what they want. And getting what they want is the essence of their lives. These people have far surpassed mere privilege. They decide how much 'privilege' the rest of us get to have. We can hold the ones you've picked out on the tenth floor until it's time to move them to the island for showtime. The party starts the moment the clients arrive there, and the camera in the wall will be active."

"You're still trying to do that? Even if nobody notices the hole for the lens, people will see the flash, Clayton."

"They will. And at the same time they stand back out of the way to have their acquisition photographed as part of their receipt to the Movers, the hidden camera will also be photographing them. One flash, two pictures."

"I wish you'd do all this yourself."

Clayton just smiled and pointed at the door, inviting her to walk out if she felt like it. "Anytime you prefer the street, who am I to stand in your way?"

"Oh, so you would let me go?"

"Of course not. I'll shoot you in the back if I have to. But it isn't going to come to that. We are better than that, you and me. We have an understanding."

Allison ignored the gesture and turned back to her reflection with the powder puff.

"Nothing for tonight, Allison. You can wipe that stuff off and go to bed." He walked out of the room without looking back, hoping he left her feeling the same way Father Young had left him feeling earlier in the day.

11

THE BLACKBURN-NIGHTINGALE RESIDENCE

SAN FRANCISCO

February 24th
* 2:00 a.m. *

THE LATE FEBRUARY AIR hung with a heavy chill outside Golden Gate Park atop the Sunset District. The city had cooled to barely forty degrees, and the neighborhood was saturated with fog. All the lamps in the Blackburn and Nightingale home were extinguished, leaving the house looking just as dark inside as it would be after they left the city. Inside, Vignette, Blackburn, and Dante were sound asleep, with no one awake to look out the window and see, in the thick silence of the foggy darkness, a lone male form approaching westbound along Lincoln Way. He wore soft-soled shoes that made no sounds. His clothing was dark. A cloth cap sat on his head pulled low over the ears. Since nobody was out at that hour to see him and take note, he may as well have been invisible.

When he neared the front of the house, he glanced around in all directions, found the coast clear, and ran on the balls of his feet up the walkway to the house, onto the porch, and directly to the front door. There he withdrew a house key from his pocket and inserted it in the door lock, turned the key, and quietly pushed the door open. He removed a small knife from the same pocket and stepped inside.

He had made only the faintest of scratching and scraping sounds while he worked, and if the guest in the house were sleeping upstairs as predicted, there would have been nobody downstairs to hear him.

The mistake lay in the quality of information he was given.

A huge crash rang through the house and propelled Blackburn off of his mattress. Next the sound of Vignette's wordless voice came from downstairs, growling like a rabid canine. Blackburn stumbled over his shoes in the darkness and fell into the nightstand, knocking his pistol under the bed. Downstairs, more crashing noises followed, sounds of things hitting the floor and shattering.

"Randall!" came Vignette's voice, clearly panicked. There was no time to seek out his weapon. He flung open his bedroom door and ran down the stairs, taking the steps three at a time.

In the living room, he confronted the sight of a strange man staggering around the room while Vignette punched at his face and Dante rode his back and slammed at his head with a fat book. Blackburn dove at the invader and tackled him at the knees.

Vignette stepped back when the man fell, but Dante rode his back all the way down and continued slamming at his head with the book after they hit the floor.

"Dante!" Blackburn called out. "Dante! You can stop!"

But Dante was in a frenzy. He continued slamming away at the invader, who was now curled into a ball with his hands over the sides of his head.

"Dante!" Vignette spoke softly and put her hands in front of the man's head to stop Dante from swinging again. He abruptly stopped, looking at her in surprise. She gently pulled him from the man in a backward crab-walk while Blackburn reached down, picked up the little knife the man had dropped, and pulled the intruder to his feet.

"Hey!" shouted Dante. "Look at this!" He stepped across the room and retrieved the door key where it had fallen to the floor and skidded away. "He had a key to your door!"

The man was in his thirties with the thin body of an alcoholic who drinks his meals. His skin was heavily pockmarked, and his teeth were broken and yellow. Blackburn held him by the lapels and studied him for a moment, then said, "Vignette, Dante, will you please go upstairs and wait for me in my room?"

"What do you want us to do that for?" Dante asked, but Vignette held her finger to her lips and pulled him toward the stairs, adding, "Randall, Dante said he heard the man open the door. He grabbed the book and waited out of sight until he came in."

"I did, and then I bashed him in the head."

"Good job."

"I wish it was a brick. Is he here after us, or is he just a thief?"

"He's no ordinary thief. He had the key I left at City Hall. I need to have a talk with this fine gentleman, so why don't you two go on up? I'll meet you up there in a few minutes."

"You gonna turn him in?" Dante asked while they traveled up the stairs.

Blackburn looked at the intruder, then back to Dante, and smiled. "Nope," he replied. "No cops this time."

"Then what are you—"

Vignette pulled him away from the upper landing and escorted him upstairs. Blackburn noticed Dante appeared oddly comfortable with what had just taken place. As if the violence of the street and the infected souls who walked it had conspired to harden his eyes for violence, especially when he won. The living room went quiet but for the perpetrator's raspy breathing. Blackburn clung to the man's jacket, stared into his milky eyes, and came to a decision. He tucked the knife into his palm and pulled the man outside onto the front porch.

As soon as they were out in the dark, Blackburn softly asked, "You know who I am?"

"Yeah. I know you, Randall Blackburn. Big-deal private dick, used to be a cop."

"Impressive. Now let's talk about you. I see you let yourself in."

"Nothin' to say."

Blackburn closed the front door behind them with one hand and lifted up the small knife to hold it in front of the man's eyes. "Don't want to tell me your name?"

"I can't."

"What, you don't recall?"

"They'll kill me. And they don't kill you soft, they kill you hard."

"See, now we're getting someplace." He put his mouth close to the man's ear and whispered, "Truth? I don't give a shit what your name is. And I'm not going to turn you over to the cops, either. I'm going to decide what to do with you, all by myself."

"Do what you want."

"Okay." Blackburn punched him square in the mouth. It hurt his knuckles a bit, but he felt the man's weak teeth collapse in his mouth while he staggered backward. He bellowed in pain, but Blackburn rushed forward to shove him back against the house siding and slapped his hand over his mouth. He held on tight.

"Little cuts."

The man looked at him in confusion.

"Little cuts. You don't get it?" He raised the knife and swiped a shallow incision across the side of the man's throat. The man's yelp barely produced a sound beneath Blackburn's thick palm. He swiped the knife across the other side of the man's neck, leaving small incisions on either side of his Adam's apple. Blood began to flow.

Panic lit up his eyes, and he grabbed at Blackburn's arm, trying to pull the big detective's hand away from his face. Blackburn smiled in a deliberate display of cruelty and said, "No, no, no. Not allowed to make a sound. Not one, unless you want to talk to me."

The man glared in fear and outrage, gasping through his nose. After a moment, he slowly nodded. Blackburn released a smidgeon of pressure.

"Okay, who are you?" He released just enough pressure to allow speech.

"My name don't mean a thing in this."

"Yeah, probably not. Why are you here?"

"The boy."

"What were you supposed to do?"

The man just stared. Blackburn moved the knife to the back of his neck and drew another slice. He let this one bite deeper, clamping his hand down hard again to make sure no sounds of distress found the neighbors. This time the man gave in to panic and did all he could to nod and moan and indicate a willingness to change his mind about talking.

"Same question. What were you supposed to do?"

"Strict orders: stab him, let him bleed out, and leave him here in your house for the cops to find."

"I bet somebody told you to phone the police after you got clear of the neighborhood. Pin it on me, right? Right?"

"Somethin' like that, yeah."

Blackburn held the knife blade up to the man's eyes. "I'll bet you think life never treated you fair, don't you? And for that, you were willing to take money to visit evil on a young boy. You could see yourself doing that, because life's been unfair to you. Here's a thought: how fair would it be for the boy when you came to murder him in his sleep?"

The man with the unimportant name glared and did not move.

"What you are going to do is this: tell whoever hired you I'm coming for them. You have disrespected my home and put my daughter and her guest in terrible danger. You even intended to frame me for a dreadful murder. So for your punishment, I'm electing you to be my messenger."

Blackburn surprised the man by pulling him close to his chest, wrapping his left arm around the back of the man's head, spinning his back to him and holding him tight while his right hand plunged the knife deep into his right buttock. Unlike the other stab wounds, this one was far more than a scratch. It was a stab and would bleed heavily. Blackburn kept his hand over the man's mouth while he stabbed him once again in the other buttock. The knife blade was only about four inches, so he drove half of it in.

The perpetrator arched his back in an instinctive attempt to avoid the blade and screamed out a cry that would have awakened the whole neighborhood if his mouth could have opened. As it was, his noises of distress failed to reach further than the front walk.

The bleats subsided, and Blackburn again eased his grip just enough to allow him to speak. "You don't have to tell me your name, but you have to tell me who sent you. I already know the key came from City Hall. Did the mayor send you?"

"Mayor don't know nothing. I'm supposed to keep clear of City Hall. I get orders from the police desk sergeant, and I pick up my pay at the same place."

"Who leaves the orders for you?"

"I don't know! I don't know. They just call me with orders and leave my pay with the desk sergeant.He don't even know what it's for! He gets an envelope and holds it for pickup. Orders come from all sorts of different people. Listen, I got nothin' against you. A man's gotta eat."

"You mean drink?"

"All right, all right. I wasn't gonna enjoy it or nothin', so don't confuse me with that Salsedo bastard. He likes to kill 'em by the crowd."

"There's a familiar name."

"You know who I mean—same guy killed your son. And I swear, I was not after your girl tonight! Hand to God: they sent me for the boy. Kid's nothing to you, right?"

"Wait! Wait! Wait! What did... Killed my son?"

"Andrea Salsedo. You know about him. He told me. When that guy starts drinking, he's a different man! Went around bragging about how you knew he killed the kid, but you could never prove it in court, and how you were too scared of him to look him up yourself."

Blackburn did not make the slightest move. He appeared not to breathe.

The perpetrator caught the look in his eyes and understood he had stumbled into quicksand. He effortlessly decided it was a good idea to provide more information. His mouth moved of its own accord.

"Said...his pals...got him his old typesetting job back east. New York City."

Blackburn's voice came out in a guttural snarl. "He told you this when?"

"A few days ago, that's all. Just before he got on the train."

"To New York."

"Yeah. Y'know, the city."

Blackburn stared into the perpetrator's eyes without moving. Seconds passed. Nothing moved. The perpetrator got the message, and a wet stain formed on the front of his pants.

After another long moment, Blackburn released the man and smoothed down his lapels for him. "I'm letting you go now."

"What?"

"You are my messenger boy. You are going to go back and hand the desk sergeant a message for this Andrea Salsedo, which you are going to write out yourself. Since the sergeant is apparently being paid to avoid arresting Salsedo, don't tell him what you know. Just say it's for whoever gave him the envelope."

"Yes! Okay! I can do that!"

"And what you will write in this message is that I'm coming after him. Our trip only delays the consequences. I will come after him. And I believe whoever is behind this will get the message, word for word. You just do it like that."

"What for? Salsedo's gone. On his way to New York."

"Yeah. Handy, isn't it?"

"Handy?"

"We'll be on our way there in a few hours. Isn't that something?" Blackburn spun the man around and pushed him toward the front steps. "Every time you try to sit for the next few weeks, that's me giving you my opinion of your way of life."

Blackburn had no need to tell Mayor Rolph how upset he was. The phone call he placed to Sunny Jim's home shortly after two in the morning was a message in itself.

"Detective, you have got to believe me! I had no idea the key was stolen, and I certainly did not send anyone to your home!"

"Mayor Rolph, I don't know who I can trust!"

"Understood! Understood! This is the same problem we had during the parade bombing. Corrupt employees selling us out to some high bidder. I am going to shake the branches here until I find out how that key was lifted from our files. I promise you that!"

Blackburn sighed. He rubbed his hands over his eyes in frustration and transferred the earpiece to the other side of his head.

The main purpose of his call had been to tell the mayor what he had just learned about Shane's death. But it occurred to him the information could compound the issue. He had no sense that Mayor Rolph was conspiring against him, but the mayor seemed vulnerable to being undermined from within. And if the parade bombing was any indication, Blackburn had to suspect the loyalty of anyone working at City Hall.

"There'll be more trouble coming if this guy was sent by the same people we're going to investigate in New York."

"Yes, and I am so sorry about all of this, Detective, but please tell me you're not calling to cancel your trip. We need you in New York more than ever. If they can reach across the country and open the door to your home—"

"I know. Last time they blew up our whole house. Believe me, I don't underestimate their determination. You can always find some immoral idiot who'll kill for money."

"Why did you let him go? Why not hold him for the police?"

"You want me to stay in town to press a breaking-and-entering charge?"

"Point taken."

"Mr. Mayor, can you trust your enforcers to prosecute him?"

"That depends on how deep the corruption runs this time."

"Yes. And last time they got most of City Hall. So instead of trusting a corrupt system, I turned him into a messenger and sent him back to them. Mr. Mayor, our train leaves this morning at nine. Can you ride herd on your forces to see to it they finish out the house for us as we planned?"

"Yes! Yes! My God, after what you have been through, I will personally come over there and make certain everything is locked up tight and send patrols several times a day to cruise the house."

"Think they'll actually do it?"

"No need for sarcasm, sir. I have already apologized."

"I don't intend sarcasm, either, Mr. Mayor. I need information I can rely on and people I can trust, just as you do. I trust you because of our history. When the parade bombing took place, you were one of the only people still doing your job. Can you hold the line here this time?"

"I can damn well do my best, Detective, but what we know about being undermined from within is that you don't know where the contamination lies until you call upon some legitimate action and see it ignored."

Blackburn said his goodbyes and replaced the earpiece on the metal fork. There was no point in mentioning how little consolation he got from the mayor's response.

12

CITY SQUIRE HOTEL – TOP-FLOOR PENTHOUSE
LOWER MIDTOWN, MANHATTAN

February 25th
* 8:00 a.m., Eastern Time*

CLAYTON MANNERLY NURSED HIS BREAKFAST at a small table placed near the window of his study. The tall hotel building's upper views displayed Penn Station, Bryant Park, and the surrounding neighborhoods south of midtown, a lofty vantage point that usually provided him a sensation of superiority over the ant-like creatures scurrying the streets below.

This morning there was no such feeling.

He had slept an hour, maybe two, leaving his eyes gritty and his mouth dry. Nightmares regularly plagued him, and today wakefulness was doing little to relieve the hangover from the night terrors. He hated the fact that his war experiences drove him to such a state. What about other men, he wondered. Not the ones in padded cells and straitjackets, but those who could still pass themselves off as normal. How did they manage it?

And what about the women of the battlefield, stuffing the guts back into dying young men for hours, for weeks, for months at a time. How could they emerge unscathed? How could they just step back into the old life once again and dance to the same tunes?

Was he the only one failing to make the insanity and cruelty of that war leave him alone? It was as if the people who fought the war barely remembered it. Nobody talked about it. Nobody he knew, anyway.

Before he signed up for the service, it seemed obvious that as soon as the war was over, those men who fought would stand head and shoulders above those who did not. His father had made that clear to him. Abundantly clear. Who wants a coward for a son? *What an idiot mistake, hardly worth the risks.* If he had possessed more confidence in himself, he would have stayed home and left the gossip crowd hanging.

This night's dark dream began with that same weird sensation he always got from being hoisted up on the telescoping spotter's chair while they raised him high above the battlefield to surveil enemy lines. Trench warfare was a new phenomenon, and visibility of enemy movements was a life-and-death issue. Being a spotter was a terrifying job with low life expectancy. He suffered through three close calls before he bought off his lieutenant and got himself transferred to relatively peaceful hospital duty back behind the lines.

But the hospital. *Hospital.* The name tasted bitter in his mouth. Piles of amputated limbs accompanying a never-ending chorus of screams of agony and pleas for relief, soldiers crying out for loved ones, most of whom they would never see again. Praying with a priest, when they were lucky enough to get one, while they died of gas burns that had destroyed their faces and scaled the air sacs in their lungs. Many of the mangled soldiers were barely more than boys.

It was just as terrible for the women of the war, for different reasons. Few had combat injuries, although some ambulance nurses sustained horrific wounds. No, the women came in with rape injuries more than anything else, mostly at the hands of Russian soldiers. The Russians seemed to have some kind of forced-rape policy intended to crush the morale of the opposition.

Everybody in the hospital was chagrinned over it, so much so, kidnapping and rape became forbidden subjects. Unseen notions of decency created real fences. One did not discuss such things. The slog of hospital life continued, and Clayton Mannerly began to feel his heart hardening in reaction to the broth of unending misery.

Next the children began flooding in: orphans left in the world by parents already decimated in the fighting and the shelling of cities. Soon his place of work was not a hospital so much as an open field of help-lessness.

Oddly enough, helplessness was where Clayton found his true self.

Not his own helplessness, but that of others who were under his control by virtue of their condition. Somewhere in the annals of his unconscious mind, he had worked it all out: he was miserable because these people were so miserable themselves. So long as they remained helpless, they would rain down their misery upon him, and he was already full.

Instead, he made helplessness his invisible partner in crime, and a most effective one at that. Helplessness held them down for him. For in that place of death odors and screams of pain, he found sexual stimulation such as he had never experienced. Up until then, he had merely been a man who enjoyed sex with a female now and again and tried the odd male encounter when prudence allowed. All in all, sexual contact was not a significant part of his life. He had fantasies, sometimes feverish dreams, but sex mostly escaped his notice on a day-to-day basis.

But there, in that joke of a hospital, he experienced a revelation: help-less people were thoroughly compelling to him, the excitement of having them beneath him was powerful in a way he had never felt before. Stroke them into a state of please-don't-hurt-me and then look deep into their eyes while you hurt them. Teach them betrayal and pain for no other reason than you have betrayal and pain to give.

He asked himself, was it the war that changed him by stranding him in that excuse for a hospital, or did he just strike a vein of personal ore? Either way, the condition of the patients called out to him and the appeal never slackened over time.

Based on that, the future opened up to him when he received a visit one day from a local bishop who claimed he was there to offer spiritual comfort to the suffering. Clayton's personal Revelation came when, after a day of consolations, the bishop pulled Mannerly aside and quietly guided him through the strangest conversation he had ever had, jabbing him with what seemed to be random inquiries and pleasant attempts to make conversation, but which, as Clayton slowly came to be aware, tested out his level of religious study and personal conviction, as well probing his responses to society's moral limits.

Having grown up in a New York City hotel, Clayton was sophisticated enough to catch the older man's attempts to play him, but he felt interested to see where the bishop was going with his odd questions and comments. Besides, the hospital job was boring, and the action was scarce at that hour.

By the time the bishop's long preamble drew to a close, Clayton found his attention wandering until he realized there was a sexual angle at play in whatever this was. He had served his time as an altar boy until he blackmailed his way out after he caught the head priest with one of the other altar boys on his knees in front of him. At the age of ten, he could already put two and two together, meaning when he looked at his future in the wake of that confrontation, he didn't like his chances for escaping the same position in front of the same priest.

As confused and overwhelmed as he had felt in that moment, he could say—standing upright before God—he never once felt the slightest urge to get some holy man's smelly cork poked into his mouth. He swore to the priest that he would talk unless he was left alone, then ran like an escaping thief, which maybe he was for stealing the holy man's expectations.

He never went back, either. His parents tried to fight him for a while, but he resorted to telling them just enough about what he saw to give them a general idea. They both decided to drop the topic and left it alone after that.

Now he was grown, standing before a man who called himself a bishop, as if that made him better, and who then behaved in a way that proved he was not.

The only real quandary was the depth of appeal the so-called bishop's suggestions conjured. Mannerly was captivated by the jaw-dropping offer of the opportunity to buy into a constant stream of helpless human beings who would depend upon him for every breath they took, all under the guise of medical care. He would have complete mastery over a victim, to the point where the victim became little more than a product. Therefore, while they passed through Clayton's hands, they were his property.

Until he let go of them.

In this arrangement, clients could get their property to do anything at all, because the clients held the hammer. *Kill the footman and bury him in the garden. The laborer. The maid. The orphan child.*

When the bishop finally came to the point of his conversation, perspiring in hope and fear, he mumbled a vague suggestion. Perhaps Clayton would like to make a lot of cash money in a hurry...

And there it was at last. The bishop's robe was off and he may as well have stood naked. Here was an unimpressive little fellow who already had religious power over others as well as political power over many of the nation's leaders, but who found those powers insufficient to his needs. He required a deeper, frankly lethal level of power over his flock. For that, he would sup from the recovery ward.

None of which concerned Clayton as anything more than points of passing interest. It was all part of the ruined world to him. Free of moral restraint, he found the phrase "a lot of cash money in a hurry" nearly as compelling as the helplessness of those beauties under his care back on the ward. Writhing in their beds.

Because he liked, no, he *loved* owning people. He loved the way it made him feel. Fully aware of the social stigma on it, and perhaps further titil-lated by it, he discovered there was no more satisfying sensation in his pointless life than to look at another human being and know he could do whatever he wanted to do to that person. Whatever he pleased.

The cherry on the cake was the knowledge that the person you owned also knew you had all the power over them. Just as it was with any other servant, an astute owner could learn how to remind the help of their place using little more than a glance.

The bishop made an important clerical observation: there was nothing un-Christian in treating slaves like slaves, because God had dictated there should be such a thing as slaves in the first place.

That catapulted Clayton's attention level right away. Other than the prospect of an inheritance of a hotel he had no idea how to run with any success, he was going to return home cash poor. His family's humble wealth was that of the well-paid servant class. In social circles, they amounted to the status of bench players. Clayton considered this to be just as much a deformation of his future chances as a bad reputation. Worse.

On that first day, all the bishop asked him to do was turn his back for a minute while he took one of the orphans away with him for delivery to "the Movers," his name for the clients driving the trade and overseeing its administration. No records were to be made of the transfer.

The holy man turned out to be a fellow traveler when it came to his appreciation for the company of helpless human beings who could not prevent him from doing whatever he pleased with them.

Mannerly had felt himself go hard when he considered the proposal and the bishop told him a little about the people he served. "The one I have my eye on is lucky. She'll go to one of the most prominent families here in London. I won't mention which parish, but they are rich and powerful, like the church that represents them. She may have, ah, extra duties, but she will survive and be well fed. It is of the essence to our survival that we know how to manage dealing exclusively with the rich and the powerful, because nobody else can afford our product. Nothing else controls such people but fear of exposure."

"Blackmail?"

"Frankly, yes. And it's not just the men." The bishop leered. "Women too. They generally don't use their indentured servants for sex, but oh, they love to order servants around. I tell young men who come to me for confession when they are thinking of proposing marriage. I say, if you want to find out what kind of woman you have, give her a servant, tell her she can do anything she wants with her or him, and be certain she understands that there is nothing the servant can do. There is nowhere to file a complaint.

"Then see how she handles it. Nine times out of ten, you will find yourself watching a woman treat that poor servant the same way she's going to treat *you* once the shine wears off!"

The bishop laughed a bit too loud, but Clayton got the point. He laughed along to keep him loose. This was getting interesting, and mop duty was still twenty minutes away.

"But what about children?" Mannerly had asked, chasing the sexual thrill.

The bishop smiled like a kindly priest feeding the poor. "Once they're yours, you can do whatever you want. Keep them for yourself as foster children, sell them, get them jobs, or just use them for your own pleasure. They have brought you the gift of their helplessness, and it is yours to do with as you please."

That was it. They spoke the same language.

Clayton could have kissed the bishop. What a revelation! His joke of a military career had just been validated. His personal sense of purpose expanded. His entire purpose in the war became clear to him, and it had nothing to do with combat. The helplessness of others brought along with it a series of rewards that, in a fair world, might pass for remuneration for Clayton's bravery in the spotter's chair. One of those damn bullets had creased his head so close, if he had sneezed, his brains would have been blown out.

He had earned this. He was owed.

Since the women were helpless, they could easily be persuaded to cooperate using the prospect of opportunity. Males who were too young to be self-sufficient or too injured to make their way in life were as malleable as the females. The children could be absorbed into any environment chosen for them. In all three cases, whoever took control over those people could do whatever they wanted with them.

The bishop became a regular visitor. His payments to Clayton Mannerly were prompt and in cash.

Not once was a patient missed by the hospital. As for families, whoever might report them missing was likely dead, in the military service, or in a prison camp somewhere. It made no difference. The "missing" merely took their places among the countless casualties of the war. Chaos hid them from view like squid ink.

As the days went on, Clayton marveled at the ongoing performances of the bishop while the man returned to "counsel the flock" there, over and over. Clayton was astonished by how well the performances went with the bishop's audiences. The man had a perfect command of his illusion of piety and truly appeared to be doing God's work.

"God's work!" Clayton called out across the ward to him, more than once, smiling a fake big smile. It never made the bishop blush at all. He just kept waving his cross around. God's work.

Throughout the war, the rest of the world became completely absorbed in trying not to destroy itself, with no time or energy to invest in finding justice for the silent helpless. The aftermath of the war was almost as chaotic for most people and therefore a powerful distraction away from Clayton, the bishop, and a group of shadowy but powerful "clients" who turned out to be far larger than anything he had imagined at first.

He discovered a community he had never known to exist. Here were people who not only loved holding others in helpless conditions, they had the means to pay dearly for the privilege. Plus a deadly determination to keep their supply lines secret from the world.

Demand was robust. Opportunities abounded for anyone whose conscience fell into the same deep hole Clayton Mannerly soon occupied. He found the downward trip a spine-tingling ride.

Once he jumped back stateside after his commission ended, he took up the helm of the hotel his father had left him while Clayton was on the battlefield. At the time, the army could not spare him for the funeral. But for Clayton, with his mother already gone, it was a relief to have been exempted from the blubbering sympathies of other mourners.

Most of all, with his father now deceased, he was free of having to fear the devout man's reaction if he ever discovered his son's new pastime. Disinheritance and a life of working poverty was not for him. He had a busy new career planned.

Some soldiers came home with enemy weapons as souvenirs, some brought home malaria or the clap. Clayton brought home what his father would have called an "awakened demon," just waiting for his guard to be lowered so it could take control. He liked the way it felt to give up control to this demon, or whatever it was. He had a new appreciation for a certain way of being that was essentially invisible until the desired behavior manifested.

Meaning, so long as the behavior only manifested in secret, it was nearly impossible to detect by anyone who was not a direct witness. It was as good as having the ability to slaughter your enemies at will, then walk the world dripping in blood without anyone taking notice.

As the months passed, secret orgy parties went on at the hotel and the seminary in Queens. Sales went through the roof. In this fashion, a story that would have been a three-inch headline in every paper in the country instead went untold, traveling by no other means than word of mouth from enthusiastic and satisfied clients who all appreciated how quickly their lives would turn upside down if the truth got out.

Demand outstripped supply. The infected church demanded more and more for their frontier monasteries in hostile places, and the infected halls of political dominion did the same. The infected circles of the wealthy had always thrived on forced labor and now blossomed under this new iteration of the same old trade. Clayton gave in to the power of the thing without knowing what it was, and soon without caring.

Even in the present day he had no idea what to call his clients except the Movers, this club, this organization, this troop of dedicated seekers of ultimate pleasures. It was a nameless, shapeless thing existing in the unseen realm between a wink and a silent nod. Rarely was its existence mentioned by any of the participants or supporters, or especially the victims, who were universally terrified into silence.

God, how he loved it! Clayton resolved there was no way in hell he would allow the boy Dante to destroy his invisible empire. He had already wasted months slowly bringing the boy to the realization of his expected role in recruiting faceless orphans from the New York streets. It had all been carefully explained to Dante that persuasion was far safer than kidnapping and, done right, worked better all around. But the boy became increasingly morose while the truth was gradually revealed to him. He began moping about the hotel and hanging onto Eliana as if they were actually related and not two random acquisitions.

Still, no matter what Dante's problems happened to be, Clayton had to have a child recruiter. That was all. Sometimes Father Young could snag a couple of young boys using his priest's frock to calm them, but his duties at the seminary kept him from spending enough time on the streets. He was useless at acquiring small females.

The priest liked to hang around the train stations with one of the seminary students also wearing a frock, posing as two holy men doing innocent spiritual business while they sought out more of the helpless. They snagged a random boy here and there, hungry, sickly, desperate for help, boys too easy to be a challenge. But it was never enough. Beyond the requirements of staffing the seminary, Father Young appeared to be under pressure from his own list of contacts. Clayton had introduced him to the bishop, but afterward the bishop appeared to have developed a supply line for the priest that was all his own. Such was the demand, the unspoken, unseen demand. An entire industry was grinding away directly under the noses of the American people, and the only real problem was keeping it fed.

So why couldn't the boy see the opportunity and appreciate what was offered to him? Was it the field trip to Blackwell's Island? Along with the training session on how to recognize potential victims, the Blackwell's Island trip appeared to tilt the load and pull Dante completely off track. He came back to the hotel in some kind of a blue funk and stuck to Eliana like biscuit glue for two days, as if that somehow removed his new obligations.

Then the boy disappeared, and Eliana started to wonder out loud if he had been kidnapped because *"he would never leave without me."* Clayton had believed that much, then. So where was the boy now? He had no answer.

He had never made any objection to Dante's relationship with Eliana. He considered the bond between the pair an asset that might make Dante as cooperative as Eliana proved to be; she had long since learned to shut her mouth and do as she was told.

They both behaved as if their relationship was real, and their delusions mattered not at all until the boy ran off. The boy who knew too much.

So what was Dante's sticking point? Who could predict that a child with a background like his, bounced from one orphanage to another all of his childhood, would abandon a life of luxury along with a random woman he liked to call his auntie, only to take to the streets alone?

Of course the kidnapping story was ridiculous, and given a little time to think it over, he realized Eliana was a lousy actress and she wasn't nearly frantic enough if she thought Dante was actually captive out there somewhere. Her act was a put-on. It was a little show.

Once Clayton Mannerly's suspicions surged, he had to choke Eliana pretty hard to get her to say the words, "San Francisco." After that, he was satisfied she would rather die than say more, so he had let her live and sent her to clean up his study.

13

SOUTHERN PACIFIC EASTBOUND EXPRESS
NEAR RENO, NEVADA

February 25th
* Midafternoon *

FREEZING TEMPERATURES FOLLOWED THEM DOWN from high altitudes while the Eastbound Express stormed out of the mountain passes. It ran onward toward Reno and then on to flatter lands. Dante had no idea of the train's actual speed, but he could tell it was faster than anything a horse could do. With the day's temperatures already low, the air felt like liquid ice tearing at him while he sat facing into the wind on the leading edge of the dining car's roof.

Blackburn and Vignette were safe from the cold in the heated car below him. Last time he saw them they were lingering at their luncheon table. The accommodations on board were not at the level of luxury provided by the Overland trains running from Los Angeles to Chicago, but every reasonable comfort was provided, including bunk berths for first-class passengers and a fine dining car.

Vignette had been wonderful during their long ride. She offered him a book to read, but he couldn't keep his thoughts still enough for that. They borrowed a deck of cards from the conductor, but Dante's mind was not on the game. Out of frustration, Vignette asked if he wanted to learn how to pick a lock.

Minutes later, with the conductor busy in another car and the other diners gone for now, she took him to the door at the far end of the dining car and pulled out her ever-present hairpins, which she wore even when her hair itself had no need of them. She had him kneel with her to put the door lock at eye level, then said, "All right, for this we need two hairpins. You can buy lock-picking sets, but if you're caught with them, you're pretty much guilty of whatever they want to accuse you of. I suggest you think of some reason to always carry a couple."

"Like what?"

"Say you're holding onto them for your sister."

"I don't have a sister."

"Who's going to know that besides you?"

He smiled and nodded. "All right, hairpins."

"This one, I put a small curve at the end," she applied a little pressure, "like this, so it looks like a little crowbar. The other pin, we pull off the rubber bit at the end and then fold it into an L-shape, then stick one end into the lock." Which she did, adding, "All the way in, until it stops. Then we take the one with the little curve, and while we keep that folded shape in the lock, we gently slide in the tiny crowbar faceup, and lift, lift, lift, while we slowly move into the lock, lifting. Hear the little clicks? That's the tumblers moving out of the way."

Fascinated, Dante whispered under his breath, "Lifting, lifting..." His intensity of focus while he watched her was nearly enough to generate heat. His eyes remained riveted on her hands while she made the subtle moves of working the lock's tumblers. It was as if he were receiving the keys to the universe.

Vignette paused, jiggled the L-shaped pin a tiny bit, and smiled in satisfaction. "That's it." She turned the L-shaped pin, and the lock gave up the door. She opened it to the rush of the wind, then let it slam back into place. Dante went through the motions of screaming with delight and throwing his arms over his head without actually making a sound, causing Vignette to laugh out loud.

"Here," she said, dropping the two pins into his hand. "You try."

It took him most of two minutes, that first time.

"Try again." Vignette smiled. She looked happy in spite of his slow progress. Dante couldn't understand that. He had so little experience with patience from an Old One, the moment caught his attention like a jerk on his sleeve.

On his second try, he got the lock in about one minute. When he looked up at Vignette, she was still paying attention, still smiling, not looking angry or impatient at all. Strange.

About thirty seconds after he began his third attempt, the lock opened again. It was only a few minutes later when Dante returned to the door while Randall and Vignette sipped oolong tea from porcelain cups. After popping the lock almost as quickly as the conductor could open it with a key, he nimbly climbed up to the roof with no concern for consequences.

Blackburn leaned out the window a couple of times and hollered for him to return to his seat, but Dante happily ignored him, figuring no adult was going to climb out there and force him down. He was right about that much. Sometimes it came in handy to know things about how the old guys thought.

The first time he rode the roof of a train car was on the trip out from New York. As long as Eliana knew nothing of it, she would suffer no worry over it. He also felt lucky she had not been there to see him when he hopped onto yet another freight train and got an instant case of traveler's remorse when an old guy who stank of dried piss and bad whiskey latched onto him like a snake going after a henhouse. He grinned with half his teeth and began hollering incoherent crap over the noise of the train. Dante moved away, only to have the old guy come after him again. Too friendly. Too close.

Instinct told him this guy saw him as food, so in a bursting impulse he would never have followed if he thought about it first, he had swung himself out the open cargo door and scrambled up to the roof of the car.

He was fairly certain the freezing rooftop was a place old Piss-and-Whiskey would be sure to avoid, with footing far too treacherous for a man who walked the way he did. That made the frigid, rocking rooftop feel safer than anywhere else on the train.

On today's ride, the nice winter coat Blackburn and Vignette had bought for him during the cab ride to the station was soft enough to pad the wood. It also looked far better, after the weeks his old coat spent on the streets, but both coats were about the same weight. Meaning he could endure the perch atop the car for a short time, but the sharpness of the cold tightened his skin and quickly drained the warmth from him. He felt the process deep in his face, even beneath the wool scarf wrapped twice around his head. He wouldn't even try venturing out there at night.

If he could not tolerate the cold as well as he did before, it would be a grim message, a warning that he was not heading back to New York City with the same strength. He estimated an overall loss of as much as ten percent of his total body weight since fleeing Clayton's hotel, judging by his beltline. That would be most unfortunate. Even when his strength was high for a boy his size, it was too often not enough. He had never been able to consistently outrun the sour Old Ones.

As to his weakness or his strength, it was not for lack of food that he lost weight while he was on the road. He had actually been able to eat pretty well by skimming tabletops while he waited for Eliana. People walked away from cash tips and half-eaten meals, both of which he snatched without attacks of conscience. Sometimes he could even help other kids score food.

Sleep was the big problem. He learned how tough it could be to find a safe spot to close his eyes and go dead to the world for a few hours. Nobody his age was safe on the city streets. As long as human beings lived there, it made no difference what city it was. He seemed to spend most of his time on the run from somebody or other. He was successful most of the time, but the law of averages was grim. He reminded himself that he had never seen any other kid with a perfect getaway record, either.

When he won, it was because of quick thinking. Even still being the mere age of eleven, he felt the unique speed of his thought processes every time he spoke to someone else, especially if the topic was complex. When he first confronted the problem, he took it for an inability to clearly express himself. But he found all he had to do was speak as if he were dealing with children who happened to have good vocabularies. Then he communicated with most of the Old Ones just fine.

Upon first arriving in California, he took a little of his ticket money and sat down to eat in a café behind two doctors, and he overheard them talk about new tests they had nowadays to measure your intelligence and rate you with a number. He had no idea where his number would fall on that listing, but he was certain most people's thoughts ran slower than his. Intuition told him it was not just a matter of his speed in thinking but the ability to track complex trains of thought without jumbling them and getting lost in the process.

He just had no idea what to do about it. So far in life, his abilities mostly served a purpose similar to street-corner card tricks, offering random advantages now and then, but that was about it. The darkest sides of human nature proved the most difficult to outfox. There, his talents had little to offer.

Every street kid he talked to told him more or less the same thing, and it made no difference where in the world those kids came from—they were too small to keep themselves from getting snagged by the Old Ones. Once that happened, they were forced to learn most everything there was to know about the worst parts of human nature.

They all had their own words for telling him, but the stories were the same. They even stopped at the parts they had to leave out and stared into empty space in the same way. For those parts, they had no need of words.

These were the things they all knew. Humans were carriers of human nature, anywhere you looked. The race or the language or the religion of the people in question, none of it made any difference. Human nature was as dangerous as nitroglycerin.

His own roster of foster homes carried experiences of captive ordeals he was never able to prevent. He was forced to meet demonic humans who loved nothing more than the feeling of power they received from delivering shock and pain to innocent people. The art of it seemed to be something about how well they could conceal the damage they inflicted.

Dante had no trouble understanding why just making laws against things tended not to work. In those lethally lonely moments when he was forced into the company of an old man demon or an old woman demon, or even a group of old demons, he was only able to face them—and the knowledge that they walked among everyone unseen—using a secret totem he carried inside. It was formed of a series of blurred memories. There was an adult male, a man he thought of as his father, whether or not the man really was. It took place before the series of handoffs began, one so-called foster home to another. Dante did not know who the man in the dreams really was. There was no way to search him out. But he remembered the strength the man imparted, even in dreams, with his steadfast kindness. In Dante's mind, he was everything good and decent and strong. He was a model for Dante to build himself on. The kind of man who possessed the strength to destroy but only used it to build. A man with the ability to fight, but who only used that skill to defend himself or others.

Today, Dante's ability to withstand the deadly frozen blast was a suitable test of his determination. Now that they were nearly 4,500 feet higher than they were at the Pacific shoreline, his challenge was to see how far he could press himself into the cold and still keep enough of his body and soul together to survive.

The self-assurance he derived from the accomplishment would help to stiffen his resolve when he risked going back for Eliana. Most of all, it would help him if the two of them had to face down Clayton's men by themselves.

Or that was the idea. Eliana was not only all he had, she was the only source of consistent motherly affection he had ever known. He could never get enough. Being apart from her while he waited in San Francisco was like missing a limb. The inability to check on her was maddening. And so this sudden chance to go straight back to New York with Vignette and Detective Blackburn—without jumping on freight cars or stealing food—felt like a Godsend. He realized an evil-send could feel like a Godsend because of the Devil's trickery, but he had been the recipient of enough evil-sends to have a general feel for their energy, and this seemed different. No, this was a good thing. If not a Godsend, then at least a stroke of good fortune.

Call it by any name. He needed all the good fortune he could find. Eliana and the other servants were not allowed to receive telephone calls at the hotel unless they were off duty, and as the head maid—resident of the hotel herself—Eliana was never off duty. At least that's all he knew about it. The explanation made no sense, but to him old people's explanations seldom did.

During his year with her, what mattered to him was her constant presence. It allowed them to develop their practice of close contact, almost a mother-son relationship. It took a long time for him to see their circumstances for what they were. Not because he was naïve to her plight, but because he allowed himself to be distracted by her charm. She made him feel as though the two of them together could survive anyplace at all.

After a fine year with her, he only endured the separation by focusing on the mission, and for now that meant focusing on his own survival in the cold, not by staying warm but by proving to himself he could stand up to a deadly challenge. He knew he would be ridiculed for saying so out loud, but it made perfect and compelling sense to him.

Intuition told him to use the cold. To rise into the cold and take the power from the act of rising to it, and to then bring that sense of confident victory down from that swaying roof and into the passenger car with Detective Blackburn and Vignette. He repeated to himself over and over, *You have to get her out of there! You have to get her out!* While the frigid air blasted away at his perch atop the train car.

From as far down as he had started, there was nowhere to go but up. All he had to do was stay alive for a while.

Randall spent every hour of the train ride feeling sick to his stomach over the knowledge of what happened to Shane. He had yet to tell Vignette, but knew it had to come out soon. The more he delayed, the greater risk of her outrage when she realized how long he kept it to himself.

Of course it was not that simple. His dilemma was one of balance. Adjusting to big emotional blows was Vignette's weakest ability. It could take her days to regain her stability. After Shane's death, it took weeks. Yet here they were, headed into trouble they could not predict but which was certain to be dangerous. She needed to be fully awake and alert to her surroundings and to keep her attention on the details of the case in New York.

There was no practical way to tell her while they were stuck on the train. Her sense of being trapped on the moving car would only aggravate her shock and grief. No, the best time to tell her was when they were just arriving. Give her the news at the same time he gave her a potential pathway to justice for Shane, at a moment when she had the power to spring into some form of action.

With the cooperation of Commissioner O'Grady, he could present Vignette with the awful news and at least have a plan of action to offer her. Until it was time to tell her, the plan was to discuss anything else but that. He thought about once again mentioning his concerns about her tendency to pick up orphans for a meal, but he knew better than to fall into the same old conversation/debate/argument. It never seemed to resolve anything. He had recently faced the fact that anytime either of them tried to talk about her practice of picking up stray kids and buying them a meal, all they seemed to do was go away upset. He was proud of her humanitarian side but could not get her to see the danger she put herself in.

Over and over he reminded her, just because a person was young and disadvantaged was no assurance that they lacked the capacity for evil. Even the innocent ones could lapse into violence born in simple misunderstandings of good intentions made by a fearful child who was all too accustomed to betrayal and attack. He knew from a career of experience that simply being there to help was no guarantee the help would be received with gratitude. Many of those children had already been betrayed by adults so often they expected nothing else from them but pain and deceit. Some had absorbed horrible events and smashed families, while others were only still alive because of their capacity for violence as self-defense.

Randall considered Vignette safer around dangerous adults than dangerous children. With the adults, he knew she always had her guard up. With the children, her empathy left her completely vulnerable. It would only take one child with a damaged mind to slash at her with a blade. His career in law enforcement had repeatedly shown how quickly such a thing happened. As he often reminded her, *Blink once, the blade has slashed. Blink twice, the victim is on the ground dying.*

He already realized Dante was not that sort of kid, but what about the next one? What about the one after that? He had still never found a way to make her appreciate that she was running a numbers game with the law of averages. Eventual failure was guaranteed. The only question was time.

PART II

14

CITY SQUIRE HOTEL – TOP-FLOOR PENTHOUSE

LOWER MIDTOWN, MANHATTAN

February 26th

* 10:00 p.m. *

CLAYTON MANNERLY SENT THE STAFF DOWNSTAIRS, dismissing them from the penthouse for the night so he and Allison could talk in safety. Every employee knew about the secrecy required of them; they had more or less signed away their lives. Thus those few who were ever permitted into the penthouse and especially the penthouse bedroom would never be allowed to talk about the nude portraits on the walls, famous people rendered without clothing as if they had posed in that condition. Men were depicted in female attire they would never wear in public. Naked women were portrayed with full beards. Mannerly loved the way the paintings reduced their powerful subjects to absurdity at a single glance.

"All right, everybody's gone. Let's get down to it. We've got a party to plan."

"What about Eliana? Are you sure she's done?"

"She's the one I told to spread the message that everybody was to stay down in the hotel."

Allison gave him a cold look. "Are you certain you don't want to keep her around in case you feel any sexual urges?"

He returned with his best sneer. "That's what I have you for."

"Maybe once. But lately you treat me like…like…I don't know what. Not somebody you are married to, that's for sure."

"Allison, the only reason you married a man fifteen years older is for the money. You have it. You have the life of luxury I promised you."

"Yeah," she softly replied. "I sure do, don't I?"

"You do, and every one of the women we socialize with envies you for your life. But we all work, Allison. I work. You work. All our employees—"

"All *right*! All right, Clayton, Jesus!"

"For now, your job is to hit the city sidewalks, the high schools, the parks—Central Park especially—and bring me half a dozen women and girls tomorrow night. Don't involve Father Young; he's getting cocky and demanding. Just get the girls. Plenty of people are hungry enough to take any job offered to them. Pick out his six candidates and let me know. I'll take them up to Blackwell's Island and deliver them to the good Reverend Canon Richard Young myself. Just bring them here, put 'em in my own coach, and make sure it gets done right."

"I thought you were storing them to parlay if the price jumped."

"It just did. We emptied out our stock, and the Movers aren't sending another boatload for ten days, maybe two weeks, given weather. We're on our own."

"So how many guests this time?"

"Four."

"Just four?"

"The senator, his wife, and—"

"Clayton! They're old! You said I was done with people that age."

"—and two of their closest domestics. Apparently the four of them have been playing together for months. Fancy that, if you dare."

"And they want six young females, no boys?"

"They were very specific. They also indicated they may take as many as three back with them. Remember, the rejects have to believe they are all being paid cash for their time and given cab fare home. They will have no reason to think it was any different for the ones who get selected."

She sighed, giving in to the point. "Yes, that part's easy enough, if you pick them up one at a time. It's only natural to split up afterward."

"For what the three will earn us, we can run this place for weeks."

"I'm so tired of this routine, Clayton."

"Well, we have to keep this up until the economy rebounds and the hotel supports itself."

"Why do I get the feeling you won't ever put this down? To do that, you'd have to reject all the money you can make, whether the hotel is doing well or not."

"Yes. I could do that. But I would also have to accept the risk of being discovered one day and then getting subjected to the morality biddies and their 'shocked' reactions. No, no. We'll walk away from this when it's time."

"In the meantime, I have to supply six random females who will come to a party with strangers for money? Maybe do it again until your supply line kicks back in? Clayton, you need to understand, without the cover of the orphan trains and the contracts...we are alone in this."

"Just get them. These are tough times. Plenty of people are willing to do whatever you tell them for some small amount of cash. They may not be as eager as the ones who just came out of a war zone, but they will do the work. The ones who are secretly rejected will simply go home and never know anything different than that they went to a party and made some cash doing something they most likely don't want to talk about."

"It's the others who worry me. Like the ones down on floor ten. All we need is for one of them to escape, to talk..."

"Has it happened yet?"

"No, but—"

"And it won't."

"I'm not slipping them the mickey this time, Clayton."

"You're not what?"

"I'm saying...I'm hesitant to do it."

"Oh, hesitant?"

"All right, damn you. But you could get somebody else if you wanted to. It's not so much to ask."

"Funny, I was going to tell you it's okay to skip it this time, anyway."

"You were?"

"Sure. But here's the thing. You didn't know that when you refused, did you? You just openly defied me. Yes?"

"Clayton..."

"Pick out six. Give them the drink. When they're asleep, I'll come and put 'em in the boxes. We can transport them like dry goods right out the shipping entrance."

"I just feel like garbage every time we do that."

Clayton was glad he had the foresight to send the penthouse help away to work down in the hotel. It allowed him to bellow at his wife at the top of his lungs without concern for being overheard outside the soundproofed penthouse walls.

"*Don't* tell me how you feel! Did I *ask*? Do I *care*? Son of a bitch, Allison! Are you trying to kill us? We have work to do!"

"Not so loud!"

"Who the hell is going to hear me?"

"I can hear you, Clayton. I can."

"You aren't acting like you hear me, Allison. Any other concerns?"

She heaved a deep sigh and shook her head, then turned and slowly walked out of the bedroom. Clayton called after her. "Get started! Find Eliana and take her, too."

"Again? Her attitude is not very good."

"Doesn't matter. She fills her function just by being there. Two women offering charitable help. You know I can't go; a strange man only raises questions."

"I thought Father Young always takes one of his student priests."

"Nice of you to call them that. Anyway, he does it the same way you do, except he's picking up boys and young men. An older priest and a young priest wearing their robes? They look so holy, they're even trusted by atheists!" He barked a sharp laugh and sustained it much longer than the joke deserved.

After he caught his breath, he leaned in close to her and fixed her with a strict gaze. "There's an art to this, and I saw you had the talent for it when we first met. You have a nose for desperation, Allison. You have a nose for it because their desperation mirrors your own, back before you struck it rich with me."

"Clayton, I think I know..."

"Just like Father Young has a nose for desperation in the vagabonds he drags home."

Instead of swearing or stomping out of the room, Allison dropped her voice to a whisper. She kept her eyes on the floor while she repeated what she had started to say.

"Clayton...I think I know. I know what happens to the ones who try to fight back or to the ones who try to escape."

He chuckled. "Oh, I'm pretty certain you don't."

"I heard you on the phone with the priest a few days ago, Clayton. I do know."

He leveled a deathly gaze at her that would have sealed her mouth if she had been paying close attention. But she was too absorbed in making her point to notice.

"He has his most loyal followers knock them out in some fashion, probably like we do, then put them in the water offshore of Blackwell's Island. I don't know if the currents sweep them straight down the Harlem River and on out to sea, or if they get weighted down and anchored to the bottom. Either way, they're gone forever."

The room grew very still. Silence hung heavy with menace.

Allison's first clue that she had seriously overstepped her bounds revealed itself when he refused to look at her or even to glance at her when he replied, using a voice even softer than her own.

"They were going to die anyway. Back in their primitive homelands where everybody is now living as if it's the thirteenth century because of an insane war that accomplished mostly nothing. Go get six of them, Allison. The senator and his wife will be here at nine tomorrow evening. This client is a senator from the Great State of Oklahoma. His wife played a major role in getting the 19th Amendment passed last summer, guaranteeing the vote for women. Did you hear what I just told you? They get what they want. Now don't you think you had better get started?"

She stood silent for a moment, then exhaled and turned to go.

15

SOUTHERN PACIFIC EASTBOUND EXPRESS

PENN STATION – NEW YORK CITY

February 29th
* Late Afternoon *

AS SOON AS BLACKBURN, VIGNETTE, AND DANTE disembarked the train into a freezing winter wind, a young NYPD recruit called out, "Detective!" and hurried over to them, pushing against the departing crowd. "For you, sir!" he said in an official tone, loud enough to make himself heard above the chaos of locomotives arriving and departing. "Invitation compliments of Deputy Commissioner O'Grady, sir."

He handed over a small note with hands shaking from the cold. Vignette and Dante looked puzzled but said nothing.

Blackburn opened it and broke into a broad smile. "Please give her my best, and tell her I'll check in with her tomorrow morning."

"Yes, sir!" The recruit started to salute, stopped himself, and just gave a little wave instead. He took one long step back, turned around, and hurried off.

Vignette and Dante stood watching Blackburn, waiting for some explanation.

"What's all that about?" she asked.

"Greetings and a personal invite to the home of the deputy commissioner." He looked at each of them in turn, then exhaled. "All right, let's find ourselves someplace quiet to have a talk, shall we?"

"I have to go see about Eliana."

Blackburn shook his head. "I know, Dante, but everything you told me about this Clayton Mannerly sounds as if you can't go back there alone. If he grabs you and holds you there with her, then what did your whole plan amount to? Once you're inside that hotel, I can't get to you if he throws me out. It's still private property. We don't know if reporting it to the police would help or not, because he has papers on you. If he pays them off to accept those papers, you're done. I mean it, that's it. The only way to get you out of there then would be to prove the papers are forged. How long would something like that take?"

Blackburn saw despair fill Dante's face. "You've waited this long, Dante, just give me a little bit longer to come up with a plan to check on Eliana, see what she has to say, and hell, we'll all help her escape if that's what she wants to do."

"It is what she wants to do!" he insisted. "That was the whole idea! For us to get out and live someplace safe, to...to be together...and..." He stopped, shaking his head while his shoulders slumped.

"I'll go over to the hotel tomorrow and ask around. We'll get to the bottom of it. Can you trust me to do that?"

Dante exhaled hard, but he nodded in agreement.

"I can go, Randall," Vignette said. "I'll bet this is one of those times when a female can get more information."

"You can manage to look harmless and unsuspicious?"

She smiled and raised her eyebrows. "I can try..."

"Good. We'll see how that works out. Now the second thing, it's big. It's huge, really, and I've been thinking about it ever since we left San Francisco."

"Why didn't you say anything?"

"This is why." He took a deep breath. "The intruder we drove off told me something while we were out in the front yard. It's something it wouldn't occur to him to say if it weren't true. Given the way he told me, I have to think it is."

He glanced around the freezing platform and the heavily dressed people rushing back and forth. There was no good place to tell her, but this wasn't even close.

"Just come along," Blackburn said, putting his hands on each of their shoulders and guiding them off of the terminal platform. "We'll get a bite to eat."

They found a nice little tea parlor not far from the station and went inside. Once they were seated and placed their orders for tea and muffins, Blackburn watched the waitress walk away and then lowered his voice to speak.

"I placed a call from Chicago to Deputy Commissioner O'Grady, our contact at the NYPD. Since we're here to help them, I thought she might be willing to get me some special information on these anarchists and have it for us as soon as we got in." He pointed to the list. "As you see, she's a woman of her word."

"Her again. Are we going to meet her?" Vignette asked.

"Tomorrow. I think you two are going to hit it off."

Vignette did not appear convinced. "What's so special about this other information that you've been carrying since we left and you couldn't tell it to me?"

He took both of her hands and then said, "All right. Here it comes. I hate this, but what I'm about to tell you is true. It's one of the long list of evil things in this world that I can't protect you from, much as it breaks my heart, because I see you, Vignette. I have always seen you. And I know Shane was your rescuer, in many ways, and even though I can't feel what you are feeling over this, it hurts me too, and it kills me to see it inflicted on you."

"Randall, damn it."

"All right, all right." Then he quietly told her about Shane, how his death was no accident. He told her all about Shane's killer, Andrea Salsedo, an anarchist typesetter and printer of anarchist pamphlets. He told her how the order to kill was most likely issued to Salsedo by Mario Buda, the bomber who had escaped them four years earlier.

Vignette's first reaction was a guttural scream of shock. She stifled it with her hand over her mouth. Her eyes flew wide open, and she bent forward at the waist as if she might topple out of the chair. Blackburn hurried to her side and put his arms around her shoulders while a few other patrons stared in concern.

Dante felt his stomach drop at the sight of Vignette's distress. He knew there were things people did in this situation but couldn't think of what they were. He wanted to comfort her but knew he had no right to get personal with someone he had known only a few days. She had been so kind to him and seemed to be such a free-spirited person; seeing her like this made him hurt inside. But what to do? What would work, and what would only make things worse? What did regular people do for something like this? He had no idea. He could only rest his hand on her shoulder and hurt for her, feeling useless.

Evening was approaching by the time they retrieved their luggage and secured lodging. Randall walked with his arm firmly around Vignette's shoulder while she stumbled through a trance of shock. She clutched Shane's little teardrop-shaped magneto switch with both hands and stared at nothing. Dante kept quiet and just followed along.

The proximity of Penn Station to the City Squire Hotel seemed to cast a pall over the neighborhood, so Blackburn had instructed their cab driver to take them uptown to the Plaza, sitting on the south end of the great Central Park. He made the choice from memory, knowing it to be one of the most famous hotels in the world.

The Plaza felt like a familiar choice even though he had never been there, because he had picked out his house in San Francisco for its location across from Golden Gate Park. So he booked a three-bedroom suite on the eighteenth floor with a park view and gave only passing attention to the price.

He trusted Mayor Rolph not to object to the bills, given the deadly atmosphere of crime they were expected to penetrate, among whiffs of

secret slave trading and corrupt government officials. Theirs was poten-
tially lethal work.

He wondered, just how much of Randall Blackburn and Vignette
Nightingale did the City of San Francisco hire for a job that was not a job
but a mission, one already saddled with the dreaded Three U's: *unprece-
dented*, *unsupported*, and *unofficial*? He would die in combat defending
Vignette from dangers he had thrust upon her. Mayor Rolph had to know
that. Ol' Sunny Jim took it into his calculations in dealing with Blackburn
in the first place.

Blackburn had already made contact with enough troublesome
elements of the orphan train case to disregard whatever shenanigans took
place in hiring him. That was done.

No person of any sophistication would expect a victory to come cheap.

Dante kept watch from the corner of his eye for Clayton's men. It was a
relief not to see any, but that hardly meant there were none around. On top
of his anxiety over Clayton and Eliana, he nearly cringed with discomfort
out of empathy for Vignette, an Old One who had gone out of her way to be
so kind to him. She was like nobody he had met since Eliana came along.
But the desire to help Vignette told him nothing about how to do it. It left
him baffled.

He already guessed the distance from the Plaza on Central Park South
to the City Squire Hotel as something over a mile. He had no money for
transportation, but if this detective broke his promise to help him reach
Eliana, he could travel the distance on foot in a matter of minutes, if he
stayed light on his feet and danced away from the grabby ones.

For the moment, he was glad enough to stay in an environment not
substantially different than the one he lived in for a year at the City Squire.
More polished. Unapologetically luxurious. If they had rats, he figured they
wore white gloves. Dante even had been given a little room to himself in the
suite. He had no idea what to make of this. The big detective actually
respected their privacy enough to give them each a room with doors that
locked from the inside. A persistent part of Dante's brain fired nonstop

warnings. If there was an angle to this generosity, he needed to find it and fast, but he couldn't figure what it might be. Nobody was demanding anything of him.

He was eager to see what was going on with this Randall Blackburn. Ordinarily, the man would only strike Dante as one of the fakes who hide under masks but whose true self comes out as soon as they get you where nobody can stop them. But so far, this Old One didn't seem to be like that at all. Dante had no idea why. Vignette had called the detective the "best man" she knew. What a thing to say. Why would she make that up?

Still, if that was true, where were the other men like him? Where were the ones who even came close? In a perfect world, he and Eliana would find a place where such people existed, where they treated Eliana with respect and taught him how to become one of them.

Why were so many demons around? Aside from finding Eliana, it was the central question of his life.

16

THE PLAZA HOTEL – CENTRAL PARK SOUTH

FEBRUARY 29TH

* Evening *

VIGNETTE HAD ALLOWED BLACKBURN TO WALK HER along like an oversized puppet. Even in her worst distress she knew she could trust him. He guided her from their taxi into the hotel lobby, checked them in, and took her upstairs with Dante. She knew he could do nothing to spare her the pain pulsing through her, but years of experience told her he would take care of her and see her safely off of the freezing city streets and into a warm, quiet room, as he had. It was all she could ask of him and all he could do, but so long as this murderer Salsedo ran free, suffering was built into the scenario for her—into the vignette.

Strobing images alternated in her mind: riding behind Shane on his big Harley and laughing so hard she nearly lost her balance before the memory gave way to her harshest, most grinding imaginary images of his death under the wheels of the truck sent to collide with him. She could no longer dismiss it as an accident. The worst memory was visiting his ruined Harley at the police impound so twisted and mangled, stained with blood, that she could see his broken body lying on it as if he were really there. She had snapped off the magneto switch without thinking about it.

But those torturous death images swiveled to a single, beautiful memory of Shane as a little boy back at St. Adrian's, when she was still Mary Kathleen. Their two-year age difference had seemed much greater then. Shane was unlike many of the rowdy or criminally minded boys. He consistently behaved like a quiet young gentleman. She had no explanation for it, but there was some civilizing force at work inside of him, and it showed. It never occurred to her to wonder why she was able to see it in him.

She knew the friars sent for Shane sometimes—at night—just as they did to her. And yet neither of them said a word about it to anyone, as far as she ever knew. Just like none of the other kids said a word about what happened to them either.

She had known nothing of the world, but the special quality she shared with Shane was that of intuition far beyond levels expected of an ordinary child. Part of that intuition communicated with her as a warning device, a wave of nausea she could not explain.

She had felt it for the first time as a girl of what, maybe five? Maybe six? She couldn't say for certain and would never know for a fact, but the dark intuition had ridden into her mind and roiled her insides for the first time with the realization—the certainty—that some of those males were not monks at all.

Part of her sense of closeness with Shane came from her memory of looking into his eyes and realizing something inside of him was saying the same thing; they were not orphans being protected in this place. They were captives of evil men. They were on their own.

Were any of the so-called monks real monks? It seemed impossible to know now, and she figured that was good. Some of them may as well have been Old Testament demons in the flesh. It would be the same from the viewpoint of any helpless child being subjected to the most monstrous side of strangers.

These demons were no less terrifying for their lack of horns. Intuition had made it clear to her, even as a little girl, that her attackers would

behave as perfectly civilized men in the company of outsiders, and probably in the company of anyone they believed deserved better behavior.

She honestly had no idea what to do to deserve better behavior.

The question quickly ceased to matter. Trying to locate a common
ground with those adult creatures felt like inhaling deadly gas. She blocked
it all out from then on. Kept the lid as tight as a Mason jar.

The blocked memories remained in place, as she assumed they did for
Shane, because in their nine years together under Blackburn's roof, they
never discussed it. Not one time. Now, with Shane gone and this terrible
knowledge of his murder, somehow the old floodgates of emotion drew
back. Her muscles began vibrating, as if she were naked in extreme cold.
She had no control over it. She had only been able to keep on her feet with
Blackburn's support.

Migraine-level pain gripped her head in iron straps pulled an inch too
tight. The ringing in her ears was so loud she barely heard anything around
her. The demons were raping her all over again. Those nasty excuses for
human men who were not men but demons and nothing more. She knew.
She knew what they were.

Sometimes the same faces loomed over her, and sometimes new ones
appeared. She learned to imagine she was nothing but a doll, and then
used the doll to steal from them. She did it by stealing the satisfaction they
craved from seeing her shocked reactions. She gave them dead weight
instead. She also stole from them by burying her reactions to the sort of
blows that did not leave marks. She stole the pleasure their demonic
natures sought in watching a child writhing with fear and pain.

When she did a good enough job, the demon was so unsatisfied, he
never came back.

"Vignette?"

Pressure on her shoulders. Strong but gentle. Like brother pressure.

"Vignette? You with me here?"

Randall, then. It was him. Like waking up from a deep, deep sleep.
Hanging halfway out of a dream world.

"Vignette, I want you to take three hard breaths. In and out. I know you
hear me. This is important! We start on the count of three and take the first
big breath. Ready?"

She had enough love for him to make a sincere attempt to reply, but instead of saying, "All right," all she got out was, "Ahh," before she coughed and had to clear her throat for several seconds, as if she had lost her faculty of speech. So she gave him a tired smile, nodded in acquiescence, and pushed out every ounce of air in her chest before drawing in a long, deep inhale, pulling hard at it.

"One...," he counted.

She exhaled, and then repeated the cycle all over again, in and out.

"That's two..."

This time she pushed the air out, bent over forward, and began the deepest, most drawn-out inhale she could manage, puffing up as if she were trying to float away.

"My God, three! Three!" He laughed too hard. "She wins!"

He squeezed her shoulders again, that good, strong, safe touch she never felt from anyone but Randall and the brother those men stole from her. Blackburn's laugh broke her heart because she heard the trace of panic in it. She took his hand and smiled for a moment, and he seemed to regard that as being enough for now.

Randall grasped her hand and just kept on smiling that scared-to-death-but-I-love-you smile while he walked her into her room. The last time she saw that frightened smile, he had just vanquished a man with a knife from their home.

"I'll just close the door for you if you're going to be all right in here."

"Thank you, Randall."

"Vignette, we will not let this pass in front of us. We will get justice for Shane."

She surprised him by throwing her arms around him and whispering, "I have to, Randall. Now that I know this, I can't go back to my life until we do."

"I understand. Me either, actually. Tonight, let's start by getting some rest before we see the deputy commissioner tomorrow. You get in bed, and I'll try to help out Dante by calling the hotel and checking on his aunt."

"Okay." She began to pull back the covers, then stopped and quietly spoke again. "You know, don't you—or if not, you should know by now—I never forget, and I mean *never* forget, the luckiest day in our lives, for Shane and me, was the day you took us home. Some days I get scarce about showing it, but..."

"No. You show it, Vignette. I see you." He beamed. "I love you, too."

~

Randall closed her door and stepped back into the suite's main room, where Dante paced like a caged animal.

"Will you call now? Just ask for her and see what they say?"

"Yes, now I'll make the call. I couldn't do it before, because if there is any foul play involved with her, a long-distance call with questions could tip them off. Now that we're in town, I'm hoping we can move too fast for them to react. I'll start with something harmless."

"What do you mean?"

"Listen." He picked up the telephone receiver from the candlestick phone sitting on the rolltop writing desk and dialed 0.

A few seconds later: "Hello. Operator, please connect me to the main desk of the City Squire Hotel. Yes, I'm calling from a hotel room. Yes, they have a phone book. Hello? Hello?" He looked at the receiver as though it had just struck him in the mouth. "Damn, is there something about these things that makes people rude, or is it just me?"

"I don't know."

"That's okay. Not really a question."

He opened the desk's main drawer and withdrew a thick phone book. "Let's see. Yellow pages...hotels... Look here: City Squire Hotel... Here we go. Pennsylvania 6-0606." He closed the book and dialed the number. The call immediately went through.

"Ah, hello! I'm in the city for the week, and I believe I lost my watch visiting my friend at your establishment. The maid for my room was named Eliana. Any chance she's on duty and could speak with me... Last name? I don't believe maids tell people their last names, do they? So are you saying the name Eliana doesn't ring a bell?"

"What?" screamed Dante. Blackburn threw up the flat of his hand to silence him.

"Oh, it rings a bell, but she doesn't work there anymore? Answer me one more question, please: Why is this so hard? I simply want to speak to a maid about a watch she might help me find. Hello? Hello?"

He hung the receiver back on the candlestick. "And what is it with people slamming these things down without saying goodbye or anything?"

"I don't know."

"Again, not really a question. Can you think of any reason at all why she might be gone, Dante? I don't mean on a train to California, either. Anyplace else?"

"Where else? They won't let her have anything. She's got nothing. The little bit of money she had stashed away went to me. Somehow she must have got her hands on enough for a train ticket. Then she blew out of there. Maybe she's got more! Maybe she's got enough to eat and everything!"

"Dante."

"How much would that take, to have enough to eat and maybe get herself a hotel room once she's there in California?"

"Dante. You think that's what happened?"

"Yes! She managed to get out and get on a train, and now she's on her way to California and I'm not there!" Dante collapsed on the sofa and hung his head in his hands, mumbling, "Oh God, oh God, oh God."

"Hold on a minute. First thing the investigation trade teaches us is not to jump to hasty conclusions. They will take you so far off track you'll never solve your case. Right now, all we know is the desk clerk either didn't know about Eliana or had some reason not to tell us. Given the clerk's tone of voice, I'd say the clerk was caught off guard before she got her story straight. I don't believe Eliana's gone at all."

Dante whispered, "Something's wrong. Isn't it? You think they found out about the plan and took revenge on her, Detective?"

"I don't know, Dante, but I believe we are going to find out. And about calling me 'Detective,' I appreciate the respectful use of the title and all, but let's be more informal. Vignette wasn't much older than you are when we met, and she's always just called me Randall."

Dante gave him a blank stare. "Your first name? I don't usually call Old Ones by their first name. They don't like it."

"Ah."

"There's a lot the Old Ones don't like. A lot. I can't keep up. How do you do it?"

"I would never claim I can keep up, but it helps to work for myself out of an office in my own house in a job where the only people I have much contact with are the ones I investigate and the ones I interview. But that also means I hear people call me 'Detective' all the time, so let's use a name more special with us, like Vignette does."

Blackburn regarded him a moment with a rueful smile. "Why don't you and I agree to call this our arrangement? Just the two of us. Since Vignette called me Randall when she was a kid, you can too. Opinions from old people, if you hear any, won't count." He stuck out his right hand to Dante. "What do you say?"

Dante thought it over for a moment, then beamed a shy smile. He took Blackburn's hand and shook it. A small hand with a firm grasp.

Randall continued to hold onto his hand. "So what's my name again?"

Dante blushed but looked him in the eye and spoke in a clear voice. "Randall."

Randall shook Dante's hand in an exaggerated motion. "Right! And you're Dante! Nice to meet you."

He released his hand and headed toward his bedroom. "We're lucky to all have our own rooms here, Dante, but there's just the one bath. So let's all get in and out as quick as we can."

"I already went while you were with Vignette."

"Did you brush your teeth? Force of habit; I asked Shane and Vignette that for years."

"Oh. Well, yeah. I've been carrying my toothbrush in my pocket ever since I left. You never know when you'll get some clean water and a chance to brush. I've heard people in Clayton's hotel coffee shop say if you brush your teeth all the time, you can keep them."

"You always call him 'Clayton'?"

"Yeah. He doesn't like it, so I do it on purpose."

"Still don't want to tell me why?"

"Can't."

Randall nodded his understanding. "So you're ready for bed?"

"You bet. If we can't do anything until tomorrow, then I want tomorrow to get here as soon as it can."

"Okay, I'm next, then. If you wake up and we're asleep and you get hungry, don't leave the room. Just pick up the phone and dial for room service. See, the number's right on the front of the phone book. They'll cook whatever you want and bring it up. Tell them to charge it to the room."

"I know all about room service. I sometimes helped Eliana if the kitchen staff got too busy to make deliveries. Nope. Tired. I'll sleep all night long."

"Good enough, then." Blackburn was impressed by Dante's enthusiasm but too tired to wonder why the boy was selling the message so hard. Instead, he headed to the bathroom to get ready for bed.

When he walked back out a few minutes later, he noticed Dante's door was already closed. So he went to his own room, closed the door, undressed, and was asleep nearly as soon as he hit the mattress.

Dante waited a good ten minutes before he silently rolled off his bed, picked up his shoes, and put on his coat. He opened his room door, stepped out, noiselessly closed it, and padded across the suite to the exit. He picked up the room key from the small table by the door, released the main lock, opened up, and stepped outside.

17

PENN STATION NEIGHBORHOOD
LOWER MIDTOWN, MANHATTAN

February 29th
* Shortly Before Midnight *

THE CHURCH OF HUMBLE SAINTS served the community around Penn Station in multiple ways, chief among them a main entrance that was open at all hours and in all weather, marking the place as truly one of refuge. The church also ran a resident seminary school, headed by the Reverend Canon Alaric Stone. Stone's face was classic and it matched his demeanor, that of a kindly priest.

Father Stone also happened to be well known to a young boy who was, at that moment, half a block away and speed-walking toward the church's main door. The boy carried a fine bouquet of red roses recently purloined from the expansive lobby of the Plaza Hotel. There was nothing rosy in the boy's demeanor. His opinion appeared to be set hard while he skipped up the steps, yanked open the never-locked door, and stomped inside.

Dante pulled back his winter hood and looked around in the faint cathedral light until he spotted his target: the sizable "poor box" standing just inside the stately entrance. It had space for donated clothing and, best of all, a coin slot for small cash donations. As Dante knew from experience, Father Stone handed out coins like candy to poor children on all the feast days.

Dante also knew what was expected in return.

A sign on the front of the box said, "Help feed poor children."

He delivered a single, full-legged kick powered by a hop-and-skip lead-in, connecting with the box's locking device so effectively one might not be blamed for suspecting this was not his first time. The lock disintegrated with a dangerous clang and rattle while parts hit the floor and scattered. Too much noise. Whatever he was going to do, it had to be done now. He knew better than to rely on the late hour to give him cover. Experience had taught him the thinner street traffic could pose the risk of making you stand out when you needed to blend in.

He reached into the broken box and pulled out a handful of coins, jamming them in his pocket. He started to walk away, stopped, turned back, and grabbed another handful of coins. He started away a second time, stopped, turned around, and came back once again, tucking the bouquet under his arm and stooping to pick up coins with both hands this time.

Bending forward, he peered deep into the box, then straightened up, apparently satisfied. He pocketed those last handfuls, then took the bouquet from under his arm and walked away, calling back over his shoulder in full voice, "G'night, Father Stone! Pleasant dreams!"

He jogged around the Penn Station complex to the front of the City Squire. The Penn Station clock said it was still a couple of minutes before midnight, and Dante knew Eliana never checked out early. She would be visible through the main-floor windows when she came to the front desk to drop off the keys for the last shift.

Spending the past year in that hotel had taught him a lot about the neighborhood. He knew the alley across from the hotel had roofed, open-sided storage areas where kids with no place to go often slept. He had brought out food and coins to them a few times over the year, but Clayton caught him and threatened to punish Eliana for Dante's transgression if he didn't stop. Clayton considered the presence of ragamuffins detrimental to the hotel and his personal reputation.

Ordinarily, Dante might have been intimidated away from entering the dark alley, but necessity drove him toward courage he did not feel. He quietly walked down the narrow strip until all the streetlight from the boulevard faded out. He stopped to let his eyes adjust for a moment, then strolled along the front of the storage sheds looking for sleeping forms. He found one right away. A boy of twelve or so lay curled up on a wooden pallet under a pile of ragged blankets.

"Hello? Hello there?" Dante softly said. He got no reaction, so he tried a loud, "Pssst!" The boy jerked awake and bolted to his feet.

"Stay away!"

"It's okay, it's just me."

"I got a knife!"

"Good, but you don't need it. I'm not here to give you any trouble. I'm here to pay you for a minute of your time." He pulled a handful of coins from his pocket. "See?"

"I don't do that kind of stuff! Get outta here!"

"Wait, wait! I just want you to deliver these flowers to the hotel lobby over there. That's it. I've got more than a dollar here, and you can have it."

The boy looked at him, full of suspicion. "Oh, yeah? Why don't you take it yourself?"

"They know me there. They don't want me around."

"So what did you do?"

"Doesn't matter. I can't go into that lobby, but you can. Easy as pie."

The boy approached Dante and held out his hand.

"Gimme the flowers. I oughta just take your money, but I'm too tired to fight."

Dante beamed and handed them over. "Good. I'm too tired to run."

The boy kept his hand out. "Yeah, but the money first. I ain't gonna help you, then find out you run off with my money as soon as I made the delivery."

Dante poured the coins into the boy's hand. "Here you go. This is enough to eat on all day if you're careful."

"Do you want these handed to the desk clerk?"

"No, just take them to the flower display on the front desk and put the roses in with them. That's all."

"That's it?"

"Do it and the money's yours without having to fight at all."

"Why do you care about adding roses to their flowers in the middle of the night?"

"Why do *you* care? You've got your money."

The boy shot him a condescending look and simply walked away with the flowers, heading for the street. For a moment Dante was concerned that he was just going to take off, but the boy crossed the street and walked to the hotel entrance. The doorman stopped him, but whatever the boy told him proved to be good enough; he went on inside without trouble.

From the mouth of the alley, Dante stared across the street and watched through the front windows while the boy went directly to the flowers on the front desk and pushed the roses into the larger display. They blended right in. The boy turned around and walked back out, tossing a wave at the doorman as he went past him.

Instead of coming back across the street to the alley, the boy just continued on up the street without bothering to look back. Dante assumed he was off to look for someplace still open where he could spend his coins.

The church poor box had done its job, no thanks to Father Stone. Dante remembered the priest from the "training session" Clayton tried to get him to go through, which had only served to convince Dante he had to run away.

As for Eliana, if she was still there, then she would have to keep up appearances and continue to work as she normally would. In that case, he would see her at the change of the shift, and she would see their pre-arranged signal and know Dante was back in the city.

He stepped back into a large shadowed doorway and sat down to wait, just as he had done every day in San Francisco under the Clock Tower outside the Ferry Building. If Eliana was there and working tonight, she would be dropping off her keys any minute. His vantage point allowed him to see right where she always stepped behind the counter to leave the keys behind the front desk floral display.

He waited. He waited some more. Then a female worker he had never seen before walked across the lobby holding the large ring of hotel service keys. She stepped around the front desk and appeared to place the keys in the usual spot. She definitely was not Eliana.

His heart sank. The Penn Station clock showed it was already a few minutes after midnight. Eliana was never late. Clayton just wouldn't stand for it. No, she didn't show up, meaning she wasn't there.

Which meant she was gone. Most likely on a train to California. They could have passed each other's trains going and coming. Disappointment made him feel as if his body was filled with cold mud. His legs felt heavy with every step. He turned north and headed back toward Central Park and the Plaza Hotel, covered the distance in half an hour, and sneaked back into the room without waking his hosts.

He had no idea what to do next.

18

THE PLAZA HOTEL – CENTRAL PARK SOUTH

March 1st
* 8:00 a.m. *

BLACKBURN, VIGNETTE, AND DANTE sat in their hotel suite at three small breakfast tables brought up by room service. Dante had managed to get back into the room and replace the key back on the table without waking them. Now Vignette and Dante picked at their barely touched breakfasts while Randall held the phone receiver to his ear.

"Yes, Commissioner, we can be there at eleven." He picked up a paper pad and wrote while he talked. "All right, 247 New York Avenue, Brooklyn? Good. Three hours, then. We look forward to seeing you. Oh, she's going to be there, too? Excellent, I'll let Vignette know. Yes, goodbye." He hung up the receiver. "See? She says 'goodbye' very nicely. I don't understand these people who just hang up."

He drained his coffee cup and said, "We need to eat. You've both had a couple of blows, but we have to keep our strength up. Vignette, I am going to have someone for you to meet."

Dante dropped his fork. "I'm not hungry. I have to find out what happened to Eliana."

Blackburn shook his head. "The way you describe these people, they sound far too dangerous for you to be sniffing around on your own. We should send Vignette."

Vignette brightened at that. "Good! I'll go. This thing with Shane is killing me, and I need the distraction."

Dante turned to her. "You'll really go? Now?"

"Sure I will. Throw 'em off, let 'em think a woman poses no risk."

"But you'll go now?" Dante asked.

She smiled, understanding his urgency. "I realize you want to find out, Dante. I would too. But learning what happened to your aunt is only part of what we have in front of us today."

"Have you got cab fare?" he asked her, unfazed.

Randall added, "You let Vignette do her job without having to look out for you. Stay here with me." He turned to Vignette and handed her the paper pad. "We're due at this Brooklyn address in three hours."

"This isn't City Hall. It's a home address. Sounds like they've got the same troubles we have in San Francisco."

"It would jibe with what we know so far. Give yourself an hour of travel time, then we'll go to the commissioner's house and see what she can tell us."

"I don't like being around the police," Dante said.

"You'll like this one." He turned to Vignette. "And Vignette, she's going to introduce us to someone I'm sure you'll appreciate."

Less than an hour later, at the City Squire Hotel, the lock on the door to floor ten turned and the door swung open to reveal the whole floor, stripped of walls and reduced to a single giant room. The lights were dim, the air musty. The entire tenth floor had been converted into an oversized holding cell with no walls or individual cells, only a row of empty cots lining one portion of the wall. They were covered with filthy sheets. Some had bloodstains.

The cots were empty, save one, and they all had chains fastened to the bed frame. The clasps lay open on the bed in wait for the next recipient.

The sole occupant lay without moving, asleep or unconscious.

Clayton Mannerly strolled to the cot and kicked the frame. Eliana jerked awake, startled.

"You know a woman named Vignette Nightingale?"

"No, Mister. I don't."

"Well, that's odd, Eliana. She's downstairs asking about you. I told her you're busy working, but she insists on seeing you. When I tried to refuse, she started talking about coming back here with the police. You know we can't have that."

"Mister, I do not know this woman or why she is here."

"This have anything to do with Dante?"

"No, I'm sure it is a mistake, that's all. A mistake."

"Mm. You can just get yourself down there and tell her it's a 'mistake,' then, can't you? Make sure she believes you. Make sure she goes away."

"If I do that, can I have something to eat? Nobody has been up here since yesterday morning."

Clayton smiled. "Tell you what. Do a good job of getting rid of her and I'll let you go clean up and get back to work. Next time Allison and I hold a party, whether it's at Blackwell's Island or here, you smile like it's Christmas and play along with whoever shows an interest in you."

"That man was dirty."

"And now you're dirty, aren't you? Not a drop of bathwater since the party."

She could only whisper, "Please, Mister. Sir. Let me get clean."

"Fine, then. Wash up at the sink. Get rid of her, or being dirty will be the least of your problems."

Vignette rose from her chair in the lobby when she saw the woman in a maid's uniform slowly walking toward her. Observation set off steam whistles: wrinkled uniform unfitting of a good hotel; woman obviously exhausted for some reason; worry lines creasing her forehead; aged beyond her years. She could have been as young as forty but looked a decade older.

Vignette tried to put on a welcoming smile, but the woman's appearance filled her with dark concern. She extended her arm to shake hands. "Eliana?"

The woman stopped short and kept her hands folded in front of her. "My name is Eliana," she softly said. "I think there is a mis—" Her voice caught in her throat. "I think there is a mistake." Her Ukrainian accent was strong—Vignette had heard it spoken in San Francisco from time to time—but her English was clear.

Vignette looked deep into her eyes and saw nothing more than fear. It immediately convinced her there was no mistake at all. She lowered her hand and said, "I'm Vignette Nightingale, Eliana. May we sit for a moment? This won't take long."

Eliana remained standing with her hands folded in front of her.

"Do I have your name right?"

"Yes."

"You have nothing to fear from me. I am here as a friend, and I have a message. Someone you know very well misses you. Do you know who I mean?"

"Ah, no, Miss Vignette."

Vignette dropped her voice to a whisper. "Are you sure, Eliana?"

"Why do you ask me this?" Eliana murmured, barely moving her lips.

"My friend waited for six weeks in San Francisco."

Shock froze Eliana's face while she held back a gasp.

"He wonders why you are still here, that's all." Vignette stopped and waited.

Eliana was unable to smooth over her reaction. She had spent so many years suppressing her emotions in front of others, but now her self-control was only powerful enough to prevent her from bursting out in hysteria. That was as far as it could go.

"Eliana, I work as a private investigator, but the odd thing is, that's got nothing to do with how I met a certain young boy or why we brought him back to New York."

Eliana's hand flew up to her mouth and clamped down hard. She moved her hand away and silently mouthed, "Back to New York..."

Vignette continued, "I could have just been out driving around, I still would have stopped for him." She paused again, keeping her face relaxed and her expression neutral. "But the boy was in a mess of trouble, and I hated to see him get caught. I watched him dodge them, and I must say, he's resourceful and all, but the laws of chance are far too fickle for a boy to navigate among rough men."

She leaned in toward Eliana. "Do you agree?" At that moment, Vignette leaned into Eliana's personal aura. The woman clearly had not bathed in some time and must have merely splashed herself off at the last minute before coming out to speak with her. Her personal odor and her wrinkled uniform signaled a level of distress that was out of character for the establishment. Vignette wondered, was she not supposed to notice?

Eliana's eyes flicked toward the main staircase. A well-dressed, authoritative-looking man stood a few steps up from the main floor, watching them. He was too far away to hear them, but the intensity of his gaze would have alerted Vignette under any conditions. He stared as if she had burst into flame. She resisted the urge to stare back and turned away.

If he had some concern, she wondered why he kept quiet. One of the traits shared by every psychopath she had experienced so far was a lack of awareness of how they appear to others. It was especially true if they believed nobody who mattered was watching.

She looked back to Eliana and saw the woman had turned pale at the sight of the man, whoever he might be.

"Eliana, I didn't come here to cause you any trouble, but it seems as if something is wrong here. My only purpose in coming to see you is to let you know..." She took a deep breath and decided to jump in. "Dante misses you and can't understand why you never showed up. He loves you. He just wants to know what happened to you."

Eliana dropped her eyes back to the floor. "Please, Miss Vignette. Tell him to live his life. I made up the story about coming to San Francisco so he would leave without me."

"My god! Why do that?"

"When the Mother of Moses was in slavery, with all the slave babies being killed by an evil ruler, she put her infant son Moses in a reed basket, then let the Nile River float him away, all in the smallest ray of hope for that boy. Anything to get him away. We do not have to wonder if it tore out her heart. Mothers in Ukraine give away our babies to save them from the pogroms that sweep up anyone at all. They don't even ask if you're Jewish anymore. They just rape and kill. Now, you must keep Dante away so he can have hope. Not just for me, but for him. If they think he will talk, he will die at their hands. I am already likely to die at their hands."

"Who would do that to you?"

Eliana's whisper was so soft it would carry no more than a few feet. "Mister Clayton calls them the Movers. They're so rich and powerful, it doesn't matter who they are. They do what they want. If you try to stop them, they make you disappear. My plan was for Dante to disappear on his own. Before they could get to him."

"Why would anyone do that to orphans? There are all sorts of charity groups taking in orphans and displaced war victims. Do you want to know where I found Dante?"

"Please, no. It tears away my heart, but you must be strong for him, too." She glanced over again at the man observing from the staircase. He glared at her in what was a clear message to finish up the conversation. She spoke again without looking at Vignette.

"Make him forget about me. My poison must not touch him. Tell him whatever you want."

"Before you go, Eliana. How did you and Dante come to be here? Why are you here at all?"

"In Ukraine, the war left us starving. Orphans everywhere, begging, stealing. I volunteered to come to America after the war took everything and everyone from me. They told me I would get work here. They tell everyone that. Then you never see anyone you know again."

"Is Dante from Ukraine?"

"We don't know where he's from. He looks like he could be, but he speaks no other language and he doesn't remember his early life. Look at him. If not Ukraine, maybe Albania, maybe Greece?"

"What has to happen to a boy to make him forget part of his own childhood?"

"You remember all of yours?"

"Every damned minute, seems like."

Eliana answered by flicking another quick glance at the man on the staircase. She spoke in a soft, flat monotone. "I am poisoned, Miss Vignette. Help Dante and keep him away from here. Mister swears I can never survive out there without him. My heart is already broken. Please save Dante."

"From what?"

"Save him, Miss Vignette."

At that, she looked over at the man watching her from across the lobby and gave him a faint nod. She crossed the lobby to the staircase and ascended, passing the man without looking at him. He gave Vignette a smile of condescension, then turned to follow Eliana up the stairs, using his genteel professional voice to call for her to stop and wait.

19

DEPUTY COMMISSIONER O'GRADY'S RESIDENCE

BROOKLYN

March 1st

* 10:55 a.m. *

VIGNETTE'S TAXI CLOSED IN ON the modest house at 247 New York Avenue in Brooklyn. She rode in the back with hot rocks in her belly. No matter how she played it out, in the end she was going to deliver a crushing blow to Dante. She burned with guilt over the grotesque information she carried. Throughout the cab ride from Manhattan, every time the driver hit the brakes hard or took a sharp turn, the rocks shifted and seared new places inside her.

She only knew her destination was the home of Deputy Commissioner O'Grady, her husband, and four children, but little more than that. It looked as if the woman had chosen a good place to raise a family in a respectable neighborhood. Which was something of a minor miracle in itself.

It was unusual for the ruling police class to allow women to rise at all, but to allow them to carry on with their families at the same time they did important criminal work? It seemed unreal. She wondered if there was a catch. Was O'Grady somebody's favored daughter? Part of a dynasty of some sort? They certainly had such things in San Francisco, why not here?

Her cab pulled to the curb with a few minutes to spare, and she was relieved to see Randall and Dante sitting on the steps waiting for her. Randall wore his best suit, with a white silk shirt under his double-breasted vest, topped by a single-breasted wool coat and matching pants, carried all the way from California. But Dante sported a brand-new outfit that told of a stop at a clothing store on the way over. His baggy pants were suspendered and cuffed just below the knee. His calves were covered with tall leggings. As if to prove he still retained something of his own standards, the colorful end of what appeared to be a necktie hung from his front pocket.

Vignette stepped out of the cab wearing the only good outfit she brought along, a navy blue suit of wool trousers with suspenders, a white long sleeved blouse and cravat, with a matching wool jacket that gathered at the waist and flared over her hips. She hoped it was formal enough for the woman she was about to meet. Her attire was not something that usually concerned her, but everything she had heard about Ellen O'Grady made her want to know more about how this woman had managed to succeed in a man's world. She knew it wasn't the driver's fault she had rocks in her belly that burned whenever he hit the brakes. She tipped him enough to brighten his morning and waved him off.

"Hi!" called Vignette while she approached. "Isn't she home?"

"She is," Blackburn answered. "We waited for you so we can all go in together."

She felt a blush at this small indication of her value, but Dante fixed her with an expectant stare.

"What happened with Eliana?"

The question hit like a brick. She hated to pass the news to him at this hour, in this place. But there was never going to be a good time for this news. She had to tell him so they could move on. As important as Dante had come to be to her, the reason for their trip to New York was pressing on them. They needed to get into the fight if they were going to be of any use.

"Dante, I saw her for just a couple of minutes."

"How was she? What did she say?"

"It was more what she didn't say. She was dirty and looked very tired."

"Dirty? No. Eliana is always clean."

"Her uniform looked like she'd been wearing it for days."

"No! Something's wrong! She never wears dirty clothes. Clayton won't let anybody work unless they're clean."

"Well, she wasn't on the floor last night, and she didn't say anything about working today. I would have assumed she's been sick, but that doesn't explain the uniform."

"Why didn't she come to meet me?"

"She wanted to, Dante. I believe she wanted to more than anything in the world, but something stopped her. Some kind of fear. I don't know what, for sure. She tried to put a quick end to our conversation and then hurried away. Perhaps I can go back later and—"

"Floor ten!" Dante cried out, pacing around and staring into space. He turned back to them. "Floor ten. That's why. Floor ten!"

"What?" Vignette responded.

"He's got her on floor ten! That's why she's dirty, and that's why she isn't working!"

Blackburn was all ears now. "What's this about floor ten?"

Dante stared into space again, seeing something no one else could see. He began to breathe in small gasps. Finally he turned to them and spoke in a voice tight with emotion. "All right, I'm going to tell you something. Just so you can help her."

Blackburn nodded. "I'd be glad to hear it."

"Floor ten and floor eleven are the top floors There's just the penthouse over them. Those two floors aren't for hotel guests. Floor ten doesn't even have any rooms, and no walls. Clayton had it all cleared out. Now it's just this giant empty space with cots fastened to the floor. Eliana showed it to me."

"So he's booked out an entire floor, permanently?"

"More than one. Floor eleven isn't for hotel guests, either. But if she's dirty, she's not on floor eleven. You have to be clean to be there. It has rooms. It's where they have their parties."

"Damn, two floors out of commission. How can he keep the place open?"

"It's not with hotel bookings, I can tell you that."

"So how, then?"

"That's all I'm gonna say now." He stared into space for a moment. "But she's on floor ten. She must be. We have to get her. We have to go now!"

She kneeled to Dante's face level and took his shoulder in her hand. "Dante, I promise you we'll check on her again as soon as we're done here. But we also have to carry out this meeting right now, and we can't tell them about this. We don't know where the commissioner's loyalties are going to be when it comes to us. Can you control yourself long enough to just get through this meeting and then take our next step?"

"So we'll go see about her after that?"

"I promise."

He thought it over for a moment, then gave her a slight smile and nodded.

At the same hour, the Borough of Brooklyn and the Canzani Print Shop on 253 Fifth Avenue played home to Mario Buda and Andrea Salsedo. They sat in the shop's back office chuckling together like two old friends, protected from interruption by a sign on the front door claiming the shop was closed for lunch.

The men huddled over a small desk in a space barely big enough for the two of them while Salsedo worked on wiring a detonator. His large magnifying glass was fastened to a table stand and positioned so the tiny wires and connections of the device were easy to see. A small box of gunpowder and another of gun cotton took up most of the table surface, except for the small handwritten note sent by Blackburn's "messenger" back in San Francisco: *The detective beat the hit. Sez he's coming for you.* The note frightened him at first, but once he showed it to Buda and saw the way the more experienced bomber laughed it off, he felt better.

Buda was all smiles and consolation, assuring him people bluffed other people all the time, and nobody was going to stick their necks out far enough to risk their lives and come after him. It was a scare tactic, no more.

Salsedo had accepted the words with gratitude. In addition, his anarchist comrades had been kind enough to supply him with a small sleeping room above the shop, which was extra handy for bringing contraband materials up and down without being seen. The items on the table before him had been on his cot upstairs until a few minutes earlier.

Though the men were about the same age, Buda stood back and watched like an older professor grading an exam. His power had grown within the anarchist movement in the four years since the Preparedness Day Parade bombing, back in San Francisco. Even though it failed in its goal to shock America into avoiding the Great War, it was said among many of the faithful that Buda now answered directly to Signore Galleani himself on matters of strategic attacks, because he alone out of all the fighters for the San Francisco parade mission managed to actually detonate his device, create mayhem, and escape with his life to fight again another day. This same resolve was the chief reason Buda saw no other course of action but to have Salsedo eliminated. Exploded. Use him to set an example of what happens to soldiers who refuse a direct order. Let his death serve the cause one last time, and then be done with him.

No matter how his own loyalties sat within him, Buda had learned in the passing years that the life of an administrator was better than the life of a soldier. Proof: that previous June he had ordered a series of eight successful bomb attacks using powerful devices in eight US cities, all within a ninety-minute time frame. Yet it was Salsedo who was a wanted man, who now had to work under an alias and to look over his shoulder wherever he went.

Salsedo was so fiercely loyal to the cause, he remained oblivious to Buda's role in his miseries. Buda intended to keep it that way, now that he knew Salsedo was a fair weather fighter.

While Salsedo tended to the wires, he spun out an amusing story just to keep things light. "I told the prison guard, anybody who calls potassium nitrate 'saltpeter' just proved they never built a bomb! Let them go!"

Both men chuckled at the thought of idiots who failed to grasp the explosive properties of volatile chemical compounds.

Buda said, "Last month in Italy, I told Signore Galleani you could build a bomb out of bat shit and sugar!" They both laughed at that, until Buda added, "Of course, so could I."

This stopped the laugh on a dime. Salsedo dismissed it with a shrug. "Well, we've got the nitrate in the guano, but the art will come out in refining it, with the concentrations so low. You know something about crystallization I ought to know?"

"Yes. Drink only out of crystal glasses, and don't handle bat shit."

That got them chuckling again.

Salsedo happily returned to the detonator, peering down through the large glass lens. "I've been waiting to tell you, I have a new source for potassium nitrate. There is never enough of it. We should send word down the line, because every single one of our partisans can get their hands on this if they want to. Anywhere they have sand and farm animals."

"Andrea! That would be excellent news. What is this new source?"

"In all honesty, it's more accurate to say 'a new use for an old source.' You put your cows or horses in pens or stalls over a sand base. Wait until the buildup smell of ammonia is strong. Then dig out the sand and boil it in a small amount of water. Drain it, mix it with wood ash to take out the calcium and magnesium. It leaves you with an endless supply."

There was a brief pause while each man visualized the potential of world domination being helped along by piss-soaked sand. If they were meeting over cocktails they might have exploded into laughter, but in this place they merely chuckled harder. No guffaws, never that. Each man embraced caution at all times and would never allow himself to laugh out loud with neighbors nearby. They might come over to see what was so funny. But the chuckling helped to smooth things along.

Corporate executives at the companies they despised would call this a good meeting. Pleasant. Buda and Salsedo were brothers in the anarchist cause, which represented a mass of chaotic power. The atmosphere was cordial and relaxed while Salsedo worked and Buda observed.

"So!" Buda exclaimed. "You enclose the ignition pill right inside the metal sleeve along with your primer instead of a secondary sleeve?" He used an innocent face and a modest voice to imply incompetence in the friendliest possible manner. "Without stability?"

"There is more than one way to deal with time delay in chemical reactions."

"Of course. As you say," replied Buda, using a tone of voice generally reserved for very old people who wander outside.

Salsedo paused, took a deep breath, and continued to work. "Don't distract me."

"Keep working if you like, but I have seen enough and I will send a telegram overseas to assure Signore Galleani you are the one for this mission. Great mission."

He considered making up a story but decided it was unnecessary. "I already knew it when I got you the funding for your trip back here." He silently reminded himself to keep his story straight. "He just wanted me to see your technique with my own eyes and confirm that you are the one indeed. I already knew that, Andrea."

Salsedo considered that for a moment, staring into his own imagination. Then he smiled, turned to Buda, smiled again, and went back to work.

"While you finish," Buda went on, "I can now reveal the specifics of your mission. It means the life blood of our revolution. Signore Galleani needs major funding to launch his plan, and the timing is crucial. It has to happen before the presidential election here."

"What is that, eight months?"

"Close enough. My point is, once this mission is done, there will be maximum opportunity to create instability all over the world, based upon the instability here—between a disrupted presidential election and a collapsed stock market."

"What am I to do?"

"Create a set of bombs that detonate with immense force. We need the most powerful explosions we can create while using boxes small enough to move around in secret. These are nothing at all like schoolboy pipe bombs. But! Their explosive must be stable. Stable enough to avoid premature detonation in fluctuating temperatures. Amateurs could not build this bomb. Think of military-level applications."

"Say no more." Salsedo's chin jutted out with pride. "You are obviously referring to enhanced charges, specialized materials."

"I constructed a beautiful device for Signore Galleani in San Francisco four years ago, however—" Buda stopped himself. To mention Signore Galleani's utter failure in setting up the San Francisco Mint bomb attack would be to reveal his underlying contempt for the man. Galleani had far too many followers who were prepared to die for him, men who would never stand for knowing Buda felt such things about their dear leader.

He carefully went on, "Unfortunately, outside forces came in, betrayals, et cetera. Certainly nothing he could have done about it."

"I am flattered by your generosity in sharing this mission with me, but why not build these devices yourself?"

"You must not call it generosity, Andrea. Naturally, I would love to do the job, and I told Signore Galleani that very thing. He said to stay out of it, to let you show your value to the movement. I don't mind telling you I was angry about it. But he said he wants to grow the number of members who can build the sort of bombs he needs to carry out, well, more aggressive attacks. Pipe bombs will no longer suffice. His words."

Salsedo's eyes went wide with anticipation. "Enhanced charges, then? I can also increase explosive force with thermoplastics I get from grinding up Bakelite telephone covers."

They almost burst out laughing. Both felt the wave hit, but discipline ruled, and instead of giving in, they held on fast and stuffed it down inside. Nonetheless they snickered appreciatively at the thought of turning public phones into bombs to blow up the public.

Salsedo felt so respected, so well regarded, his overall sense of well-being could not have been higher if a battlefield medic shot him up with morphine. It made him want to talk.

"But more than that, Mario, my experiments tell me we need to replace the use of TNT with the ammonium salt of picric acid."

"That gives us Dunnite. Explosive D. It's far less stable."

"And far more powerful! Military-level explosions."

Buda smiled in admiration, indicating approval for Salsedo's flash of brilliance. He nodded and stroked his chin, as if giving the matter deep thought. Like a schoolboy receiving this information for the first time.

Andrea Salsedo could take all the credit he wanted, posthumously.

"All right, then. That leaves us to the specifics. We need bombs we can fit inside steel boxes with American measurements of two feet on each side and one foot inside depth."

"Anything else in the box?"

"No."

"How thick will the steel be?"

"Thin. The kind they use for making first aid kits."

"Like the kind you see in the military?"

"Like the kind you see on passenger trains."

20

DEPUTY COMMISSIONER O'GRADY'S RESIDENCE

BROOKLYN

March 1st
* Late Morning *

THE FORMAL SITTING ROOM ON THE GROUND FLOOR of Deputy Commissioner O'Grady's home displayed her gift for the tasteful use of style. The stately order of the place identified her as a woman whose children had grown up and moved away. She stood while Blackburn, Vignette, and Dante were ushered into the room by a tall, silver-haired valet.

The trio found themselves facing a stout-looking woman in her mid-fifties, slightly care-worn but steady in her bearing. People who did not fear strength would find her attractive.

As soon as introductions were made all around and everyone seated, the valet set cups of tea before each of them. The air in the room was heavy with heat from the steam radiators on the wall. Vignette did her best to smile and nod at the appropriate times, but she had to consciously avoid staring at O'Grady. This woman, who could pass for a stalwart Sunday school teacher, had spent decades working among the male police members? How?

Questions swirled in her mind. How did O'Grady do it? Where did she get the wherewithal to stand up to them? How far did she push confrontations before backing down? How much aggression could she employ to defend herself?

At that moment, Vignette realized O'Grady was speaking and she would do best to listen. She pretended to sip the tea.

"—a startling level of development since we spoke, Detectives. I was already looking forward to your presence here, but now I'm more glad than ever. This thing is so big we can only see parts of it at any one time, but if you stand back you can get an idea of what it is."

"What's that?"

"Wealthy people, powerful people all around the world have managed to establish a network through which they can ship people. They conduct an international market without the rest of the world knowing a thing about it. Try to imagine, they've set up a functioning underground railroad on an international basis! Only this one isn't set up to free slaves; it's there to transport them and to keep them a secret all during the trip. The ones who survive enter a world where they're invisible. To everyone who ever knew them, they're already dead. You don't need to believe in Hell to grasp the level of torment these people suffer."

Vignette heard herself speak words she could not remember using before. "May I speak?"

O'Grady gave a small laugh. "Might as well, Detective. It's why you're here, and we're meeting in my home instead of the office, so you can say whatever you have in mind."

Vignette was lightheaded with the effect of being addressed in a tone that indicated credibility by a woman of O'Grady's professional accomplishment and power. Why, a woman who could do all that and still marry, bear children, raise a family—and live to tell the tale? She had never seen anything like it before. Never heard of anything like it, either.

"Yes. Thank you. Um, but what you are saying is information we already have. It's more complete," she hastened to add. "But still, we came looking for something we can use to begin the hunt."

"Ha!" cried O'Grady, slapping the arm of her chair. "I've heard stories about this one! Looks like I'm under pressure to deliver now!"

Vignette threw a panicky glance at Randall, but he was beaming at her and seemed to have nothing to add.

"No, no, I just meant we came hoping—"

O'Grady turned to Blackburn with a grin spread across her face. "Nothing frivolous about your partner, eh?"

The doorbell rang, prompting a delighted look from O'Grady. "Aha! Here she is, Detective Nightingale, come just to meet you."

"Me? How would she know about—"

O'Grady talked right over her. "Oh, I just had the feeling you'd hit it off with her, dearie."

Another woman in her fifties came strolling in carrying a stack of papers under her arm, dressed in a pantsuit and matching overcoat. Her somewhat thick torso was topped by a face that signaled a distaste for makeup and a low tolerance for balderdash. "Hello, everyone. So you started without me, eh? Why? Am I late?"

"No! Never!" chimed O'Grady. "These three were early just to make you look bad! Meet Detective Isabella Goodwin, everyone. First female detective on the force, now commanding half a dozen patrolwomen. Cracks cases by going undercover like the best actress you ever saw. Detective Goodwin, this here is the team Sunny Jim sent our way all the way from San Francisco: Randall Blackburn and his partner, Vignette Nightingale. They brought our young friend Dante here with them, because they're traveling together for now. That about covers it."

Goodwin offered a businesslike smile. "Good, then. Hello, everyone."

They greeted her back, and since she did not offer to shake hands, they kept theirs at their sides.

"Vignette, I've heard so much about you."

"Me?"

"Oh yes. We keep our eyes on the independent thinkers."

"That we do," O'Grady agreed, nodding.

Vignette had no idea how they could be keeping an eye on her. The thought made her uneasy for some reason. In that moment, she hoped it was idle flattery.

"So I wonder if you're from the same family who once lived here in New York?" Goodwin asked. "They ran a small newspaper here called *The*

Nightingale for a year or so, but when it went down they moved out west. That was about ten years before your big earthquake."

Vignette felt herself blush. She seldom had to revisit her origins, and it was not a painless experience. "Well, it's a bit complicated, but my late brother, Shane, was adopted by the Nightingale family out of the orphanage where we both were staying. He lived with them for a year, but they died in the Great Earthquake and Fires. Shane and I were reunited after that, and I took the same last name for reasons of...well, I'm not certain. Closeness."

"No need to explain," Goodwin assured her, accepting tea from the valet and holding the cup in both hands. After sipping, she turned to O'Grady. "Did you tell them yet?"

"Nope. We were just getting started."

"All right, then," she began, spreading brightly colored pages out on the large coffee table. Each sheet of paper turned out to be a political pamphlet printed by anarchists and anti-American groups. Their pronouncements screamed with rage and sought vengeance for all things. The apocalyptic visual art was done in splashes of contrasting colors.

Goodwin gave them a moment before she continued, "You've already been told what we suspect about the orphan trains, but here's where it really gets sticky. You've seen flyers like these on the West Coast?"

"We have," replied Blackburn. "Flyers and newsletters printed by anarchists, communists, fans of King George, pretty much anybody who hates America."

Vignette asked, "What could that have to do with the orphan trains?"

O'Grady answered, "Nothing. Until, in the last six months or so, when we now know the infiltration of the orphan train organization was taking place. We started seeing evidence that the entire anarchist movement was experiencing a powerful influx of funds. The reason is brilliant if you ignore the evil in it. The anarchist attacks help keep the authorities occupied and disguise this new form of slavery. See? The corrupt rich bastards figured out how to make stinking anarchists support private ownership of other human beings without even knowing they're doing it. The method is as old as time: buy 'em off. Turns out anarchists are for sale, just like the people they hate. Suddenly they have money for weapons," she ticked off the list on her fingers, "explosives, signs and banners, travel and lodging for protestors. And all these little publications. Thousands of them. The money was pumped into local organizations."

"I would guess," Blackburn said with a knowing grin, "you uncovered that information using logic followed by action."

"Heh. We, ah, sweated a few of their members, and it appears the money has already been cut off. Word came down through the local organizations from who knows where, because it always comes from who knows where, and it was simple. That flash flood of cash was meant to prime the pump, just to get things started. You see how they did that? They put basic human nature to work to get them off their asses. The money let 'em all know what they could accomplish, if and when they got funding for their plans. Give 'em a taste, then say, *This is what it could be like all the time.*

"Now comes the part they must have called upon the Devil to design. After that, the money, their only chance at a steady supply, is supposed to come from smuggling people. The people they smuggle have either been captured or they signed up under deception only to find themselves enslaved, or whatever you want to call it when people buy and sell strangers. Apparently there is a steady demand."

"Jesus!" Vignette said with a gasp. "Why can't the law find them?"

"We can find them. Most of the time we know right where they are, where they work, where they live. The problem is building a case that holds."

Vignette was horrified. If she were in any other setting but this, she would walk out. But that was hardly an option; there was nothing to do but let the commissioner finish.

"Plus the natural accompaniment of children and mothers seems to more or less disappear in their system. The kids are abandoned on the trains and shipped west for display at train stops, until somebody adopts them or they hit the West Coast."

"What happens to them then?" asked Randall.

"Anybody's guess. The world just finished beating itself bloody. I don't know how the people out west see it, but here in New York, we don't get much public concern for crimes people can't see or feel for themselves."

Goodwin said, "We think they're ramping up to cause a major disruption in the presidential election this fall. The money will let them prepare for maximum damage. Somebody is pumping money into the cause right now, trying to ignite widespread civil chaos. People are so dead tired of war and bloodshed, it could be just enough to compel people to vote for, shall we say, a more vigorous level of government control."

"Anything to keep peace on the streets and in the schools."

Vignette's brow knitted. "What are they after? Do you know?"

"Just what Goodwin told you," O'Grady answered. "If they can't collapse the system—which they think they can, but they can't—they'll try to disrupt the election and throw it toward their candidate, which they might. And if they succeed, they have a man in the White House. The frustrated anarchists will still have to contend with our system, but they'll have a president who owes them. So the anarchists still win, at least a little."

Goodwin added, "But if they're able to disrupt the entire election with riots, why, the country sinks into chaos, and the anarchists win more."

"Either way, they still generate an endless supply of cash to fund their terrorism, hoping to win through attrition, knowing their future funds are secured."

"Secured by their underground market for people," said Goodwin.

"So. Not much of a problem to investigate, you're saying?"

"Wish I were joking, Detective," O'Grady said with a grim set to her jawline.

"Tell them the best part," Goodwin said. She glanced at Blackburn and Vignette. "You guys will love this."

O'Grady nodded. "As you can imagine, both of us are used to being slighted by the men in command. Not all of them, Detective Blackburn, so take no offense, but enough of them to make real waves for us."

"None taken. Undoubtedly true," Blackburn agreed.

"So I don't think twice when I have to wait in a long line to be heard by the upper brass, then wait in an even longer line for action. Getting stonewalled is what we call Monday."

"Or any other day of the week," muttered Goodwin.

"Let me guess," Vignette picked up the story. "You can't get any help from the command structure in getting to the bottom of this. Not the identities of the organizers, either. Your requests are more or less being ignored. Did I get that right?"

O'Grady nodded in approval. "Detective Blackburn, everything you told me about this young woman seems to be true."

He smiled at that. "And there's more..."

"Anyway, you got it the first time. I make requests, they get ignored. I give an order, it maybe gets followed, or maybe does not. What I learned is, Attorney General Palmer's department issued a report saying some of these were printed right here in Brooklyn. Last year. He also issued the report *last* year. Not a thing's been done."

"Son of a bitch!" Vignette blurted. "Oh. Ah, sorry."

"No need to be sorry. So when I complained to my superiors about it, asked for the authority to put the hammer down on the officers responsible —they quite helpfully told me this is the sort of thing that makes people think women are too emotional for police work."

Goodwin nodded. "Two of my staff served in the Red Cross on the battlefield, tending to men wounded with the most horrific of blast injuries, burn injuries, gas injuries, holding the hands of dying men when there was no hope. Doing it while mortars exploded over their heads. It's a dangerous thing to call them fragile, if you don't want your teeth kicked in."

"I believe my partner Vignette understands you perfectly," Blackburn said with a broad smile. "She has a few teeth on her bootheels!"

He laughed at that but noticed Vignette appeared as if she would gladly shrink through the floor while she waited for the moment to pass.

"Anyway," Blackburn continued, "in San Francisco we're familiar with this sort of planned disloyalty, set to go off like a time bomb. They used it in the parade bombing four years ago. In the end, it took a wave of mass firings to scrape off the ones who had sold out."

"Assuming it worked," added Vignette.

"Right. City Hall and the SFPD were infiltrated so thoroughly, the mayor could hardly get an order filled."

O'Grady squinted in concern. "Guide me on this if you can, Detective. Did he have *any* loyal officers left?"

He took a deep breath and gave a smile of regret. "He did. But at the time, when he had to make fast decisions, there was no way to tell who was on the level and who wasn't. The mayor's own police chief turned on him."

O'Grady nodded. "I spoke with good old Sunny Jim earlier today. He sends his regards, and he gave me an earful on what it was like for you folks back then. I had to tell him it all sounded familiar to what we're facing now."

Goodwin said, "But we think our status as outsiders in the department may actually turn out to be our saving grace here, Detective Blackburn. The people behind this didn't dare approach Commissioner O'Grady or myself with whatever they're offering as bribes or threatening for extortion."

"I wish they had," O'Grady muttered. "Though they might not care for my response."

A moment later, she and Goodwin both burst out laughing at whatever their imaginations showed them regarding O'Grady's response. It took a few moments to slow things back down.

Goodwin spoke first. "Most of those little publications were done up right here in our home borough of Brooklyn, New York. Perhaps not all of 'em. I don't know. Doesn't matter. You will be able to identify the ones done here, because," she dramatically flipped one flyer over to reveal, "they print their contact information on them to drum up more business! Ha!"

There was an awkward pause while Randall and Vignette tried to figure out why this was relevant.

Goodwin added, "One would think this angle had been thoroughly investigated long ago. When I first reported it, all I got was the pleasure of seeing my orders ignored. Detectives, I regret starting you off in town with a tedious task, but please track down each of the printers listed on the backs of these flyers. Someone among these people is working for a faceless group who wants to use this evil underground railroad to pay for their war on society. This is being done by people with the money and power to make it happen and keep it secret, and they are taking the risk that these same anarchists won't turn on them later."

"I'd put money on it," Blackburn said.

Commissioner O'Grady summed it up, "If you find the printers, use kid gloves with them. Do nothing to indicate you are anything more than a potential customer. Do nothing to alert them. Do not cause them the slightest concern or raise their fears in any way."

Blackburn chuckled. "Can we talk to them?"

"If you have to," she replied. "And only if you can do so without provoking any alarm. Check the details of every print shop you enter. Observe everything around you with the eyes of eagles. Is there anything at all to cause you to suspect they are not just printing pamphlets but are in league with terrorists? If you find anything of substance, come back and give us time to organize the proper response."

"Will your response include the rest of the force? The ones who are...um..."

"Men?"

"Well, yes."

"It will if they think there's a promotion involved. We have to give them enough evidence to keep them from turning away."

The silver-haired valet glided into the room and bent to whisper in O'Grady's ear. Her eyes widened for a second, then she stood. "Well, on to other matters. You will organize your hunt as you see best, correct? Detective Goodwin is in charge, and I'm deputizing both of you. Please each take one of the deputy badges there on my desk. A little welcome present. Try not to show them unless you have to, but sometimes a little brass can be just the thing to open a stuck door. Goodwin has my utmost confidence. Thank you, and I'm quite sure we'll meet again soon. Something big is coming."

She looked at each of them in turn, done now, and waited.

They filed out one at a time.

21

CITY SQUIRE HOTEL
LOWER MIDTOWN, MANHATTAN

March 1st
* Early Afternoon *

DETECTIVE GOODWIN TOOK ADVANTAGE of her flat's location in Greenwich Village, not far from the City Squire Hotel near Penn Station. She had the taxi drop them at her place; they would need time to get their wardrobes ready while Randall and Dante scouted print shops.

Vignette was floored by the apartment itself. Goodwin was single but had a boyfriend who apparently spent a good deal of time there; his tasteful accoutrements were all over, creating the appearance of a man who was young and athletic. The fireplace mantel boasted a display of Goodwin's considerable civic awards. It was clear she had a reputation for her undercover work, and in spite of being a somewhat known public figure, she continued to fool unsuspecting perpetrators and bag big arrests.

One look into Goodwin's "costume closet" did a lot to explain it. Uniforms of all kinds and outfits for an array of services hung side by side. Blue-collar work outfits had their own section, with assorted tool kits on the floor beneath them.

Vignette found herself staring at Goodwin, who reached down to pick up one of the tool kits and said, "We'll have to do some alterations to make an outfit suit you, but I can do most of it with safety pins."

Detective Goodwin smiled. "Got any experience with plumbing work?"

Vignette and Detective Goodwin approached the City Squire Hotel on foot, talking quietly as they went.

"Posing as a plumber is like dancing on a high wire. You have to look like you know what you are doing and be so confident that nobody gets in your way, but at the same time you want to avoid actually doing any plumbing work. You could wind up doing something wonderful like joining the sewer line to the water supply. It's not that hard to do, if you're ignorant enough. In a fancy hotel like this one, a plumber is invisible. People who can afford a place like this have no desire for contact with the help. Most of the time, they don't even look at you."

She ran her eyes up and down Vignette's frame. "You don't make a convincing male, but nobody is going to look at you close enough to realize it. They see the clothing, the tool kit: boom. That's all they need to know. We walk in and hide in plain sight." She stopped at the big front entrance to the hotel. "After you." She smiled, holding the door.

As soon as Vignette walked past, Goodwin followed, whispering, "Walk hard. Like this. Don't swing your hips." Goodwin sauntered to the front desk like a bored blue-collar worker eager to get on with the job. Vignette kept her eyes on the floor partly out of fear of being recognized but mostly because she feared meeting Goodwin's eyes and laughing out loud.

So this was another woman's version of "moving things around," she thought. This was Goodwin's version of Vignette's secret talent for manipulating perpetrators into getting spooked and doing something reckless enough to get them caught. Where Vignette used silent breaking-and-entering skills, moving a perpetrator's personal items around in a manner calculated to induce confusion, Goodwin liked to put on a false face and walk straight in the front door. She not only moved things around, she invited others to watch her do it.

"Afternoon," she said to the desk clerk in a deepened "male" voice. "Yeah, so we got a call to check a water leak? One of the upper floors."

The desk clerk looked at Goodwin and sniffed. "I know of no such leak. You may be misinformed."

Uh-oh, thought Vignette. She got ready to make a run for it. But Goodwin just exhaled in relief and broke into a wide grin.

"Whoop-dee-doo! False alarm on this one! I mean, let's agree dat's what it is, all right? 'Cause I'm ready to call it a day, anyhow." She turned to Vignette. "Let's go, Steve."

To the desk clerk, she said, "If water starts runnin' down into the lobby here, give us a call. Main thing is to catch it before pieces of the ceiling start falling on your guests."

The clerk went pale in the space of a heartbeat. But Goodwin pulled Vignette away, taking her by the arm and saying, "Quittin' time! Let's get dat beer we was talkin' about."

"Wait! Wait a minute!" called the clerk. "Wait, wait, don't go yet. I suppose someone else could have, ah, made the call. No sense taking risks."

"You sure? 'Cause we don't mind quittin' early, I tell you!" She turned as if to leave again.

"Stop right there. I just told you we aren't taking any risks. Go ahead on up and make certain there's no water problem. This master key works for any lock in the public portion of the hotel. Don't go higher than the ninth floor. We're doing work on floors ten and eleven, and the top floor is the private penthouse." The clerk handed over the large key. "We respect the privacy of our guests. You must call out 'Maintenance' in a clear voice every time you knock on a door."

Goodwin started to take the key but stopped. "Okay. So, you *do* want us to go up then, right?"

"Yes! Yes! What's wrong with you? Go on up. Go now!" The clerk forcefully pressed the key into Goodwin's hand.

"Okay, pal. No need to cry about it. Let's go, Steve."

Vignette followed Goodwin to the elevator banks in a state of wonder. She spoke in a whisper, "Steve?"

"Why not? You could be a Steve," said Goodwin while she pressed the call button.

"I look like a Steve?"

"You could be a Steve. I'm telling you."

Vignette grinned. "Steve, then."

They got on the elevator and called for the operator to take them to the ninth floor. When they reached the floor, they stepped out and waved off the operator, waiting until the car was gone while they looked up and down the empty hall. It was too early for much hotel activity, so the hallway was empty at the time.

"All right, Dante says if she's here, Mannerly is holding her on the tenth floor. Floor eleven is private, too, but they keep it clean, he said. They wouldn't put prisoners there." Vignette looked down the hall and spotted a sign for the stairway. "If that key also works on the fire doors, we're home free."

She and Goodwin walked over to the fire door leading to the stairway, tried the key, and easily got past the lock. "There we go," she murmured before stepping through, then signaled Vignette to hold still for a moment while she did the same, listening for any sound that might betray someone else's presence.

With a last check up and down the hallway, she nodded. They entered the stairwell and allowed the fire door to close behind them.

They climbed to the tenth floor, and Goodwin inserted the key in the fire door's lock. "Let's just have a quick gander here."

The key failed to turn the lock. Vignette stepped forward, pulling out two of her unnecessary hair pins. A few moments later, the tumblers had been lifted and the lock opened. Goodwin smiled at her and pushed the door open just enough to see out and down the hall. Vignette stood behind Goodwin and peered over her shoulder.

A chilled blast of air hit them. The entire floor was empty: a single, giant room, just as Dante had told them. Every radiator on the floor was shut down, leaving the space miserably cold. Blasts of freezing air came in through two open windows at either side of the giant room in a misbegotten attempt to air out the space. In spite of the breeze, the stench of unwashed humanity and human waste combined with sour traces of fear and despair to impart the atmosphere of a medieval dungeon. Slightly more modern but just as wretched.

About two dozen army surplus field cots were screwed to the floor. Each cot had a set of cuffs for the wrists and legs, with stains from human waste on the canvas and in some places on the floor, which had been stripped down to the concrete pad.

Vignette felt her pulse jump. The stress of seeing this place activated deep feelings of terror and revulsion left over from her time of captivity with the monks. This place was different than the orphanage where her tormentors imprisoned her, but very much the same in terms of the misery inflicted on the people who passed through.

Old skills in the back of Vignette's mind leaped up out of her memory from the time when every detail she took note of could be the one that either threatened or saved her life. She instantly recognized the room's salient aspect; each cot had the identical frame of thin wood, strong enough to support a canvas bed, fit for any campground.

None of them were strong enough to restrain a determined victim, however, and even a sick or injured person might find enough strength to snap the wood and slide off the restraints. And yet the wood frames showed no signs of damage or wear, even in spots where stains proved that at least one desperate person had been held.

In this place, the victims did not fight their restraints. She knew that. She knew what it was to spare herself torment by ceasing all struggle and becoming everything short of dead. And because of that, she read the scene before her in a glimpse.

She took a deep breath and shook off the dark grip of memory. Part of stealing power from those merciless memories was to pretend they didn't exist. They had nothing to say to her. She had learned to sleep despite knowing the monster was under the bed.

Goodwin asked, perplexed, "How the hell could they ever keep so many prisoners quiet?"

Vignette replied, "Fear works just fine. Especially if they've already seen you beat or kill one of them first."

The images in her brain caused Vignette's head to ache so deeply it was difficult to stand up straight. In that moment, the bloodstains on the floor seemed to rise up and speak through her.

She whispered to Goodwin, "Detective, what do you suppose happened to the people who were here?"

Goodwin looked up and down the rows of cots for a few long moments. "Keeping people alive costs money no matter how badly you do the job. Logic says they got put on the market with all possible speed. Move 'em down the line. The lucky prisoners find a buyer."

"What about the others? The ones who don't get..."

"Accepted? Taken? Bought?"

"...Yes."

"Good question." Goodwin took one last look around. "Haven't heard about any of them coming to the police."

Vignette was at the end of her strength for this. "I think, once you absorb the misery of the place, there's not a whole lot to see up here."

Goodwin nodded. "Whatever happened to Eliana, she's not here. Let's get going."

"I'm right behind you."

After picking the eleventh floor lock, they found the entire floor deserted, but with an otherwise normal hotel hallway lined with doorways to individual rooms. At the time, all the room doors stood wide open, as if the cleaning crews had just left, but the resemblance to a hotel stopped there. Every room had a large bed—but nothing else. No capacity to house a guest with any creature comforts at all. Not a chair.

As if the activities in these rooms were entirely horizontal. Apparently there was no need for security concerns over the open doors because nobody was on the floor to do any mischief.

Goodwin spoke in a voice nearly too soft for Vignette to hear, despite being so close.

"What the living Hell is this?"

"Apparently you only come to this floor to..."

"Mm-hm. Let's just say use the bed." Goodwin turned to Vignette, wiggled her eyebrows, and walked back into the stairway. Vignette snorted and followed her.

They made their way back down to the ninth floor, then left the stairway and walked to the elevator stop, called up the car, and rode back down to the lobby. Goodwin glanced at the elevator operator and then to

Vignette in a silent warning not to talk. As soon as they reached the lobby level, they stepped out and headed back toward the front desk.

Goodwin plopped the large key down in front of the clerk. "Welp, nuttin' drippin' up there, far as we can tell. Nice and dry." She beamed at the desk clerk, who seemed to find her impertinence revolting. Ignoring her, he palmed the key, dropped it in a handy drawer, and began to study the register as if she were not there.

"Hey," said Goodwin, holding up both hands. "I can take a hint. Time to go, Steve."

Without looking up from his work, the clerk muttered, "Yes, time to go, Steve."

Goodwin took Vignette's arm and walked her to the entrance, chuckling.

"What was that about?" Vignette asked as soon as they were outside.

"If the boss comes around and starts asking questions about us, all that guy's gonna know for sure is somebody named Steve showed up with another guy to check for a water leak."

"Meaning what?"

"Meaning we gave them something useless to remember. It makes them focus their attention where it doesn't do any good. Cardsharps do it to suckers all the time."

"Fine with me," Vignette said, glancing back over her shoulder toward the desk clerk. He continued to scribble away at something, pointedly ignoring the pair who had just surveilled the place right under his elevated nose.

22

OUTSIDE THE CITY SQUIRE HOTEL

March 1st
* Immediately Following *

BLACKBURN AND DANTE STOOD ON THE SIDEWALK just outside the City Squire Hotel, at an angle that put them where people inside had no view of them. As soon as Vignette and Goodwin appeared, Dante waved to them and shouted, "There they are!" He turned to Blackburn. "They're dressed funny, but it's them. Let's see what happened!" He started toward them, but Blackburn put a hand on his shoulder.

"Wait. Let them come to us so nobody inside the hotel puts them together with us."

Moments later, the four stood gathered in a recessed doorway just down the street from the hotel. Goodwin cut to the chase. "She's not up there."

"Randall, Detective Goodwin was uncanny! She just walked us right past—"

Dante spoke over them, "You saw the place? Floor ten? Floor eleven? You actually *saw* it?"

"Yes, Dante," Vignette replied. "Detective Goodwin got the clerk to give her a master key, so we also checked in on those floors."

Dante spoke through tight lips. "So you saw everything, right? Not the people, but the place at least. You saw the whole place, right?" He turned to Blackburn as if to say, *See?*

Blackburn gave Goodwin a steady stare. "There's more, of course."

"Floor ten is some sort of giant holding bay, for maybe two dozen people at a time. Chained to cots. It's been used, Detective Blackburn. More than once, judging by the stains on the concrete floor."

"Tell him about floor eleven!" Dante interrupted. "Tell him!"

"Right. Give me a chance, son. But as the lad says, floor eleven is also not an active hotel floor, but is set up for something completely different than the floor below it. On this floor they have rooms furnished with nothing but beds. Nothing else."

"Party rooms, Clayton calls them. I've only seen them that one time when he made me go see what they do, part of it... They're not good places."

All four were quiet for a long moment. Finally Goodwin spoke up. "I'm afraid the workday is over on this case, for me. I have a full load on my plate already. I think you'll do best if you communicate exclusively with Commissioner O'Grady or myself on police matters. Before I go, let me urge you to stay within the law while you investigate this. There. I'm on the record as having told you that."

She turned to Vignette and gestured toward the canvas tool bag in her hand. "Since you can't change back into your clothes here, just drop off the costume when you get around my neighborhood."

Vignette could not conceal her disappointment. "What, that's it? You can't spare us more time?"

Goodwin was sympathetic but stood firm. "Wish I could, but not for now. We have to have more evidence. Something definitive. I know what the police brass will respond to and what they will not, especially if the complaint comes from two out-of-town private detectives and a couple of the females he has no choice but to allow on his force. So make sure you get solid evidence. The sort of stuff fancy lawyers can't talk their way around."

Blackburn gave a dry smile. "And stay within the law."

"But of course." A mischievous grin crossed her face. "That said, if I had stayed within the law over the past thirty years—entirely within the law—there would be more than a few dangerous criminals on the streets instead of upstate making license plates. So, Detective, your turn. Please tell me you learned something from our friendly Brooklyn print shops."

"We checked six of them," Dante broke in.

Blackburn continued, "None of them showed any sign of being attached to a political group, especially any of the ones calling for violence. They all just seem to print up whatever jobs they get hired to do."

"We played like we were customers," Dante announced.

"Yes, actually, the last one we hit was the Canzani Print Shop over on Fifth Avenue. The man who printed one of your samples was on duty. Only time that happened out of all the other shops. Guy must live there." He held up one of the flyers and turned it over to show the shop's trademark. "It's this man. Tony Tazio."

"Thank you for your work. Good start. Give me that one to take for the case file."

Blackburn handed it over. "Can we toss out the rest of these?"

"Be my guest. If you stay in town long, you'll see plenty more of them."

23

THE PLAZA HOTEL – CENTRAL PARK SOUTH

March 1st
* Minutes Later *

IF DETECTIVES BLACKBURN AND NIGHTINGALE had a little less on their plates, they would have noticed Dante's deep silence all the way back to their hotel. He had been consistently excitable since they had arrived in the city, moody but alert. Now he sat in their taxi and stared out at the street with an empty gaze, as if he were seeing nothing of what was in front of him. He only came alive once they were back in their room and Blackburn broke the silence.

"Well, Dante. As strange as all this was today in terms of what we learned, it doesn't tell us anything about Eliana or her whereabouts. I believe the best thing in your corner right now is that Vignette went to Mannerly's hotel to see about her. Now he knows people are out here who give a damn about her."

"That's us, Dante," Vignette added. "We care about her, and we won't forget her."

Dante appeared grateful. He dipped his head and whispered, "Thank you. I know Eliana would want me to be sure to thank you. For everything."

"Mannerly runs a hotel. He doesn't dare draw down the heat of a kidnapping investigation upon himself. Now that Vignette let him know you're with us, I don't see how he can do you any harm, or Eliana either."

"Detect... Randall..." Dante began to breathe in shallow, irregular breaths. "I have to tell you now. We're at the part where, if you don't know, you're likely to get hurt. Or worse. Then it would be my fault, too. But you've both been so kind..." He took a deep breath. "He always told me, over and over, he has all these people in the police department and City Hall. See, he's got pictures of a few of them, too. Proof that they were there. And so they make sure nothing happens to him."

Dante glanced from Vignette to Blackburn with panic boiling behind his eyes. "Nobody finds out how dangerous he is until it's too late for them to do anything about it. Do you understand?"

They were all quiet for a long moment.

"Thank you, Dante. I'll keep that in mind. I know Vignette will, too."

"Quite right," she agreed, then brightened and said, "Now what say we order up dinner and get some rest for tomorrow?"

"That sounds good," Blackburn replied. "I'll call down for us."

"Time to go change into my own clothes." She stepped off to her room, calling back over her shoulder, "You should have seen Detective Goodwin today, Randall." She stopped and broke into a laugh. "Next to her I look timid! Ha!" She walked into her room, chortling under her breath, and closed the door.

Blackburn picked up the phone to call down their dinner order. "You guys trust me to order for us? Otherwise, speak your piece now. Going, going..."

A moment later someone came on the line, and he began the process of ordering up the same dinner for each of them. He seemed to have a bit of a problem getting the other person to realize he wanted three of the same thing. The call ran long.

Dante sat in silence with his imagination swirling with worry. It made no difference that Eliana was a grown woman and he was still a boy. The string of concern linking him to her was strong. He had made her welfare his own concern, and that would never change. It brought a madhouse display of memories. Experience taught him the customers who came to Clayton's parties were all bluster, meaning they might get all excited and scream foul things at you, maybe shove you around, but would not cause any real harm. That went for Eliana as well. She was only drafted into party work when an upcoming party lacked enough similar samples. Dante was revolted by the ones who committed their twisted ways on Eliana, but he also knew she could survive them, just as he had. They mutually held one another above this river of sickness.

What stuck the fishbone crosswise in his throat was sometimes one or two of the Old Ones decided they had to use violence to have a good time. Even when they were told not to damage the merchandise, sometimes a crazy one got in and made a problem. A few were women. The others were men, all types of men. Dante knew the numbers averaged out to show slightly more than one scary demon for every twenty ordinary old customers.

In his year at the hotel, Dante knew of children who came through floor ten for a few days before disappearing to the next market, or sometimes a westbound train. The lucky ones never had to go through a party up at the island before they were shipped west. The far less fortunate were rounded up and made presentable. Then they were sent off for a brief stop at Blackwell's Island to meet the orphan train sponsors. And simply never came back.

There were a rare few who claimed to have escaped captivity from people who certainly sounded like Clayton and his Movers, but from everything Dante had overheard, none of these victims could point a specific finger at anybody. Faceless handlers had passed them along, much like postal clerks handling packages.

Any of the authorities who somehow got wind of the slavery ring were immediately presented with more money than they were likely to see in several lifetimes. They reliably disappeared. Not one ever turned down the offer.

Clayton called it the cost of doing business. He talked about it enough.

Before Dante knew it, the Plaza Hotel kitchen had made three meals appear on little wheeled carts. Vignette came back out, and the three of them ate like people too hungry to resist the food but too tired to enjoy it. It worked well for Dante that both of the Old Ones were content to leave him to his thoughts.

In the year he spent with Eliana, she had taken him under her wing and helped him open up to the world. He saw her as brilliant. She spoke better English than many Americans and constantly pushed him to work on his. She had not merely taught him to read, she taught him how to continue teaching himself, then gave him his prized pocket dictionary—the power to continue learning without needing her help or anyone else's.

He didn't know of anything more beautiful in the world.

From the start, she was the first old one in a long time who neither approached him for sex nor threatened to hurt him if he did not comply with whatever the order of the moment happened to be. She did, however, slowly steal the hate and resentment festering in him by taking interest in him and maintaining it over time, over hours and then days and then weeks, and within months he had stopped counting and just lived there with her.

No matter what her own mistreatments were on any day, she always turned away from them for the sake of goodness. And without preaching a word to him, she showed him what actual goodness looked like in motion. She kept him away from Clayton as much as possible. She was not privy to Dante's private treatment in the man's company, but she recognized the fear and loathing in the boy's eyes whenever he was in Mannerly's presence.

Eliana took a clubbing on Dante's behalf when Mannerly walked in one day carrying a piece of two-by-four pinewood around two feet in length. She immediately saw rage and madness in his eyes. Something in his life, something having nothing to do with them, had set him off. Now they were there alone with him to bear the brunt of his infantile outrage. Mannerly started to say something about using it to replace a wall stud, but instead abruptly sprang into action like a hunter pulling an ambush.

But Eliana jumped in front of him and tried to sweep him aside with her body. Though Clayton's swing was aimed at Dante, the board struck Eliana on the side of her head.

The blow put her on the floor. The moment Eliana went down, Dante jumped in between them to protect her, exactly as she had just done. Eliana was on the floor, still conscious but too disoriented to react. She tried to scream and only managed a strangled cry.

There it was. Dante stood shivering in fear while he nevertheless held his place, glaring back in defiance of this man and at the indecency of his wooden club.

Clayton sneered in mock disgust to protect his sense of himself and threw the wood across the room before storming away. But Eliana got to her feet and enveloped Dante. She cried and cried, to have brought him into such terrible danger.

At the time, Dante was completely stumped for a response. Why wasn't she happy? There was plenty he wanted to say, but he could not process what he was taking in from the person in front of him. He wanted to break open and soak up her goodness and offer her his love in return, for whatever that might be worth to her.

In the end it mattered not at all. Day after day, she walked around in that hotel getting her difficult and sometimes degrading work done while also giving a damn about him, whether he knew of it at the moment or not. Dante would not have been able to verbalize it and had never heard Eliana try. They both just seemed to need it.

Clayton forced Dante to begin learning the skills he would need to help run the place one day. Meanwhile she saw to his good nutrition and the regular brushing of his teeth and made him keep his sleeping room clean at all times. She hid books from the hotel library in her cleaning cart and smuggled them to him. After reading them, he was expected to give her a breakdown of the book.

Of course he did not have to cooperate. All he had to do was give up that warm rush he got when her eyes twinkled with pride while she looked at him. He could feel it; every time he honored her with his behavior, it confirmed her beauty to herself. It lifted her out of the dark cellar she lived in, trapped in that multistory hotel, and demonstrated something of her true value. He realized Eliana used her mind to create a ray of light for both of them.

And so he wanted nothing more than to please her and to shine in her eyes. When he saw her look at him with pride, his whole mess of a life suddenly felt as if it made sense, even if just for a moment.

Toward the beginning of his time in the hotel, they both thought he might be able to stay and find some way to survive, despite living so close to the Movers. For a while it seemed as if he would be able to keep his head down and go more or less unnoticed. That empty hope was abandoned on the day Clayton took him aside and explained it was time for him to learn his role in that part of the family business having nothing to do with hotels.

No, the real family business. The one that actually paid the bills. The Moving business. The one that brought Eliana there to the hotel, and later also brought Dante. She seldom mentioned the Movers to him. For her, the past was a thing of torment, not just in terms of the treatment she endured because of her rotten husband's gambling debts. It represented the losses she suffered when she was snatched out of her life and shipped off against her will to answer for them.

Dante knew the more monstrous of the Old Ones hurt her in all sorts of ways. He knew they had been hurting her for a long time in those naked parties down under the penthouse. Mostly they hurt her by terrorizing her into accepting life as an indentured servant, which Dante knew was a fancy term for a slave.

In terms of his concern for her and his desire to help her, it made no difference that their ages were reversed. They needed one another in equal degree. They developed a relationship that might as well have been mother and son. Over time, for Dante, the binding force between them grew more powerful than any other emotion. And while Eliana seldom spoke of her feelings, she was clear in her actions. No matter how she suffered from the boss because of it, her arms were folded around him all the time.

From the moment he hopped the train to San Francisco, Dante had begun to realize his own sense of well-being depended upon having her in his life. Eliana's presence, her beautiful company, was melded into the picture of everything that meant anything to him. Beyond that, logic had nothing to do with it.

Waves of muffled traffic sounds rose from the streets. The Plaza Hotel suite went quiet and still, but Dante did not sleep. He lay with his eyes wide open and his brain on fire.

In the hallway outside the room, the completed dinner dishes sat in their trays on the floor. An astute observer might look close and notice something about the white linen napkins; only two had been left with the dishes. One linen napkin was missing, along with one of the hotel's sharp steak knives, the ones with robust carved handles and serrated steel blades, guaranteed to cut and slice.

24

CITY SQUIRE HOTEL – TOP-FLOOR PENTHOUSE
LOWER MIDTOWN, MANHATTAN

March 1st
* Simultaneously *

CLAYTON MANNERLY ADJUSTED HIS CRAVAT in front of a mirror while Allison put the finishing touches on her hairstyle. She took full advantage of her perfect widow's peak hairline, sweeping her mane over the top and to the side, where her tresses cascaded down to just below her shoulder line.

She primped with the concentration of a surgeon. In a few moments, she would have every curl twisted into place.

Clayton spoke in an unnecessarily soft tone. "So tonight we're all taking a private ferry over to Blackwell's Island. Leave aside the gaping public. Allow these celebrities and people of wealth to enjoy the auction like the royalty they are."

"Clayton. You call these leeches royalty?"

"Don't smirk! Be careful about that. Ask yourself, what else but royalty could pay for all this? Paying more than you or I ever could, to be sure. And it isn't just the unique marketplace. These people love to be able to drive around the island and see the impressive buildings of the asylum. The structures look like stone castles."

"Mm, if you ignore what goes on inside. I think everyone who visits the place goes with the same question in mind: How much of myself or my family members am I going to see in these afflicted people?"

"You know, if you pay for a ticket, you can get close enough to taunt them and watch their responses."

"Clayton, damn it!"

"I didn't make the rule and neither of us has ever used it, but that's what they do. What's your objection?"

"I believe you know my objection comes from having my conscience dropped into a vat of whatever produces such a thought."

"Allison. This auction was Father Young's idea, but it's a gift straight to us. It'll give you enough time for you to pick out your mark. By the time the party gets started, you will already be reeling them in. I don't care who it is, with this crowd. Any one of them. Just get the mark in front of the camera so they can never deny they were there."

"You've never been so indiscriminate before."

"We've never had an opportunity like this before. Anything you hit, scores! They're all good. They're all wonderful. They came this far, paid this much, you can bet they're ready for a party like this. We give them free drinks for half an hour or so, and then we run the whole group out for a lineup and let our guests start bidding. So. Do we have an understanding?"

Allison replied via mirror reflection, "Of course we do, Clayton. We understand: I do what you want. And you understand, we will not indulge with children. I never want to see that again."

He refused the bait and replied in the same tone, "You don't have to, then. What you must understand is, you are not my slave; you are my partner in building for the future. While you don't want child partners, some of them will, and we're not there to stop them. Demand is so hot, this batch is going straight up to the island without stopping here at all. I don't know how they plan to have them ready for inspection. Line them up and hose them down, maybe."

He shook it off like the negative thought it was. "Allison, unless they come from royalty, few women walking this earth will ever get *near* experiencing anything like the powers you already have over everyone who passes through here. You are privileged beyond the comprehension of most people."

He flicked off a bit of imaginary dust from his silk jacket and stood, keeping his eyes on her. "The collective wealth and political influence of our guest list this evening could alter the course of history for more than one major country. And yet these titans need people like us." He laughed at the thought. "Come along, then."

Clayton gently crossed over to her seat at the vanity table and sat next to her, then indulged himself in the wonderful feel of her sumptuous, perfectly coiffed hair while he thrust his fingers into it and pressed them across her scalp like the best scalp massage in the whole wide world. He wiggled his fingers, tousling her locks, pulling apart the careful curls.

He could feel her need to kill him. It was just the sexiest thing.

25

THE PLAZA HOTEL & BLACKWELL'S ISLAND

March 2nd
* Just After Midnight *

THE HOTEL ROOM'S DOOR SOFTLY CLOSED. A moment later, the lock turned. Out in the silent hallway, Dante's heart beat with such force, he could hear his pulse when he opened his mouth. He waited for the elevator while his anxieties mounted. He felt certain Blackburn would have his hands on his neck in seconds, grabbing him the same way the twisted Old Ones did and demanding to know how any orphan could be so ungrateful to people who tried to be his friends.

It was a fair question. He strongly hoped to live long enough to explain. Over and over, he had been impressed by the generosity and good will of these friends, but there was far too much he could not tell them. It was impossible to sit still and trust any of the Old Ones to actually help him find Eliana and get her out of there. With the exception of Eliana's love for him and support of his development, he had nobody to credit for his growth. There were plenty who had helped him learn to loath and distrust strangers, and while his optimism still helped him overcome their deadly messages most of the time, the weight of it all grew by the day.

Darkest of all among his thoughts was his fear of what would become of his new friends if they somehow got caught up in whatever sort of plans the Movers had in motion. If they did, the new friends would learn of his shame. Perhaps they would even see him shamed in front of them, humiliated by the same foul behaviors Eliana had been forced to endure in front of her neighbors back in Ukraine.

After another long moment with no elevator car in arrival, he headed for the stairway. He began to trot down the eighteen flights, moving on the balls of his feet for maximum silence.

His destination of Blackwell's Island was a place boasting numerous sanitarium buildings, places where people were sent when society had no idea what to do with them. In spite of the fears twisting inside him, or perhaps because of them, it felt good to be in motion. Doing nothing would not help him or anyone else, as far as he could see it. The simple acts of moving his legs and pushing out into the night made him feel stronger than he had in days.

He reached the ground level and made his way through the lobby, hurrying past surprised hotel workers who didn't expect to see a child at that hour, but who were not quite concerned enough to stop him. Chasing after him would only add to the labor they already had to shoulder in the course of their work shift.

He slipped out the lobby entrance.

He knew the Plaza Hotel faced north because it looked straight up the length of Central Park. With the park to the north, east had to be to his right. On the street facing the great park across from the hotel, he turned to his right and headed east, for the water. He navigated by guesswork because most of his time in Manhattan had been spent almost exclusively inside of Clayton's hotel, leaving the city itself a foreign place to him.

The night was frigid, with a stiff breeze that made the cold hurt worse. His teeth began to chatter while he pulled his new coat tight around his throat and hurried away. He moved along at a brisk jog to keep himself warmer. On this night, all he knew for certain about finding his destination was if he traveled a few more blocks, he would come to the East River, a few hundred meters of water flowing between Manhattan and Queens.

Blackwell's Island was a narrow strip of land sitting dark and insignificant underneath a massive bridge. He had seen it once before, a perfect place to be close to the city but isolated from it. Free to experiment with unimaginable torments called "therapy" on voiceless "patients" who had the misfortune of being committed to the care of the state. Or, as Dante had witnessed for himself, those with the even greater misfortune of being committed to the care of the Reverend Canon Richard Young.

He zigzagged at every other corner, just to throw off anyone who might be following. Not that he saw any pursuers at the moment, but his long antennae had kept him alive so far.

He maintained eastward travel by alternating streets, counting down the avenue numbers from Fifth Avenue toward the river. Before long he could smell the water and had no need of any other directions. Soon there it was, the giant bridge mounted on enormous stone piles straddling the thin island like a pair of rude legs. The bridge itself floated from the Manhattan side over to Queens without ever touching down on the island below it, appropriate to a tiny landmass where Dante knew all hope was abandoned by the few who found themselves there and recognized it for what it was: a place where those who leave alive only do so if they depart without their souls.

Clayton Mannerly had ignited a fire in Dante's core. He would find Eliana at any cost. There was no risk he would not take.

Boats and ferries were the lifeline of the tiny island. The darkened shoreline of the Manhattan side offered a series of finger docks poking out into the water and giving berths to a random population of bobbing rowboats, oars neatly tucked, most of them humble workboats too old and cheap to steal.

Dante stole one anyway. Selecting the smallest rowboat for ease of propulsion, he untied the line, tossed it aboard, and hopped in. There were no witnesses down by the water in the frozen midnight air. Nobody saw the wiry kid watch the current for speed and direction, then settle in and row for the island. The distance appeared to be no more than four or five soccer fields in length. In warmer weather, a strong swimmer could easily cross the water.

On this post-midnight winter morning, the water would kill in minutes.

He had learned of Blackwell's Island from his first and only trip, when Clayton brought him to Father Young for "training." More accurately titled, it would have been: How to help the Reverend Canon Richard Young to reel in new boys by canvassing the streets and back alleys. All for that seminary thing he claimed to be running over in Queens. Dante was glad to have never seen the place. During his one visit to Blackwell's Island, Father Young had said he always needed more boys because they got a lot of paying visitors. That much was bad enough in itself, but it was not the killer element.

For a few frozen moments, a patch of night fog swirled up and away from the water, and then there it was, looming in silhouette: Blackwell's Island, the place where the big secret auctions were held, and where later, the rejects were processed. Some of the gray, foreboding stone buildings stood abandoned, giving the tiny island a fearsome appearance.

Dante righted the oars and began to pull. The boat was old but light. He put his back and arms into it, and the little craft leaped forward. River fog swirled and enveloped him while he headed out onto the water. There was plenty of random traffic on the East River. Workboats, mostly, occupied by men hard at work on their midnight shifts. While their countenance was grim, they presented no real danger. But he knew men with bad intentions might also get ideas if they came across a single boy in a rowboat. He had considered getting a pistol a few times in the past but never got around to it. That hesitation felt regrettable now.

His journey among the other isolated craft would take a few minutes, if all went well, or could be his last if all did not. He aimed the boat toward Blackwell's Island at a steep angle to combat the push of the current and fell into the strenuous rhythm of propelling the boat across the water through the fog. His thoughts overtook him as if they, too, swirled around him in the eddied mist.

On that terrible day when Clayton had dumped Dante off for a day of "training" in Father Young's care, Dante learned the truth—every child who came in through the Movers and passed through New York, if they were to make it onto the orphan trains, first had to help with "processing the rejects" for something called a "full fatal." Every one of them had to do it at least one time.

The processing lesson was the killer element, the part that stopped him in his tracks, gave him back his voice, and set him to screaming in outrage at being told his "work" entailed such a thing. Once he saw the retired and decaying Hydrotherapy Wing, the sunshine of that daylight visit did nothing to reduce the horror of the place. There was plenty of hydrotherapy left to go around.

The place had a double row of huge bathtubs once used for immersing hysterical patients in cold water. He had soon learned "improvements" were added by the Movers at some point in the recent past. Now it was a place where blindfolded rejects were tied up and made to sit in the big tubs filled with the cold waters of the East River, near freezing on any winter day. All the tubs had heavy wooden lids hanging on chains several feet above each tub.

Clayton had proudly described how troublemakers were placed inside, still blindfolded, and then the tubs were filled to the brim with water while they sat bound and helpless, unable to see their plight. Then...the heavy lid was lowered onto them.

It forced the patient under the water and held them there.

After thirty panic-stretched seconds, the lid was to be raised, and Dante was assured people usually survived it. He was told, as a rule, only one treatment was needed to secure workable attitudes from the patients. It really calmed them down. If they did not survive or if their elimination was necessary, then the river could have their weighted corpses.

What he had failed to understand at the moment was why Clayton and Father Young would tell him such things. Why show him such a place?

He soon learned it was because a big auction was planned for the coming weekend, and it was time for him to learn how to operate the chain system to raise and lower the heavy wooden lids. There would be rejects, there would be troublemakers, there would be slave adults who refused to bend to the whip, and slave children nobody wanted. He would be sinking one of the troublesome ones that night. At least one.

When Dante stiffened at the news, Father Young consoled him, "Just a fifteen-second job this time. Or thirty. Half a minute. Say half a minute to start off with, then. Not the full fatal."

An adult male was dragged in by two of Father Young's seminary conscripts, accompanied by two armed guards. They went about their work like marine recruits out to win a weekend pass. Whatever drove them, Dante could tell they might as well be automatons. No help for him would be coming from that direction.

The victim was already bound and gagged, with a blindfold over his eyes, but he fought them with surprising strength. Dante realized the victim was hardly behaving like someone who thought he would be submerged for only a few seconds.

Dante felt Clayton and Father Young glaring at him, *willing* him to execute their chosen victim, to use his muscles to pull the proper two chains in the right balance, allowing the heavy lid to press down, slowly pushing the victim's head lower while it sank.

There was no way. Terror filled him and sent urine down the front of his pants and set his leg muscles into spasms that nearly put him on the floor.

Dante had felt certain he was about to suffer this same awful fate unless he cooperated as ordered. And he still could not pull the chain and lower the lid. He wondered for an instant if it helped to have died bravely when you go to meet God, to have refused to turn to evil. Could it add any shine at all to a soul such as his?

His musing did no good. Clayton grabbed his much smaller hand, squeezed it around the chain, and pulled it downward, then slid the hand up and pulled downward again, slid it up once more and then began pulling on the chain a third and final time to lower the lid into place.

"Hold your breath!" Dante cried. The words seemed to burst out of him. He recoiled in embarrassment at his useless advice. Even if the victim somehow heard him, wouldn't he think he was simply being mocked?

"Hold your breath?" Father Young repeated, scoffing.

Now the weight of the big tub's thick lid forced the victim under the surface, sending the excess water over the edge and down the sides of the tub, to flow away somewhere under the floor. Dante hated himself for being relieved not to hear the victim beg or scream.

The moment the lid dropped, Father Young snatched Dante and pulled him away from the control chain. When Dante began to shout in protest, Young also covered his mouth. He held him tight for a minute that felt like an hour, then released him. Dante leaped away from him and skidded to the floor on the opposite side of the room.

"What are you doing?" he screamed. "Why did you do that? Lift the lid! Lift the lid! Get it off of there!"

Father Young offered a small, sad smile, then pulled the chain over and over while the heavy wooden lid slowly rose into the air. The victim was underwater, not moving.

Young spoke in a voice dripping with false kindness. "There, you see? He's already gone. We cover their mouths and eyes out of courtesy to the chain operator, so they don't have to see their faces or hear their cries for mercy. Everybody wants mercy. What they never understand, it seems, is that snuffing their lights out *is* mercy, for them. They are spared the lives of slaves, exchanging them for eternal Life in the Kingdom of God. Not a bad deal, wouldn't you say?"

"Kingdom of God?" Dante gasped, backing away. "Do you even believe in God?"

Father Young studied Dante for a moment, then walked to him and leaned down to whisper in the boy's ear as if to convey some grand secret. "All that matters is whether *your* pretty little head believes in God, my boy. If you do, then you can believe you just sent this man to a better place."

Dante could not avoid turning to look at the drowned man again. The visible part of the victim's face appeared to be contorted in agony, or perhaps the attempt at one final scream.

Clayton tried to calm him down, assuring him there was no shame in his survival. Just about everybody they challenged with the lid drop went along with it. It was so effective, none of the few who escaped the place wanted to talk about it. When Dante, raging, demanded to know what happened to the ones who refused, Father Young threw a pointed glance at the nearest big tub. He favored Dante with a benevolent smile and used the same tone he would employ in a homily for a small room: "*Remain silent. Do as you are told. Go in peace.*" He repeated it several times.

Without having to ask, Dante understood most of the condemned people found themselves in that position merely because potential buyers considered them undesirable. Their great crime was in sticking up for themselves and hungering for freedom, which got in the way of an organization of people who had nothing but contempt for others, for all others, for anyone who wasn't them.

He stomped and shrieked for the rest of the day, impossible to placate. At last Father Young told Clayton to pack him off to the hotel. The day was wasted. They would have to cover for him in the coming auction, then get him ready in time for the next one.

"Unless you chose him wrong?" Father Young suggested to Mannerly, reeking of innocence and friendly concern.

"I did not, I repeat, did *not* choose 'wrong' about any damn thing with that boy! He's going to step up. He just doesn't know it yet."

"Wonderful, I pray for nothing less."

They agreed to give Dante a few days to calm down and to start up again after that. Mannerly considered the training much too important to forgo. The boy could hardly take up his duties without it, and these duties justified his safe and secure life with Clayton and Allison Mannerly whether he wanted to be there or not. Ungrateful bastard.

Later that day, alone with Eliana, Dante told her what had happened during his "training." Her face filled with dread at the news. She stood and began pacing.

"This is it, Dante," she fretted. "The time for you to go has come whether we want it here or not. You cannot remain without having your soul turned to trash."

She counted out their small stash of cash and coins by hand.

The next day he was gone.

The thin fog evaporated, revealing a makeshift landing other small boats had already put to use. Dante thought the improvised pier looked like it was built by pirates. Two long ladders had been fused together, end to end, and floated out over the water on small pontoons that looked like volley-balls. The other small rowboats floated on short ties, proving other visitors shared his desire to traverse the island without official notice. Apparently, they all had their own reasons for avoiding any form of official arrival at the island's main landing dock. Blackwell's Island was a deadly place, as Clayton Mannerly pointed out to him, where convicts and crazy people were hauled in from all over, *to mostly disappear from the world.*

He started to tie up to the floating ladders at the closest spot to the shore, but even if he were to go over the side, that still left him having to wade ashore chest deep in the frigid water. He looked for alternatives, gazing around at the shoreline. He saw plenty of places where he could hit land and tie up, but none that afforded access by foot. He would again be left to swim or climb very dicey terrain in wet boots.

Perhaps, in daylight and warm weather, he could disembark there and walk away dry. On this dark, ice-cold morning, it was not going to happen.

He swallowed hard, then quickly took off his pants and his coat and his boots and socks and even his underwear, using the coat for a "hobo's hand-bag." He lay sideways and eased himself over the side to avoid splashing, one arm held high in the air with the handbag, moving slowly to avoid attracting notice from anyone who might bring trouble. Even out here, he knew he had to assume they were out there. That kind of thinking had kept him out of trouble more than once.

His left leg went into the water first. His entire body wanted to scream in protest at the cold water, which immediately began to suck away at his body heat like a giant leech. His determination to find Eliana kept his jaw clenched tight and his lips sealed while he lowered the rest of himself into the water and stood up.

He dialed the shriek back to more of a tortured grunt and waded toward land, aiming for an opening that looked like an animal trail leading up from the water. *Animal trail...what animals?*

It took eight agonizing steps to clear the waterline and come fully onto land. His leg muscles began to shiver uncontrollably. His knee joints buck-led, and he went down to his knees with one hand flat to the ground and the other straight up in the air with the bundled clothing.

The clothing remained dry, but he arrived ashore like a drowning swimmer who finally breaks the surface. He gave himself three giant gasps before he forced himself to get to the vital business of getting the garments back on his soaked body.

He dropped his clothing onto branches to keep them off the ground, then decided to sacrifice his underpants to the task of blotting the rest of himself enough to safely put his clothes back on a body that was not quite dry but was at least less wet.

He got the blotting job done in a matter of seconds, but the finer movements of redressing himself required function from muscles now shivering and shaking to the point of seizure; even common movements took too long. He kept losing more valuable body heat to the struggle with every second his condition forced him to remain unprotected. The cold itself became a living thing. It knew him. It hated him and wanted nothing more than to suck the life from him.

At last he got the socks on, by far the hardest part. Just in time. His hands and feet were becoming wooden. He shoved the pants on, forcing them over his blotted skin. The fabric wanted to stick to his damp flesh, but he pushed each leg through and got immediate relief from the worst of the cold's pain. He got the top button closed with his thumbs working like sticks of wood but left the others.

He jammed his feet back into the boots and got them on well enough. He knew better than to bother tying them at the moment and instead donned his shirt, also not fastened. Last, the heavy dry coat. Perfect. He squeezed his hands beneath the armpits of the coat garment, feeling the elation of having managed to save his own life. It was as if the verdict just came back in and he was going to be allowed to continue to exist.

He stumbled out of the thin tree line and looked in all directions. Directly ahead of him was an old stone building anyone could see was abandoned. A bunch of smaller places surrounded the big building like good soldiers, also abandoned now.

Clayton had made certain Dante knew what once went on in those buildings. The system had housed and fed a huge number of employees, people who had no reason to want everybody to be well. People who inflicted "treatments" that would drive a perfect person mad.

He felt a lonely sense of satisfaction, viewing the places where once such power was wielded over the lives of so many helpless individuals, because the building before him was now as dead as the bodies of criminals executed there. He knew the experience of staring at the recently dead while they were still recognizable as ordinary humans, people who were most likely baffled by everything going on around them and who were swept away in a terrible wave of history.

He rounded another copse of small trees to see a tall gas lamp shining ahead, illuminating the front part of the main landing dock. The private cobblestone road leading from the dock ran straight up to a big wooden building, three stories high. The building was long. The walls stretched far in the distance.

Instinct told him to walk using quick, small steps to keep his blood pumping. He skirted the deserted horror castle and made for the big building over on the other side of the landing. A handful of lighted windows were visible there. *Good enough, then. Does a place like this use lookouts from a distance? Not likely. Why do the work?*

After a minute or two, he stood within a few feet of the last lighted window of the lowest rooms on that building. A simple door had been installed a few yards down from his spot, with a set of plain concrete steps leading from the ground. He looked in all directions and decided he could enter at that door and, once inside, avoid the lighted rooms and travel only in the direction of the dark windows.

He decided his hands were warm enough to finish fastening his clothing and tying his boots. He only exposed his bare fingers in such cold but for one grim realization: if he had to run, he needed to be wearing clothing tight enough to run with him.

A fairly stiff breeze gusted in over the water, rustling the onshore shrubbery and whistling through the treetops, helpful in concealing any noises he might make. He finished fastening the buttons and steeled himself to make his bold venture inside.

The sound of the wind was the only thing he heard while he touched his fingers to the door handle. At the same instant, a big hand clamped over his mouth in a deadly grip and a strong forearm wrapped around his neck, forcing him to breathe through his nose and to soak in the fumes of a chemical-soaked rag.

Dante tried to struggle but quickly lost control of his limbs and then forgot what struggling was supposed to feel like. He stepped straight off a cliff and went into free fall. While he plummeted, his last conscious thought was one of surprise: there was no upward blast from the air...

And that was it.

26

THE PLAZA HOTEL – CENTRAL PARK SOUTH

March 2nd
* Shortly After Sunrise *

THE ENGINES OF THE CITY WERE UP AND RUNNING, rumbling the sidewalks, fouling the air, and fraying the nerves. Randall Blackburn and Vignette Nightingale began their day huddled in a rear corner of the hotel's pricey coffee shop, sitting near a sign proudly bragging: *"We Never Close!"* Each wore winter boots and layers of clothing for warmth, with a large winter coat lying to the side. They looked like people who were headed downtown and intended to walk.

Observers, if any, could have hardly been blamed for deducing the pair as father and daughter, likely having an unusually sincere conversation about something they could just as easily talk about at a better hour. Only a couple of other tables were occupied, with most working people long since on their way, and nonworking people still asleep. It was more of an hour for people who had slept little that previous night.

Neither of them had slept at all after three o'clock that morning, when Blackburn found himself awake and put on a hotel robe to have a seat in the suite's sitting room. He had to pass Dante's room to get there, noticed the door was open, and glanced in while he passed.

The bed had been empty, but the bathroom door was open and the light was off. So he had knocked at Vignette's door. Waited. Knocked. Waited.

At this point he had begun a steady tapping guaranteed to produce madness and sustained it until the door was pulled back by Vignette. She looked more than a little annoyed.

"People sleep," she grumbled.

"I know. Apologies. But Dante's not in there, correct? Maybe he got scared in the night? Just being thorough, here."

She merely glared at him for a moment while she processed the words... understood... realized he was right... and slumped in resignation. "Damn it. He took off, didn't he?"

"Impressive deduction."

She nodded, then exhaled hard.

"All right," he said, "if you ask me, this kid is essentially a cunning wild animal who happens to speak English and is smarter than most people. We're going to have to hope he's bright enough to keep himself out of trouble out there. There's no way to hunt him down."

He placed one hand on her shoulder and looked closely at her. "Vignette, I have to ask you to let go of this for right now. He left. He can come back. But we can't have our lives disrupted anymore on his behalf."

She took a breath and then nodded. "Yeah. Yeah, I know. I hate it, but you're right."

"Come on, since we're up, let's go get breakfast."

They had nearly finished eating when a young man of about Vignette's age, though a foot less in height, walked into the coffee shop and stepped up to their table. He spoke in the voice of a church choir tenor.

"Excuse me. Good morning. My name is John Smith, and I'm with the *Daily Herald*. The commissioner's office told me I might find you here, and I thought I'd start early. Paid off, too. May I sit?"

Vignette started to point to the empty chair next to her, but Randall stopped her, saying, "Excuse me, but may I see some identification, 'Mister John Smith'? Keeping in mind I will be personally disappointed in you if you're not what you say."

"Yes! Of course! Why, I only knew you from descriptions, and still I had to guess, and in my case I can't expect you to..." He pulled out a card. "Here, see my New York driver's license. John Smith. Right there."

Vignette shook her head. "Has any restaurant ever accepted reservations from you?"

"It's not the problem you might think. I find if one speaks with confidence, one can generally—"

Blackburn grinned and interrupted, "Okay! You proved your suspicious name is just your suspicious name. Now why do you think we would want to speak to the press?"

Smith ignored the empty chair at their table and grabbed one from the adjacent table, then scooted close to them without bothering to ask first. "Commissioner O'Grady told me you're in town for some sort of investigation that affects New York City and San Francisco, meaning it affects the whole country."

"Why would she tell you that?"

"A bargain. She told me that much so I wouldn't go to print with what I already have. You can learn a lot by reading between the lines. She didn't know I was guessing at some of it, but she confirmed it. In return, I promised her to keep it quiet until she gives the okay. All I want is to help you in your investigation, break the story as it happens, so to speak."

"Damned nice of you," Blackburn said in an even tone.

"It's not a question of being nice, Detective. It's that this is a great country for somebody like me because I can start as a stringer, which is what I am, and end on the regular payroll, for no other reasons than my brains and my reporting! There's something big here, I know it. I want to break it and win the Pulitzer. Know what the Pulitzer is?"

"I've heard of it. Started three or four years ago, right?"

"We had the fourth annual ceremony in June. Cash awards for great reporting. But I need the material, the story. And I have a feeling you two are going to walk into the middle of it. I can be handy to have around,

Detectives. You could look forever and never find a guy with more motivation than me!"

"I don't think so, Mr. Smith."

"Just tell me this much: Where are you going right now? You're up this early, you got something in mind, right? I'll promise to hold it until you're ready to release it. You'll see you can trust me."

"I'll tell you, but it's no scoop." He pulled out his small stack of flyers. "Yesterday we spent the day canvassing print shops in Brooklyn. We stopped for the day at this one: the Canzani Print Shop."

Smith took a look and broke into a wide smile. "Hey! Canzani Print Shop! I know this place. I've been backgrounding a piece on anarchists and some kind of connection to smuggling people."

"We know that much. What we need are details."

"Same thing I need. But that top flyer right there is Tony Tazio's work, all right."

"Yes, the name's on the back. You know him?"

"Nah. You see enough pamphlets like this, you get to know their personal styles."

Vignette asked, "Even if you don't know him, did you ever meet him?"

Blackburn glanced at her with a little smile of admiration.

"Nope. Know *of* him, though. Everybody in the news game knows about him, and we all know we're gonna be writing stories about the people he kills before it's all done. You from out of town, though, right?"

"San Francisco, actually," Vignette replied.

"San Francisco? What do you know from out there? The woods, right? I mean, they had gold for a while, but hey, what have they done for us lately, know what I mean? Ha!"

"Tony Tazio, Mr. Smith."

"Tazio, oh yeah," he replied, making it sound like *aw yah*. "Fake name for an agitator with a history of building and setting off bombs for his anarchist cause." He gave them a conspiratorial grin. "But like I said, I'm keeping files. Background project, you know, spare time, all that. And with the right breaks I will nail his hat to the door!"

"You'll do it even though law enforcement has failed so far? How?"

"Any cop will tell you, reporters can find out things the authorities can't, because we're not constrained by their procedures. Beyond that, I don't reveal sources."

"Keep your sources to yourself and just tell me how you think you can bring down this man."

"I expose him to the world! That's how I accomplish it. And under his real name. Make sure every employer, banker, law enforcement officer knows—make sure nobody is ever fooled! This name 'Tony Tazio' is fake. An alias. But the man using it is an actual anarchist bomb builder named Andrea Salsedo."

Vignette was caught with her teacup two inches off the saucer. It fell back in place, although the excellent china held together. She did not move. Instead she stared into the cup as if she saw something there. Blackburn watched her with a burning gaze, but he too said nothing.

For a few moments, Smith was proud of the reaction he had garnered. These people truly seemed to appreciate his potential to them, with all his insider research and whatnot.

But still they each said nothing, and after a few more seconds the interlude itself became the message. He had said something wrong. Smith cleared his throat and waited for one of them to tell him what the hell had just happened.

Blackburn glanced at Vignette and raised his eyebrows in a questioning gesture. She gave a barely discernible nod. He took a deep breath and turned to Smith.

"As you see... What you've just told us...ahem. Mr. Smith, we recently learned in addition to all the things you mentioned, this man, Andrea Salsedo, is also the murderer of my adopted son, Shane."

"My brother," Vignette added. She spoke softly, but her teeth were clenched.

"My God! Why isn't he in custody?"

"Because nobody will ever prove it," Randall replied. He signed the breakfast bill and turned back to Smith. "Therefore, I hope you'll understand when I tell you we have to leave."

He and Vignette both stood and began to don their coats. Smith stood along with them.

"So your destination is the Canzani Print Shop in Brooklyn."

"Among others," Blackburn replied.

"Here's the thing. I decided to bet on myself and buy a car so good, I would have no choice but to succeed in selling my work to the papers."

"I thought you're with the *Herald*."

"Well. Stringer. You know? They like my work so much they will pay me for it so long as I bring them a good story. *Capiche?* We say that here. It means 'Do you get it?'"

"You're unemployed?"

"Freelance, Detective. Like you, eh?"

"All right, you're a freelancer, but you might tell people you're only a stringer right up front."

"Sure. Then I can watch all the people not talk to me. Did you hear the part about how I need to get a good story?"

Blackburn stepped back from the table. "Good day, Mr. Smith."

Smith raised his voice but otherwise continued as if he had not heard Blackburn at all. "So like I said, I bet on myself and bought the most spacious, comfortable four-seater on the market. It's called the Nash Touring Car. For driving around people I interview, people who help me get a story, all that. The streets were clear when I got here. I was able to park next door." He smiled.

Blackburn turned to Vignette. "Want a ride with the freelancer here?"

She smiled, but there was no humor in it. "More than that, if Mr. Smith is planning to write about people like that, I want to find out if he's brave or crazy."

Smith laughed. "You're hoping brave, right?"

"Probably. Crazy can be fun sometimes."

"Off to Brooklyn, then," Blackburn said, gesturing toward the door.

"Somebody better be about to say something worth calling me at home so early."

"Commissioner O'Grady, it's Randall Blackburn."

"Detective Blackburn, I expect my home telephone number to only be used as a necessity. Tell me this is one."

"The printer who did the pamphlet from Canzani Print Shop is using an alias. This so-called 'Tony Tazio' is actually a wanted man named Andrea Salsedo."

She picked up without missing a beat. "Salsedo. Well, that's perfect. Just got a bulletin about him. Another Galleanist. Wanted for a string of cross-country bombings last June."

"That's him, and I have to confess to a personal interest now. We just learned this is the man who murdered my son, Shane. Vignette's brother."

"Oh, Jay-sus H. Christ, Detective! Now you're personally involved?"

"I want to be there to see the arrest, Commissioner, and most of all I want Shane's sister to see his killer hauled in."

She let out a deep, slow exhale, then cleared her throat. "And in return?"

"And in return I won't call it in anywhere but right here with this phone call. Everything after that comes from you. I'm hoping you can put Detective Goodwin and her squad of policewomen on the arrest."

O'Grady slapped the table, sending a sharp thump down the line. "Ha! As if you believe I would do anything else! Yes and yes! I believe I'd like to see this myself. Here's what you do: meet us there, but stay away from the print shop until we get there. Do not go inside. Don't set off any bells. We'll be there soon enough."

He avoided promising anything. "See you there, Commissioner."

27

BROOKLYN

March 2nd
* 8:30 a.m. *

THE BRAND NEW NASH TOURING CAR sat close to the curb nearly a block up the street from the Canzani Print Shop, far enough away for discretion, close enough for a good view. The vehicle's body panels were finished in gleaming ebony black and highlighted by silvery glints of chrome accents. John Smith sat behind the wheel while Blackburn and Vignette occupied the back seat, elbows on their knees. They all kept their eyes on the shop's front door.

"Well, that's it," Smith abruptly spoke up. "I need to pay another visit to the filling station down the street. Use the facilities."

"I could do that too," Vignette agreed.

"Me too," said Blackburn. "So Mr. Smith, you go on ahead. We'll take turns and keep the shop covered. They should be about ready to put out the 'open for business' sign. After that we can split up and cover the back door, too."

"I'll volunteer for that, Randall," said Vignette. "That guy won't get past me."

"That's what I'm afraid of. Let's hope it doesn't come to that."

They stepped out of the car and let Smith drive away some two hundred yards to the filling station. Even at that distance they could see him get out and go inside.

"You know," Blackburn said, "they think I want a printing job done. I could pop back in there and pretend I was checking on the job. Make sure Salsedo is working. I mean, we saw him go in, but we haven't been watching the back."

"Why would he leave this early?"

"He probably wouldn't. But it can't hurt to check. Don't worry. We won't do anything to make the commissioner unhappy."

"All right. The only time he saw me, I was in my leathers and wearing the helmet. I'll just be feminine and helpless. That's all he'll see."

"You've done this before, haven't you."

"Who, me?" She pretended to fan herself with the flat of her hand.

"Good," Blackburn said with a grin. "He'll never make the connection. Just remember all we have to do is verify he's there."

"I want to talk to him."

"You can't, Vignette."

"I want to talk to the bastard, Randall!"

"Can you do it so calmly that he will have no idea you're onto him?"

She stared hard at him for a moment, then slumped in resignation.

He patted her shoulder, understanding. "Let's go see what's up in there."

Moments later the sign went up declaring the shop open for the day, and they quickly made their way inside. Despite the early hour, the place smelled of printer's ink, machine oil, and body odor. The room was fairly dark, with only natural light coming from the windows and small lamps attached to the top of each working press.

Vignette held Blackburn's arm as if she were a young woman accompanied by her strict father, a convincing bit of misdirection. She also made it a point to keep her face turned away from the windows. They already knew they were the first "customers" to visit since the place opened, but the presses were pounding away on jobs already scheduled.

Four printers, three male and one female, worked with fixed concentration.

Blackburn spotted Salsedo at the same press he had been operating the last time. He made himself smile at the printer and waved.

"Hi!" he called out. "I was passing by with my daughter and thought I'd pop in and see if you think you might have time to do that job I talked to you about yesterday? For the church picnic?"

Salsedo impatiently waved him off. "Come back this afternoon. After lunchtime." He immediately focused on his work again.

"Okay!" Blackburn cheerfully called back. He started for the door, but Vignette was still holding onto his arm and her feet did not move. Her nails dug into his arm with her breathing shallow and her eyes riveted on her brother's killer.

Blackburn spoke without moving his lips in a voice barely above a whisper. "Let's go. Gotta go. We're *going*." On the last word he walked away, putting power into his steps and pulling Vignette along with him. They made it to the door without any of the busy printers taking notice of her reaction.

After they hit the exit, she maintained her angry silence while they moved several doors up the sidewalk and stopped at the curb. Blackburn gave her an admiring smile. "Respect to you for your self-control, my dear."

She had to take several deep breaths before she could respond. Finally she met his eyes for a moment with a small smile. "I actually thought it was stronger. Thank you for helping me out of there."

"I should have gone in alone. Are you going to be okay?"

"I'm grinding my teeth down to nubs, but we do it because we can't allow anything, not one single thing, to mess up this arrest, right? We have to see this guy brought to justice. This is our chance to do it, yes? I mean, without having to take care of the job ourselves."

"Hold that thought!" Blackburn interrupted. He continued in a whisper, "Taking care of it ourselves is something we only talk about if nobody else is around. And only if we whisper."

Vignette smiled, playing along. "Okay," she whispered. "I believe the message was sent and received."

John Smith proved his comic timing by picking that moment to hit the

Touring Car's blaring horn and pull up in his fine piece of luxurious machinery. He called out, "Ah! Much better now. I can taxi you over to the station if you don't want to walk it."

Vignette muttered, "The man appears determined to do us favors." She slipped Randall a mischievous grin. "I've noticed how often you get up to pee at night. Maybe you should go first? Let him drive you. I can wait."

He responded with a resentful smile. "Counting my bathroom trips is not something for you to be proud of." He started to object further, but his sense of truth stopped him. "All right, damn it. I'll go first. What's that they say? Age before beauty?"

"Who says that?"

"Beautiful young people."

"Consider the words spoken."

Blackburn made a pained face and took a step toward Smith's automobile. Then another. Then shook his head and strode over to the car and got in.

Smith made some joke she could not hear which he seemed to find hilarious. Blackburn ignored it. They drove away to make the journey of a few hundred yards in comfort.

All three were comfortable again and waiting in Smith's luxurious car when three official-looking vehicles rolled around the corner, approaching without sirens or lights. They quietly pulled up in front of the print shop, and within twenty seconds, Deputy Commissioner Ellen O'Grady, Detective First Grade Isabella Goodwin, and four female policewomen emerged and took places a few yards back from the shop's front door, positioned at an angle to conceal them from anyone inside.

Vignette watched, riveted, while she and Randall climbed out of Smith's car and the policewomen gathered for action. "Hey, look at this, no men today." She said it like someone who had just found a five-spot on the sidewalk.

Blackburn nodded. "Yep. Just Detective Goodwin's policewomen. I thought we should be sure to attend for this. Now listen, I am trusting you to withhold your responses when you see him. It's crazy, the things that can get a guy off on a technicality. Don't give his lawyer a technicality, Vignette."

She met his stare with difficulty and swallowed a hard lump. She knew he was close to the truth of her without even asking her about it. She dropped her gaze and hurried ahead to greet O'Grady and Goodwin, flushed with amazement to see such a serious situation being handled entirely by female law enforcement. She had never seen anything like it. For her, there was nothing more inspiring.

These female police officers proved her initial judgment, way back as a little girl, that the supposed paucity of options for her adult life was untrue. As it turned out, there was a wide range of choices between the straitjacket of marriage and the dry life of a spinster schoolmarm.

There were jobs and careers with meaning and challenge. How glorious it was to see it played out on this day with the arrest of the man who had stalked and killed her brother. The man who drove Shane and his police cycle under the wheels of a borrowed garbage truck, for the love of God— oh, it was going to be fine. The women were here today. They had come to grab a murderous monster and deliver notice; he was done killing them and their babies. He was all done killing their families.

Vignette showed respect to the working women by standing back far enough to avoid any interference but remained close enough to observe. Deputy Commissioner O'Grady and Detective Goodwin each caught her eye for an instant, offering acknowledgment with a nod while they formed everyone into a huddle and got together their arrest plan.

Detective Goodwin sent one of the policewomen in ahead of the rest, clearly tasking her with scouting the place. Vignette wondered how she would do it, inquire about printing rates or something, she supposed.

Everyone proceeded to stand around and try not to look suspicious for what turned out to be a period of three anxious minutes. At last the officer emerged from the shop and calmly walked until she was also out of sight from the shop's windows. Then she quickly huddled with the others.

Moments later, O'Grady looked directly over at Vignette, pointed to the shop, and nodded, confirming he was still in there, unaware of the police presence. He had not scooted out the back way.

Vignette spun to Blackburn and gave him a delighted grin of anticipation. He responded with a cautious smile.

Goodwin directed two of her policewomen to stand guard on either side of the door, hugging the walls to hide their presence while they protected against attempts at escape. O'Grady and Goodwin each had one armed policewoman backup while they carefully stepped to the door. Goodwin held the door for O'Grady, who would have been pleased by the gesture, but it turned out there was no time to proceed inside.

A sudden swell of roaring automobile engines approached at top speed, followed by the attention-grabbing spectacle of four police cars plus a paddy wagon peeling around the corner, then aiming their rumbling circus of noise at the print shop. They skidded to a halt on screeching tires.

Every one of the vehicles was driven by and occupied by men. Four to a car, two in the paddy wagon, eighteen in all. Blackburn had them counted before the last car stopped. The first man out of the first car wore a formal uniform, epaulets on his shoulders and stripes on his sleeves, stars on his collar, with white gloves on his hands. He was a portly, middle-aged man with a thick brush mustache, and anyone could see he was in charge. He stood calmly tugging at the base of each glove while the other men leaped out and formed around him.

O'Grady slumped and muttered, "Well, shit. Double shit." She turned to her officers. "It's Commissioner Enright. The conversation killer. Stand down, officers. Let's see how the land lies here."

"O'Grady!" called Enright. "Pull your officers away from there!"

She waved the women away from the print shop and sent them to wait two doors up the street. Then she stomped directly to the commissioner wearing an expression that revealed how hard it was to control her temper.

The other officers recognized her, of course, but it was an indication of how loyalties and politics came together that the men unconsciously closed around Commissioner Enright when O'Grady approached. Vignette watched her make a spirited argument with Enright, although clearly to no avail. She stood with her back ramrod straight while he made his sneering, dismissive reply, spun on his heels, and waved to his men to proceed with the raid on the print shop.

With a resigned expression, O'Grady waved to her policewomen to stand down. Vignette's heart sank to see it. She stepped next to Blackburn and took his arm. All they could do now was watch the men of the force handle this.

"I'm sorry it turned out like this, Vignette, but it's a local matter."

"I know. I just need to see him go to jail. That's all."

"Will it be enough?"

She looked at him, puzzled by the question, then sighed. "Maybe," she replied. "Maybe it will."

She was surprised to see the policewomen taking it all in stride. It appeared to be familiar behavior to them. O'Grady and Goodwin walked over to them while the male officers pushed their way into the print shop, shouting for everyone to put up their hands.

"John Smith isn't around," Blackburn observed. "I wonder if he phoned this in from the gas station?"

"Sure, why not?" said Goodwin. "He greased his path with the commissioner by tipping him off and kept things in the old boys' club."

"He won the day," added O'Grady, "but it's also a textbook example of what we are up against in this city. Drop by my place this evening around seven, won't you? Let's talk about the realities we have to contend with if we are to make any progress on the larger case."

"I look forward to it," Vignette replied.

O'Grady and Goodwin turned to rejoin the policewomen, who were getting back into their cars.

The noise of commotion inside the shop came back through the door, but they could not see what was happening until, after a minute or so, two men came out with Andrea Salsedo between them, hands cuffed behind his back. He appeared to have been struck on the head during the struggle and gazed around with blank eyes.

Vignette very much wanted to make eye contact with him, but he never looked at her. There was no way she could let it go. She jumped in front of Salsedo and his two escorts, momentarily blocking their way.

"Get away from the suspect!" Enright bellowed at her, but she burned her gaze into Salsedo until he focused on her at last.

"The man he killed was my *brother*!"

Even Commissioner Enright paused for a second at that. It was all

Vignette needed. She bored her gaze into Salsedo's eyes to drive her words home. "His name was Shane Nightingale. I will follow everything that happens to you, and if the police can't cure the world of you, I'll do it myself."

The killer stared at her is if she were a ghost. He appeared to believe her.

Commissioner Enright snorted in impatience and gestured for his men to pull Salsedo to the waiting paddy wagon. "He tried to go out the back! Make sure his cuffs stay on until he's in a cell!"

Vignette thought the order sounded rather obvious but guessed Enright needed to put his stamp on the event. The last of the cops were filtering out of the print shop when John Smith came driving up and pulled to the curb.

"You missed it," Vignette called to him.

"He caused it," Blackburn said, walking up behind her. He took her arm and walked with her to the reporter's vehicle. He leaned down to speak through the passenger window.

"So you called from the filling station. Probably on your first visit, yes?"

"Detectives, you have to remember, I'm a journalist!"

Vignette scoffed. "I think we should have remembered that before we trusted you."

"I need good stories to get on staff full-time, and that means front-page work! This event would never make the lineup of major stories with women doing the arrest. It makes it sound like, how tough could these guys be, you know? That's just the way of the world, folks."

"She mentioned that we trusted you."

"Trust? If you aren't doing anything wrong, of course you can trust me. But if you step outside of how things are done, I know where my bread gets buttered."

Blackburn smiled. "I noticed you didn't say 'outside the law.'"

"That's right, Mister Blackburn." He got out of the car. "Good day, Miss Nightingale! Best of luck to you."

With that, he walked over to Commissioner Enright and shook his hand. Blackburn heard nothing of the conversation, but he could see the commissioner smiling and being receptive to Smith, who knew where his bread got buttered.

28
———

ABANDONED ASYLUM BUILDING
BLACKWELL'S ISLAND

March 2nd
* Late Afternoon *

THE REVEREND CANON RICHARD YOUNG stood in the musty shadows of an old tie-down room in the abandoned building, where dozens of hapless individuals once lived after being judged, fairly or unfairly, incapable of managing their lives. The shadows were described by the oil lantern in his hand, the room's sole source of light. He spoke but did not look at the person he was addressing. Instead, he stared at the blank wall as if he could see a better world through it.

"I don't believe anyone has come to tell you where you are, so I'll do it. You were moved from the seminary in Queens here to this retired mental institution. We're currently on Blackwell's Island, and this is what was called a tie-down room. In here, people could be tied down and rendered helpless, and the operators could then do quite anything they pleased for them, with them, to them. Anything at all, you know, for their own benefit. Which rather goes to our purpose here today."

The voice from the shadows was raspy and weak, coming from a man

sitting on a new army cot placed amid the trash and clutter of the abandoned room. "Taunt me if you like, Father Young. God knows I repent of all
my sins, but perhaps I still deserve it."

"Quite right. But I am unaware of any priest giving you absolution. I'm
certain I didn't authorize it. Don't you think you need absolution from your
church?"

"My soul needs it. To be sure."

"There is a way for you to get it, too. But only one. You tried betraying us
by talking about what we do. It put you here. If you seek absolution, you
will eliminate two of our problems tonight."

Friar John looked at him with deep skepticism. "What are these
problems?"

"They are your task for tonight."

"What can I possibly do to help you solve problems? I can barely walk
down the hall."

"I'm certain you can do more if you need to. Now, you already saw the
isolation tubs, and I'm sure you don't want to end up in one."

"Nobody wants that. Even those of us who know we need to suffer."

"Exactly so. And when the young boy and his auntie are delivered to
you, you will place them in the tubs and lower the lids, then go outside and
say your rosary three times."

"But that would...would..."

"You can do as I require, earn your absolution, and go to God with a
heart full of joy, or you can refuse," he leaned in toward Friar John and
whispered, "and pay for all eternity."

Friar John's pale yellow skin turned gray with horror. "You would never
do that to another child of God."

"Maybe not," Father Young tossed back, "but I'll do it to you."

He stepped out and closed the door. There was no need to lock it.
Where would a weakened and crumbling escapee go?

∽

"Are you certain?" O'Grady said into the telephone receiver. "All right, damn it all. Thank you." She disconnected the call and turned to Blackburn, Vignette, and Goodwin.

"That's it. Andrea Salsedo was never signed into the county lockup. Or any of the city jails."

"But the police have to know where he is, don't they? They're the ones who took him."

"They know, all right. We're the ones who aren't supposed to know. Us and everybody else. There's only one place he can be."

"Where's that?" Blackburn asked.

"The fourteenth floor of Number 15, Park K Row. Which is the office of the Bureau of Investigation, run by the Justice Department."

Blackburn frowned. "How do you hold an inmate in an office?"

"By making sure the public never finds out there are holding cells there. They exist precisely because nobody thinks to look for them. It's where they put inmates who are in...sensitive investigations."

Blackburn shook his head. "Sensitive investigations about blowing up innocent men, women, and children?"

O'Grady gave a grim nod. "It's outside the law, but so far the people who do know about it are giving it a pass. They know we need some place to interrogate terrorists without having their attorneys making everything impossible—"

"Wait a minute," Vignette interrupted. "That reporter, Mr. Smith, said the reason he called in the police instead of letting you make the arrest was the papers wouldn't make anything of it unless conventional male police did it. They figure if the crime was serious, the NYPD would send in the men."

"He's probably right about that. We've seen it before, the desire to trivialize the role of women on the force. Some of them find us to be infinitely threatening."

"But," Vignette persisted, "if Salsedo is being held in some secret location, the papers can't print the story at all, right? The police and City Hall won't allow it. It's too much of a scoop."

"So long as Salsedo is alive, they will want to hold him in secret. Part of it is to protect him from his own men. If they decide he's likely to talk, he'll never live until his trial."

O'Grady said, "And part of it is to keep the place secret for when they need it next time."

"Bet they don't have to try very hard. It's the same in San Francisco; the public doesn't want to know about places like that. They want to get home in time for dinner and get a good night's sleep."

Detective Goodwin said, "If this had to happen, I'm glad it was today, so you both could get a clear idea of what we're up against."

"Buyers of children in addition to adults," replied Vignette in a grim tone.

Blackburn shook his head. "Raising money for politics that way? I don't think either of us could bear it if Salsedo is able to escape justice for this."

"That's the size of it. Detectives, your mayor told me today he can't guarantee that the people who make up his administration can be trusted on this. I let him know I have the same problem. He repeated how glad he is that you're here, because he trusts you. And with that endorsement, I'm trusting you, too. Our principal challenge is to keep this investigation small. We have to be able to take our time and let them make a mistake we can use."

Blackburn gave a rueful smile. "Well, Commissioner, our home's going to be pretty empty with nobody there. California's a long way off."

O'Grady made as if she hadn't heard a word. "I can see you're both exhausted. It's been an eventful day, and more so for you than us. Why don't you go on back to your hotel and get some rest?"

Vignette stepped between them and addressed O'Grady with a tactful smile. "Good idea. Thank you. We also have to see if Dante came back. He was gone when we woke up this morning, and we're hoping he just went to take in the sights."

"Do you think that's what he did?"

"No."

◇

Dante hugged Eliana as tightly as he could while he also pounded on her back with the sides of his fists, crying so hard he could barely get out the words. "Never, never, never do that again!"

"I'm so sorry, Dante!" Eliana sobbed, holding him. "I didn't know how to protect you! You had to get away from that man and his miserable wife! Every day you spent there was, was..." She couldn't finish the thought, but there was no need.

"I know. I know. He was trying to steal my soul. Wasn't he?"

"Worse than that. He was trying to get you to give it away. For his lies."

They remained in that position, slowly rocking each other in the pitch darkness of one of the hospital's abandoned holding cells. He had been dragged in by Mannerly, still unconscious from something he knew they used to keep the prisoners under control. There was enough light from Clayton's lantern to recognize him in the few seconds before he had stepped back out and locked the door behind himself.

Dante quickly threw off the grogginess when he heard Eliana's voice and realized they were alone together, but it took him several long minutes to calm down and become rational after he demanded to know what happened to her.

Eliana just held him and kept repeating motherly words of love to him. She knew her words would eventually soak in because she knew her Dante. One of the reasons she sent him away was knowing he had already seen far too much of her degradation at Clayton's hands, at the hands of his clients. She had faith that Dante's goodness of heart and sense of honesty would someday lead him to understand her despair, that he would bleed for her as she bled for him. He would see her actions as the desperate gesture of hope they were. She trusted him to see it.

"When they stole my daughters from me and took me away from my home, they told me my girls were sold to rich people far away. People who lost their own children in the war and don't care how they get new ones. Their names were taken from them, so I have no way to look for them or know if they survived. At first, I was going to try to escape, but after a while I realized there was nowhere to go. My heart was too heavy to start life again." She looked at Dante. "Then you showed up, and I saw your goodness right away. I couldn't protect my own goodness, but I had to help you protect yours. It's the only reason I tricked you."

"I know, Eliana," he whispered. "I mean, I guess I know, but we stay together now, right?"

She gasped a sob without meaning to and clapped her hand over her mouth. "Yes. Yes if that's what you want."

"It's what we both want."

She nodded. "Yes, it's what we both want."

He took a long inhale, then whispered, "I have a boat tied up down at the—"

The cell door flew open and hit the opposite wall with a heavy thud. Clayton Mannerly stood glaring at them by the light of a gasoline lantern. The door was only eight or nine feet from them, so the light played over them, forcing them to squint. Clayton Mannerly even controlled whether or not they could see.

"I have seminary students patrolling every building, Dante. How stupid can you be?"

"I figured Eliana would be here because she wasn't at the hotel."

"She was going to help entertain a few guests, but your arrival put the kibosh on that." He raised the lantern to get a better view of him. "You killed her, Dante. How does that make you feel?"

Dante leaped up to attack him, but Eliana held him back. "He never killed anybody!" she cried. "That's better than you can say!"

"Dante killed you, all right. He did it by coming back. Not here to the island but back to New York." He sneered at Dante. "You must be too ignorant to understand, you had it made! All you had to do was keep your mouth shut and stay out of the public eye. But you had to play the hero."

He turned to Eliana. "And you..." He chuckled. "Well, you were never going to leave the island, anyway, after you two betrayed me. At least you would have had the courtesy of knowing nothing about your coming death, and then the sleepy rag over your mouth, and then the big tubs before you wake up. Easy. For you, for everybody. Finally, weighted down on the bottom of the East River for all time."

Eliana slowly got to her feet to face him. She pointed a trembling finger directly between his eyes. "I curse you," she quietly said. "I curse everything

about you and your life. I curse you to the fate of dying by your own fool-
ishness. I curse you to cause your own death."

He laughed. "Pray tell, when?"

"Soon, Mr. Mannerly. Very, very soon."

"Mm. I wonder if it will come sooner than yours, which is arriving this
evening right after the guests leave." He reached for the door handle and
pulled the cell door closed. They heard the bolt slide home in the
doorframe.

Eliana shouted after him, her voice echoing in the empty building. She
slammed her hands against the door and screamed at the top of her lungs.
"The curse is on you, Mister! There is nothing you can do to escape it!
Nothing!" She stood panting at the door, listening for a response. None
came.

She rejoined Dante, and they sat in silence for a few moments. Then
Dante said, "Those big tubs are the ones he showed me before I ran away."

"I know. As soon as you told me about them, I knew we had to get you
out of here. But, oh God, Dante you're back, and I don't know what we can
do now!"

By way of answering, Dante pulled the steak knife from his beltline,
unwrapped it from the dinner napkin, then went to work picking away the
wooden frame around the barred windows. While the glass was long gone,
the bars were still deep-set and strong.

Before long, Dante realized there was no way to dig out the bars
without hours of labor. His chance of doing it in time felt immeasurably
small. He only kept working because there was nothing else to do.

Friar John lay on his cot listening to Clayton Mannerly ridiculing his two
prisoners in the next cell. Mannerly's condemnations were much like those
he often hurled at Friar John. They reminded him of his own condition as
an object of ridicule. Too many others treated mockery as if it had some
healing power. As if mocking and humiliating someone might correct
whatever their flaws or misbehaviors might be, if only the mockery were
done hard enough, long enough.

Perhaps mockery also worked that way in Friar John's life once, long ago, serving to set him back on a more correct path. But personal regrets, combined with his brutal incarceration, had performed a kind of alchemy on him.

The change went down to his bones. Every aspect of his personality that once made him a unique individual had long since fallen away. While he could still feel hunger, and to some extent pain, his capacity for pleasure of any sort was gone, burned away by shame, done in by the cruelty of a sinful condition. Because for many years, as if in a trance, he had set upon the orphaned children left in his care. He had plucked out his favorites as if he were walking through an orchard and gathering low-hanging fruit.

All the while he had no idea he was building his own stockpile of pain. Most painful of all was to wake up years later and recognize the horrors of what he had done.

Satan had fooled him good. The Beast had turned Friar John into the selfsame demon he spent his early life avoiding. Building calluses on his knees from hours spent praying to be delivered from temptation. For so many years, he had received no answer. Deliverance from temptation never arrived.

Friar John decided the Devil hated everyone whether they followed him or not. You could go onto your knees to the Great Liar, and he might laugh at you and strike you down anyway.

Some of the church's highest-ranking officials were twisted to a degree that beggared belief, and they appeared to have dodged any sort of accountability. Their corruption brought no consolation to Friar John, however. Their time of Judgment would be their own.

His time of damnation had already manifested, bringing its most painful lesson: You do not have to die to go to Hell. That dreadful place was already his home, in these closing days of his life in this plundered world.

And so it was that Friar John discovered Damnation, for all its solitary horrors, to be a condition offering a form of freedom all its own. Clayton Mannerly ought to have locked the door to his cell instead of trusting the friar's weakness to chain him down. While it was true Friar John had no way to escape the island in his wasted condition, he was surprised to discover the man he once was still had one strong move left.

The old non-friar gradually powered his body off of the cot and into a standing position, swaying slightly while his muscles adjusted to this new challenge.

Bolstered by adrenaline and rage, he took one shaky step, He took another, then another. Before long, he had crossed the little cell and was at the door. Pulling it open. Stepping through and out into the hall.

Dante and Eliana heard the rattle of the door bolt being lifted aside. Dante figured Clayton had a few more points of mockery to drop on them and so was surprised when the door swung open and there was no lantern light. He was startled by the sound of a rasping voice.

"The Lord works in mysterious ways," Friar John said, coughing at the end of the phrase. He cleared his throat and continued, "Come with me. Let's get you the hell out of here."

Dante and Eliana were not about to argue or question his motives. Out was good. Once they were all out in the hallway, they headed for the only door in the building. When they reached it, they paused to study the lock. Moonlight and a little starlight were enough to show them the door had locking bars that could be dropped either inside or outside, depending on the direction of a threat. Friar John leaned against the doorframe, gasping. "Do you—do you have some ability to get away from here?"

"I have a boat tied up down there by the shore, if we can dodge the patrols," Dante replied, keeping his voice as quiet as possible. "I don't think they do anything about empty rowboats tied up at night. Their idea is to catch people near the buildings. When they got me, they didn't do it until I was right at their door."

"Then you can avoid them because you know to look out for them. Go, then!" Friar John told them. He turned to Eliana and said, "We can still save one of them. Get him out of here!" He put one hand on each of their backs. "Go!"

Eliana hesitated. "What about you, Father?"

"Do not call me that! I lost...the right."

"Mister Clayton will know you helped us! What will you do?"

Friar John smiled for the first time in ages. "I'm going to earn my absolution."

He pushed them again, and this time they ran, checking in all directions for patrols and staying in the shadows. They both had enough strength and motivation to move like frightened rabbits.

Friar John watched, nodding, while his lips formed a grim smile. He stepped back into the building and quietly closed the heavy wooden door. He leaned his back against the thick planks and gave in to the sin of pride. He realized his spiritual error, but oh, it was a thrill to hear the desperation in that man's voice. It was a sensual joy to be the cause of it. Sin or no sin.

"Dante!" Clayton Mannerly called from the other side. "Lift the bar! What the hell are you doing? Dante!"

Father Young's voice also bellowed, "Dante! This will do you no good, young man!"

Friar John was crystal clear on his duty in that moment. Keep the men on the other side of the door from going anywhere for as long as possible. Because once the men discovered the others were already gone, they would sound the alarm and the hunt would be on.

"Dante!" Clayton called out again. "All you're doing is making me very angry! I have a sledgehammer and an axe out here, and if I have to beat this door down, you'll regret it with every drop of your blood!"

For an old evaporite long since accustomed to misery and isolation, the sense of pleasure in the feeling of power over these filthy men and all the men like them was more seductive than a wink and a come-hither smile from the Whore of Babylon. Add to that the opportunity to defy the rotten imitation of a priest, a demon in the flesh, and contravene that demon's authority. To mock its power. Oh yes.

His heart hammered in his chest. A dying man's last strength surged through him, and he found his full voice.

"They don't want to talk to you, Father! You either, Mr. Mannerly! They said you should go look for wives in a dog kennel!"

He laughed enough to start up a coughing fit that forced him to stand with his hands on his knees. But it felt good, though. So good. Sometimes sin was the best choice going.

Besides, he had this absolution he was in the middle of earning, so maybe he could just lump that sinful pride in with all his other character flaws and score forgiveness for that, too.

Because this was it. Absolution time.

"Well, gentlemen, they told me to say you're just gonna have to go to work with that axe and sledge! Oh, and something about reproducing with pigs. I'm not too sure about that one."

For the next minute, Friar John was engrossed in the actual state of prayer Father Young was likely faking on the other side of the door. Then he began to feel the axe slam into the thick wood door and begin making quick work of it.

He knew he would soon die. The prospect of being slaughtered here on this humble hospital floor filled him with anticipation as well as fear.

He was sorry to be so afraid, but he could see it clear as day. Clear as Saul on the road to Damascus. The blows raining down upon the door were actually those of his own hands, beating on the gates of heaven. "I saved them!" he cried out. "Surely that's something, Lord! I saved them!"

At that moment the heavy door caved in on its hinges. It fell inside, striking Friar John on the head and drawing a heavy flow of blood. It pinned him to the floor.

"Where are they?" screamed Clayton, still in the doorway.

"Dante!" Father Young shouted into the building, in his most powerful Sunday homily voice. Nothing.

Both men pushed inside and began to hurry down the hallway.

"You're wasting your time!" Friar John cackled like a man who could see his own salvation coming around the bend. "The stone was rolled aside! The tomb is empty!"

On that last syllable, Clayton ran back and swung the axe full force at Friar John, striking him in the back. Friar John instantly knew it was a killing blow. He felt like a bride. This was his absolution. No doubt. He had faith. Even the pain felt good, like fire burning away his countless flaws. He found himself lying flat with his cheek pressed to the cold floor. Surely this was absolution. It had to be.

"Oh, thank God," he whispered. "Oh, thank God." His facial muscles could no longer manufacture a smile, but they would have, if he had his way about it.

Mannerly and Young had no time to chase Dante and Eliana and guarantee silence from them. Their guests had already arrived, and the proceedings were about to begin. They would have to trust the sentries to hunt them down. Allison was with the party guests, holding the event together, but both men had to reappear soon if they expected the evening to succeed.

They did, because the Movers demanded sales and would expect the proceeds tomorrow morning. The real underground railroad operating in this day and age created an invisible cash flow into their coffers with each sale and each trainload. After all, they had politicians to buy off and media moguls to control. They had the magic of photography covertly capturing the misbehavior of leading financiers with photos taken by his hidden camera, wired to the main camera the guests thought was photographing the victims while it also captured their images with the same flash. Clayton had personally put the cameras in after seeing how effective they were at his hotel.

He knew the Movers would appreciate photos for future influence over the powerful dopes of popular culture. A little something to have them all dancing on a string while the Movers called the tune.

They covered the short distance without raising any alarms. Their caution kept them from being spotted. As soon as they reached the boat, Dante realized he would have to get into the water again to retrieve it. Instead, he took Eliana's hand and led her into the nearest boat. Once they were in, he rowed around to the little stolen rowboat and jumped aboard it, helping Eliana join him. The boat went down to within a few inches of the water-line but floated. He retied the larger boat and began to untie the smaller boat, but its line had become tangled in dead branches under the water. He pulled out his knife and this time felt its worth, slicing through the rope with ease.

There was no room to sit side by side and row. He had her stay in the bow and took both oars in his hands. Before starting out, he craned his neck to see the main building where Clayton's party was scheduled. He knew the victims would already be inside while the enormously rich clients milled about in front of the entrance, anticipating the marvelous and unique experience to come. He knew, from hearing Clayton talk about it on his penthouse telephone, there were politicians, entertainers, bankers, and rich people who did nothing but live on their holdings. One and all considered ordinary morality something for the unwashed masses.

He rowed in earnest and rapidly pulled away from the shoreline. In less than a minute, the fog swallowed the island and the little boat was lost in the darkness. The few remaining rowboats silently bobbed and nodded.

In a few minutes more they struck the Manhattan side of the narrow river. Their landing spot was close enough to the boat's original mooring that they quickly steered it back into place, tied up, and jumped out.

They huddled in the befogged darkness and looked inland in all direc tions, straining their senses to confirm they had arrived undetected and could safely walk away.

29

THE PLAZA HOTEL – CENTRAL PARK SOUTH

March 2nd
* Evening *

BLACKBURN AND NIGHTINGALE made the short walk from the taxicab to the door of the Plaza Hotel feeling spent. They had been given little time to recover from their long train trip before being thrown into the middle of this case, and it was taking its toll.

Vignette gave up a big yawn while they walked into the lobby. "I have to say, Randall, as tired as I am, it's going to be hard to sleep without knowing where Dante is."

"That's two of us, then."

"I'm glad we got Salsedo, but that Department of Justice office building doesn't sound like an ideal place to hold a mass murder suspect. What can they do in offices? Tie him to a desk?"

"Good question. We'll check up on him tomorrow and be sure they have him someplace secure."

"Suits me," Vignette replied while they headed for the elevator.

"Detectives!" John Smith stood up from one of the big lobby chairs and waved.

Vignette dropped her head and muttered, "Oh, damn it."

Smith hurried up to them holding his hat in his hands. "I just wanted to—"

Blackburn held up his hand. "Mr. Smith, you betrayed our confidence today."

"Hey, you still got your arrest, didn't you?" He looked back and forth between them. "Come on! We both won! No hard feelings, right?"

Vignette exhaled hard. "Why are you here, Mr. Smith? We're tired."

"Yes," agreed Blackburn, "get to your point."

"My *point* is I can still be of use to you! And I don't mean for merely arresting some anarchist bomber."

"He's more than that to us."

"Either way, he's small fry. I can get you much better quarry than a mixed-up bastard who builds bombs. Salsedo wasn't even the reason you came out here all the way from California, was he?"

Blackburn and Vignette both stiffened. Blackburn replied, "How would you know that?"

"Please. I told you I keep meticulous files, and I've got information you could use to bring people to justice."

"Why haven't you used it yet?"

"It's not for lack of trying. I've reported this three times! The reports generate no action at all. I go ask why—all I get is a runaround. I'm here tonight because I need someone on the inside who hasn't been corrupted and still has the authority to get some action."

"That's funny, Mr. Smith. We can't seem to find anybody with authority to get some action, either. The deputy commissioner and her policewomen were ready to do just that when the men you called swept in and the commissioner himself stole the arrest. Now Salsedo's at the Department of Justice instead of a proper jail cell."

"Uh-oh. The fourteenth floor?"

"That's what we hear."

"Jesus. That's where they beat them till they talk, you know."

Vignette spoke up. "Any other time, I would find that upsetting. In his case, I've got no sympathy."

Blackburn added, "Plus, if he volunteers the information they need, he won't have to take any beatings at all."

"Good, then can we forget him now?" Smith asked. "Believe me, you have much bigger fish to fry. I've got files on this six inches thick! You know about a man named Mario Buda?"

"Do we? He was behind the San Francisco bombing four years ago. We nearly had him, but he slipped away."

"Slipped away and came back here, is what he did. Laid low for a while, then got back to his old tricks."

"Why the hell would an anarchist get involved with monetary elites like bankers and corporate owners?"

"You mean rich bastards? Buda says it helps if you think of them like that."

"Okay. Rich bastards."

"They're planning something, Detective. It has to be something big. Why would the country's rich bastards get in bed with anarchists?"

"A common goal of some kind. I have no idea what it could be."

"There you have it! What do you say, Detectives, water under the bridge? No hard feelings? We have important work ahead of us."

"All right," Blackburn said. "You go see Deputy Commissioner O'Grady tomorrow. If you can convince her to let you in on this, we'll work with you."

"Randall!" Vignette hissed. "He ruined the arrest of the man who killed Shane!"

"Not ruined! Not ruined," Smith chirped. "They got him, didn't they? Besides, if they have him at the DOJ, my story will never see print, anyway. They have to keep the place from the public eye."

"You went from the prospect of having a minor story to having no story at all, didn't you?"

"No need to rub it in. My profession is subject to the vagaries of chance, just like yours, Detectives."

"All right," said Blackburn. "We'll leave it like this. If I get a call tomorrow from Commissioner O'Grady telling me you're on the team, you can track this investigation with our cooperation. Otherwise we have to freeze you out."

"Which we would certainly do, otherwise," added Vignette. "You made no friends with that stunt."

Smith closed his mouth, smiled, saluted them, then turned and walked away in the wrong direction. He realized it was the wrong direction, stopped, and reversed himself to travel across the lobby and out the front door. His ability to quit while he was ahead was part of what made him a successful interviewer.

"See you tomorrow!" he called back with a jaunty wave.

Blackburn just waved. Vignette replied under her breath, "Maybe."

Vignette and Randall arrived at the room to find Dante home again, fresh from the bath and wrapped in a towel, sitting on the floor next to the bathroom door. Steam rolled out the door while he sat laughing over something or other. From inside the bathroom, a woman could be heard laughing along with him. They remained unaware of the two tired detectives who had just shuffled in.

Dante went on, "I didn't think having a pocket dictionary was all that humorous, but she seemed to find it so funny. I mean, it practically made her scream!"

The female voice came from inside the bathroom, making a mock scream of terror.

They both laughed again at that.

Dante was mid-laugh when he realized they had company. He stopped, but the woman was still laughing while she walked out of the bathroom, one towel wrapped around her while she dried her hair with another. Her laugh stopped there. She looked at Dante.

He leaped to his feet, looking the picture of awkwardness.

"Dante!" Vignette happily cried. "You're back! Where did you—"

"I had to look for Eliana, you guys! I had to do it."

Vignette spoke right over Dante, "It's all right! It's all right!" She turned to Eliana. "Hello again, Eliana," she said, gesturing to Randall. "This is

Randall Blackburn." She met his eyes and smiled. "He's my father. We also work together."

Blackburn smiled and said, "Hello, Eliana. We've heard a lot about you. Dante thinks very highly of you."

"Yes, hello," Eliana replied, then touched her fingertips to Dante's cheek. "I did not want him to look for me, but he did. He came to save me."

Vignette turned back to Dante. "I'm so glad to see you. To see you both."

"I am too! It was wonderful to have a place to go, to take her. And we both needed to get all cleaned up."

"In that case, I'm glad the place was here for you too," Blackburn said. "Dante, we don't have to do it tonight, but sometime soon I would love to hear about whatever has gone on with you since we saw you last."

"No, Randall. We can't do that."

"Why not?"

"When you tell, it puts you back in the... It puts you... I mean, it feels like I managed to get out, and thank God I'm out, but now I'm supposed to turn around and go back? I tell you, my bones feel cold when I think of doing that."

"All right. I understand. Whatever happened, you dealt with it and over-came it. You two got yourselves back here. We can just be glad for that."

Eliana responded, "Thank you, Mister. I don't know what to say. I am so grateful to see my Dante again."

"To be expected." Vignette glanced toward the bathroom where Eliana's rags lay on the floor. "Ah, Eliana, let's check out my suitcase. I think we're close enough in size to get you something to wear for now."

Eliana's face flushed, and she nodded in gratitude.

"Don't worry, Auntie." Smiled Dante. "We're together now, and we're both away from Clayton and the Movers."

"Where did you find her, Dante?"

"Blackwell's Island. I couldn't tell you before."

"Why not?"

"Well...look, I'm sorry. But I had to take care of it myself. What if you sent a bunch of cops there and got Eliana killed? Or what if they kidnapped her and took her away?"

"Why would anyone do that?" Blackburn asked.

Eliana responded, "It's how I ended up here in America."

"As soon as I found out she wasn't at the hotel, I knew she had to be on the island at the old asylum."

"Old asylum. Why would it even occur to you to go there?"

"Clayton holds the special parties there sometimes. They had one last night. They have big empty buildings and nobody is around who can tell on them. Part of the hospital is still open, but if any of the patients ever got wise and tried to tell anybody, who would listen? After we tried the hotel, I had to check the island."

He looked over at Eliana and then asked Blackburn in a small voice, "You'd never send her back, would you?"

"What?" Blackburn exclaimed. "No. Trust me, it's obvious, the two of you belong together."

Vignette nodded. "Even though we don't have a clear picture of everything going on, we know you both needed to be out of there."

"All right," said Blackburn. "We're all beat. Let's put this down until tomorrow."

"Good enough for me," said Dante. "Eliana, you take my room. I'm gonna sleep on the sofa out here."

Eliana touched his cheek with her fingertips again and smiled.

In the morning, the hotel staff tucked a copy of the *New York Daily Herald* under their door, and while Eliana and Vignette took turns using the bathroom, Blackburn sat reading a small article buried on page six: *Crazed Asylum Inmate on Blackwell's Island Kills Priest Sent to Comfort Him.*

Dante had told him a little more about the escape last night, scant details, but the newspaper story sounded wrong. Blackburn wondered who possessed the authority to slant a news story so far from the facts. Why did they get away with it?

He was about to ask Dante about it when the hotel room phone rang on the other side of the suite. Blackburn laughed when he heard Dante say, "Blackburn and Nightingale, Private Investigations."

After another moment, he said, "Yes, ma'am! Here he is." He covered the mouthpiece and said to Blackburn, "It's Commissioner O'Grady. She wants to talk to you about an apartment."

Blackburn walked to the phone and took the receiver, wondering what an apartment could have to do with their case. O'Grady quickly set him straight.

"Good morning, Detective," she began in her usual brisk, no-nonsense tone. "It's becoming clear your visit will have to be an extended one, unless you refuse to help us and decide to leave."

"We haven't given any thought to leaving, Commissioner."

"Good to hear, but I caught your remark yesterday that it's difficult to stay gone for so long. It struck me because, as it happens, my husband and I have a rental property here in Brooklyn and our tenants moved out last week. We've both been too busy to deal with it. My idea is to lease it to the city for as long as you are here, and have you stay there. As long as I don't lose money on the proposition, my husband agrees to it. City will pay fair market rate. However, the Plaza is so expensive I fear the city might send you home just to save money, and leave us in the lurch. In fact, if any of the people involved in this corruption ring are involved with that decision, I'd say they'll get you out of here as quick as they can. So let's not give 'em an excuse. What do you say?"

"That's, ah, that's generous of you, Commissioner."

"Nonsense. It's practical for all of us."

"I understand, but last night Dante returned with his aunt, who was indentured to Clayton Mannerly. There's something very wrong going on with that man and his hotel, although I don't have enough details yet. I have no intention of turning her in for breaking her contract to a man like that, and I hope you won't either."

"Not my fight, Detective. You can trust me on that. By the way, the place has three bedrooms, plus a small library you could convert if you want to. Room for Dante and his aunt, everybody will fit. Save 'em a bundle."

"Remarkable generosity, Commissioner."

"More or less. It's also a good way to keep the woman around."

"Eliana."

"Right. We might need testimony from her. Never know. It'll be helpful to have a place to meet where my office subordinates can't pick up gossip."

Blackburn laughed at that. "In that case, Commissioner, it sounds as though you have a plan and we'd be wise to sign up for it."

"Good. Can you move today? The desk told me checkout time is at one o'clock. Just come to my place, and I'll walk you over."

"One o'clock, then. It's clear you don't let any grass grow under your feet. We'll see you at your home today. And thank you for this most generous—"

"Knock it off, Detective. I'm taking care of my own business here, too. See you this afternoon. Good day." With that, she rang off and the line went dead.

"Doesn't mince words. Says 'goodbye,' though. Hey, everyone, change of plans. Commissioner O'Grady has an apartment near her home where we can stay for as long as we need. Having a private place is always better than a hotel. Dante, I know I don't even have to ask Vignette first to say you and Eliana are welcome."

"He's right," agreed Vignette. "He doesn't. You are."

"The Commissioner says you'll have room for both of you to stay awhile. Start putting your lives back together."

"Oh, this is so good!" Eliana replied. "I would be happiest to keep Dante close to me."

"Me too," Dante said, beaming. "We talked about it first thing when we were back together. No more sending me away anyplace. She's never allowed to forget how important she is to me."

Eliana smiled at him and touched his cheek with her fingertips again. "I touch his face like this. To say 'I love you.'" Then she stood straighter and looked them both in the eyes. "I will earn my way by keeping up the apartment and doing the cooking, shopping for groceries. These are things I can do for us all."

"Don't you want to take some time to recover?"

She gestured to Dante. "This is my recovery."

"That settles it, then," Blackburn said. "Let's get ready to make the move, then go downstairs and hail a cab."

"Suits me," Vignette replied. "I don't want to leave town until we know what happens to Shane's killer." She stepped into her room, gesturing for Eliana to follow, and opened her suitcase while she pressed her point. "I want them to make him talk. I want to know why he did it." She removed several different items of clothing and began to hang them in the closet. "Most of all I want to know if there was anyone else involved. If there's anyone still out there..."

Blackburn saw no reason to express his own suspicions about that.

30

MARIO BUDA'S COBBLER SHOP – BROOKLYN

March 3rd
* After Midnight *

MARIO BUDA HUNG UP THE TELEPHONE RECEIVER and let his shoulders sag. Another ultimatum from the Movers, delivered by a voice he did not recognize in a call from a location he did not know. He had come to depend on those filthy people, and now it was all coming back to him in terrible ways. So far in life he had only survived by employing caution at levels near paranoia while maintaining his pose as a mere cobbler. Lately that pose had forced him to lease a cobbler shop he could never afford, if not for help from the Movers, along with a small used truck that he affixed with a "Cobbler" sign on each side door. No matter how he felt about it, he was in bed with them.

Their help was vital, but their interference was infuriating. The worst part by far was having to waste his time in the fixing of boots and shoes, just so he could have something to point to if the police came sniffing around. After the arrest of that idiot Salsedo, such a visit seemed guaranteed to occur soon. He regretted not killing him when he had the opportunity.

He was enraged by the moron's carelessness. He thanked his lucky stars that the night before, hours after Salsedo's arrest, it had occurred to him to sneak into the print shop and clear out anything Salsedo left behind, anything that might give the authorities information on the coming operation.

His lock picks had managed to get the lock open, but the door could barely be pushed inward an inch before it was stopped by a thick chain on the inside. He was forced to go around to the more exposed front of the shop and use his picks there. Despite his fears, he made it inside without being spotted.

He struck a match inside the darkened shop and looked around in the amber light. Salsedo's press was free of pamphlets or flyers, and the small back room where Buda watched him assemble a detonator showed no trace of anything involved with explosives.

The shop was clean.

Next he climbed the narrow stairs to Salsedo's sleeping room above the shop and picked his way inside with ease. Buda took a quick look around and shook his head. He knew the authorities were watching Salsedo's home, his wife, his children. There was nothing for the man to do but accept these humble circumstances.

As far as Buda was concerned, the two men's backgrounds explained their deep differences despite their ideological agreements. Buda grew up as an impoverished son of a common laborer, motivating him to learn his trade early in life to guarantee the ability to work, no matter where he traveled. He could repair shoes on his kitchen table if he needed to.

Salsedo, however, depended upon being an employee at a print shop. Getting hired, keeping the job, avoiding conflicts with other workers. Keeping those fellow workers in the dark about his real work while he maintained a front that allowed him to walk the streets as a working man. It was too much deception to maintain for long, and Salsedo obviously failed at it.

Buda spotted a sack of dirty laundry on the floor beneath the cot, which he realized was a good disguise element; who wanted to handle someone else's dirty laundry? Buda did, at that moment. He snatched up the laundry bag, tossed it behind himself, and got down on his hands and knees to have a look.

"Idiot!" he shouted without meaning to. He slapped his hand over his mouth and glanced around, then relaxed as he recalled the shop was empty. Still, there they were; Salsedo had left two extremely powerful bombs and their detonators under his bed, just waiting to be discovered. No lockbox of any kind. No sealed cabinet. So proud of his work, he apparently wanted to sleep on top of it and keep it unboxed where he could easily see it. Buda guessed the fool thought that since he worked right downstairs, he could guard them well enough.

He located Salsedo's sole suitcase, opened it, then realized it would not hold even one of the bombs, let alone both. He kicked the suitcase aside and took one bomb under each arm. The devices were heavier than they looked, each in excess of fifteen kilos.

He felt satisfaction in their heft. Although the bombs were built by Salsedo, it was done with techniques he could never have known how to employ if not for special tutelage under the Bomb Maker Nonpareil. Buda set the bombs down, opened the door, picked them back up, and set them down again on the other side of the door long enough to relock it, then hoisted them again and made his way downstairs and to the front entrance, carrying enough explosive power to kill and maim hundreds of people at a time.

If he were a praying man, he might have offered up thanks for the police officers who were so blind in making Salsedo's arrest, charging in behind their headline-grabbing commissioner and allowing their excitement to prevent them from thinking things through while they were still at the scene. He loved stupid police officers, the dumber the better, but since they would have found out where Salsedo was living shortly after they began their interrogation, they would no doubt be back to search the living space above the print shop in the morning. Maybe even before sunrise.

Let them come, he thought. *There'll be nothing for them to find. They'll go away thinking they stopped him before he could do anything.* One of the few things in this life Mario Buda loved even more than stupid police officers was the incompetent police work they performed.

He carried the bombs to his truck at the curb. An odd mixture of giddy excitement and grim determination came over him. The bombs were now in his hands, and he might even have time to wire up several more of the petulant little sweethearts, so long as the people paying his bills believed they were needed. He got all the way back to his cobbler shop two miles away and carried the bombs inside without seeing another soul.

To keep up appearances, he would have to call overseas and speak to Signore Galleani about this loss with Salsedo's capture. He knew Galleani would issue a black mark against Salsedo; the man knew far too much. Nobody could hold up under the terrible things the NYPD was known to do to prisoners. He would talk. He would sing like a bird at sunrise. And if the consequences of his confessions were dire enough, they could threaten the entire overall mission with regard to the upcoming election, along with its glorious potential to keep their movement funded over the long term.

Once back inside his shop, he sat down and began working, fitting one tall boot onto his iron shoe stand while he sized the other with a boot stretcher, correcting shoddy work done by some other cobbler. With barely more than six months to go before the big operation commenced, he could not risk getting himself picked up the way Salsedo was.

He opened a paper bag with the remains of the prior day's lunch and sat back with a contented sigh. He felt comfortable with the night's excursion and carried no anxiety at all. His thoughts began to wander in lazy circles. Clearly, the insight he displayed by realizing Salsedo's place had to be emptied out was complemented by his resourcefulness as the Bomb Maker Non—

A heavy knock sounded at his door.

It was still dark outside. Buda's brain went into overdrive: Police? No, the knock was not forceful enough. They liked to intimidate and frighten people when they came calling. A salesman? Not at this hour. A potential customer? No, for the same reason.

A thief? Perhaps. A robber checking to see if anyone was inside...

Who else would it be? Surely, it was some filthy capitalist bastard hoping to have the chance to break in and take advantage of a working man. Steal his money and leave him in the lurch.

Buda picked up a heavy leather hammer and stepped to the door. "Who's there?" he called in his toughest voice.

"Mr. Buda!" came a man's voice from the other side. "My name is John Smith. I'm with the *New York Daily Herald*. Nothing to worry about! May I talk to you for just a moment?"

"How did you find my shop?"

"Public record of new business leases in Brooklyn this month. Only two cobblers, the other place is run by a Chinese guy, so, not you."

"Yes, but how did you know I would be inside here?"

"It's funny, but I actually fell asleep at the wheel while I surveilled the place, and the only thing that woke me up was you slamming the shop door when you left a while ago."

This man saw him leave? His heartbeat hammered in his mouth.

Buda slowly opened the door a crack. This John Smith turned out to be a young man around twenty or so, a bit on the short side. Harmless looking in a doughy kind of way.

"Hello!" Smith said with too much enthusiasm and a smile that did not belong on Buda's shop porch at that hour. "Name's John Smith, like I said. Reporter."

"John Smith, reporter, why would you come here at this hour?"

Smith was instantly apologetic, "Oh, I wouldn't! I never would! I mean, people need their sleep, yes? I proved that this evening by falling asleep when I was trying to do surveillance. Ha! No amount of discipline makes up for fatigue, correct?"

"That's the second time you mentioned surveillance. Why would—"

"So I followed you when you drove off in your truck—" He paused, then added, "To the Canzani Print Shop over on Fifth."

There was a long pause while Buda looked at Smith with eyes like a hungry shark. "No hard feelings, Mr. Buda! Believe me! I don't want to cause you the slightest trouble. May I please come in and talk with you?"

"Afraid to talk out here? In case someone else is also doing surveillance?"

"Ha! Funny! I didn't know you were funny! See? People need to know more about you! Understand your thoughts. For example, your English is almost as good as a native speaker. Information like that can generate the kind of respect worthy of the 'Bomb Maker Nonpareil.'"

The term struck Buda like a nightstick to the head. How would this little man know that name? Consternation ruined any pleasure he would ordinarily take in hearing his title. He could not imagine where this so-called reporter learned it.

"Wait a moment." Buda closed the door, picked up a blanket, and tossed it over the bomb parts on his kitchen table, then stepped back and opened the door wide.

Smith wasted no time hurrying in. Buda closed the door behind him but remained standing next to it, watching. Smith pulled out a chair from the kitchen table and gestured to it. "So, good, this is good, mind if I sit? Right about here? Won't be but a minute or two."

Buda eyed the blanket covering the pile on the table, but Smith behaved as if nothing was there. "State your business."

Smith broke into a smile. "Publicity! Plain and simple. We like plain speech in this country, so here's the thing: if you have a friend on the paper, you can get stories slanted to suit you and not your opponents. Hot diggity! Want to hear more?"

Buda slowly moved to the kitchen table and sat across from Smith. "I know this already. Why am I hearing it from you?"

"All right. Cards on the table. I'm a stringer for the *Daily Herald*. If I bring them a great story, I'll get hired on full-time. You are a great story. Your thoughts, your struggle."

"Some of your readers want to see me put to death."

"Sure, and some of them want to bring back the slave days. They don't get to have what they want, that's all."

"But you. You can get me what I want."

"Possibly. I can't if we don't try, though, can I?"

"What, specifically, do you need from me?"

"Only what you want to tell me, nothing more. You control the flow of information, I shape it. Think about it: for years you've had to read whatever the papers wanted to print about you. I'm offering to put the reins in your hands!"

Smith lowered his voice to a whisper and leaned across the table. He spoke directly over the pile of covered bomb parts, which he persisted in not noticing. "Let's face it, the elites of our society get to tell the public anything they want to say, using news services they own and control. Why shouldn't you get in on some of that?"

"And in return, you bring me..."

"I'm inside the investigation into the Movers."

"How soon will you be dead if they find out?"

"I don't like showing my cards, Mr. Buda, but sometimes I have no choice, to persuade people to talk to me. In your case, I'd say there's an enormous opportunity in talking."

Buda caught Smith's gaze flickering down to the covered pile for half an instant before Smith looked back at him and smiled a smile that was still too broad and too happy for the occasion.

He held Smith's gaze while he leaned over to the counter, picked up two glasses and a bottle of grappa, then dropped one glass in front of Smith and placed the other in front of himself. He poured.

"Maybe we talk a little more."

They raised their glasses in an informal toast before tossing back the grappa. The pile of blanket-covered bomb parts lay directly between them. Neither man so much as glanced at it.

CITY SQUIRE HOTEL – TOP-FLOOR PENTHOUSE
LOWER MIDTOWN, MANHATTAN

March 3rd
* 8:30 a.m. *

THE REVEREND CANON RICHARD YOUNG stood next to Clayton Mannerly, directly behind one of the oversized penthouse windows. He stared down at the extraordinary views of the city below them. Not Paris, to be sure, not even London for all that. But in the fresh energy of morning, Manhattan was a powerhouse of a metropolis clawing its way to international dominance with every passing year. Daylight revealed its true nature, beyond the din of traffic chaos, the fumes, and the trash. It laid bare the slabs of muscle operating the city and showed the anatomy of a seething creature trapped in new skin already too small, hungry for growth in all directions.

The iron of war had served its purpose, Clayton mused. A decade earlier, the Movers decided to shift massive amounts of wealth and industry on a worldwide basis, so they bought chains of newspapers and newswire services around the western hemisphere and spent a couple of years manipulating public opinion and making certain very few people ever got the chance to hear anything more than what the Movers told them. The quicksand of their war pulled in North America and all of Europe, along with parts of Asia.

Germany was only the trigger charge on the entire powder keg of Western Europe, and Clayton had nearly poured his own blood into the cause. Now the gold of peace lay strewn before him across a field of opportunity. He had just finished telling Father Young that he and everybody else who survived the Great War deserved their share.

The Reverend Canon did not care to engage on the topic. "Concentrate, Clayton. We are not here to discuss government payouts, or whatever bits and pieces Uncle Sam chooses to share with us. We're here to look for ways to sustain ongoing payouts from the people who run those governments, whether the public knows about them or not."

Clayton kept his gaze out the window and down on the streets. "That's what we've been doing all along. Isn't it?"

"Clayton, concentrate! What will you tell people about your wife? You need a believable story."

Clayton's entire body stiffened, but he did not shift his gaze from outside. "Do you think she was aware of anything when it happened?"

"No chance. I sent the same young men after her who caught Dante. Told them they needed to make up for letting the boy escape, and the best way to avoid temporary tub time for them was to put Mrs. Mannerly in the tub. For permanent."

"Well, ah, it's done, then? By now?"

"She's either settling to the bottom of the East River or riding an underwater tide along the bottom and on out to sea, even as we speak. They know how to attach those little air bags so the weighted body will float underwater for a while before the air leaks out someplace downstream, maybe even someplace out to sea. Fish get 'em. Crabs."

"I wonder if she thought it was me grabbing her? Do you think she had time to wonder about that?"

"The chloroform is virtually instantaneous. A moment of concern on her part, and she knows nothing after that. Unconsciousness, submersion, rapid drowning, processing the body for a trip down the East River, in that order."

"I wish there was another way to take care of the problem."

"Listen, you're worried about the one part we can control ourselves. It's everyplace else along the supply line where we stand vulnerable to other people and their stupid mistakes. But we can be expert at cleaning out our houses. As we did last night."

"Okay, I just, I don't want to hear next week some fisherman pulled her out of the water, you know?"

"Pulled her... Clayton, you can't forget the main reason the Movers use us, *need* us, is our ability to utilize the hospital to get rid of rejects! Their rejects! Untraceable disappearances. They can buy, rent, or borrow other meeting houses in plenty of other places. You think your hotel is so unique?"

"Excuse me, it's also located near the train station and in the middle of Manhattan. In its own way, it's as sheltered as Blackwell's Island."

"Right, and once again, they can buy that anyplace. But! A reliable system to eliminate and dispose of any man, woman, or child who is too sick, too crippled, or too ornery for the slave trade? Golden! Pure gold! Not even the Movers are powerful enough to withstand the reaction if all this were to be exposed. You can't forget that."

"It just seems so wrong. Allison was only trying to chat up the governor and his lieutenant. Then you got that phone call."

"She used the word 'slave,' Clayton. We can never say that. We call them indentured servants. When she referred to them as slaves, she more or less called the governor, his lieutenant, and every rich and powerful bastard at that party a slave trader."

"She didn't mean—"

"It's 1920, Clayton. Nobody wants to be called a slave trader anymore."

"She was my *wife*, Father Young."

"I know. Out of courtesy to you, I had my best men do it. It's also why I can guarantee you, she had no time for any but the briefest flash of concern. Perhaps a quick prayer. All to the good, in that case, eh?"

Clayton fought to remain calm and conceal his state of alarm while the priest seemed to swell in size like a parade balloon. He realized he was trapped. There was nowhere else to go and nothing to be done about it.

"Yes, Father," replied Clayton's meek side. It was a relief to surrender control.

32

O'GRADY'S LOANER APARTMENT & O'GRADY'S RESIDENCE
BROOKLYN

March 3rd
* Midmorning *

THE BORROWED APARTMENT WAS A THREE-STORY brownstone done in finely crafted masonry on a street lined with similar structures. The flat occupied the ground floor, boasting wide windows for maximum light. There was plenty of open space, with rooms as large as those in a private home. The apartment came with indoor toilets, still a luxury in some quarters, basic furniture, a functioning icebox in the kitchen, hot and cold water, a working telephone bolted to the wall, and a brand-new phone book. More than enough for their needs.

They chose their bedrooms, an easy job since all were good choices. Then Vignette popped into the kitchen long enough to check the cupboards and cheerfully announce they had a supply of old but service-able dishes along with enough pots and pans for cooking.

Dante and Eliana made grateful noises while they stumbled off to their rooms, where they each lay down on their beds without undressing. The apartment grew quiet while Blackburn and Vignette unpacked their few things and checked out the unit.

The telephone rang with a loud jangle. Vignette snatched up the receiver on the first ring in hopes of not waking Dante and Eliana. "Hello?"

"Detective Nightingale?"

"Good morning, Commissioner."

"I see you found the keys I left for you. Sorry I couldn't be there. I've been dealing with the Salsedo case and mostly getting nowhere."

"Can we help you with that?"

"I wish you could, but the whole department has gone silent on me. Even at my rank, I can't find out anything about his case. I've learned they do in fact have him buried over at the Department of Justice, in one of the holding cells they don't have, for interrogations they don't conduct. But that's about it. I only have one informant over at headquarters, while it seems like half the department's compromised."

"Compromised by whom, Commissioner?"

"Let's not say more over the phone."

"Agreed. I hope it's all right, but I'd like to leave Dante and Eliana here. They're going to need time to rest."

"That's fine. I called to ask you and Detective Blackburn to come by my home, and it's best if they're left to themselves. I also called my secretary and told her to explain to any visitors that I'm out on a case all day today."

"Does she know about us? I mean, is it all right for us to call you at your office?"

"No."

"Can she not be trusted?"

"Who knows? She draws a fine salary, but how badly does she think she needs money? Does her husband gamble? Maybe she refuses to cut her coat to fit the cloth she's got, so she never has enough cash on hand. Can I trust her, then, with these 'Movers' slinking around passing out cash like candy?"

"I'm guessing no."

"Fact is, I don't trust her because I can't, and that's a heartbreaker because I like her. But sometimes people you like will still betray you. So I treat her as if I do trust her while I remind myself not to."

"Commissioner, that sounds like me on any given morning."

O'Grady laughed. "So you're in the right place! See you in thirty minutes or so? It's an easy walk. Less than a mile."

"Yes. See you soon," she replied, and put the receiver back on the hook. It often felt odd, trying to end a conversation over a telephone line. But Vignette was intoxicated by this woman, a self-made powerhouse who actually addressed her as a colleague. None of Vignette's other-ness appeared to make any difference to her.

She turned to Blackburn. "Commissioner's house in half an hour. What say we walk it?"

"Good. I could use the exercise."

Vignette looked in on Dante and Eliana. Both were sound asleep, dead to the world. She didn't have the heart to wake them just to tell them she and Randall were going to see the Commissioner. Instead she left a note on a scrap of paper torn from the phone book.

Their coats were more than enough to keep them warm while they left the brownstone apartment and took the brisk hike to O'Grady's home. The weather was sunny with a chill wind, fairly mild for a late-winter day.

John Smith sat parked down the street in a nondescript Ford jalopy he got from his landlord, who was more than happy to make the trade for the day. The delighted landlord had driven away laughing in Smith's luxury Nash Touring Car, while Smith climbed into the Model T to bump his way over the potholes in the city streets.

The sacrifice paid off when Blackburn and his daughter or whoever she was passed by him without so much as a glance. His engine was already running, so he allowed them to gain a few car lengths and then fell in behind them. His eyes were blurry with fatigue, but he had a supply of hot coffee in his unbreakable Stanley Thermos Bottle. He sipped while he drove with one hand.

Smith's parents often cited the dangers to journalists who dared to expose the underbelly of things. Smith, on the other hand, was drawn to the work for the chance to do precisely that. He had chatted up O'Grady's secretary for half an hour before she revealed that while her husband did not gamble or drink to excess, she still never seemed to have enough money. It cost Smith the equivalent of two car payments to convince her to part with the detectives' new address, but now while he drove along behind them, he was glad to have spent the money.

He would get the Touring Car paid off somehow. After he finally brought this story in, and did it no matter how high up the levels of society it climbed, he would own the damned car outright. Drive it to the folks' place for Sunday dinner and step out like it was nothing.

"So here's the part I didn't want to discuss on the telephone," Commissioner O'Grady began as soon as Randall and Vignette were seated. "I mentioned earlier, I have this one informant at police headquarters. I received a call from him this morning."

"Him?" asked Vignette.

O'Grady smiled. "One of the good ones."

"See?" Vignette said to Randall with a wide grin. "You're not the last one."

"Oh no," he modestly agreed. "Top ten, maybe."

"At any rate, I've just learned that the down-low gossip around our illustrious headquarters is saying three of the department's top administrators were at a spontaneous market set up over on Blackwell's Island last night. One of the abandoned hospital buildings. Apparently they do it periodically, and the organizers call them 'soirees.'"

"Let me guess," Vignette said. "Soirees that are actually markets. For people."

"Short answer: yep. But if you ask, you'll be told they're merely selling high-value, high-priced contracts. Legal instruments. Contracts for indentured labor, meaning the so-called indentured people all signed contracts, trading away so many months or years of their lives in return for some form of badly needed payment. That amount becomes their selling price, plus interest. Anyone with the money can buy or sell their contract and take them home."

Randall spoke in a dry tone, "It's 'not slavery,' because the contract is mutual."

"They can claim they're only selling contracts, not people." Vignette snapped it out harder than she intended. "Essentially, a magnet for evil. That's what we're looking at here, aren't we?"

O'Grady nodded and replied, "We aren't through brightening your day just yet, Detectives. No, no, proving once again that the Devil really is in the details, the owners of the contract are in possession of fine print which enables them to charge back the 'indentured' person for food, medicine, certain other expenses. If the indentured person goes into the hole on expenses, as they must surely do, their only recourse is to sell more time. More pieces of their lives. Most will never come close to working their way out. The adults sign up out of sheer desperation, and the kids get dragged into it because they've got no say."

Randall threw a glance at Vignette, which she caught and understood. Something was about to spring here. He spoke up, "Did your, ah, informant attend?"

"No, no, just gossip. Like I said. Which is a perfect lead-in for today's message. As you can see, we have to know more. Fast. Soon. Manners take a back seat, all due apologies. But information against these people is at a premium, nearly impossible to come by. So, then, who has this information, or at least some of this information, besides your two guests currently asleep in my apartment?"

Vignette realized the commissioner was talking about having Dante and Eliana testify. She leaped to her feet. "No, Commissioner. Not yet! They need to be left in peace. They need time to—"

"Hear me out, now!" The commissioner somehow managed to shout without raising her voice. "I don't want to have to put them into protective custody, but I will! I know they've had a hard time of it. But I also know a lot more people are having the same hard time *while we sit here*." She took a couple of paces behind her desk, then turned back to them. "No. The only way I can see to leave those two walking the streets is if they are staying at my place. With you."

Randall looked at her in consternation. "As you know, you have that already."

"For now."

"Commissioner, it's very difficult to leave our home in San Francisco and be away from our other work for a long period of time, and we've already been gone longer than—"

"I spoke with Mayor Rolph this morning. In addition to sounding terribly hungover, he assured me your home is safe and regularly patrolled. You may have your city services turned back on the moment you arrive, restoring your home to full function the same day. Next week, next month, as you require. You should hear how he talks about you! Both of you! Walk on water! He'll see to it you can return to San Francisco the moment your judgment fails you and you deliberately leave New York. As far as your work goes, do either of you want to tell me you've got something going on more important than this back home?"

There was an awkward pause. "Eventually," O'Grady continued in a soft, careful tone, almost a whisper. "I'm going to need...we're going to need...Dante and Eliana to testify against Clayton Mannerly. I know you hate it, but if we can get this into a courtroom, the case will need them."

"That's a big if. In the meantime, they've refused to say much of anything. I don't want to force them."

O'Grady sighed and nodded. "Here it is: we can try it the kind and gentle way, but if it fails, we still need results. This case cries out for answers. The three who attended the soiree, they couldn't have had the money to buy somebody's contract. So why were they there? Security service for the elites? Out of the rest of the brass, how many others are compromised without attending the thing? Detectives, I need you in New York because at a time when we most need the united power of the NYPD, we don't know who to trust."

"Outside our little circle," Randall muttered.

Vignette felt a heavy weight on her chest. This woman she so admired, and whose approval felt so fine, seemed not to understand what it might do to Dante and Eliana to be dragged through all that again, and to be put at risk of retaliation from the Movers. Back in San Francisco, Dante had loudly proclaimed himself to be "shed of it." Faced with such a prospect, he would undoubtedly grab the first opportunity to flee and take his chances on the streets.

Vignette shared a level of knowledge with Dante about the depths of depravity displayed by the "old ones," as Dante called anyone no longer a child. She knew too much to tolerate the idea of him living out there alone. It could not be allowed to happen.

She and Randall reluctantly agreed to report back if either of the pair showed any signs at all of wanting to go on the run. And if Eliana and Dante had a conversation between themselves, either Randall or Vignette was to try to listen in. Put them under a microscope and keep them there.

And in return, Randall and Vignette could keep a bubble around the pair that might allow them to recover in peace. Randall assured the commissioner they would remain vigilant for any details about the way these so-called Movers were able to operate. He shot Vignette the "don't argue" look and flicked his eyes toward the door. She immediately stood, and he followed right behind.

They made for the door and got underway out on the sidewalk as quickly as tact would permit.

33

THE LOANER APARTMENT
BROOKLYN

March 3rd
* Afternoon *

RANDALL AND VIGNETTE ALLOWED Dante and Eliana to sleep into late afternoon before they woke them for a talk, and also gave them both time to get washed up and have a meal before they got down to business. Randall delivered most of the message, since he had the greatest amount of experience with the mind-set of serious crime perpetrators such as those they faced. He came right out and told them what O'Grady asked of him and Vignette, about how important it was to stop the Movers, or, given the size of the organization, to at least interrupt its function.

If it could be done.

"So it comes to this. I can't begin to imagine what you have both been through because of Clayton Mannerly and his cohorts."

Eliana replied, "He is one of many. They are like ants, roaches, mice. Remove one, another steps right in."

"She's right about that," Dante solemnly agreed.

Vignette felt his words in her chest. She ached to think of what the young boy had been forced to come to know that would cause him to agree with something like that.

"Commissioner O'Grady wants us to stay in New York for the time being. Weeks, maybe months, we just don't know."

"Here?" Dante hopefully asked.

"Yes, here, but it's not good news, Dante. She plans to put you and Eliana on the witness stand and make you tell everything you know about these Movers and the way they operate."

"What?" Dante shouted. "How are we supposed to know how they operate?"

"What about you, Eliana?" asked Vignette.

Eliana dropped her gaze to the floor. "All we know is what they did to us."

Randall had watched in silence until Eliana spoke. Then he made up his mind. "I thought the situation was something like that. It might be worth suffering through a trial if it put people away, but what I'm seeing here is you may risk your lives, waste your time on a prosecution that will be corrupted from within, and then be left to deal with the repercussions alone."

"I fear you are right," Eliana said.

"Me too," agreed Dante.

Vignette put her palm over her eyes and shook her head. "Damn it, Randall."

"I know, I know. But I have an idea. You might as well all three hear it at once, since it concerns all of us."

"What is it?" asked Dante, eager to hear about anything other than testifying.

"It's you and Eliana. You've talked about how she got you started on reading, took care of you."

"She did!"

"As it happens, we might not have the money for a private school right now, but we can sure see to it you get schooled at home until the day comes that we do."

"You want to be my teacher?"

"Nope, I want Eliana to be your teacher. And to make it happen, I'm offering to hire her to live in our San Francisco home with you. You can both watch the house, and she can teach you just the way she was doing before."

Eliana looked too stunned to speak, but Dante jumped up and threw his arms around her. "Yes! We will! Yes! Won't we, Eliana? Yes! Yes! Yes!"

She laughed at his excitement and looked as if she wanted to go along with the proposal, but then concern crossed her face. "How long will you be gone?"

Vignette spoke up. "Meaning how long can you stay there? Well, Randall didn't ask me how I felt about this plan because he didn't have to. I also don't have to ask him about this next idea, because I know he agrees. So here it is: What if you don't leave at all? It's a big house, plenty of room for you."

She took the thin chain holding the teardrop magneto switch from around her neck and put the chain around Dante's neck. "I know you'll be there when we get back, Dante. I'm trusting you with this."

Dante regarded the little switch as if it were encrusted with jewels.

Randall smiled at Vignette and put his arm around her shoulders. "I think we're both ready to let someone else live in Shane's old room."

"Now that they have his killer in custody, changing out Shane's room does feel right. And Dante, there's room in the attic to put in a bedroom for you after we get back."

"When do you want us to go, Randall?" Dante excitedly asked.

"Now. That's the reason we're having this discussion. I know you both will need time to get better after that ordeal, but there's no time to do it here. We can't let the NYPD decide to put you in protective custody and then force you to testify."

Dante said, "Because they won't take care of us when they're done."

"Right. These Movers have proven they have the means and determination to take revenge. But if you're out of the way and you don't testify, they won't have any reason to care about you anymore. So let us deal with them. It's why we came here."

"I think Randall is saying we have to get you both to the train station right away."

"Yes. I'll send you with the house keys. Eliana, can you drive a car?"

"No, I am sorry not to have learned."

"You will. In the meantime, just take public transportation. I'll start you off with two weeks' salary for travel money and mail you a check every two weeks after that."

Dante stood beaming like a child who had just seen proof Santa Claus was real. Eliana's eyes were wide with surprise, but she still seemed afraid to accept the idea.

Vignette spoke up to soothe her. "Of course, neither of you has to stay. You could leave at any time. For example, Eliana, if you wanted to go back to your country, you could."

"No. I can't do that. Ukraine was so badly damaged by the fighting, there's no place left for me. My home and family were destroyed, and the soldiers shamed me in front of our village. They... I will never go back."

"And you, Dante?"

"I'm staying with Eliana. She wants to stay in America. So will I." Dante spoke with determination, and Vignette and Randall both noted he didn't bother to ask Eliana and she didn't bother to disagree.

"Okay," Randall smiled, "but we have to move quickly. We have no idea if and when the commissioner will change her mind about allowing you to stay here instead of putting you in custody, or when she might get over-ridden by the command structure and they have you called in, regardless of what O'Grady wants."

"We can buy you some basic items on the way to the train station, and I'll send you with the two weeks' salary in cash. My car and Vignette's motorcycle will be fine in the electric stable, so don't worry about them."

Eliana still looked stunned by the plan. "We could actually be free of those horrible people?" A nervous giggle escaped her. "Can that be true? It seems unreal."

Dante held her tightly and whispered to her, unashamed in front of Randall and Vignette, "We're already free, Eliana. We got away. Now we can stay away."

PART III

34

MANHATTAN, NEW YORK

May 3rd – Two Months Later
* Morning *

THE WEATHER WAS FAIR AND COOL on that spring morning, so John Smith drove from Manhattan to Brooklyn with the driver's window down. He was now three payments behind on his Nash Touring Car and had taken to parking it in a different spot every night to avoid having it repossessed. In the long weeks since Salsedo's arrest, he repeatedly poked and prodded Mario Buda for action, trying to heat up his story from within. So far all Buda was willing to do was use his contacts in the movement to push the rumor that Salsedo was talking to the cops, doing the unthinkable and naming names. In this way, even if Salsedo ever got out, the soldiers would finish him. He was done. One less risk to the cause.

Smith even fed Buda the Brooklyn address where Randall Blackburn and Vignette Nightingale were staying, hoping to poke him into some form of sensational action Smith would write up with the proper degree of righteous outrage and proven fact. His research told him it was an odd arrangement. They were staying in an apartment owned by NYPD Deputy

Commissioner O'Grady. He knew the boy and his auntie had disappeared, but with people like that, it was to be expected. They weren't the story; the Movers were the story, and he still knew almost nothing about them. Buda told him they had always been a secret, murky group and always would be.

"They have so much power, it ruins their eyes," Buda had said. "They see nothing outside of their own pleasures and odes to themselves. I'm glad they are so foolish as to give us money and think we won't use it against them. I say, why shouldn't we? Why not?"

Smith knew an attack on the commissioner's loaned-out apartment would instantly elevate his story to the front page. True, a successful bomb attack would kill both the detectives. That was terribly unfortunate, but sacrifices had to be made if journalism was going to provide the necessary service of exposing these Movers, whoever they were. He would mourn the loss of the erstwhile detectives while he paid off his car loan.

Soon he found himself pulling to the curb across from the detectives' borrowed apartment. He parked his Touring Car, threw a snappy wave at a few neighbors who stood about gaping at the luxury vehicle, and trotted up the narrow sidewalk leading to the building.

When Vignette heard the knock at their front door, she was reading the latest note from Dante, who wrote for both himself and Eliana to tell them things were good at the house. He tossed in a couple of good-natured complaints that Eliana was making him study too hard and being strict about his lessons. Vignette hoped that part was true.

Randall opened the door to reporter John Smith, then took a step back to allow him to come inside.

"Have you seen this morning's papers?" Smith asked without bothering to take off his hat or even sit down.

"Not yet," Randall replied. "What is it?"

"Salsedo's dead."

"What?" Randall and Vignette both said at once.

"My paper is reporting he died around two o'clock this morning."

Randall and Vignette regarded Smith with astonished expressions while he continued, "Found him on the sidewalk before sunrise. Fourteen floors, straight down."

"He jumped?"

"Jumped, got thrown. He didn't fly, that's for sure. A couple of seconds falling, then poof. Nice and quick. Gone with the breezes. I didn't see it myself, but my paper is reporting he splattered when he hit. I mean, fourteen floors, yes?"

"Did you break the story?"

"Nah, damn it, I was at home asleep at the time." Smith noted that of the two detectives, the female appeared far more upset.

"Why would he do that?" she asked.

Randall added, "How would he even be able to make it to an unprotected window by himself and then climb out without being stopped?"

Smith gave a grim smile. "Maybe we can't assume he jumped. Maybe your questions are proper and he couldn't have done it alone."

"Damn it!" Randall shouted. "This makes no sense at all!"

"The corruption?"

"No, that part I understand. But the authorities needed him to testify at trial. Why kill him?"

"My contacts tell me he was taking regular beatings—every day, mind you—and still not giving them enough information to work with. Maybe they got tired of feeding him."

"Or maybe," Randall said, "they beat him until he couldn't take anymore and he found some fleeting opportunity to break for the window and dive. The natural human reaction to avoid a fall from heights might be overcome by the need to escape torture."

Vignette sighed and put her hands over her eyes. "I have to tell you, Randall, I'm having a hard time feeling any sympathy for this bastard. It would have been nice to see him go to prison, but any prison presents the possibility of escape or even parole at some point. He might have been executed after his trial, but perhaps not. From prison, maybe he could send out bomb recipes from his cell. At least this way, he's gone forever."

"Yeah. I would have loved to hear his testimony, though."

"Me too," Smith agreed. "Looks like he found the only way to guarantee being able to clam up."

"If NYPD officers threw him out, that's basically summary execution, and you can't get much more illegal than that," Randall said. "Do you think they'll investigate the cause?"

"Based on my experience, I say they'll launch a major investigation, learn nothing, wait for public outcry to die down, then bury the story."

Vignette's hands were still covering her eyes. She kept them there and muttered, "Well, shit, shit, shit."

"Cheer up. Salsedo's gone, and you don't have to wait through his trial and maybe even an appeal. Besides, maybe the police did manage to get some good information out of him. They know ways to hurt people most folks will never think of. They can produce excruciating pain and leave no marks. Remember, they had him for eight weeks. Think of the damage you can do to a guy in that time."

Vignette removed her hands and looked Smith in the eyes. "Do you expect to see any action against the Movers coming out of it?"

"All I can tell you is, I'm thinking the revelations coming out of him implicated some of the most powerful people in our country. What you're really asking me is, do the authorities have the power to go silent on this and then keep it buried over time?"

"Okay, start there."

"Yes."

~

That afternoon, Mario Buda sat in his tenement room listening to the mice scratching around inside the walls. Even though he had the wherewithal to rent a much better hotel, he felt out of place in fancy establishments. Four years earlier, he had learned a solid lesson in San Francisco when he watched Luigi Galleani give in to temptation and accept a rich man's offer to stay in his home. Of course the man betrayed him. It was a mistake Buda never intended to make.

He considered the life of the Bomb Maker Nonpareil to require a vow of poverty proving him above the materialism that drove the capitalists. Anyone could take a look at his room and see he was not one to seek out luxury, meaning the wealthy elites held no power over him the way they did over the anarchists who accepted their unearned luxury and cash, corrupting the movement's purity. It accomplished the goal of silencing attacks until the big day came, for maximum impact, but it ruined the hard edge true anarchy required. Infighting and mutual theft among members was becoming rife.

In his estimation, there was nothing more revolting than wealthy communists, wealthy socialists, or that most contemptible of fools, a wealthy anarchist.

Andrea Salsedo had been impoverished as a good anarchist ought to be but lacked conviction. He never lived long enough to find out, but his refusal to kill the boy back in San Francisco hung a death sentence around his neck. If he did not meet his end in that fall, he would have when he was blown to bits in a death that would have looked as if he mistakenly set off his own device. Their leader Luigi Galleani needed true soldiers, not debutants posing as believers. The weak were dangerous. They talked too much.

The Movers knew Salsedo was headed for a torturous interrogation as soon as the male police force learned of his whereabouts. They could have warned him and gotten him out of there, but after his refusal to accept the San Francisco mission, the only reason they brought him back to New York was to give him his final task. The job was in fact a nonexistent piece of fiction, just enough to "assign" him to deliver one of Buda's bombs for him, then die when it exploded early. Anarchists frequently died ferrying around their own creations. Nobody would think a thing about it.

A proper end for one who refused to follow orders. Even that was unnecessary, and they had saved themselves the bomb they would have needed for his execution.

Now Buda had to eliminate Clayton Mannerly himself. With six months still to go until the presidential election, he also had to sit back for now and let Mannerly continue to throw his twisted little slave sales and accumulate cash to fund their bribery schemes and guarantee their candidate's victory. When the time arrived, he would also be in possession of finished versions of more of the superb bombs he had taught Salsedo how to build: the ones with great explosive power but which could fit in a steel first aid kit.

Like those on passenger trains.

Patience was a prominent weapon in his tool kit. Buda's anarchist soldiers were running out of their newfound cash, and few were open to listening to reason about questioning its origin and purpose, for the time being. He was delighted to see that the glut of free money had been mostly spent away. Now the soldiers would become hungry again. Angry again.

Ready for action again.

~

Commissioner O'Grady paced her living room while Randall and Vignette quietly sat and gave her time to work through the shock of their news.

"You see it now, don't you? Why I've been campaigning so hard for you to stay in town? That man was in police custody! Whether he jumped out or got thrown out that window, it's a massive failure for the entire department. How the hell does a newspaper reporter get information on police business before I do? And now you say the news services are going with the story that he committed suicide?"

"They have to," Vignette began, "the alternative—"

"Yes, yes, the alternative is that he was summarily executed. If that's the case, was it because of something he knew? Or something he did?"

"His wife is already talking about suing the city. The reporter spoke to her, and she's convinced the beatings made him crazy and threw him into despair, so he saw a chance and jumped. She's saying they drove him to it."

"Son of a bitch!" shouted O'Grady. "Excuse the outburst, but of course she's going to sue! Wouldn't you? If he was thrown, the cops who did it not only made the whole department look bad, they made it look like he knew something dangerous."

"Maybe he knew something that would throw the investigation toward some of the city's elite? People too powerful to go after?"

"Nobody should be too powerful to go after," Randall objected.

O'Grady smiled. "True, but some are too powerful to convict."

"As for Salsedo," Vignette said, "our theory is they interrogated him for the past eight weeks until they finally gave up."

"You see why I need you here? I can't get any action out of my own department on this. If we had a committed force on it, we might have broken the case by now. I've got Detective Goodwin and her small force of policewomen, but that's it, and they already have their hands full. Now tell me, how are Dante and Eliana doing after you defied me and sent them out west? You can see how much I need you by the fact that I haven't had you arrested for interfering with the investigation."

Randall and Vignette both showed pained expressions. Randall self-consciously cleared his throat.

"Uh, yes," Vignette responded. "They seem to be in good spirits. She's got him reading two books a week. They're keeping the place occupied for us."

"Then you can spare more time here. Surely you can. I need you in New York, Detectives. Even if we never catch these people, if we stay on it, I'm certain we can mess up whatever they have planned."

"And avoid bringing in the department so they can't muck it up?" Vignette asked.

"Precisely." She looked back and forth between them. "Get us enough to ruin their plans, then go home. Do that, and you'll have the keys to the city here in New York as well as your own hometown. Just agree to stay and get back to work. Shall we do that?"

"What else would you have us do at this point, Commissioner?"

"Keep up the rotating stakeouts on every print shop in Brooklyn. Find a place where they don't just do someone else's job, but where they're putting out their own propaganda. Those people will either be in on it themselves or they'll know how to find the ones who are. We've got four months before they restart the orphan trains. The whole process was shut down when the problems came to light, but there is still a massive wave of orphans produced by that war. There are just too many to discontinue it. So our obligation is to see to it these criminals can't get themselves involved again. I think we'll find our lead time goes by fast."

Randall cast a sideways glance at Vignette. She gave him a rueful smile. They both realized there was no way to abandon the hunt with so much at stake. Personal inconvenience had no standing in the equation.

"We'll stay," Randall said.

"Of course we will," added Vignette.

35

MANHATTAN, NEW YORK

September 12th
* Morning *

THE SUMMER OF 1920 INCLUDED PASSAGE of the 19th Amendment to the Constitution, extending the right to vote to all women. When it was ratified on August 18th and became the law of the land, Vignette and Randall took that day off to celebrate, drink just a bit too much, and thank their lucky stars for living in such a modern era.

After his wife disappeared, Clayton Mannerly had surmised for the press that she ran off with a younger man. Few people believed him, but nobody had any idea where Allison might be.

By the time summer was done, most of the city's people had forgotten about the disappearance and had their hands full with their own concerns. Randall and Vignette were not among them. Vignette's only relief from the drudgery of the investigation was the Ace four-cylinder motorcycle she rented from a local dealer, along with an added sidecar. She had already convinced Randall to ride with her back in San Francisco, and while he preferred to drive his rented auto, he frequently rode along with her. They both appreciated the ability to weave in and out of traffic.

Still, four months of exhausting stakeouts had taken their toll on both detectives. None of the anarchists with criminal records seemed to know anything, and Vignette broke into enough of their places of working and sleeping to be assured they had nothing to contribute. Inside their homes and hotel rooms, she moved around enough of their personal items to cause chaos and panic among them, but it didn't flush out any bombers.

Time pressure was growing intense with the deadline approaching for restarting the orphan train program, but stakeouts were always the worst part of detective work. If not for the enormity of the risk involved, they would have apologized their way out of New York City and returned to San Francisco. They decided as soon as the orphan trains were successfully restarted, it would be time for them to get back home at last. They both looked forward to spending more time with Dante and Eliana.

John Smith invested enough time and energy into Mario Buda over the summer to be convinced he had the man in his palm. He already knew Buda had something big planned in their city, not Washington, DC, and he knew Buda needed him. That meant the bomb maker needed positive publicity if he was to gain maximum results from his "propaganda of the deed," as he liked to call it.

Now he watched Buda from the corner of his eye while he drove him down to the waterfront on the East River, heading for a general store to buy copper wire for his bomb-making work. The bomb builder sat in the passenger seat, idly rubbing his fingertips back and forth on the fine leather upholstery. He had derided the luxury vehicle at his first sight of it, calling it another sign of Western decadence. Smith noticed, however, Buda seemed to have little difficulty getting comfortable in it. The reporter grinned and shouted over the wind rushing through the windows, "I see you've gotten used to the ride! Maybe you should have taken some of that free money when it was being pumped into your community and bought one for yourself!"

Buda's emotional response caught Smith off guard. Although the man was smaller and more wiry than Smith, he grabbed the vehicle's stick shift and threw the car into neutral, then reached over with his left foot and stomped the brakes. The engine revved impotently while the car screeched to a halt, causing drivers behind them to honk wildly and shriek insults from car to car, using a new form of social communication which people were just beginning to discover.

Smith managed to pull the car to the curb while his passenger bellowed at him.

"Do not confuse me with fair-weather anarchists! Or fake communists and socialists who cry out against rich people and then take the dues paid to their organizations and spend them on fancy houses and cars! Let me tell you, Mr. Smith, I will ride in your decadent vehicle, but I would not be caught dead owning one!"

"All right! All right! Jesus Christ, Mr. Buda, I made a little joke."

"No joke to me, Mr. Smith. The purpose of that money was the same as any other free money. It bought loyalty. It temporarily salved old wounds. All that means is the attacks will have more impact when they come. I would never put it to work for personal use." He smiled, but the words that came out were harsh. "Unlike you, a capitalist pig."

"Capitalist? Fair enough. No apologies." He reengaged the transmission and pulled back into traffic. "So why don't we talk about your plan instead? Yes, yes, I know it's a big secret and everything, but sooner or later I have to know. The election's a little more than six weeks away. If you're gonna make a move, I'll have to file this story soon."

Smith took a brief pause, then made his closing argument. "You need to think about the fact that I have other members of the anarchist movement who would love to be featured in a story."

Buda glared at him with such intensity Smith thought he might throw a punch, but the smaller man took a safer route. "Ego-driven fools. Send them to an alienist. Whatever they can tell you won't be about this operation because they don't know. All they know about what is coming is they are supposed to pile on and attack however they can, as soon as they see the process of destruction begin. The smart ones stay out of the news."

"Lucky for me that doesn't apply to you, eh?" Smith said with a broad grin.

"Bastard! What do you know? I will be in the news as a *sacrifice*, Mister Newsman! I will be a public enemy so the authorities won't search for the others. I will be protecting my brother and sister anarchists when I step forward."

"But you'll step forward *after* you've fled the country, correct? I mean, that's what I would do, but then I'm a capitalist pig..."

Smith knew he was pushing his luck to the limit, but so far nothing he said had persuaded this madman to open up to him. He may have been lying about having other anarchists who would feed him a good story, but he was truthful about his need to file one. The petty local crime stories of the past few months barely paid his rent, let alone his car payments and other costs of living.

Buda gave him a sideways glance but didn't respond for several minutes. Finally, just when they pulled up in front of the store and Smith shut down the engine, Buda turned to him and said, "You like to talk about how dedicated you are to this line of work, this 'journalism' of yours. Well, do I have your word—your word as a journalist—that you will sit on what I am about to tell you until I say to use it?"

"You already have it. I've told you, sir, I am a reporter. We have a strict code of honor. I write all the news people need to read, and I sit on all the news they're not ready to hear. You know I want this story."

"Yes," Buda said in a dry tone. "And that is what will keep you quiet until I am ready to tell it: you won't be given everything you need until the day you go to press with the story. Do you see how greed and ambition work in your capitalist life, Mr. Smith? I have trapped you with your own greed. Because of it, you will not betray me."

"Fair enough, I suppose. What can you tell me about, today? Come on, Mr. Buda, keep me from going to another source."

Buda made an obvious effort to quell his boiling blood before he responded, "Banks, Mr. Smith. Bankers depending on Wall Street for their prosperity because their customers depend on Wall Street as well. Bankers who will receive notes warning them of bomb attacks unless they close down, followed by more bomb attacks to convince them of the danger."

"Can you tell me how many men you will use for the operation?"

"No. We have secret groups all over the country, and they are all waiting for the signal to bomb banks *en masse*. The number would astound you, Mister Reporter. But all they know is to wait for the signal when they hear the train bombs have gone off, and then to start planting their bombs in the banks they have targeted.

"I learned from experience that someone always has a spouse or a lover or a best friend, some person they have to confide in. The San Francisco operation four years ago fell apart because of it. This time, if you are looking for information about the coming attacks, you can't get anything from anyone but me."

Smith exhaled hard. "Mr. Buda. That can't work. No bank is going to cooperate with a threat like that."

Buda smiled. "As Signore Galleani likes to say, poor research on your part, Mister Reporter. They will cooperate after the Wall Street explosion is followed by dozens or hundreds dead on the orphan trains. After we hit a select few of the biggest banks in the region to prove our intentions. After people become too afraid to even enter those banks. Once people die because they're doing their banking when the bombs go off, panic will infect the rest of the country. An education in government, Mr. Smith, just in time for the People to address the system causing the problem by electing our man."

Smith's face went pale with shock. He appeared to struggle with taking it in.

Buda sneered in satisfaction. "That is when my brothers and sisters will spring into action. Of course, I will be long gone by the time your story appears. So tell me, do you think that election story is big enough for you?"

Smith stared at him for a moment, still trying to swallow what he had been told. He croaked out his response. "Oh, yeah." He cleared his throat. "Yeah. It's big enough."

∽

"Hello?"

"Blackburn, it's Bone."

"Ah. Louisiana Bone."

"It's okay, you can say 'Lazy Ana,' everybody else does when I'm not around."

"You won't hear that from me, Miz Bone. What can I do for you?"

"Not a thing. I've gone by your place a few times to check on your guests. It all still looks good to me."

"Well, thank you, Miz Bone, but you can stop now. Dante's letters sound as if the two of them are settling in just fine."

"Okay, but that was just the good news. It's not all. Got a tip for you. Two guys was in here drinking themselves under the table last night, and one of 'em starts bragging about the orphan trains."

"Great. What about them?"

"Something about the trains starting up again after being shut down for months."

"Yes, they'll make the first trip cross-country on the sixteenth. You think they're gonna inject more captive kids?"

"Nope. But I'm sure they're going to blow them up."

"You actually heard them say so?"

"No, but they were way too happy about orphan trains. The drunker they got, the louder they talked. And these anarchists love their bombs, don't they?"

"All right, Miz Bone, we already suspected as much, but this indicates it's true. You may have just saved a bunch of kids."

"You make sure Mayor Rolph knows I called, right? Keep his men away from my place?"

"Miz Bone, if this is the tip that lets us stop them, I think you can forget your legal troubles for a long time to come."

John Smith drove his Nash Touring Car through the early morning darkness to the offices of the *New York Daily Herald* with his heart pounding. The story was done, his exposé complete, and it was certain to blow the tops off the heads of the reading public. Idiot Buda did his best to give him nothing, but he was pliable under the effects of a good bottle of grappa.

Smith had extracted just a few nuggets of information to add to the picture he was building, but it was enough. Buda had no idea how much Smith already knew from his own investigations. The files on his seat outlined the Movers as a subset of America's elite rich and contained names of the organization's members.

But that was not the scoop. Oh no.

The scoop came from the *Herald*'s own accounting office, after Smith paid the lead accountant a hundred dollars cash to look at the main set of books. It only took him twenty minutes to find it: a long and detailed list of wealthy donors who had sent money to various anarchist cells via the paper's bank accounts, using the paper's confidential knowledge of where to find the leaders who would disseminate the cash to their fighters. All the sponsors had to do was send the money to the editor-in-chief to handle for them. Smith thought it safe to assume other papers were doing the same thing across the country. Selling access to their confidential files on political criminals because the authorities were prevented from seizing them.

A national scoop on the news business itself. It was too good to be true.

Over the past few months, the picture finally revealed itself. Nobody could tell when the Movers began; they seemed to have always existed. Nobody even knew what the Movers actually called themselves, if anything. But by quietly buying up many of the country's leading newspapers, bribing public officials, and blackmailing those who refused to cooperate, they not only had a lock on their black-hearted slave trade and the purchase of children, they had the guaranteed loyalty of their clients and full control of the public's perception. Any time an investigator got too close, the Movers could manufacture gigantic emergencies to overwhelm the flow of news and wipe out the inconvenient story.

Except now, with the amount of detail and provable charges Smith was about to unleash, even the most powerful of the Movers was going to have to run for cover. He also knew about Mario Buda's plan to bomb the first of the renewed orphan trains and Father Young's plan to have the children he had accumulated from their slave parents also on that train. They would conveniently vanish without a trace in the planned explosion and conflagration, the first of many major attacks on the American capitalist system.

At this point in his long months of research, he could specifically name a dozen small groups of anarchists waiting in the wings for the explosions to begin, at which time they would pile on with bombs and fires of their own, overwhelming the American system and creating chaos across the country. The knowledge that innocent children would die made his chest hurt a little, but he felt better when he thought of paying off his expensive car and earning a permanent place among the newspaper's salaried reporters, perhaps even a top position with his Pulitzer.

He reached the *Herald* building and parked. Nothing left to do then but go inside, type up the story, hand it to his editor—and let that beautiful rain of money and respect fall down upon him.

Inside the giant waiting area of Penn Station, two Bible-toting nuns who oddly looked like Vignette Nightingale and Detective Isabella Goodwin surreptitiously watched the passenger lockers. They sat on hard wooden benches ironically shaped like church pews, and since Goodwin had long since learned most people would avoid a nun with an open Bible in her lap, they kept theirs wide open and pretended to read.

Goodwin's other duties prevented her from spending as much time on stakeouts as Vignette and Randall were doing, but the train station vigil was more immediate than watching local print shops and gathering up samples of anarchist flyers and pamphlets.

They had been there for the past three days, taking the busiest day shift while Goodwin's policewomen filled in on the other two shifts. After the tip came in from Louisiana Bone, Goodwin had pressed reporter John Smith for information and assured him he would go to prison for any charge she could dream up if he withheld information and tragedy occurred because of it. He had then grudgingly told her there was good reason to watch the largest sets of lockers there, the ones designed for heavy suitcases, in the days leading up to the first departure of the resumed orphan trains.

Detective Goodwin saw no reason to trust Smith's word, but their quarry had proved to be so cautious and the Movers so invisible, there were no other leads to follow.

Now here they were, dealing in hope, which neither trusted much.

Goodwin was under pressure to return to the office. The men she reported to were usually supportive of her, but that was based on her past successes at bringing down con artists and thieves with her disguises and undercover work. This time, the NYPD brass seemed not the slightest bit curious about rumors of slave auctions, anarchist bombers, or fixed elections.

She had applied for a search warrant for the Penn Station lockers twice. Both requests were ignored without comment. Setting up a stakeout was all they could do.

And for three days, nothing. Goodwin had her other policewomen taking turns around the clock, phony nuns one and all, and yet there had been no suspicious activity. She and Vignette were about to abandon the quest as a waste of time.

Vignette muttered under her breath, exasperated, keeping her head down as if she might be praying out loud, "This makes no sense. Why would Smith give us a bum lead?"

Goodwin replied in the same soft voice, "Who knows? Maybe the lead was good and someone else changed their mind."

At that moment their replacements arrived, so Goodwin quietly informed them this was their last shift before she shut down the stakeout. To anyone who noted their entrance, the two newly arrived ersatz nuns added to the illusion, since most people had not adjusted to the idea of policewomen with full powers to detain and arrest, whether they were dressed as nuns or not. She and Vignette quietly closed their Bibles, stood up, left the other two to take up the watch while they walked out of the station.

One of the dozens of travelers sitting on the wooden benches had his feet up on his small suitcase while he pretended to sleep. In truth, he was following orders like the proud soldier he was, guarding the lockers holding tomorrow's bombs, moving from seat to seat and periodically changing clothes in the men's room to avoid notice. He had traveled from Italy with the Signore himself, a week earlier, so the great leader could oversee the operation. In keeping with the order to maintain a tiny roster for this giant operation, the honor of protecting the bombs was his alone.

Until tomorrow morning, the lockers were not to be disturbed for any reason, by any person. This Galleanist was a loyal follower. Unless the lockers were opened by one Mario Buda, whoever was foolish enough to do so would take a bullet in the back. Of course the act would cost him his life. As a godless materialist he had no hopes of eternal reward, but he was willing to settle for a glorious reputation in death.

The Galleanist had noticed the nuns coming in and staying without getting on a train, relieved by other nuns who also sat without going anywhere. Fishy, sure, but nuns? Nuns who somehow had an idea what was in those lockers and were setting up a watch on them? How could that make any sense at all?

He decided his imagination was working overtime, and that a week of occupying hard wooden benches and trying not to sleep was taking its toll. What was he supposed to do? Tell Signore Galleani some nuns were onto him? If the police knew, they would be there, would they not?

If the nuns knew, apparently they said nothing about it to anybody except other nuns. The idea was pleasantly absurd enough to make him laugh. Two of them had left the building, anyway. Here in the final stretch of his long watch, a little humor was a big relief.

Early that evening, Mario Buda opened the door to his tenement hotel and beamed with pleasure. "Signore Galleani! Wonderful to see you! I trust my directions got you here without trouble?"

Galleani ignored the question. With his cap pulled low and his collar high, he stepped inside and looked around the room with obvious distaste. By way of greeting, he said, "How can you live in filth like this, Mario?"

"Signore, our surroundings here are poor and this building is not kept up well, but as you see, I am a clean person. There is no filth."

Luigi Galleani had recently turned sixty years old, and the Emigration Act of 1918 made his presence in the United States illegal. He was deported from the US a year earlier under suspicion of numerous political bombings. On this day, the only difference American law made in his life was he now attended the United States in secret instead of walking around broadcasting his presence. As far as he knew, the Americans thought he was still back in his hometown in Italy.

"Filth, mess, poverty, call it what you will. This hotel looks like it hasn't been decent for fifty years, and I believe simple dignity requires one to have decent surroundings."

"Certainly true for you, as the leader of our movement. But I am content to spend my money on equipment for the revolution and not upon myself."

Galleani's genius at manipulating people to do his bidding had not deteriorated over time. Instead of arguing further, he gave Buda a fatherly smile. "That is only one of the reasons you are fairly called the 'Bomb Maker Nonpareil,' Mario. Your level of devotion to the cause does me proud."

Buda broke into a wide smile, enthralled with his mentor and drunk on praise. "I have the explosives ready for tomorrow, all to fit into the onboard first aid kits. These will set off a shock wave the entire country will feel. As you see, nothing is here. Even if the police came tonight, they would not find a thing. They are already in the storage lockers at the train station." He lifted up a set of locker keys strung together with a bit of twine.

Galleani affected a look of concern and worry which he knew would get Buda's attention.

"What is it, Signore Galleani?"

"I was hoping you would have one of your devices here."

"Why is that?"

"According to the Movers, you have one more job to do before tomorrow's work. I assume all your devices are incendiary?"

"Just the ones for the train. The one for downtown is not, but it has maximum explosive power and it's packed with lead curtain weights."

"They will bloom like flowers, no doubt. But we need one of those incendiary devices for tonight."

"Tonight? How can we—"

"Our contact at the hotel is finished. We have no more need of his services, and the Movers are eager to get on to safer new bases of operation."

"He knows too much?"

"Far too much. The Movers can't abide the risk he presents, and neither can we."

"What do we do?"

"You, Mario. I can't do anything. You are the point man on this just as you have always been. The Movers don't want the authorities to be able to figure out how they do it, so they want Clayton Mannerly's hotel burned."

"I would like to eliminate this man, but sir, before the operation?"

"Yes, and that's the point. Do it before the operation. Set your device where it will gut the place with fire. Your fire will occupy a large number of fire and police, which means they won't be downtown. The plan is to begin after midnight, when the skeleton shift is on duty. Go to the train station early and get one of the incendiary bombs. Are they in suitcases?"

"One per case. They're just the right size to fit into the first aid boxes."

"Bring one in its suitcase cover to the City Squire Hotel. Walk into the lobby as if you own the place and ride up to the top floors. Plant the device where it will spread the most fire. The Movers don't want any evidence of Mannerly's detention floors."

"Forgive me, but why do we care what they want?"

"We have to live in the present time, Mario. And that requires vast sums of money to create political change. Now, we know Mannerly is done with the parties and auctions for the time being, so he is surely going to be in bed at that hour. With a bit of luck, you'll cure two problems in one stroke. As soon as you plant the bomb, drift back out the front door without looking as if you are doing anything wrong. Then return to the station lockers and begin the real work. Mario, listen to me: this operation will make you famous among every anarchist in the world. They will tell their children stories about you.

"I am honored to have this opportunity."

"Good. Now let's see you smile. One train car full of orphans has just been spared so you can carry out this work."

36

PENN STATION & THE CITY SQUIRE
HOTEL

September 16th
* 1:00 a.m. *

ALL OF THE POLICEWOMEN DISGUISED AS NUNS were issued copies of Mario Buda's likeness and kept themselves on high alert for his face. They knew all too well that if they became careless or inattentive and allowed chaos to occur, the males in the department would use it to "prove" women were not capable of the more serious aspects of the job.

Which is why the two nuns on duty were not fooled by Buda's affected casual attitude while he strolled into the train terminal. Eyes were on him before he reached the lockers, and by the time he opened one up, the nuns silently moved in his direction without looking at him. They stood face to face as if lost in a quiet conversation and watched from the corners of their eyes while he pulled out a medium-sized suitcase, leaving the locker empty.

He was so certain of his secrets, he never even looked over his shoulder while he traveled across the terminal floor and back out into the night. The nuns were both trained by Detective Goodwin, so they knew how to remain in character to maintain the illusion and how to follow at a practical distance to prevent their quarry from detecting them. Their orders were clear: *do nothing to stop him until you know where he is going.* They remained behind him while he walked away projecting the persona of a traveling man looking for a hotel.

However, minutes later when he turned at the entrance to the City Squire Hotel and revealed his destination, the more senior of the police-women realized she could not permit a man with a bomb to walk into an occupied hotel. She shouted, "Mario Buda! Stop right there!"

Buda jumped, startled, and whirled to face them. His face registered consternation when he realized he had just been called out by a couple of nuns. Whatever they were, they weren't pointing guns in his direction at the moment, so he turned and fled into the hotel. They gave chase, but the distance they successfully maintained for secrecy now worked against them while they lost precious seconds closing on the hotel. They burst into the lobby just in time to see that it was empty at that hour.

At the elevator banks, one of the car doors slid closed.

The junior nun looked more frightened than her partner and asked, "What do we do now?"

"Go to the front desk and commandeer the phone. Call Goodwin. I'll watch to see what floor he stops on."

Randall Blackburn picked up the receiver on the telephone. "Hello?"

"This is Detective Goodwin. I just spoke to the commissioner, and she said to call you out to the City Squire Hotel. Her undercover officers followed Mario Buda there from Penn Station."

"You think he's leaving town?"

"I don't know, but he was carrying a suitcase he retrieved from the lockers. I told them to stand back and not follow him further into the hotel. We have to assume it's a bomb, and we don't know when it might go off. They're starting to evacuate the guests now."

Randall was already grumpy, coming out of a sound sleep. The news only made it worse. "Ah, damn it!"

He called out in the direction of Vignette's room. "Vignette! Wake up!

They spotted Mario Buda! We've got to go!" Speaking into the phone again, he said, "All right, you can tell her we're on our way. We can travel fast at this hour."

He hung up without waiting for a response and hurried to throw on some clothing while he called out again, "And bring the keys to your bike!"

Vignette came out of her room hopping into her leather pants, looking partially dressed and fully alert, as if the sudden knowledge that they were finally getting a crack at bomb-maker Mario Buda had gone through her like electricity. Her face showed a combination of fierceness and elation.

Buda had the tenth-floor elevator door jammed open with his belt buckle shoved underneath it. Galleani had told him the Movers knew about floors ten and eleven, and they considered it imperative to avoid letting the authorities gain any insights into the operation. The explosion and fire would take care of all that, and he felt more cheerful than he had in a long time while he kneeled next to the suitcase bomb and completed wiring the circuits, which he always left incomplete to avoid an accidental discharge. He connected the last wire to the final screw post and stood back to admire his work. At thirty-six, his knees creaked a little when he straightened his legs, but he stood up feeling good—until a harsh voice hit him like a knife in the back.

"What the hell are you doing? Who are you?"

Buda whirled to find Clayton Mannerly, red-faced with outrage. He had been alone in his penthouse when the front desk called to say the police told them a terrorist was in the hotel and had traveled to the tenth floor. He had run down the back stairs from the penthouse to floor ten in seconds.

Buda recognized Mannerly, but it made no difference now. The bomb was active, the fail-safe was armed. No matter what anyone did to it now, it was going to explode and the two cans of oil on either side of it would spread liquid fire in all directions. By the time the fire was out, the hotel would be gutted and all useful evidence of the Movers' work obliterated.

He rammed Mannerly with his shoulder. It was barely enough to push past him, though Mannerly seemed more interested in the suitcase than the man who had brought it. Buda broke for the stairway and charged into the stairwell to make his way back down to the lobby.

Mannerly resisted the urge to follow the man and tackle him. Instead, he forced himself to address the more pressing problem and kneeled to the suitcase. He found himself looking at what was clearly an explosive device. The oil cans fastened to it with twine still had their labels. It took no expertise to recognize it as a firebomb. Right there in his hotel.

But the Movers had underestimated Clayton Mannerly's dedication to his inherited hotel, no matter his contempt for the hotel business. The place was his grand claim to fame and his key to obtaining pliable sexual partners. It was worth everything else demanded of him.

He leaned in close to the bomb and studied the wires for an intense minute, then exhaled with relief when he isolated the red power wire coming out of the battery and the ground wire next to it. He didn't need to know anything about bombs to realize a bomb could not explode if its detonator was robbed of power.

With a satisfied grin of determination, he grabbed the false power wire and yanked it free without finding the true power wire running out of the other side of the battery. The fake power wire had been keeping the electrical charge away from the explosives until the real power line was activated, but if it was removed, power would flow from the battery to the detonator.

Which it did.

The explosion pureed him before he could register his mistake, throwing fire in all directions, blasting through the roof of the elevator car, and sending a pink cloud of Mannerly mist up the shaft and onto its walls. It would not be there for long. The fire immediately began chewing its way through the hotel's wooden inner structure like a starved animal.

Buda made his way down the interior stairs with some of the faster evacuees, all in various stages of nightwear while they tripped and stumbled down the steps. He heard the explosion high overhead just before he reached the lobby. When he arrived, he found chaos already supreme. He positioned himself directly behind two obese women and made his way through the lobby while panicky guests filed out onto the sidewalk.

Once outside, he kept calm and moved with ease, much too wise to run despite the urge. He was soon down the street and away from the gathering crowd, on his way back to the nearby Penn Station.

Inside the train terminal, he checked the locker area for stray nuns. He had to admit it was pretty clever of the American cops to use them, although he could not understand why nuns would do police work. At any rate, religion held no interest for him, and for all he knew, the Catholics had their own hit squads paid by the Vatican. He chuckled at the idea while he scanned the locker area. All clear. He took the remaining locker keys from his pocket and grabbed a nearby rolling luggage cart to pull over to the lockers.

Within a few minutes, he had gingerly removed the suitcases containing four remaining bombs plus one with his own purpose-built device and loaded them onto the rolling cart. The suitcases perfectly disguised their contents while he rolled them across the terminal heading for the track for the Westbound Express. The low-end passenger cars were already in place and being serviced prior to departure, giving the platform a helpful buzz of activity for him to blend into. *Just an early passenger, folks. Nothing to see here.*

Vignette powered her Ace-four through the light traffic on the early morning streets, with Randall riding in the sidecar. The powerful engine produced a deafening roar and a sensation of danger whenever she accelerated. Randall tried not to wince every time she came within inches of another vehicle, which all looked huge from his perspective.

The pair reached the hotel after fifteen minutes of hair-raising swerves and high-speed cornering, only to find the bomb had already detonated and the hotel's upper floors were burning away. Panicked guests in bathrobes and pajamas had already gathered outside.

Firefighters were on the scene from nearby firehouses, aiming their hoses impotently toward the top floors and falling five floors short. The blaze also appeared not the least bit intimidated by the fire hoses, and worse, nothing was inhibiting the flames on the inside. This was odd, because Randall and Vignette both knew when the garment district fire of 1911 killed 145 workers—mostly young women and girls—the city passed a law requiring sprinklers in all buildings over ten stories tall. This building stood twelve floors tall, and still the flames blazed away without inhibition.

They entered the lobby and began helping people to the door who were too old or infirm to make it out on their own. A few were injured in the panicked rush. It occupied precious minutes to assist each victim while the blaze claimed the building, which appeared to have suffered a complete failure of its sprinkler system. In truth, Clayton Mannerly's late father had paid a small fortune in cash bribes to have the inspectors sign off on his nonexistent sprinkler system years earlier. It was a canny financial move, and even after all the bribes were paid it had saved him a bundle.

For now, no one realized the entire system was missing. That would come with daylight.

Randall heard one of the hose captains order the men to focus on everything from the eighth floor down and stop trying to hit higher floors. The water pressure produced by the engine pumps was unable to throw a stream any higher, but the captain thought they might save the bottom half of the building.

Randall pulled Vignette away from the guests. "We know Buda was keeping that bomb in a locker at the train station, meaning this hotel attack was likely not his reason for being in town. It wouldn't have required him to store his suitcase there."

"We don't have to ask why he has bombs at the train station."

"The orphan train. Damn it, the whole point of the early departure was to keep it from the public as much as possible." He pulled out his old silver pocket watch and flipped it open. "It's one forty. The train leaves in about twenty minutes."

"God, Randall. Do you think he's that sick? Would he actually kill dozens of children just to prove a political point?"

They looked at each other for a long moment, then both turned and ran to her motorcycle, sped the short distance to Penn Station, parked illegally outside the front door, and rushed inside.

37

PENN STATION – NEW YORK CITY

September 16th
* Simultaneously *

ON HIS WAY TO THE WESTBOUND DEPARTURE TRACK, Mario Buda passed a rack of pegs on the outside station wall where workers hung wet raincoats. He snatched one without slowing down and within seconds had the garment on his back. Now he looked like any of the other workers milling about at their chores, possibly a hired man loading equipment.

With only four bombs left to plant on the train, his risky work went by with all due speed. He left the cart on the platform and stepped onto the first designated orphan car and walked to the end of the car like a man who knew what he was doing. There he found the first aid box bolted to the floor next to the exit door. He set his suitcase down and removed the bomb, unclasped the kit, and scooped the first aid contents into the now-empty suitcase. He replaced the items with the bomb, which fit with barely a millimeter left over.

He twisted the last connection wire to guarantee the detonation, closed the kit, grabbed the suitcase full of medical supplies, and stepped back out of the car. Time to move on to the next device.

The Reverend Canon Richard Young guided the six children into the crowd of passengers and blended them in with the orphans scheduled to depart. He was well aware of the sneaky orphan train shipment because John Smith liked to talk, and it was with great relief that he gathered up his accumulation of half a dozen children of various women who had passed through the system and been taken away. The children had been held in the cells on Blackwell's Island since winter, but their health was declining and he needed for them to be gone.

They had all been forced to do their hydrotherapy duties. The horror and guilt would keep them silent, and they were too weak from mistreatment to have the capacity to resist. There was no need to force them; each one found it a welcome prospect to get on a train and leave the good father behind.

Young looked around at the handful of matrons assigned to watch over the kids. They were vastly outnumbered and overwhelmed, just as he had hoped. He gathered the kids around him like a mother hen and patted their heads the way an actual priest might do, and told them to stay with the crowd of kids and board the train whenever they did. He wished them well and made the sign of the cross over them in case anyone was looking, then turned without another word and walked away.

Not one of them would have to be told twice to get on the train.

On the way out of the station, Young spotted a beautiful young man of twenty or so, looking around like he was lost and confused. He looked at Father Young as if he hoped a priest might somehow come to his aid. Young felt a thrill go through his body. He smiled and approached the young man with a face full of fatherly concern.

"Hello. If you don't mind my saying, you appear to be a bit troubled. Maybe this old priest can be of service to you?"

The young man beamed with relief. "Oh, Father, yes! I came to the city to get work, but I've run out of money. I came here to sleep in the lobby, but they keep rousting me and moving me along. I'm just so tired."

"In that case, maybe we have proof of God's goodness here, because my name is the Reverend Canon Richard Young, and I run the St. Adrian's Seminary over in Queens. If you don't mind a quick subway ride, I happen to have an empty dormitory where our seminary students sleep. They're all out on a charity mission this week. You can pick your bunk."

The young man lit up. "Oh! Father, that would be terrific!"

"God is good." He extended his hand to the young man, who took it and pulled himself to his feet. He happily accompanied Father Young to the nearest subway stop and followed him down the steps leading under the city.

The young man's patience was about to be rewarded.

Years of rage and months of planning had met with days of surveillance to bring him to this happy spot. He already knew the seminary students were gone because he had surveilled the Queens location. And he had been over on Blackwell's Island creeping through the darkness when he found Father Young in the process of rounding up the children in their cells and ushering them to the train station.

At first he feared his plans would have to be postponed once again, but while he had followed the little crowd onto the local train to Penn Station, a spontaneous idea formed; he already knew about the priest's personal habits in gathering young boys and men. He could use that against him and let the priest think he was picking up another naïve fool, someone ready to be turned into another victim.

The young man noticed the entire underground platform was deserted at that hour. It was late for weeknight excursions and still early for commuters.

In moments, the subway train approached with a roar of chilled tunnel wind and piercing squeals from steel on steel. Just before the conductor car reached them, the young man casually put his hand on the shoulder of the Reverend Canon Richard Young and spoke the exact words the priest said to him as an eight-year-old, the first time Father Young visited his bed, long before he had broken for freedom and run for his life.

"I think you need to relax."

"Mm?" Father Young responded.

"You still don't remember me? It's what you said to me, Father. Maybe I changed too much since I was eight?"

Young stared at him, searching his memory. Then there it was: a flash of recognition. "Are...are you..."

"You need to *relax*!"

Those were the last words heard by the Reverend Canon Richard Young before he felt himself shoved with great force off of the platform and down onto the tracks. He had a quick instant of realizing he had just been murdered by one of his boys before his head struck the electrified third rail. Mercy he did not deserve left him instantly dead and spared him any awareness of going under the steel wheels and being ground into pieces.

The subway engineer somehow missed the deadly event, being busy operating the train, which made no additional noise while it tore up the Reverend Canon. There was no one to witness his demise or to feel the least concern. On the young man's way up the steps and out of the subway station, he passed another fellow about his own age, attired in an elevator operator's uniform and heading down to the subway platforms.

He called to the elevator operator the way friendly New Yorkers do, looking out for one another, "Might want to take a taxi today. Some drunk priest just fell on the tracks and got electrocuted. He's all ground up."

"Really?" gasped the elevator operator. His eyes widened, and he hurried away to be the first rubbernecker to observe the final condition of Father Young's mortal coil.

While the departing young man was now a murderer, he harbored no consciousness of guilt. Instead he made his way into the night feeling light as a feather. He took deep breaths, somehow pulling air deeper into his lungs than ever before. In the following minutes, he got away just as clean as the good father himself had done, for all those many years.

Mario Buda stepped out of the last targeted passenger car carrying the fourth suitcase used to conceal his train bombs. Like the others, this one was now full of medical items replaced by his explosive device. He moved smoothly along the platform among the loading passengers and the working porters, doing nothing to attract attention. He tossed the suitcase onto the luggage cart with the other loads of medical supplies, then grabbed the last untouched suitcase—the one containing his most powerful bomb. For this one, the space used by the oil cans on his incendiary devices was instead occupied by two additional sticks of dynamite on either side of the detonator. He had not constructed such a powerful bomb since he had built his shaped charge device for Signore Galleani back in San Francisco.

From somewhere nearby, a male voice shouted, "Buda! Stop!"

Alarm stabbed through him. He spun to see that damned San Francisco detective and his partner staring straight at him over the heads of dozens of milling children. *Bastards!* He turned and fled in the opposite direction, clutching the heavy bomb to his chest. All the strangers in the dense crowd around him were now his friends in the cause. To reach Buda, the capitalist thugs would have to push through the crowd carefully enough to avoid causing injury to the travelers.

Others of weak willpower could fail the mission, but he would not. Under no circumstances could he allow these monstrous fools or anyone else to stop him. If they got close, he would detonate the bomb himself, taking all the little piggies with him. With plenty of shrapnel riding the blast waves to make a chiffonade of piggery. Confirming forever his reputation as that devoted anarchist Mario Buda, Bomb Maker Nonpareil.

Vignette started off in pursuit of Buda, but Randall knew excitement was clouding her judgment. He grabbed her by the shoulder and held her in place.

"Stop, Vignette! You could get killed for nothing. Look! He's only got one bag! He's already set up the other bombs onboard and the train's pulling out. We are not splitting up now."

She glanced back at the train and took a deep breath while the sight brought back her focus. All the children were aboard, and the cars were very slowly beginning to move.

She took a deep, shuddering breath, thinking, *To hell with that murdering son of a bitch, for now, anyway.* If she and Randall survived the morning, Mario Buda would be on their capture-or-kill list until one or the other took place.

There was nothing to discuss until they got aboard, so they sprinted to the nearest car and sprang onto the steps while the train slowly gathered speed.

One of the strong-faced matrons noticed them leap aboard and stepped in front of them at the doorway. "I believe you are on the wrong car. This one is for children."

Randall was glad to have the chance to use the deputy shield for the first time. He pulled it out and held it up so she could see it was real. "Ma'am, we're here on an investigation, and we won't be bothering the children at all, but we have to take a look around in this car and the other three orphan cars."

She inspected the badge with a keen eye, but her job was also law enforcement; she recognized the valid shield. Her attitude shifted from strong and defiant to compliant and resentful. "Go ahead. Don't even touch one of the kids unless I'm there with you."

Vignette offered what she hoped was a reassuring smile. "Ma'am, there's no need to search the passengers, but we've got to look into any of the large bags or trunks."

"Help yourself." While she spoke, she casually reached down to pull two boys apart who were tussling over something, forced one to sit down and moved the other to the opposite side of the seats. It took about two seconds.

Randall had already done a visual search on the car and realized the little suitcases and children's bags were too small to contain a terrorist's bomb. Without a word, he started down the aisle, taking in every detail on both sides of the car until he reached the end.

The largest container in the car, the only one of any substantial size, was a steel box bolted to the floor and marked "First Aid." He gave it a quick once-over while Vignette approached behind him.

"Randall, none of these kids has a trunk and a big suitcase. I don't see where..." She followed his gaze to the large metal box. "Oh."

"This box hasn't been moved. The thing is inside." He withdrew a pocket knife and extended its thin blade and kneeled next to the metal box.

Her eyes doubled in size, and she managed to yell while whispering, "Wait-wait-wait! What if he wired it to blow if it's opened? Buda's famous for his trick bombs."

"I know, but this could also go off at any second. Why would he bother with a long time fuse once the train is underway? By the time we get the engineer to stop the train and pull the passengers off, it'll likely have done its work."

Vignette stared back down the length of the car and the unreal sight of dozens of children, many not yet teenagers, who sat listless and mostly unmoving. A few talked quietly, one laughed at something. From the rest there was only a cricket chorus of sniffling and coughing. A mood of defeated acceptance tinged with vague hopes filled the car. It made her heart so heavy she had to look away, reminding herself to stay focused, and that the children were in terrible immediate danger.

She put her hand on Randall's shoulder and nodded. It was all he needed.

Randall lay on his side with his eyes directly in front of the lid's leading edge. He studied the two fastener snaps holding it down. The hardware was fastened on separately from the box itself. It revealed no point where Buda could have rigged the clasp, given the brief amount of time he had aboard to work in secret. He would have needed a tool kit and a workshop.

He lightly traced the outline of each one with the tip of his knife and felt no rough spots. He looked up to meet Vignette's eyes while he took a deep breath and thought, "All right, the clasps are okay." He only realized he was speaking out loud when he heard himself say it.

He gently opened them and felt the grip on the lid release. It raised a fraction of an inch when he twisted the blade, allowing him to study the entire rim. There were no wires attached to it, so he slowly lifted the lid. He and Vignette both breathed sighs of relief when nothing happened.

And the first aid kit was revealed to be anything but. The thin steel box now contained one of Buda's explosive devices, constructed to fit perfectly in the space with almost no room left over.

With the lid open, they could both now hear the ticking of the clock wired to the detonator. Buda had kept his detonator simple; the clock hands would connect the two wires in fourteen minutes. A number of other wires ran in and out of the clock with no hint of their function.

"Jesus, Randall, we're almost out of time!"

He stood to look out the window. They were still in heavily populated territory. He bent back down and slowly lifted the device, gauging the weight at something less than thirty pounds. There was no trip wire. Once again, Buda seemed not to have been concerned about people finding the bombs and ruining his plan. Obviously the first aid boxes were supposed to cover his tracks for just long enough for him to be long gone and for the train to be well on its way to delivering death to its passengers.

"Vignette, can I have your coat?"

She took it off and handed it over without asking for a motive, and he promptly displayed his intentions by wrapping it around the device so it was impossible to tell what it was. He held the covered device out to her. "Can you carry this much weight?"

She recoiled at the sight of the device but nodded, took it from him, and bore the weight with ease. "Now what?"

"Take it to the caboose, set it down on the exterior platform, and stand guard over it. Nobody touches it for any reason until I can get back with the other three."

"You think he has one on every orphan car?"

"We can't gamble that he doesn't. Vignette, no matter what, stay between any curious people and the bomb. We're safe enough for fourteen minutes."

"Thirteen now."

"Get going!"

Vignette made it to the caboose unimpeded; a woman toting a cloth-covered bundle caused no concerns, but at the end of each car she had to put the bomb down, open one of the car doors, go through the door, then pick the bundle up again. When she reached the caboose, she crossed to it from the final car prepared to intimidate anyone who tried to stop her, whether she had to show the badge or the bomb.

It took up twelve of the available thirteen minutes for Randall to make three more trips to and from the orphan cars, using his own coat to disguise

the remaining devices while Vignette stood guard. Then they found themselves standing on the train's rear platform with a stack of four bombs and
no time to negotiate with reality over it.

The train was just then crossing into New Jersey, speeding over populated but uncrowded land. The tracks at that point ran over a tall right-of-
way formed of large stones covered with fist-sized granite rocks.

They were out of time.

He lifted the top bomb from the pile and tossed it perpendicular to the
tracks. It made it all the way to the bottom of the right-of-way and landed
on the pulverized rock. It flipped twice, then detonated with a deafening
roar and a ball of flame that rose fifty feet into the air. The sloped right-of-
way deflected the blast up and out, leaving the tracks secure.

Vignette realized they needed Randall's greater upper-body strength for
this task and settled for lifting each bomb and handing it to him so he
could throw with all possible speed. In this fashion they got two more of
the bombs over the side. Each bomb was also jarred by the impact with the
ground and exploded early with force that would have been devastating
inside the passenger cars, surely killing everyone. The absence of buildings
or people in the immediate vicinity rendered the spectacular display as a
thing of great curiosity but causing no actual harm.

Then somebody onboard the train pulled the emergency brake line.

Randall and Vignette were both thrown into the back of the caboose
while the train wheels locked and began to drastically reduce their speed,
making it difficult to get back up. By the time he was able to grab the last
bomb and give it a Hail Mary pass, the train had already slowed to a fast
walking pace. This one would detonate much closer to them than the
others.

The bomb exploded when it struck the base of the right-of-way, just as
the others had, but without favorable distance. Due to the angle of the
heavy stones, the explosion again blasted rock shrapnel away from them.
The concussion wave hurled them into the back wall of the caboose, but
this time it struck with much more force and both were knocked senseless
for several long seconds.

After Randall was able to clamber back to his feet and saw with relief that Vignette was also rising, a flood of guilt ran through him. He had nearly gotten her killed. There was no way to sugarcoat it. He placed his arm around her shoulders as much to assure himself as to comfort her while they made their way outside into the fresh air and early morning darkness. He pulled her aside amid the jumble of frightened children, emotional railroad workers, and a few random civilians from the area. It took him a moment to compose his thoughts.

"I want us to get back aboard and go on to San Francisco," he told her.

"What, now?"

"I've been looking for a way to convince Commissioner O'Grady for the last couple of months. This'll do. Vignette, we aren't going to beat these guys, and neither is the commissioner."

Her eyes widened. "I've never heard you say anything like that."

"We helped these kids. We have to take that as our victory. Now we'll stay on the train to see to it they make it to San Francisco, and Mayor Rolph can personally guarantee them legitimate adoptions. As for this organization, these 'Movers' or whoever they are, we'll never stop them. We're up against human nature."

"So what do we do? I know you're not saying to give up."

"We will keep on fighting them, and once in a while we will win one. Like today. But we could make every Mover in the world drop dead right now, and tomorrow, more would pop up."

Vignette felt herself sag with relief. She drew a deep breath. "Thank you for saying what I've been thinking. We've been chasing the wrong things."

He nodded. "We can catch criminals, but we can't tamp down human nature."

They took a moment for a hug before they got to the task of answering questions.

38

WALL STREET, NEW YORK CITY

September 16th
* Minutes Before Noon *

AS A RULE, MARIO BUDA HATED NEWSPAPERS. All they did was remind him how much injustice roamed the land, making him feel powerless in the world and unable to offer any meaningful objections to mankind's cruelty. All he could do was make explosive barks of protest. He was painfully reminded of this when he drew near to the corner of Wall Street and Broad Street and passed a newsboy hawking his wares. The *New York Daily Herald* had put out an early morning EXTRA!

He pulled his rented horse-drawn garbage cart to the side and squinted at the headline: *4 Bombs Explode Along N.J. Train Tracks!* With a sub-headline: *Miracle! Nobody Harmed.*

Impossible, he told himself. It was not true, of course. Capitalist propaganda. He had built each of the bombs himself, planted them himself, and nobody ever touched them except him. A Mario Buda bomb never failed to go off, but that did not and could not guarantee they would take out their intended targets. They could be stolen or prematurely triggered. Bombs were maddeningly democratic in that regard.

He stopped himself when the thin coating of disbelief fell away. There was no avoiding the truth. Somebody had managed to find them in time and get them out.

In the past his creations were always outfitted with mercury switches, designed to react to changes in gravity if the bombs were moved. But this time—this one time—he had eliminated the switches to protect against bumps on the train ride and to make room for a few more ounces of explosive material.

The Bomb Maker Nonpareil's expertise had failed him. No. It was worse than that. His very judgment had failed him. The bombs were not removed because of any lack of skill on his part; they were removed because he had made a stupid mistake. Caution abandoned: a beginner's move.

He felt as if he could rip his head off his shoulders, throw it down the street, and still manage to scream in frustration without it. He tossed a coin to the boy and unfolded the paper to reveal a horror show. The details proved it. Two unnamed private detectives from San Francisco were aboard, found the bombs, and tossed them from the back of the train. They reportedly spurned offers to return to the city and elected to ride back home to San Francisco.

Pain clutched at his chest. He ground his teeth so hard his jaw throbbed. The exploded orphan train was to be the signal for the others to begin their attacks, assuring them they had true power on their side. What the hell was he supposed to do now? He had already mailed the threats to the heads of every bank in the district, guaranteeing them "the same fate as the orphan train." The deaths of children would have left no doubt of their seriousness.

Now his letters would become jokes, items passed around at cocktail parties to coax laughter from expensive whores and crooked businessmen. Nothing would wake them, not their post-war inflation, slow war recovery, labor riots, or the rising crime rate. Nothing could make the greedy fools let loose of their criminal financial system and greed-based labor policies.

He stopped the cart in front of the J.P. Morgan offices, a most fitting location, and picked up a nearby garbage can, carrying it to the cart and adding the contents to the little pile he had already made on the way there. Nobody ever bothered a man carrying garbage, nor would they look closely at him. The rented horse probably lived a terrible, boring life, and the trash cart was nearly worthless, so his soundly sleeping conscience rolled over and scratched but did not awaken while he reached into the cart, pushed aside some of the garbage, and set the timer on this non-incendiary, high-explosive device for 12:01 p.m.

Three minutes away.

The overall mission was already a lost cause, of course. He would complete his part out of loyalty to a world he imagined populated with people who did not disgust him. That was about all he had left. This orphan train debacle was the final failure. It was growing too hard to garner support from partisans. Everybody wanted a comfortable life. So few were willing to sacrifice by living in poverty and working in isolation.

He was leaning against a stone wall around the corner half a block away when the canon roar of his device filled the downtown area. Giant billows of smoke rolled in all directions. There was a stunned pause of silence at first.

Then the blood-curdling screams began. Buda's traditional exit music.

Buda walked on without bothering to go back and look; he could read about it later. It was more important to be far away now. He dropped the paper with that morning's news and walked away from that afternoon's news while the smoke rolled between the tall buildings.

But in so doing, he missed the one bit of consolation that might have lessened his pain. It was a small notation on the second page: *Daily Herald Stringer Missing*. The two-inch story had slight information, only that police were searching for *Daily Herald* stringer John Smith, who was known to drive an expensive luxury car found stashed in an alley blocks away from the *Herald* offices. The trunk had been left open, and there was blood on the bumper. There had been no response at his apartment. No one had seen or heard from him.

Everybody who worked at the paper had been questioned, but there was no good information. The editor-in-chief was quoted as saying Smith had not written anything much in recent months, but he was supposedly working on a big story.

The editor claimed no one at the paper ever saw it.

Maybe, the editor speculated, Smith was only faking his disappearance to seem important. Make himself out to be a celebrity reporter. He never made it a secret about wanting a full-time job on the *Herald* staff.

Alas for John Smith, his final scoop would never have the proper cap to it with news of his demise. There would only be mystery. His body had been weighted down too well. It might have rolled along the bottom of the East River for a ways, driven by the strong current, but it did not rise to meet the surface and was never seen again.

39

THE BLACKBURN-NIGHTINGALE RESIDENCE

SAN FRANCISCO

Two Months After the Wall Street Bombing
* 9:00 a.m. *

RANDALL BLACKBURN HELD THE TELEPHONE receiver tight to his ear while he leaned into the receiving box bolted to the wall. He made it a point to speak directly into the cone in an attempt to make himself clear, but the call from O'Grady's New York office came over the wire sounding as if someone was crumpling up balls of newspaper in the background. His own voice had a tinny echo that blurred his words. He wondered if conversations in Hell sounded like that.

He struggled to make out O'Grady's words while Vignette and Dante passed him carrying a small wooden desk up the stairs to the new attic bedroom. Vignette kept her eyes on the desk to avoid collisions with the walls, but Dante flashed Randall a delighted grin while they went by. He was eager to get off the living room sofa and into his own room.

O'Grady continued, "Sorry it took us so long to get to it, but your things were safe at our apartment. The motorcycle was easy to return the day after you left, but I had to wait until my own people could get on the job of finalizing everything."

"That will be fine, ma'am. Everything we really need was already here. Any word on Mario Buda or his boss?"

"You mean that Galleani character? Officially, he was never here and is still under deportation in Italy."

"Unofficially?"

"He and Buda sneaked out of town once they realized their plan to disrupt the election failed. My guess is this time they really did leave the country. For now. Just because their plan fizzled, there's no reason to think they won't try again."

"Will the news services ever come out and tell the people Mario Buda did this?"

"Maybe if the two of us buy our own newspaper. Otherwise it's officially a mystery."

"And the explanation for the bombs on the train is still holding up?"

"Protests by anarchists, which they were, but which went off without doing any harm because two unnamed officers got rid of them at the last instant."

"Thank you for keeping us out of it."

"Glad to. That kind of fame isn't good for anything but trouble."

"What about that reporter?"

"Smith is still missing. Maybe he'll turn up someday. You know, being a reporter and all, he's a guy who likes to see his name in print. If he's alive, we'll hear from him, but it's a big if."

"He told me he was close to breaking the story."

"And I'm guessing he got too close. Another example of how they keep things quiet. Get too close, disappear. Because 'Movers' is just what we call them. What they really are is a cancer that has invaded everything. And the public doesn't want to know about horrible things they can't stop. It's easier to say it's all impossible and dismiss it."

O'Grady sighed. She cleared her throat and continued, "On a better topic, what about you and Detective Nightingale? Are you going through with this new living arrangement?"

"Yes, we are, and to make room here at the house, Vignette and I are biting the bullet and renting an office space across from City Hall. I can't think of anything I'd like better than to keep Dante and Eliana here. Vignette and her brother, Shane, reformed my whole life. I'm ready to do it again."

"I'll let you get back to it, then. Tell your partner if she ever wants to try law enforcement in New York City, she's got a job anytime she wants it."

"I promise to tell her nothing of the kind." They both laughed and ended the call.

Randall hurried up the attic steps to help Eliana and Vignette finish up the adult tasks in setting up Dante's room, while Dante hung pictures on the wall taken from books he had begun accumulating upon their arrival. He was like a boy having his best birthday party ever. Eliana hummed under her breath and wore a smile of delight.

"Shane!" Vignette called without hearing herself. It had been years since she cried out in her sleep, but on this night she tossed in the grip of the strangest dream to ever visit her. When it began, Shane was alive and back with her. They were teenagers fresh from a ride on his big Harley. Elation filled her as it always had when riding with him, but instead of just laughing and speeding away with her once again, Shane began to fade from view. His body became nearly transparent.

Fear seized her. "What's going on?" she cried out. "Shane!"

But Shane merely reached out his hand to her with a loving smile on his face.

"No!" she cried. "Don't go!"

He seemed not to hear her. When he finally spoke, his voice was faint, already disappearing along with him. "Take care of your brother," he said, looking into her eyes with the purest love she had ever felt.

"How do I take care of you? You're not here! I'll never stop loving you, but how can I take care of you? Please tell me what you mean!"

Instead of explaining, he simply touched his fingertips to the side of her face. She knew that gesture. She had seen Eliana touch Dante that way many times.

"Take care of your brother," he said again, and this time his eyes shone so much love into her, everything else exploded into light. After that, she could see nothing of Shane's face, but she felt the fingertips he held to her cheek, soft and warm.

Vignette awoke with a start and sat up in bed. Emotions swirled inside her. She still felt the pain in her heart that would never go away, but there was more: a loving remnant for her waking world, as if a part of Shane remained with her.

But the light in her dream was gone, and the bedroom was pitch dark.

She got out of bed, threw on a robe, grabbed a match, and lit the oil lantern on her dresser. She carried it up to Dante's new room in the attic.

The door was unlocked. She walked in, moving by the lantern light, and sat on the edge of the mattress where Dante lay sleeping.

There was something she and Randall had discussed that day, and which they had decided to wait for the right time before revealing it to Dante. Randall had left it up to her to decide when that time was.

Tonight she could not and would not wait one more minute. She reached out her hand and touched his face. Her fingertips were cold with anxiety, and though they barely made contact with his skin, his eyes snapped open, his body convulsed into the fetal position, and his arms came up over his face and head. He did it without making a sound.

Vignette was so taken back she had no words. Before she could come up with any, Dante lowered one arm, peeked out, and immediately relaxed. He rotated to sit on the edge of the bed with a sheepish smile but made no attempt to explain. Vignette had no need to ask. That was one of the reasons he was so welcome in her life. She already knew.

After a moment, he smiled up at her and reached out to take her hand in both of his. He held onto her fingers while he met her gaze.

"Dante," she whispered, "I have to ask you something. Randall and I have talked this over, and you don't have to answer me right now, but I just can't wait anymore. How would you like to have an older sister?"

His face reflected doubt. He appeared genuinely confused. "Don't I already have one?"

Vignette felt a sob of surprise and joy tear from her chest. It would have been painful if it was not such a relief. She took one of his hands and placed his fingers in the same position on her cheek as Eliana did. "Kiddo, you do now," she replied.

"Eliana stays too, though. Right?"

Vignette smiled at that. "She already agreed. And don't be upset with her for not telling you. I asked her to let me tell you. Not tell you, but ask you. Because in case you didn't want to, well, I mean you would have the right not to stay at all, and I wanted you to have a fair chance to, you know, to—"

"You aren't gonna go soft and get weepy on me, are you?"

She laughed but noticed he did not. They held that position for a few moments, until Vignette gasped with a new idea. Her eyes flew open. "Hey! Want to go for a ride in the park? I left my bike out front last night. We can be gone in two minutes."

"It's still dark."

"Right. The park's great for riding in the dark. Shane and I used to do it all the time."

Dante gave her a mischievous grin unlike anything she had seen since Shane was alive. He hopped out of bed and, in a matter of seconds, pulled off his nightclothes, slipped into trousers, a shirt, jacket, and shoes, and started to walk out the door with her. He stopped at the doorway, held up one finger, and hurried back into the attic room.

At the dresser, he picked up Shane's teardrop-shaped chrome magneto switch and pulled the string over his head. He looked at her and smiled. "Okay. Let's go."

Randall woke to the sound of the front door closing, just as he had back in the days when young Shane and Vignette also thought they were sneaking out. In the silence of the hour, he distinctly heard the big Harley engine fire up and rumble out in front of the house, then listened while the bike-sidecar combination pulled away, did a U-turn, and made for the park. He easily sound-tracked it eastward down Lincoln Way, then to the right turn at Sunset, then moving back again to the west inside the park. It sounded, Randall thought, as if the big bike was actually flying back there behind the trees, somehow cruising along just below treetop level, blasting past them all in the darkness.

He heard Vignette crank the engine to a full Harley roar while Dante's own cry of gleeful defiance added a top note of joy. Her voice joined him, and they screamed in harmony.

He wondered if he had the strangest family in the city and felt a swell of pride at knowing he probably did. Remarkable for an unmarried man. He and Vignette had agreed to the new arrangement that afternoon, and she had obviously told Dante. Now it was time to embrace whatever came from it. Hearing the delight in their voices amid the darkness of the hour told him everything he needed to know. An official new addition to the family, then. They could not change the darkness, but they could create joy within it.

He went downstairs to brew a cup of tea and wait for the young ones to return and found Eliana already down there heating up the water. She was wrapped in the thick, ankle-length robe she had proudly purchased with her first wages after she and Dante had arrived there.

Neither needed to ask the other why they were up. They each smiled in recognition. There were countless questions left to come, but each had seen too much harshness and betrayal from the world to fail to understand the need to let it out slowly, in small steps over time. There would be plenty of that now.

They were so alike in their thoughts and feelings about those two young people out there in the darkness, the moment of shared concerns felt telepathic to each of them. There would be answers to questions about the past, as if the answers could make much of a difference. But within the moment itself, each fully understood the other.

He looked into her eyes and smiled. "Thank you, Eliana."

The words caught her off guard, and she stiffened just a little. But after a moment, she relaxed, then exhaled with a self-conscious smile. He could see it was hard for her to take in the words. She was heroic in keeping her ghosts out of their home, but Randall knew enough about such things himself to see the telltale traces in her. No doubt she had voices in her head tormenting her, just as he did. He felt certain hers were so persistent they would surely try to ridicule her moment of joy and to somehow assure her she was not worthy.

Except she now had three people on her side with no intention of allowing her to suffer and a determination to convince her of her value to them. Condemnations were not welcome in their house. In their home.

When the tea was ready, they both sat before the big living room window, looking out into the park, listening for the howl of the approaching motorcycle. A few other engines were out and about at that hour, and so a roar of pistons did not necessarily indicate Vignette's Harley. When it arrived, the unique voice of the 1,000-cc twin-cylinder engine would be capped by the voices of two young maniacs, shrieking with joy.

ACKNOWLEDGMENTS

Back again from Book #1 comes Landon and his brother, Cohen; Matthew and his brother, Daniel, still two beautiful young boys and still two rising young men. They are each in this world to create respected places in their futures, all because of how they were nurtured at home by Jill and Trevor for the boys, and Heidi and Steve for the young men.

My gratitude goes to Publisher Cate Streissguth for allowing me the opportunity to offer up this story in series form. It has been a wonderful opportunity to spend more time in the company of Randall and Vignette, Shane, Dante, and Lazy Ana Bone. I also celebrate Severn River Publishing for giving my stories and characters a home. SRP is the brainchild of CEO Andrew Watts, to whom we are all grateful for this platform.

Thanks to editor Kate Schomaker for her application of skill to Books 3 and 4 of this series. She works with surgical precision reflecting a deep understanding of the elements of style, the structure of good storytelling, and the use of language to facilitate it. She also catches those quirky details that sit right there staring you in the face, undetected. A pleasure to work with on both books.

The privilege of working with this SRP team came out of the faith in this book series shown by literary agent Lindsay Guzzardo, representing for Martin Literary Management. Thank you, Lindsay. Said it before, and I happily say it again: every writer is grateful for faith shown in their work, and I am no different in that regard. Every book is an attempt to live up to expectations, our own most of all. Validation is rain to the garden.

As always, deep thanks to my wife, Sharlene, Beta Reader Nonpareil.

And of course to you, the actual Readers, one and all.

— A.F.

ABOUT THE AUTHOR

Anthony Flacco is the New York Times and international bestselling author of *Impossible Odds: The Kidnapping of Jessica Buchanan and her Dramatic Rescue by SEAL Team Six,* which won the USA Book News Award for Best Autobiography of 2013. His *Tiny Dancer* was selected by Reader's Digest as their 2005 Editor's Choice for the magazine's commemorative 1000th Issue, and he received the 2009 USA Books News True Crime Award for *The Road Out of Hell: Sanford Clark and the True Story of the Wineville Murder.* Flacco's *The Last Nightingale,* book one of the Nightingale Detective series, was originally released to acclaimed reviews including a NYT rave, and was nominated by the International Thriller Writers (ITW) as one of the top five original paperback thrillers for 2007. Anthony resides in the beautiful Pacific Northwest.

anthonyflacco@severnriverbooks.com

Sign up for Anthony Flacco's reader list at
severnriverbooks.com/authors/anthony-flacco

ABOUT THE AUTHOR

Anthony Flacco is the New York Times and international bestselling author of *Impossible Odds: The Kidnapping of Jessica Buchanan and her Dramatic Rescue by SEAL Team Six,* which won the USA Book News Award for Best Autobiography of 2013. His *Tiny Dancer* was selected by Reader's Digest as their 2005 Editor's Choice for the magazine's commemorative 1000th Issue, and he received the 2009 USA Books News True Crime Award for *The Road Out of Hell: Sanford Clark and the True Story of the Wineville Murder.* Flacco's *The Last Nightingale*, book one of the Nightingale Detective series, was originally released to acclaimed reviews including a NYT rave, and was nominated by the International Thriller Writers (ITW) as one of the top five original paperback thrillers for 2007. Anthony resides in the beautiful Pacific Northwest.

anthonyflacco@severnriverbooks.com

Sign up for Anthony Flacco's reader list at
severnriverbooks.com/authors/anthony-flacco

Printed in the United States
by Baker & Taylor Publisher Services